Peter Martin

TP 1000:
The Bishops

First published in Great Britain in 2018 by Heggerwood Realms

Copyright © Peter Martin 2018

The moral right of Peter Martin to be identified as the author of this work has been asserted in accordance with the Copyright, Designs and Patents Act of 1988

All rights reserved. No part of this publication may be reproduced, stored in a retrieval system, or transmitted in any form, or by any means (electronic, mechanical, photocopying, recoding, or otherwise) without the prior written permission of both the copyright owner and the publisher of this book.

All the characters in this book, except for those already in the public domain, are fictitious, and any resemblance to actual persons living or dead is purely coincidental.

Front cover: Heggerwood Realms

Typeface: Garamond 11pt

ISBN-13: 978-1720602057
ISBN-10: 1720602050

For Katijah, my wife, my love, my life

Acknowledgements

My family, for putting up with my quirks over the last three-plus years while researching and writing this book.

Tina Whiteside, my first cousin once removed, whose Martin family tree helped inspire one of the themes in this book.

Richard Cornock, the funkyfarmer, for invaluable information about life on a dairy farm.

Sally Cholewa, archivist with the RBS Archives for her very thorough research on my behalf into dormant bank accounts.

Evan Bromfield, Urban Vertical Project, for his help in better understanding hydroponic and vertical farming techniques.

Critique Circle, for a great writers' feedback platform and the following critters Benzehabe, Caroljones, Clareeast, Fcsc, Mayaone, Reindeer, Rellrod, Sbeaulieu, Joan Szechtman (Unohoo), Tjamesl and many others, for their invaluable suggestions and help in polishing my writing.

Angela Ackerman and Becca Puglisi, for their fabulous thesauruses which were of so much help in giving some depth to my story.

Last, but by far not least, my editor, **Ray Bell** of Heggerwood Realms Copy Editing Service, a slave driver in true Roman style, without whose encouragement and help, this book would never have seen the light of day.

Chapter 1
Monday, 6th March, 2006 – Yorkshire, England

Chest tight, his sight blurred by unshed tears, Mark Bishop set the red ceramic urn on the limestone mantelpiece. The ashes of his cousin David would rest here in his study, kept company by those of his parents' and his sister. Head bent, he grasped the mantelpiece with both hands and closed his eyes as the full weight of loneliness pressed down on him. Thirty-one years old and the last of his relatives gone.

Only five weeks ago, Mark and David had discussed plans for David's wedding. Two weeks later, David's fiancée called to say a car had skidded on black ice and hit David's car head-on.

Memories of the last time he had seen his parents and his younger sister, Stephanie, who had just celebrated her sixteenth birthday, rose in his mind. Stephanie had been excited to be attending her first formal company dinner and dance with her parents... a drunk driver had shattered these plans and their lives.

He ran his fingers over the ceramic urn and read the metal plate–"Stephanie Ann Bishop, 1985-2001." His throat burned.

Mark did not have time to wallow in his misery, his farm

manager was waiting and patience was not one of Bill Marsh's virtues. Bill had worked for Mark since he had bought Keldthorpe Farm just over three years ago and was among the few people he called a friend. Bill's weather-worn features bore testament to his farming experience, the legacy of a lifetime of outdoor work.

Mark had been away for a fortnight attending the funeral and sorting out his cousin's affairs; it was time to return to work.

Mark took two deep breaths, opened the office door and walked past his large mahogany desk to where Bill was waiting. The sweet smell of burning apple wood in the fireplace eased some of his grief. Mark slumped in to the armchair opposite Bill. 'Any news on the new tax advisor?'

'She'll be 'ere next week,' the gruff Yorkshire man said. 'Supposed to have a farmin' background.'

'She?'

'Aye. A Miss Grainger, from ovver Richmond way. Jim Bradley sez she's one of 'is agency's top advisors.'

'Great. Likely some old biddy. Still, she can't be any worse than the others; the last chap was bloody useless. You'd have thought he worked for the damn tax man. I told Bradley, if this one's no good, I'm changing firms,' Mark retorted, running his fingers through his chestnut coloured hair.

'If yer'd not spent so much money addin' all them extra rooms t' farmhouse and all yer pricey furniture, yer'd a' been better off.'

Mark grunted. 'I just wanted a decent place to raise my own family.'

'Yeah, an' we know what Claire reckoned to that idea,' Bill muttered.

Mark's eyes narrowed at the mention of his ex-fiancée.

TP 1000: The Bishops

Bill looked out of the window and cleared his throat. 'Anyroad, we're rollin' an' fertilizin' t'fields and therza few 'edgerows to finish an' some fence posts to replace. Maintenance men are comin' tomorrow to check the solar panels and gerrem cleaned up. There's a lot to do before we let the girls out to graze and...'

Jenny Marsh snorted from the door. 'Well, it's not goin' to get done if you two stay glued to them chairs all day, is it?'

Jenny was Bill's wife and Mark's housekeeper, cook and, Mark often thought, the real boss at Keldthorpe Farm. Certainly no-one you wanted to upset. And considering she needed no help lifting fifty-pound bags of flour, he tried not to get on her wrong side.

Hands on hips, her snow-white apron pulled tight across her considerable bosom, she glared at Mark. 'I thought yer were goin' to finish that there bookcase in the basement? Yer've been messin' wi' it for ages. And there's the closer on' front door what needs fixin'...'

'Come on, Bill. Let's get out of here before she gets us cleaning the kitchen.'

'If yer think, for one minute, I'd let yer stumble around my kitchen mekkin' a mess, yer can think agen.' Jenny herded them towards the front door. 'Now gerrout and be useful. Go on. Shoo!'

Mark strolled to the stable where Lucky, his mustang, greeted him, snorting as if to say, a*bout time you came.* After a few frisky minutes, Mark held him to a steady walk, both of them moving smoothly together. He spent the rest of the morning riding along the flanks of the hills overlooking his farm, checking the dry stone walls for damaged or collapsed sections. Stretching, after replacing several fallen stones, he gazed out over the valley. The green fields, outlined by the complex pattern of their encompassing walls, changed from their chequered shades of green to a sombre dark grey as the shadow of a cloud passed over.

The solitude brought his mind back to his family's fatal accident. How different things might have been if he had followed them to dinner five years ago instead of going to his friend's party. His chest tightened remembering his parents' amused smiles as his sister twirled around showing off her new evening dress, while Mark teased her not to trip in her high heels.

Mark continued to brood on 'what ifs' as he returned for lunch. He hung his jacket in the hall and Jenny cornered him. 'Are yer goin' t'basement to see to that there bookcase after yer eat?'

'Yeah, why? Is there something else I should be doing?'

'As long as it keeps yer from mopin', that'll be fine.'

He winced. 'I'm okay, Jenny, honest I am... only every now and again...'

'I know, luv, I know.' She saw the grass stains on his jeans and his dirty hands and frowned. 'Now you can go an' get yerself cleaned up. Yer not gettin' any lunch lookin' like that.' She turned and stomped back to her kitchen.

Mark smiled as he went upstairs. He had been fortunate in hiring Bill and Jenny. Under Bill's tutelage, he soon found out running a dairy farm in Yorkshire was a far cry from mining operations in West Africa.

Two days of steady cleaning, sanding, staining and sealing the thirty-foot long oak bookcase helped him unwind. The attention needed around the intricate carving absorbed his mind, leaving no room for thoughts of the past. Back aching, he decided to take a break and sort out his cousin's effects stacked in his study.

David had been an amateur photographer and amongst his effects, Mark found several boxes of photo albums, packets of negatives and camera equipment. Flicking through one of the albums he stared at a photograph of his parents and sister; his remorse returning at these reminders of what he had lost.

He put aside a box of power tools and a pile of books to check later. Another had a few souvenirs from David's holidays in Europe. In the last box, underneath a stack of battered notebooks and files, he found a cloth-wrapped package. He removed the cloth, and the faint musty smell of ancient paper arose. It was a heavily bound old family Bible. When he opened it, his breath caught in his throat.

The first entry was from 1740. He read through a list of over fifty names and dates of births, deaths and marriages, written by different hands over the years. The last entry was of his sister. Gently placing it on the table, he sat and flicked through the files. He found an assortment of records—birth, baptismal, marriage and death certificates, tax records, maps, old newspaper articles, rough-drawn family trees and all kinds of other information.

David had traced the family tree back to an Edward Bishop in 1620. There was not much information in the notebooks before 1740, but David had complied detailed notes for later years. Mark even found one or two intriguing hints his family had originated in Germany; supported by the occasional German names such as Helmut, and especially Markus, the 1660 Germanic form of his own name.

Mark became intrigued as he read David's notes, and tried to imagine what his ancestors' lives had truly been like. Over the weekend, he managed to push the family tree back to Henry Bishop, born in 1513. He compiled all David's notes into a detailed genealogical chart, ending depressingly with the last box. It bore his name and date of birth. It looked to him like a tombstone for all the Bishops.

Blackie and Fritz, Mark's German Shepherds trained to herd cows, started barking.

Bill nudged Mark and nodded towards a dark blue *Ford Focus* entering the farmyard. 'Ey up, we've gorra visitor.'

Mark left the musty warmth of the barn, dusted his hands on his faded jeans and strode across the yard towards the tall woman who had approached the front door.

'Who are you looking for?' he called out. She had striking Mediterranean features. Olive skin, emerald-green eyes, and raven-black hair tied in a neat bun, and only a few inches short of his own six-foot frame.

The visitor stared at his torn sweater and stained jeans. 'I have an appointment with Mr Bishop.'

'Well, you've found him.'

She smiled and extended her hand. 'I'm Pauline Grainger, your new tax advisor. I believe Mr Bradley called to tell you I would be coming today.'

Mark frowned and shook her hand. She was most definitely *not* the old biddy he had been expecting.

'Alright, follow me.' He strode to the house; the door banged open. *Shit! I forgot to fix the closer.*

Jenny entered the hallway. Mark readied himself for a tongue lashing, but she stared past him. Her scowl disappeared, replaced by a look of surprise.

'Pauline? Pauline Grainger?'

TP 1000: The Bishops

'Mrs Marsh?' Pauline's face lit up with a brilliant smile. 'How are you? How's Mr Marsh?'

Mark raised an eyebrow. 'You know her?'

'Of course!' Jenny replied, pulling her in for a hug. 'Known 'er since she was a bairn. Her mum's an old friend and her dad, Georgie Grainger, used to farm out towards Hawes.' Jenny released Pauline, but held her hands. 'I'm sorry t' 'ear abart yer dad passin'. 'Ow's yer mum doin'?'

She glanced at Mark before answering. 'She's doing well. We sold the farm after dad died and bought a house near Richmond to be nearer my office. I, er, didn't know you worked here.'

'Well, me and Bill are helpin' 'im run this farm ov 'is. But what're yer doin' 'ere?'

'My firm sent me as Mr Bishop's tax advisor.'

'Bill said a Miss Grainger from Richmond was comin', but I didn't think it were gonna be Georgie's little girl. Well, that's good news. All I've heard from 'im is a lot of moanin' and groanin' abart the last one.' She grinned at Pauline. 'Don't worry, 'is bark's worse'n 'is bite. Now, I'll be off to mek some tea.'

Pauline turned to Mark with a thin smile.

'Er, right,' he said, rubbing his neck. 'Come this way.'

Pauline stepped onto a thick-pile beige carpet. The large desk facing the door and the three dark brown leather office chairs looked expensive. This luxury extended to the matching leather couch and armchairs near the window. Making an L-shape with the desk, in a corner of the room was a matching bookcase holding several neatly labelled files and books on a multitude of farming topics. All very different from other farms she normally visited. They usually had flagstone floors, files stored on window ledges with the kitchen table doubling up as a desk.

Mark sat behind his desk and Pauline sank into a chair opposite him. She passed two files across the desk to him and set up her laptop.

He opened the first file and his body stiffened. 'These are the damn returns the other idiot submitted.'

'I am well aware of that. Now, look at the other file.' She returned his glare in full measure.

They were still scowling at each other when Jenny came in and placed a tea tray on the coffee table. ''Ope yer like the tea, Pauline. 'e prefers it black but there's milk an' sugar if yer want, and 'omemade shortbread.' She turned to Mark. 'Now you, mind yer manners and stop lookin' so grumpy.' With that, she marched out.

Pauline pointed to the second file, *'This* is a list of all possible claims for a farming business. Now let us identify what claims we can make for the last three years.'

Pauline questioned him relentlessly for four hours. Mark was exhausted, however, he had grudgingly to respect her thoroughness. He was pleased he could show her receipts for everything he had ever paid. He had learned his lesson the hard way from the finance department at the mining company, and occasional rants from his father. No receipt–no claim!

'All I need now are copies of those receipts,' Pauline said as they finished.

'No problem,' Mark replied and downloaded copies of all three years' receipts onto a flash drive and passed it to her. 'Here you go.'

'Ah, thank you.'

He smirked at her surprised expression. 'My pleasure.'

'Are there any other assets subject to UK tax regulations?'

'Only my personal bank account. There's some foreign investments and an account in Singapore, and an accountant settles my taxes over there. I'll give you a break-down of it all.' He took back the flash drive and wondered what she would think after she reviewed it all.

TP 1000: The Bishops

'I believe that's all we can accomplish today.' She checked her organiser. 'I can be back at the end of the month with an estimate of your total rebates and a letter for the *HMRC*. Will nine-thirty on the thirtieth be suitable?'

'Fine.'

As Mark escorted her out, Jenny came to say goodbye, giving her another hug. 'Give my love to yer mum when yer see 'er.'

'I will, Mrs Marsh. Thanks for the tea,' Pauline said, before making her way outside. 'I'll see you on the thirtieth, Mr Bishop.'

'I hope you'll have good news and it won't get screwed up again.'

'Mr Bishop, I am not in the habit of making mistakes.'

He flinched at her icy stare. 'Okay, we'll see.' He turned back to the house, not willing to let her have the last word.

'So 'ow did it go?' Jenny asked, when he came through the door. 'Get yer taxes sorted?'

'Looks alright I suppose. Might get a bit back from the tax man, if I'm lucky.' He gave Jenny a nervous look, not wanting to criticise her family friend. 'She *seems* to know what's she's doing. We'll have to wait and see.'

'What I 'eard is she's a pretty smart lass. Attractive... single an' all,' Jenny announced, and retreated to the kitchen smiling, leaving Mark open-mouthed and no chance to respond.

The last thing he had expected was Jenny acting the matchmaker. No matter how damn professional Pauline was, there had been enough gold-diggers in the past for him to hold out any hope— especially after she found out he had extensive foreign assets.

Pauline banged her fists on the steering wheel. 'I'll give him *hope it won't get screwed up again*. I've never *screwed up* an account in my life.'

She looked daggers at the blameless sheep grazing in the passing fields as she drove back to her office. She was dreading having to unravel the puzzle of paper inside a shoebox which was another farmer's idea of filing receipts. Pauline was grateful when five o'clock came around.

Once Pauline was home, she kicked her shoes across the living room and collapsed on the settee.

Her mother settled her slim frame next to her. 'Rough day, luv?' she said, patting her daughter's arm and smiling at her theatrics.

'Between Mr Taylor's shoebox filing-system and that Mr Bishop at Keldthorpe Farm, I've had it with farmers.' She pulled at her hair. 'Must admit though, I wish all my clients were as organised as him. Oh, by the way, I saw Mrs Marsh at Keldthorpe. She sends her love.'

'Jenny Marsh from over Reeth way? What's she doing there?'

'Near as I can tell, she's the housekeeper and cook and her husband works on the farm.'

Pauline's phone rang. She reached into her briefcase and smiled when saw the caller ID. 'Sorry, Mum, talk later, it's Julie.'

'Pauline! How're you doing?' Julie's voice bubbled over the phone.

'I've had better days.'

'Aah, your new client. You said it was a straightforward job. Check his claims and resubmit.'

'It is, but he's an arsehole.' Taking a deep breath, she related the details of her visit. Her voice hardened. 'I can understand him being angry over the mess old man Jefferson made, but that's no reason to doubt my ability either.'

'Ignore him and do your job. That's what I do with the moaners and groaners. Anyway, you still coming at the end of the month?'

'For sure. I'll be there Friday after work.'

'Great. We'll have a whole weekend to shop 'till we drop.'

'Don't forget there's a stamp fair on Saturday.'

'Ugh! You and your stamps. Anyway, try not to kill your client between now and then.' Julie laughed as she hung up.

'You shouldn't be too hard on Mr Bishop, you know,' her mother said when they sat for dinner.

Pauline balled her fists. 'But he's so damn rude, I could...'

'Maybe so, but I reckon he has his reasons.' Her mother leaned forward, her elbows on the table, clearly relishing the chance to impart a bit of local gossip. 'What I heard in the village was, five or six years ago, he lost all his family somewhere in the Far East. When he came back, he bought Keldthorpe farm. Spent a fortune extending the farmhouse. One of them contractors said it took nearly two years and cost over a million pounds. After he'd finished, he went and spent another small fortune decorating and furnishing it before he was married. A month after he'd finished, his fiancée calls and breaks off the engagement, saying she'd changed her mind and wasn't going to live on some farm in the middle of nowhere. That was about nine months ago.'

'Oh, that's bad.' She understood all too well the pain of failed relationships, but she still reckoned he was an arsehole. 'But there's no need to take it out on me. I've only just met him.'

Pauline hummed along to the radio as she drove out to Keldthorpe Farm. She had spent most of the fortnight making sure she had nailed every possible legitimate expense. She had found claims for over twenty-five thousand pounds for the last three years as well as reducing his future tax bill by a substantial amount.

When she had reviewed his other assets, she had had a shock. Mark was a lot richer than many farmers. Besides the farm account, he had a personal account with over £198,000 in London, and a large portfolio of rare stamps. In addition, he had several foreign investments, including a forty-percent stake in a private software development company in Singapore. Also a separate bank account there with the equivalent of seven-hundred and fifty thousand pounds, just sitting there collecting dust and little interest; an appalling waste of money.

Jenny gave her a hug when she answered the door. 'Just a minute, luv, I'll go an' get 'im. Just make yourself comfy, won't be a minute.'

Pauline sat at the desk. She could hardly wait to see his face when she showed him the rebates he could expect.

Mark entered the room. 'Hope you have good news for me.'

She took great pleasure outlining the rebates he should receive in five or six weeks time and the amount of tax he would be paying in future. She watched Mark's frown disappear, replaced by a growing smile.

'Now *that* is good news.'

'Mr Bishop, I've reviewed your overseas holdings and have some suggestions to make, but first I have a question. Exactly what is it you want to achieve here? Why are you keeping so much money in Singapore at half-a-percent interest when you could be investing it in the farm to reduce costs, and diversify farm products to increase profits?'

'No-one's asked me that before.' he gazed at the ceiling as if gathering his thoughts. 'I want this farm to be a profitable example of good environmental management and as self-sufficient as possible. As for the money, what do you suggest?'

'First of all, you could upgrade your biogas generator and

increase the number of solar panels. My figures show sufficient surplus electricity to sell to the energy company, meaning more cash flow.' She took a file from her briefcase. 'Also, there's diversification of farm products, such as implementing hydroponic produce, adding cheese production and—'

'Hold it, let me call Bill. He should sit in on this.'

Feeling vindicated, she gazed around the room while she waited. It was stark. No personal touches anywhere—no photographs, mementoes, nothing. Her inspection ended when Mark and Bill came in. She stood when she saw Bill smiling. 'Nice to see you again, Mr Marsh,' she said, shaking his hand.

Mark pointed to the couch. 'Let's sit over there.'

Pauline spoke for over an hour about hydroponic crops, ice-cream, cheese and yoghurt production. She used her laptop to show them calculations and charts, and fielded questions from them both.

'Start-up costs could be up to two-hundred and fifty thousand pounds, mainly for capital equipment and establishing a production and storage area. A lot of those costs can be used to offset your taxes. Packaging, advertising, *et cetera*, would add to this cost. However, some farms are realising three to five-percent more than from milk sales alone.'

'What about honey? I reckon it would be a useful non-dairy product,' Mark asked.

Bill groaned and rolled his eyes. 'Don't get 'im goin' abart bees, will yer? 'E's been bendin' me ear abart 'em ever since 'e spent a few 'undred quid on wild flower seeds last year. As if we don't have enough on wi' a 'undred and twenty cows and calves, a small flock o' sheep and a dozen chickens.'

Mark turned sharply toward Bill. 'I've seen what happens when the environment's damaged. Bee numbers are dropping mainly because wild flower habitats are being destroyed.' He jabbed a finger at Bill. 'Just you wait and see how many people starve to death when there's no more bees or butterflies.'

Pauline's jaw dropped. Taken aback by the passion and anger in his voice, she tried to defuse the situation and suggested he read her report and do his own research.

Mark's jaw was still clenched when she stood to leave. She said a hasty goodbye to Bill and followed Mark as he strode along the corridor to the front door.

As they approached her car, his faced flushed. 'I'll check out your ideas and see if they make any sense.'

Before she could reply he was halfway back to his house. This dismissal of her work fuelled her own anger. *What was his problem?*

Chapter 2
Friday, 31st March, 2006

Pauline had a miserable drive to Leeds, the windscreen wipers barely coped with the downpour. After an exasperating four days sorting out Mr Taylor's shoebox, she was in dire need of an escape and looked forward to a weekend with Julie. Her spirits rose when she pulled up in front of Julie's house and made a dash through the pouring rain to the front door. Dropping her weekend bag, she threw her arms around her old university roommate; Julie's slim figure and golden blonde hair, a sharp contrast to her black-haired, more voluptuous friend.

Julie prised herself loose. 'Looks like you could do with a nice cuppa tea.'

'Actually, I'm starving, what's for dinner?'

'You're always starving. I don't know how you keep your figure. I swear you haven't changed a bit since the day you won the freshman swimsuit contest at uni.'

Pauline grinned and struck a couple of exaggerated poses to show off her figure. Pauline's laughter was infectious and triggered Julie's.

After dinner, they caught up on the latest gossip. Pauline was struck by how many of their university friends were now married, either with children, or expecting. Julie's relationship with her boyfriend, Hugh, a professional photographer, was becoming serious—he had even mentioned the 'M-word'. Uncomfortable at the matrimonial direction the conversation was taking, Pauline changed the subject to their respective clients. Julie was a tax advisor for a small company and they soon started swapping 'war stories'.

'So, what's the plan for the weekend?' Pauline asked.

'I thought tomorrow we could spend the day shopping. I've made us a dinner reservation at an Indian restaurant for eight o'clock.'

Julie rolled her eyes when Pauline reminded her of the stamp fair this weekend.

Pauline pleaded. 'Come on, pretty please? We can go in the morning, and shop after lunch.'

They had been wandering around the stamp fair for thirty minutes when Pauline spotted Mark at a well-known dealer's stall.

'Damn. There's my new client. Come on, before he sees us.' Pauline pulled Julie towards the nearest stall and started rooting through the material on display. She soon became engrossed in her search and picked out an envelope with its original letter and a neatly cancelled *Penny Red* stamp. After a little bargaining she bought it for thirty pounds and continued rummaging through the rest of the offers.

'Miss Grainger, I didn't know you collected stamps,' Mark's deep husky voice said, from behind. Startled, she dropped her recent purchase. Mark bent to pick it up, his brow furrowed as he studied it.

'Ah! A good clean envelope dated February 1846. Obviously plate fifty-five, see the 'E'-flaw and horizontal line above the 'B'? This is a good example of the late use of the *Maltese-Cross*. They stopped being used with plate forty-five in 1844. How much did it cost?'

'Er, thirty pounds,' she answered, flustered.

Mark's eyes widened. 'That's a real bargain, believe me. Probably worth at least fifty.'

Pleased with this news, Pauline asked, 'Have you bought anything?'

'Aren't you going to introduce me to your friend first?' Mark asked, looking at Julie.

'Sorry, this is Julie Parker. I'm staying with her over the weekend.'

Mark shook Julie's hand. 'Miss Parker, pleased to meet you. You know stamps were printed from different metal plates. When one became worn out, they prepared and used another one. It's the first eleven plates I'm interested in. They were originally printed with black ink, then in 1841 they changed over to red ink to prevent cleaning and reuse.'

Mark turned back to Pauline. 'In answer to your earlier question, yes, I did buy something. I'd arranged to meet Andrew there.' He pointed towards the dealer he had been talking to earlier. 'He called me to say he had something I've been trying to find for ages.' Mark took out a leather pocket book from his jacket and opened it.

Pauline gawked at two beautifully exquisite *Queen Victoria Penny Black* stamps with original gum from a corner of the sheet showing part of the usage instructions along the top. The first postage stamps ever printed.

'How... how much did you pay?' she gasped.

'Andrew let me have them for twenty-five thousand. Lovely,

aren't they?' He put them away.

Pauline and Julie gaped at him, speechless.

'Well, I have to be off. Congratulations on your find, Miss Grainger.' Mark turned and strolled away, leaving the two young women standing like a pair of marble statues.

Pauline stared after him and muttered, 'bloody show-off!'

This brought Julie out of her trance. 'That's the arsehole? He's a bit abrupt, but damn it, girl, he's gorgeous... and that voice! You could do worse than tackle him.'

'You're joking! Not a chance. I don't care how good looking he is.'

'Up to you.' Julie's tone became more serious. 'Look, it's been five years since that bastard screwed up your life. You have to come out of your shell sometime.'

'Maybe, but not with *him*. Come on, let's go shopping. I've had enough of stamps for one day.'

After putting their shopping away, they changed and Julie drove them to the restaurant.

The waiter showed the two young women to their table; set in a shallow recess, outlined by a Mughal style plaster arch. He presented menus and soon returned with poppadums and finely chopped salad and chutney in small steel bowls to snack on. Pauline pointed to the delicately carved wooden arches dividing the restaurant in to semi-private dining areas. 'The décor is fantastic. Just look at that intricate carving.'

'The food's good too,' Julie replied, and popped a piece of crunchy poppadum and chutney into her mouth. 'I came here shortly after they opened. The tandoori chicken is to die for.'

They had finished an excellent meal and had started on a dessert of mango-flavoured frozen kulfi, when Pauline saw Mark approach their table.

She put her head in her hands. 'Oh, not him again.'

'Are you following me, Miss Grainger?'

'I beg your pardon?' She raised her head and glowered at him.

'This is the second time our paths have crossed this weekend; I'm beginning to think I'm being stalked.'

Pauline's face flushed with indignation. 'For one thing, I didn't know you would be in Leeds this weekend.' Her tone became more forceful. 'And for another, Julie made the reservation and I didn't know about it until yesterday.'

Mark rubbed his chin, seemingly undecided; his grey eyes boring into hers as if reading her innermost thoughts. 'Mmm. Did you enjoy your meal? Malik's a great chef.'

'Malik?' Pauline asked, flustered by his intense gaze and change of subject.

'Malik is the owner, an old friend of mine...'

A tall thin Indian man with a worried expression came to the table, his gaze swivelled between Mark and Pauline. 'Is everything alright?'

'Fine, Malik, fine. I was saying hello to Miss Grainger and Miss Parker here.'

'Good, good. If you need anything, please ask.' Malik rushed off to another table.

'Well, enjoy your meal, ladies.' Mark wore a faint smile as he walked away.

Julie turned to Pauline. 'What was that all about?'

Before Pauline could answer, Malik came back to their table.

'Ladies, how is everything? I see you know Mark.'

'Sort of,' Pauline answered. 'I'm his tax advisor.'

'Oh good. He is a very nice man. We have known each since we were teenagers in Singapore. He and his family were regulars at my uncle's restaurant.'

'So you've known him for some time?'

Malik sat and leaned towards them. 'Oh yes. My uncle had such a shock when his family died in that accident. Terrible, terrible.'

Pauline stared, and hoping to better understand her new client, asked, 'What happened?'

He looked around, and lowered his voice. 'Oh, it was six years ago, they were coming home from a late-night function when a drunk driver raced through a red light and smashed right into their car.' He shook his head at the memory. 'His parents and the other driver died instantly; his sister was taken to hospital in a critical condition...'

'Mr Bishop wasn't with them?'

'No. Mark was at a friend's house.' His eyes lost focus. 'When he arrived at the hospital, his sister had passed away moments before.'

'That's terrible,' Julie cried, and Pauline's expression softened in sympathy.

'Yes. He was nearly out of his mind. If it had not been for his friend, Jimmy Chen, I do not *what* would have happened to him.'

Back in Julie's living-room, Pauline and Julie talked about what Mark must have gone through. Pauline related what her mother had told her. How he had spent a fortune on a home to raise his own family and then being jilted by his fiancée.

'No wonder he's bitter,' Julie mused. 'But I reckon there's more to it than that. Being dumped by one person surely doesn't change a person that much?' Julie added.

Pauline considered her own situation. 'Maybe.'

The next evening, after a relaxing Sunday with her old friend, Pauline drove home. Approaching Dunkeswick, the traffic started to build up and slow down. She spotted flashing lights ahead where a *Jaguar* and tow truck half blocked the road. Mark was standing by the tow truck, watching his car being readied for towing.

Pauline found herself pulling over. *Too late to back out now,* and sighed.

She walked back towards him, shivering in the icy wind. 'Need a lift?'

Mark spun around. 'Miss Grainger? Yes... yes, thank you. Let me fetch my bags.'

'Come on, it's freezing out here.' She hurried back to her car, her breath forming clouds in the frigid air.

Mark tossed his bags in the back seat and opened his coat as he sat. 'Thanks. Much better.'

After ten long minutes, Mark cleared his throat breaking the silence and asked if she knew anything about Mr Jones, the previous owner of his farm. 'I got a run-down from the estate agent. Late-fifties, no known family, a bit of a gentleman farmer leaving his hands to run the farm, and killed by a lightning strike.'

'Same as I heard,' Pauline replied, keeping her eyes on the road. 'Nobody saw much of him from what I understand. He kept to himself most of the time, but was always polite if you met him in the village. The village gossips said the farm was barely breaking-even.' She glanced at him. 'Why are you asking now?'

'I've spent a lot of time in the basement renovating a grimy old bookcase. It made me wonder why anyone would build a huge thirty-foot long bookcase, in oak no less, in a basement. Seemed a bit strange to me.'

More silence followed while they drove along the dark two-lane country road until Mark asked, 'By the way, do you know what happened to all the contents of the house? It was pretty bare when I bought it.'

'Everything was auctioned off and the money donated to various charities and the local secondary school. I don't know where he got them, but the art pieces realised enough to build a new physics lab,' then added, 'Funny thing, I heard nothing personal was ever found. No photographs, personal letters... nothing.'

The uncomfortable silence resumed until Pauline asked if he had bought anything else at the stamp fair.

'No, most of it wasn't in good condition. There must be good material out there, but it's either hidden away in collections or forgotten in someone's attic. Either way, I've not found much lately.'

Hearing the frustration in his voice, Pauline stole a quick glance at him.

'You know,' he continued, 'the problem with postal history is we know a lot about the general running of the postal service, but the small personal details are what's missing most of the time. Imagine... if you could travel back in time to find out for yourself. There's a village in Derbyshire, for example, where the records indicate some form of postal service from the early 1840s. We know the name of the first sub-postmaster, but he wasn't appointed until 1852. So, what was happening in those twelve years? Was the same chap running the service? Who was the driver of the gig-cart who sent and delivered mail every morning and evening?' Mark's hands were doing as much talking as his mouth. 'What problems did he encounter? How did he manage to keep to a schedule during bad weather? It's those details I'd track down.'

Pauline could not ignore his excitement. 'What got you interested in the first place?'

'Besides the postal side of things? The day-to-day lives of the people involved, fascinates me. My father had a large collection, a lot of it belonged to my maternal grandfather. They left extensive notes and I've been building on it over the last few years.' Mark proceeded to describe his collection.

Pauline was embarrassed when he asked about her collecting interests. A haphazard accumulation better described her own stamp collection.

Discussing Victorian postal history coaxed Pauline to mention her own obsession with Victorian England and her extensive library on the subject. She also discovered they had another shared interest, horse-riding.

'You should ride over one day. There's some good cross country trails around the farm.'

Pauline was non-committal. Despite the apparent change in his manner, she was not ready for anything except a professional relationship.

When they turned off the motorway, Pauline asked what Bill had meant when he mentioned wild flower seeds at their last meeting. Mark straightened in his seat and expounded on the destruction of habitats for pollinators in the name of higher production. 'It's criminal. Suicide on a global scale. Damn short-sighted! Grow as much food as you can and make as much money as possible. Don't worry about future generations.'

He was still holding forth on the subject when Pauline turned in to his farm.

'We're here.'

Mark sat up and looked around. 'Oh! Yes. Thank you for the lift, Miss Grainger. I'll review your ideas and get back to you shortly. Goodnight.'

Pauline headed home with a faint smile; *maybe he wasn't so bad after all.*

'What time did yer get back last night?' Jenny asked Mark at breakfast the next morning.

'Miss Grainger dropped me off around ten-thirty,' he mumbled around his scrambled eggs.

Jenny eyes widened in surprise. 'What? Where's yer car?'

'It broke down and Miss Grainger gave me a lift.'

Mark finished his meal, oblivious to the knowing smile on her face.

'If you need me, I'm off to finish that bookcase.'

As he strolled towards the basement whistling, he was unaware of Jenny's beaming grin.

By Friday evening, Mark had finished except for a tricky panel in the last section with two knots. He stood back to admire his work. The bookcase gleamed a beautiful dark golden-brown, with black, carved roundels along the frieze, and uprights separating the five sections.

'Nearly finished. It looks great, even if I say so myself,' he told Jenny later. 'Well, I'd better get started on those proposals from Miss Grainger.'

TP 1000: The Bishops

As Mark read Pauline's report, her question of what he wanted to achieve kept coming to mind. She had made detailed suggestions for improvement and diversification, meticulously documented; demonstrating a deep insight into sustainable farming. Not only was she knowledgeable and professional, but, more important to him, she did not seem at all impressed with his wealth—and definitely had no problem putting him in his place. So different from the women who had fawned on him, or rather his bank account, when he first came back to England. He shook his head and smiled, remembering Jenny's remarks after Pauline's first visit—smart, attractive... and single.

With an energy he had not felt since his failed engagement, Mark started work. He recalled the advice his father had given him after Mark had quit his job in Africa. "Figure out what you really want to do and work backwards. Identify every step and every option that takes you from there to here. Then go for it."

He applied everything he had learned in running a mining operation, plus the tips he had picked up from his father and Bill, to his plans for the farm. After ten days of non-stop research, phone calls, emails, calculations and off-site meetings, he completed a lengthy business plan.

After dinner he went over his plans with Bill who shook his head and asked whether Mark had finally lost it. At this underwhelming show of support, he decided to call Pauline the next morning.

'Miss Grainger, I've been studying your proposals, and they got me thinking. Can you come over and review some plans I've made and give me an honest opinion?'

'I'm free tomorrow morning. Will nine o'clock be alright?'

'Great. I'll see you in the morning.'

Pauline, curious and puzzled by the weariness she had heard in Mark's voice, arrived at the farm ahead of heavy rain clouds and saw him waiting for her. Startled at his blood-shot eyes and the dark circles underneath, she asked, 'Mr Bishop, are you alright?'

'Yes, yes, I'm fine. Come, let me show you my plans.' He dragged her through the front door and shouted, 'Jenny, coffee for two in the office, please.'

He barely gave her time to take her coat off before he pushed a thick stack of paper in her hands. 'I need you to read through this and recommend loans and possible grants, and help fine-tune the financial section. Feel free to make notes.'

Flicking through, she looked at Mark in amazement. The amount of work he had done since her last visit was incredible. No wonder the bags under his eyes resembled overweight luggage.

Mark paced back and forth while Pauline read and scribbled comments. She waded through short and long range plans, projected cost and production levels, budgeted profit and loss and cash flow, all the while oblivious to Jenny bringing more coffee and biscuits.

A hydroponic complex with four greenhouses and laboratory—heated and powered by the biogas generator and electricity from solar panels, to grow lettuce, tomatoes, chillies and mangoes. Fell-side terracing and tree planting, wildflower meadows and an herb garden. Beehives, honey, cheese, ice-cream and yoghurt manufacturing with berry plantations for sale of fruit and for flavourings. Overseas marketing plans. All *this* from a two-hundred acre farm?

She looked at Mark. 'Have you any idea how much work this involves? How much money is needed?'

'Well it was your idea.'

'What?' she squawked. 'I never suggested anything like this.'

'Maybe not *exactly* like this, but you started the ball rolling when you asked me what I wanted to achieve here.' His smile had now become a full grin.

'But this is... it's staggering. Are you serious?'

'You asked why I kept so much money in Singapore, well, it was my sister's life insurance money and until now, I couldn't bear to touch it.' He pointed to the stack of paper in front of her and stared at her with a determined expression. 'It is worth using it for this.'

They worked until four o'clock when a severe thunderstorm broke, making talking difficult. They had called it a day when Jenny informed them the police had called to say the road to town was flooded with the additional risk of landslides.

'How am I going to get home?'

Jenny tried to reassure Pauline. 'Don't yer worry, luv. Call yer mum and tell 'er what's happened, and yer'll be staying 'ere until it's safe.'

Pauline turned towards Mark.

He shrugged. 'Not a lot of choice, unless you want to sit in your car all night.'

Pauline found herself being led away by Jenny. 'Come wi' me luv. I'll show yer the room and yer can call your mum so she don't worry.'

Jenny led Pauline upstairs. 'There's four spare bedrooms up 'ere. Yer in the one facing the back—not so noisy in the morning.'

It was a large room with a queen-size bed. Jenny pointed to a door. 'Shower and bath tub's in there. There's towels and toiletries if yer want to freshen up before dinner. I'll leave yer to it, then.'

Pauline bounced on the bed, wriggled her toes in the thick pile carpet, and admired what resembled a deluxe hotel room. Cream walls hung with rural watercolour paintings, armchairs either side of a coffee table, and an internet connection by the small writing table. She called her mother to explain what had happened, and had to listen to not-so-subtle hints about how eligible Mark was. A hot bath, liberally sprinkled with the lavender bath salts provided, removed the stiffness from sitting all day. Wrapped in a thick cotton bath towel she walked back to the bed and dressed.

As she entered the dining room, the aromas coming from the kitchen distracted Pauline from her discomfort. She had hardly eaten all day except for a light working lunch. Conversation over dinner centred on the business plan and what specialist staff to hire. They agreed Mark would need one to run the greenhouse and hydroponic complex and another to look after the outdoor work.

The conversation continued until Mark said, 'Good Heavens! It's nearly midnight. Sorry to have kept you up so late. You'd better wait until Bill sends word on the road conditions before you set out.'

'Goodness, it *is* late. We'd better go to bed.' She realised how her words could be misinterpreted and blushed. 'I mean, er... I didn't mean...'

Mark just chortled.

Chapter 3
Friday, 31st March, 2006

'Time to celebrate,' Mark said, with a smile.

After seven days of intense work, the Keldthorpe Farm Business Plan sat on the desk between them. Pauline's boss had proved more than willing to let her concentrate on Mark's project, he had even reassigned her other clients to enable her to focus on it.

Working together, often until late at night, a closeness and better understanding of each other had developed. Pauline found Mark's dry humour and deadpan expression when relating anecdotes from his travels, side-cracking at times. Mark, in turn, was astonished at Pauline's depth of knowledge of farming and Victorian life.

Both owned their own horses—Pauline's grey Anglo-Arabian, Princess, and Mark's buckskin mustang, Lucky—and over dinner, they talked of their mutual love of horse riding.

After dinner, Mark and Pauline relaxed over a bottle of 1985 vintage wine and discussed local news and gossip.

Pauline leaned back in her chair. 'You know the bookcase in your basement? Well, I met Tommy Mitchell and his wife in the village last week. He used to work at Briggs' furniture shop before he retired. Anyway, he remembers helping deliver it back in seventy-four or five. He said it was only a month after Mr Jones finished extending the original two-up two-down built in the fifties. Funny thing was, Mr Jones had said, "You deliver the sections, I'll assemble it." Rumour has it, the door was locked afterwards and no-one allowed to enter.'

'Strange,' Mark muttered. 'I've nearly finished cleaning it. Want to see?'

At the bottom of the basement stairs, Pauline looked around. The bookshelf dominated the room. It stretched the entire length and the full height of one wall. Four-foot high polished wooden panels lined the walls at the two ends of the room, with a large stone fireplace in the centre of the far wall.

Mark pointed to two doors on the wall opposite the bookcase. 'I added those two small storerooms and put in a dumb waiter to the kitchen; saves a lot of carrying. Later, I'll put in wooden flooring.'

Pauline stood back and gazed at the bookcase. 'It's beautiful. It almost glows.'

'Yes, but cleaning out years of muck around the carvings was slow work. The shelves were straightforward except where they meet the uprights and around the scrollwork.' He pointed to far end of the bookcase, 'I only have that bit at the end to finish.'

Examining the shelves nearest the fireplace, she noticed two knots, two-feet apart, at the back of the middle shelf. 'Why would he use cheap timber here? These knots could fall out.' She turned to study the rest of the bookcase. 'The rest is such excellent quality.'

Mark looked at where she was pointing and poked at the left-hand knot.

TP 1000: The Bishops

Click.

'Did you hear that?' Pauline asked.

'Yes, and I felt a little give...'

Pauline pushed the other one and they heard another faint click. Pauline raised an eyebrow. 'Together?'

A six-foot high section swung away from them. Mark leapt back, almost knocking Pauline over. She grabbed his arm. 'What the—'

Mark pushed again. A grating sound came from the bookcase and dry dusty air wafted over them. It came to a halt with a loud click, at right angles to the opening.

They stared, transfixed, at a small brick-lined chamber. Mark grabbed a torch from his workbench and, illuminating the room, Pauline saw two wall lights and a curved rail on the floor and ceiling. The room was approximately ten-feet deep and seven to eight-feet wide, the corners festooned with cobwebs. Two dusty biscuit tins rested on a wooden shelf on the right-hand wall, with a calendar pinned to a cork board above them. Two metal cabinets sat in the back corners of the room with four wooden boxes stacked between them.

Mark dashed in, grabbed the tin boxes and calendar and brought them out to the workbench. 'Let's see what we have.'

Pauline nodded, excitement overcoming her initial shock. The calendar showed July 2002, earlier pages torn off. After wiping off the dust, Mark shook the smaller of the two boxes and heard something rattling inside. Hesitant, and after a quick glance at Pauline, he opened it and saw a purple European Union passport for James Adrian Jones, born ninth September, 1940, two airline tickets and a pocket notebook.

'Mmm, looks quite young for somebody who's sixty years old,' Mark commented, as he studied the passport photograph.

One airline ticket was for a *British Airways* flight to Paris for twenty-eighth July 2002, the other for *Swissair* to Geneva for first August returning to Paris on the eighth.

'Wasn't that just after he died?' Mark asked.

'Yes. Looks like he kept all his personal stuff in there.' She looked towards the hidden room. 'I wonder what else he tucked away.'

When Mark opened the larger tin box, they both gasped and stared at four neat stacks of money, each with a handwritten label.

Mark picked them up and read, 'ten thousand pounds, five thousand euros, five thousand dollars and ten thousand Swiss francs. Who was this chap? Maybe there's something in this notebook.'

It contained lists of European cities with dates, names and telephone numbers of hotels. The last page had only two entries, a hotel in Paris and another in Zurich.

Mark nodded to the opening. 'Let me call Bill and work out how to secure that door.'

When Bill and Jenny saw the opening where the bookcase used to be, Jenny stared open-mouthed while Bill was more expressive. 'Bloody 'ell! What in the name of 'eaven 'av yer done now?'

Mark laughed and pointed to the money on the workbench. 'If you think that's a surprise, look there.'

'Well, I'll be...' Jenny sputtered.

'Bill, come and give me a hand to figure out how it works before we go digging around.'

Bill found a mechanical locking device holding the bookcase in place. 'Well, that's simple. Let's get 'rest o't stuff owta there.'

'Now you two be careful in there. Don't be doin' anythin' daft, yer hear?' Jenny admonished them, as they entered the small room. Pauline nodded in agreement.

They took out the four boxes stacked at the back of the room, and rolled the two metal cabinets outside on their heavy-duty castors.

Mark assumed a solemn expression and turned to Pauline. 'It's after nine o'clock, Miss Grainger, shouldn't you be getting back before it gets too late?'

Pauline stared at him, her hands planted on her hips. 'Mark Bishop! If you think for one minute I'm going anywhere before we find out what's in there, you've got another think coming.'

Mark chuckled. 'Thought you'd say that. Has anyone ever told you your eyes sparkle when you're angry?'

Between the shock of finding the room and his teasing, the compliment left her emotions imitating a manic roller-coaster.

'Jenny, you better make up a room. Seems Miss Grainger's staying again.' Mark smiled as he spoke.

As Mark and Bill opened the boxes, Jenny and Pauline crowded in around them. They took out old racing magazines, going all the way back to the early seventies, and several thick notebooks.

Mark examined the notebooks and read a couple of entries, *M.Z. Istanbul eighteenth July, 2001-16:00. A.M.S. Jaipur eleventh September, 2001-10:00*

He checked a few more pages and put the books on the workbench. 'Looks like lists of appointments. No names—only places, dates, times and initials.' He frowned and checked the thick clothbound books. The earliest entries comprised lists of horse racing results from 1973 onwards, from all over Europe and the USA. Next to each entry was a sum of money, ranging in hundreds, to thousands of pounds, with a smaller sum in brackets underneath.

'Well, if them are bets and 'is winnins, it explains where he got 'is money from, anyroad.' Bill leant over Mark's shoulder. ''Ow the 'ell did 'e get so damned good at pickin' winners? 'E must a' bin a bookie's nightmare.' Bill's accent was thicker than usual. 'Look, its gerrin' late, let's get cleaned up. We can start agen firs' thing in t'mornin'.'

'Good idea,' Mark dusted his hands on his jeans. 'That room hasn't been cleaned since old man Jones died.'

After Mark locked the notebooks and money in his study, they all sat in the dining room and discussed their find.

'One thing's f'sure, looks as if 'e made 'is money on t'ponies. Must 'ave 'ad a bloody crystal ball tucked away,' Bill declared, shaking his head.

'Race winnings are not taxable in the UK, so it was tax-free as well,' added Pauline.

Jenny looked puzzled. 'Don't explain why 'e was so secretive though.'

'It does,' Mark said. 'If you could pick all those winners, you wouldn't go bragging about it. Never mind the publicity, you'd be blacklisted by every bookie in Europe.'

Pauline tossed and turned until the sun peeked through the window and awoke her. She rubbed the grittiness from her eyes, and a hot shower relieved the stiffness in her muscles before she stumbled downstairs.

Mark was already at breakfast. 'Good morning, good morning. Didn't sleep well?'

Pauline scowled. *How could anyone be so damned chirpy at six-thirty in the morning?*

She gave Mark a black look. 'Your Mr Jones is damn aggravating.'

'They're all aggravatin', believe me,' Jenny replied, bringing fresh coffee. 'Well, yer'd better get yer breakfast inside you, 'is lordship's champing at the bit to get started agen. Next time yer can't sleep, just pop into t'kitchen and help yerself to a hot cup of cocoa or hot chocolate.'

Next time, what next time?

Mark opened the top drawer of the first cabinet. 'Let's see what we've got.' He retrieved four more passports, two old-style blue British ones and two purple EU ones. 'Hey, look at these, considering they span almost forty years, he didn't change much at all. Hope I weather as well,' he joked. The next two drawers had half-a-dozen coin and antique jewellery reference books and a first edition book in *Latin*, dated 1482, on *Islamic* medicine. The last drawer contained a leather-bound notebook. They scanned a few pages; it appeared to be a diary or journal.

In the second cabinet, the top drawer held three black velvet boxes. When Mark opened them, they found gold and silver jewellery, all mounted with gemstones.

'Jeez! These should be in a museum.' Mark went to fetch his camera.

The remaining drawers held another twenty-four velvet cases with more antique jewellery. Mark took photographs and made notes.

Pauline examined an ornate silver crucifix, with embedded green stones. 'Oh! This is beautiful. I've never seen anything like it,' she exclaimed, holding it against her neck. 'It's fabulous.'

Mark chuckled. 'Well, if they're not stolen, you can keep that cross you're drooling over... just like a woman.'

Pauline flushed. 'I am *not* drooling, I'm... admiring.'

Mark chuckled. 'Well, it's time to call my solicitor.'

Twenty minutes later, Mark was back. 'I contacted John Prentis. He helped me buy the farm and dealt with Jones' legal firm. He'll contact them regarding the will, and ask an expert from York to come over this afternoon to do a proper valuation.' Mark laughed. 'I can't wait to see Bill and Jenny's faces.'

Mark and Pauline had displayed the opened boxes on the workbench. Jenny was wide-eyed and speechless, and Bill, true to form, uttered several choice imprecations.

'Nice, aren't they?' Mark asked.

Bill stared at him. 'Bloody 'ell! Is that all yer've got t' say?'

'Well, it is a bit odd, I must admit, and God knows what it's all worth. It might be stolen for all we know. Once John gets on to it, we'll have a better idea of who it belongs to and what's going to happen to it.'

Jenny leaned over the workbench. 'Look at that beautiful butterfly brooch with all the fine silver wire and them coloured stones.'

Mark cast a sly grin at Pauline. 'Women! See what I mean? Ow!' Mark yelped, rubbing his arm.

'How can yer play around at a time like this?' demanded Jenny.

'He's being aggravating,' said Pauline.

'I told yer before, they all are.' Jenny glared at both men. 'Now, what are yer goin' to do about this lot?'

'We'll put them in the boxes and lock them in my office. Bill, give me a hand, then we can have lunch.'

During dessert, Mark's phone rang. It was the jewellery expert asking directions to the farm. Mark left Pauline in the dining room and went to wait for him.

'Good afternoon. Mr Bishop, isn't it?' a smartly-dressed, portly middle-aged man asked, and shook Mark's hand. 'My name is Paul Harrison. Mr Prentis told me you had found an antique jewellery collection. I've been in this business for over thirty years, and from what he's told me, it sounds most intriguing.'

In the office, Harrison examined the pieces through a jeweller's loupe. 'Most remarkable. This crucifix is very likely Sixteenth or Seventeenth Century Spanish.' He looked at Mark, eyes sparkling. 'The collection appears to range from early Moghul to late Victorian England. It will take me at least six hours to examine these and provide you with a tentative valuation.'

Mark looked at his watch. It would be eight o'clock before Harrison finished. He arranged refreshments, and when Harrison had his laptop set up, left him to it. Meeting Jenny, he told her Pauline would be staying another night. She nodded and told him Bill was looking for him over at the milk tanks.

Mark was kept busy with a sticking valve, then evening milking came around. When he returned to the house, he found Pauline fast asleep in an armchair. She looked adorable—curled up like a kitten. He reflected on the last few weeks. It had been a long time since he had been this comfortable in a woman's company, and not have to consider any ulterior motives. In fact, her only interest in him seemed purely professional. His mobile phone rang and Pauline started awake.

'So, *Sleeping Beauty* awakens,' Mark teased. 'That was John checking in. Mr Harrison should be finished soon, let's find out what he has to say.'

'Okay,' Pauline mumbled rubbing her eyes, only half awake. 'How long have I been asleep?'

'Three or four hours. It's eight o'clock. Look, by the time we're finished it'll be dark, so I took the liberty of telling Jenny you'll be staying another night. As sleepy as you are, it'll be safer than driving.'

Pauline looked at him through bleary eyes. 'I suppose you're right. Let me freshen up first, and call my mum.'

Her mother's comments, were, to say the least, sarcastic. 'Again? Should I pack your things?' She went downstairs wondering what else was in store for her when she arrived home.

Mark introduced Pauline and asked, 'Mr Harrison, what did you find out?'

Harrison greeted them with a wide smile. 'Miss Grainger, Mr Bishop, a most unusual collection. I do not believe any are stolen. Mr Prentis asked me to check that before anything else. As to the collection itself, although modest in size, it is certainly *not* modest in quality. Whoever put it together must have dedicated a lot of time and effort. The ages are wide ranging, from Sixteenth Century, all the way to late Nineteenth Century.'

Mr Harrison, hands shaking slightly, picked up a pair of earrings. 'This, for example, is typical Sixteenth Century Indian craftsmanship. It's called a *Karanphool Jhumka*. Karanphool means a flower for the ear, by the way. You see, the gold is set with uncut diamonds, pearls and cabochon rubies. The two strands of pearls are taken around the ear to support the weight. This projection at the rear is attached to the hair to minimise the weight on the ear.' He cast an envious look at the earrings. 'They are perfect for a connoisseur's collection.'

'I have been conservative with my estimates. I will need to check recent auctions for more accurate figures, and contact a colleague who specialises in Islamic jewellery. But, because of the excellent condition and scarcity of the collection, it may realise a hundred and seventy to two hundred and fifty thousand pounds in auction. Maybe up to twenty or even thirty percent more to an avid collector.'

Pauline voice cracked. 'How... how much?'

'Up to two hundred and fifty thousand, especially taking in to account the older pieces,' Mr Harrison confirmed. 'If I may have copies of your photographs, I will double check with the police to make sure none are stolen.'

'Right... Fine... Not a problem,' Mark whispered. He pulled himself together and remembered his manners. 'Would you like something to eat before you head back?'

Mr Harrison declined, saying he needed to drive home. Mark put his photographs on a flash drive and escorted him back to his car. 'Thank you very much for your help, Mr Harrison. I look forward to any further information you or your colleague might have.'

Mark called Bill and Jenny to his office and repeated what Mr Harrison had said.

Bill looked stunned. 'Bloody 'ell! Yer mean to tell me it's all been sittin' in there since old man Jones died?'

'There are some legal issues to settle, but I should know something in a few weeks or so.'

'What are you going to do with it all?' asked Pauline.

'It's not mine yet. We'll have to wait and see what John and the police say,' Mark replied. He rubbed his hands together and looked at Jenny. 'Now, what's for dinner? I'm starving.'

'How can you be so damn calm about it?' Pauline scowled at him.

'Eyes, remember?' Mark told her with a grin.

She glared at him, her face flushed. 'You... you.'

'Dinner will ready in a minute,' Jenny announced and headed for the kitchen, a broad smile plastered across her face.

Mark took Pauline's arm, pulling her towards the dining room. 'Come on, let's eat.'

After dinner, they took their coffee to the living room. Mark sat in an armchair, his feet resting on the rich deep-red and cream Turkish wool carpet; the ivory leather matching the textured cream wallpaper.

Pauline's gaze took in the furnishings. The couch and armchairs sat in front of a large screen television and customised *Bose* music and sound system at one end of the room. The rest, a sitting room with comfortable looking armchairs and bookcases between each window. 'This is a beautiful room.'

'I wanted somewhere I could switch off and put my feet up. I don't get as much time to enjoy it as I'd like.'

'I'd make time, believe me.'

'You want to watch a movie?' Mark asked. 'Choose something from the rack over there.'

Pauline examined what appeared to be a couple of hundred CDs and DVDs, sectioned off and labelled by genres.

They talked throughout the movie. About Mr Jones, the jewellery and why he built the hidden room. They speculated on how he had become such an uncannily successful gambler; what was his secret? Their discussion raised more questions than answers.

When the movie ended, Pauline stretched. 'A nice hot bath

and I'll sleep like a log.'

'Me too. It's been a bit exciting the last of couple of days, hasn't it?'

Pauline's eyes widened. '*A bit!* That's got to be the understatement of the year. You're a quarter-of-a-million richer than you were two days ago, for one thing.'

'*If* it's mine and, if it is, my offer of the crucifix still stands,' Mark replied with a warmth in his voice Pauline had not heard before.

Pauline blushed. 'Mark... Mr Bishop... I couldn't accept. It's far too valuable and...'

'Nonsense. It'll look lovely on you. The emeralds match the colour of your eyes. Anyway, it's getting late and I have an early start. I'll say goodnight and see you at breakfast.'

Pauline lay in bed, her thoughts jumping all over. She had given up expecting to find a decent man after all these years; it was like searching for a diamond in a coal tip. She felt exhilarated, thrilled, but the fear of another heartbreak put her in complete turmoil. The pain associated with thinking about starting a relationship again, robbing her of sleep. Eventually, exhaustion solved the problem.

It was an awkward leave-taking after breakfast. Pauline tentatively went to shake hands while Mark raised his arms for a hug. With an embarrassed laugh, Pauline embraced him. His arms tightened around her and, though lasting only a few seconds, heat rose from her chest to her neck.

She drove home, her mind in a whirl. Working closely with Mark these last few days, she now saw a very different person from the bitter and cynical man she had first met two months earlier. A much more confusing one.

After Mark watched Pauline drive away, he puzzled over Jones' seemingly mystical ability to pick winners. He went to his study. It occupied the far end of the house and ran the full width, giving a clear view of the fell-side to the north, the fields and pastures to the west, and the farm buildings across the yard. Here he kept his family's personal effects, photographs and their ashes. The pen-and-ink drawings of his mother and sister he had completed a month before their accident, framed the fireplace. Along the inside wall, he had built a fire-proofed, climate-controlled room for his stamp collection and other important documents, and where he had put everything they had found in the basement.

He took out the leather-bound book they had found and sat in a well-upholstered armchair. It did indeed prove to be some sort of journal. Mr Jones had listed various trips made since 1995, including Argentina, India and Japan.

The last entry was for third of July, 2002 and detailed his plans to move to California to meet people from an organisation called 'Tempus'. Apparently these 'Travellers', as he called them, would be there to investigate the effects of a large earthquake near San Simeon. Mark had never heard of Tempus and found no relevant references on the internet. The only earthquake near San Simeon was a 6.6 magnitude quake in December 2003, but Jones had been dead eighteen months by then.

Mark rubbed his forehead and stared at the diary. It had been one Hell of a thirty-six hours. First, a secret room, then a treasure trove of antique jewellery hidden away, those records showing an incredible number of winning bets on horse-races, and, to top it all off, here was this journal entry. Mark was puzzled. How could Jones be arranging to meet people to study the effects of something that had not even happened by then?

Chapter 4
Thursday, 27 April, 2006

While Mark puzzled over Mr Jones, Pauline was getting a grilling from her mother. She was reminded, for the umpteenth time, her cousin Jean had given birth last month.

'Your Uncle Tom and Aunty Elsie now have four grandchildren and your Aunt Lily has two. Now her Mary has gotten engaged, she can expect more.' This was followed by a tart reminder that Mary was Pauline's *younger* cousin.

Her mother had never been particularly shy about hinting at marriage whenever Pauline met, or spent any time at all with, any half-eligible bachelor. Her standards of eligibility had been dropping, until two arms, two legs and breathing seemed to be the current criteria. It had become worse over the last two months—Mark Bishop was much more than half-eligible. Pauline's two-night stay at his farm had only fuelled her mother's ambitions.

Worst of all, Pauline understood where all this was coming from. Her mother was lonely.

She had had a busy, active life on the farm until her husband died, and she had to sell it. They had bought a semi-detached house with a small garden—a far cry from the eighty acres she used to live on. With Pauline at work every day, a grandchild to take care of would be her idea of Heaven. This only made Pauline feel more guilty.

'What the bloody 'ell are yer doin'?'

Bill's voice shattered Mark's thoughts and he looked around. The cows he had help move to a new pasture, now ambled back along the lane. The gate he was supposed to have closed was swinging wide open.

He had been thinking about the last few days, especially about Pauline; how relaxed he felt in her company, and when he would see her again. He was not going to tell Bill that or he would never hear the end of it. Bill herded the cattle back into the field and glared at Mark.

'Sorry, my mind was wandering.'

'Well, wherever it bloody-well wandered to, get yer body over to it and do summat useful.'

With this rightfully deserved rebuke, Mark headed back to check on the biogas generator.

Three o'clock Saturday morning, two cows decided to calf at the same time, one of them a breech birth.

'Arse first' as Frank Gough, his farm worker, succinctly put it when he woke him. The other needed little help. This was her third calf and it was soon suckling happily, the mother making soothing grunting noises. Mark and the vet spent a couple of hours pulling, sweating and cursing before another new heifer was added to the herd.

Mark had barely sat in his office when Bill came in. " 'Lectric's gone agen in t' milkin' shed."

'That's the second damn time this year. The whole bloody system needs chucking.' Pauline's suggestion for an upgraded power system now appeared prophetic, and very attractive.

They had the back-up generator running an hour after the usual milking time and the cows made their impatience known with a cacophony of bellows and snorts. One of the young cows had become crankier than the others over the delay. Already exhausted from the breach birth and lack of sleep, Mark fumbled attaching the milking cluster. The distressed cow kicked out and sent him flying backwards. With the exception of his damaged pride, the only injury appeared to be a bruised backside.

He picked himself up as Bill came over, chuckling. 'I reckon yer'd better take rest o' day off. Yer need to have yer wits abart yer with these lasses. I know yer a karate expert an' all, but yer outweighed by five-hundred pounds at least.'

When Mark turned to limp back to the farmhouse, Bill shouted, 'Don't forget t'extra cushion on yer chair.'

Mark took the opportunity of the enforced rest to spend the weekend in his study, reading the notebooks they had found. The last entry was for twenty-ninth of July, 2002, eleven days after Mr Jones had died, with results for Ascot, Nottingham and Newcastle, but no sums of money as in the other entries. He checked the internet—they were identical to the actual results.

Mark's phone rang, interrupting his thoughts; it was Pauline.

'Mark, I am free Tuesday morning. I wondered if it was convenient to come over and help prepare the advertisements for the specialists you will need.'

'Yes, that'll be fine.' Despite the rain outside, the day seemed brighter, and the forecast for Tuesday looked even better, never mind what the weatherman had to say.

Jenny greeted Pauline with a smirk when she arrived. 'Come t' visit t'invalid?'

Pauline frowned. 'I'm sorry, Mrs Marsh, I don't follow you.'

'His lordship got on the wrong end of a cow's hoof, now 'e's hobblin' round like an old gaffer,' she chortled.

Before she could go into detail, Mark limped over. 'Thank you, Jenny. I'm sure Miss Grainger is not interested in a minor accident.' Mark led Pauline to his office and gingerly lowered himself into his chair, grimacing.

'Are you sure you're alright?' She knew a kick from a cow was no laughing matter.

'Just a bruise, that's all,' he responded, shuffling the papers on his desk. 'Now let's tackle those adverts.'

After they drafted the advertisements for agricultural trade magazines and various newsletters, Mark saved the final versions on his computer. 'I'll get them out tomorrow. Now I want to show you something else.' Mark bent down, reached into a drawer and passed a book to her. 'I've been skimming Jones' notebooks;

look at this last entry, it's a bit strange.'

Pauline's brow furrowed as she read then looked up. 'It's just another set of bets. What's strange about that? Seems to me gambling was his main source of income.'

'Yes, but see the date. The races were eleven days after he died; I checked the actual results, they were identical. I mean... how could he possibly have known eleven days in advance?' Mark rubbed the back of his neck. 'There's something else in that journal. It's in my study. Come on, I'll show you.'

Pauline followed Mark to the end of the corridor, where he punched a code into a keypad on the wall. He held the door open, and gestured for her to enter. 'My hobby room, as Jenny calls it.'

The imposing local limestone fireplace drew her eyes. Four ceramic urns on the mantelpiece with a pen-and-ink drawing of a woman on either side piqued her interest. One was an older lady while the other, an obvious teenager.

'Wait a bit, I'll fetch the journal.' Mark went to another door at the end of the study while Pauline examined the room.

It was as luxuriously furnished as the living room. No wonder her mother had said he had spent a small fortune on decorating. A light-brown, well-upholstered couch and matching armchairs near the windows exuded comfort. A thick-pile beige carpet covered the whole floor. On top of low bookcases, polished wooden carved African figurines stood neatly displayed, and on the walls hung several pen-and-ink sketches of local scenery.

Her first impression of an internal decorator's luxury showroom was spoiled when she looked in the corner by the nearest window. An old shoebox, pens and loose–leaf files cluttered a standard office desk. Above it, an annotated mosaic of *Ordnance Survey* maps showing the area around the farm and northeast Derbyshire.

Mark interrupted her perusal. 'Here we are.' She turned from her examination to see Mark holding the journal they had found.

'Mark this is a beautiful room. Who did all these drawings?' She pointed to the two sketches by the fireplace. 'Those two are excellent.'

'I did. Those are my mother and sister.' A pained expression crossed his face as he passed her the journal.

Damn, I should have realised who they were.

'See the last entry. Check the date.'

She opened the book to the last page and read the date. 'It's a month before he died.'

'I know, but according to my research, the earthquake he mentions happened a year and a half *after* he died.'

Pauline read the entry, raised her eyebrows and gasped. 'But... how?'

'Damned if I know, but I'm going to check that room again.'

As Mark gently levered himself out of his chair, she asked, 'So, what happened with you and the cow, anyway?'

With a sheepish look, Mark related his weekend adventures. Pauline burst out laughing. It was infectious and Mark's affronted expression changed and he joined in. She could not resist it. 'A pain in the butt is what you get for being a pain in the butt.' The wounded look on Mark's face made her laugh even more.

Pauline's phone rang, interrupting their laughter.

A few minutes of 'yes', 'alright', 'no problem', followed, and with laughter still in her voice, she said, 'That was my boss. I'm sorry, I have to see another client.'

Unnerved by Mark's intent stare as they stood by her car, she rocked from foot to foot. She had not felt this awkward in a long time. Unsure she could handle a repeat of their last hug, she held out her hand.

'I'll, er, be in touch,' Mark said, taking her hand.

'Right. Ah, anything else you need, give me a call.'

Pauline blushed as she realised she still held his hand and quickly let go.

A glance in the rear view mirror showed Mark waving to her as she drove away. A shiver passed through her, whether of fear or desire, she could not decide.

In the afternoon Mark received a text message from Pauline.

"Busy for rest of week. Any more news about Mr Jones, call me."

He was surprised at the disappointment he felt. 'Enough. Time to take a damn good look at that room.'

Mark checked the wall lights. He noticed they used standard batteries, not mains electricity. *Old Jonesy must've really wanted to keep this place off the grid.*

Replacing the batteries, he soon had sufficient light in which to work. After he vacuumed the floor, he examined the brickwork for defects. On the far wall, he noticed two bricks at shoulder height; both dark-yellow, in contrast to the other reddish-brown ones. He looked at the position of the two knots and examined the two bricks closely. When he pushed the right hand one, he heard a familiar click and felt the same give as before. The other was the same. Pushing both together the wall moved.

'Not again,' he muttered. 'The canny old bastard built another room behind this one!'

Mark pushed harder and a four-foot by six-foot section of the wall swung away. When it had moved right back, he took out his torch. The room resembled a short corridor roughly eight-feet long; bare, concrete-lined with the same curved rails on floor and ceiling, but instead of a wall at the far end, all he could see was a black hole. He held up the torch and his mouth dropped open at the sight of a set of stairs going deeper in to the ground.

The thumping of blood rushing through his ears was deafening as he took his first tentative step. His knuckles white on the handrail, he counted each step. The smell of dust and stale air became stronger and he noticed light fittings along the concrete wall. He had counted to forty before he stood at the bottom. He figured he was around forty-feet below ground altogether, and thirty-feet to the east, under the farmyard.

Shining his light, Mark found himself standing in a corner of what appeared to be a large room with ceramic floor tiles and plastered walls. He could not see all the way around, but made out a workbench filling the opposite corner. Going back upstairs, Mark closed the bookcase door and collected a box of batteries from his workshop.

He fixed the lights on the stairs and the wall lights around the new room—now he had his first good look at this second basement. It looked to be twenty-five feet by twenty by eight, with a table and chair in the centre of the room; everything coated with a thin film of dust.

At head height, next to the stairs, was an opening covered by a metal grill and below, a set of steel doors with a portable generator inside. Now he knew where the power for all the wall sockets came from. On top of the bench in the corner, was a fume cabinet with the exhaust running to the grill. The rest of the bench held a multi-compartment box of electronic components and a soldering iron sat in a spring mount.

Along the wall next to the stairs was a six-foot high bookcase, which, at a cursory glance, was full of books on various science and engineering subjects. Next to it was a padlocked steel cabinet. Standing alone in the corner, was a large cage made of quarter-inch copper mesh and lined all the way to the ceiling with reflective insulation. *A Faraday cage? What was that doing down here?*

TP 1000: The Bishops

Along the end wall stood five standard four-drawer filing cabinets with another metal grill above them. Mark coughed from the dust and stale air and looked at the two grills. *Hope they're for ventilation. This place certainly needs it.*

In the far corner was a plain desk and office chair. Standing by the desk, Mark scrutinised the room. *Why would anyone go to the effort of building a workshop forty-feet below ground?* Except for the Faraday cage, there was not anything unusual here.

He decided to keep this quiet for now, but was looking forward to seeing Pauline's face when she returned.

The next day he bought a bolt cutter and a more powerful portable generator. Within a few hours, he had power and the ventilation system running. He spent the next two days mopping, dusting and wiping. At least he could now examine everything without sneezing his head off all the time.

The Faraday cage had roused his curiosity and he could not wait to find out for what it had been used. Mark opened the metal gate and, seeing two more lights near the top, replaced their batteries. In the centre of the cage was a plain wooden cabinet with two deep drawers. The top one contained a foam pad with empty cut-out shapes. The bottom one contained a dull silvery metal box, the same size as a portable computer. Placing it on top of the cabinet, he saw 'TP1000' incised at the bottom right. Mark found a sliding catch on the side and it opened like a laptop. A small screen and keyboard with several labelled buttons and indicator lights occupied the lower half, the lid covered in what appeared to be gold-coloured miniature solar panels.

His stomach flip-flopped when the device beeped and a red light flashed above the words 'Battery Power'. He wiped the sweat from his forehead. Whatever this was, it appeared to be working. 'At least it didn't explode,' he murmured.

As there was nothing he could do until whatever it was, was fully charged, he examined the filing cabinets.

The drawers, labelled by years from 1970 to 2025, puzzled him, and he wondered if Mr Jones had been a Futurist. In the 2005-2006 drawer, he found files categorised by currency exchanges, property prices and gold prices. He found a range of tables and graphs covering 2000 to 2015 even more shocking. There was one labelled '*Bitcoins*', whatever they were, and in the one labelled 'Gold', tables and graphs showed gold rising from a low in February 2001 to the current price, and continuing to a peak of 1,912 US dollars in August 2011. Another graph showed US dollar trends against sterling, indicating a coming drop to 2.10 in 2008 and another below 1.50 in 2015. Stunned, he sat at the table and stared at the cabinets.

Mark closed the computer-like device, and switched off all the lights except the ones along the stairs. He moved the books and files from the 2005-2006 drawer to his study and checked the tables and charts of currency trends on the internet. They were accurate up to today's date. He took a few deep breaths to calm himself... this was becoming scary.

With mixed feelings, Mark looked through the one of the files with horse racing results right up to 2015. He found the results for the current week; a winner at Redcar at 50-1 and another at 14-1 odds. 'If these are right...' His mind spun at the implications. 'Well, there's one easy way to check,' he muttered and put thought into action. He packed an overnight bag, and told Bill and Jenny he was off to York for a couple of days on urgent business.

TP 1000: The Bishops

After breakfast he visited several different bookies in Thirsk, Ripon and York, betting ten pounds on different races at each one. Restless and nervous, he roamed the old streets, oblivious to the thousand years of history surrounding him, until it was time for the first results. Every bet had won and, by the end of the day, the three hundred pounds he had started with was now over nine thousand.

Back at the inn where he was staying, he sat in a corner of the taproom and tried to wrap his brain around everything that had happened of late. He had barely touched his drink when the barmaid called closing time. This was not turning out to be the quiet countryside life he had envisaged when he had bought the farm.

Mark had always prided himself on his decision making abilities, but what in Heaven's name was he going to do with all this information? It was one thing to tell people about the second basement, it was something else altogether to tell them what was going to happen for the next twenty years.

Mark's mind kept running over the implications of what he had discovered and after a restless night, he drove home. As soon as he could get away from farm business, he headed for the new basement. His first decision was to charge the device in the Faraday cage. While the red light continued flashing, he took the bolt-cutter and opened the steel cabinet.

He laid the contents on the table—over forty notebooks and a box of meticulously painted model soldiers; apparently lead by their weight. He removed several loose documents, passports, a World War II identity card and ration book, and a California driving license, dated 2001.

Mark gulped when he took out one of the last objects in the cabinet. It was a one-kilo *Credit Suisse* gold ingot, with a dozen more like it, just sitting there.

'Bloody Hell! That's over a quarter of a million US dollars.' He stood there, looking at the ingot he was holding, and the others in the cabinet.

A sharp beeping sound from the Faraday cage made him nearly drop the gold bar. Rushing over, a row of green lights glowed above the 'Battery Charge' sign and the screen titled 'Log-In' displayed a box 'New Operator'. Hands shaking, he touched 'New Operator' and the screen changed to a set of instructions. Following the instruction, he entered his name, date of birth, current date and time and a twelve-digit password. Finally he placed his left thumb on the thumb-pad, and felt a slight tingle. The screen changed to 'New Operator Accepted. Welcome Mark Bishop' and displayed a list of menus including specifications, operating instructions for new operators, and a 'Warnings' section.

His eyes glazed as he read the information displayed from the various menus. His mind was numb at what it all implied. This explained how Jones could predict what was going to happen, but he still could not take it in. The 'TP' stood for Time Portal and the '1000' meant that with it, he could travel one-thousand years into the past. It had to be some incredible hoax.

As soon as Jenny had gone back to her cottage after dinner, Mark went to his study and checked several locations, noting their latitude and longitude, and downloaded photographs of them at various times in history. Unable to sleep, he went back to the basement and put the device on the table. He selected 'Travel Location' from the menu. He entered data for 'Origin: Latitude and Longitude'. the same for 'Destination' plus date and time. He pressed the 'Enter' key and two status lights changed to a steady green.

Mark switched on the video recorder he had set up, and turned to the Portal device. He wiped his clammy hands on his jeans and gulped. *Okay... moment of truth.*

TP 1000: The Bishops

He placed his thumb on the pad and hesitated. 'Here goes,' he murmured and pressed 'Initiate Gateway'. A shimmer appeared in the air six-feet in front of him. It quickly resolved to a window giving a clear view of Buckingham Palace in 1819 with Marble Arch in its original position, where the famous Palace balcony is now.

'This is incredible,' he whispered, as he watched a carriage pass pedestrians in period clothes on a morning stroll.

Excited, he reset the coordinates for the bank of the River Thames and the date to first of September, 1666, the day before the Great Fire of London. The shimmer resolved into a fantastic view of old London Bridge. The height of the buildings was amazing—some of them seven storeys high. The bridge itself appeared narrow with all the houses and shops built on it and there was a crush of people and carts crossing it—two carts barely able to pass each other. He shuddered at the sight of spiked heads of executed criminals mounted above the Southwark gatehouse. On the Thames, small river barges plied up and down, and he watched one small boat capsize as it passed through the narrow arches.

He shut off the device, and the weight of responsibility hit him. Could he keep this to himself? *Should* he keep this to himself? He had to do one more test to be sure. He had pulled some pretty crazy stunts in his life, but thinking about this one made him break out in a cold sweat.

Chapter 5

Saturday, 6th May 2006

Eyes itching and stomach growling, Mark dashed upstairs, nearly knocking into Jenny coming out of the kitchen.

'What were yer doin' down there?'

'I, ah, couldn't sleep. I went to do a bit of cleaning.'

'Well, it looks like yer didn't sleep at all. Yer go get freshened up, breakfast'll be ready in a jiffy.'

He ignored Jenny's questioning looks through breakfast and headed for his study, leaving her frowning.

He paced around the room, sitting for no more than a few minutes before he resumed pacing. His thoughts raced round and round like a crazed carousel. He stopped by the fireplace and stared at the urns on the mantelpiece. *Dammit! I've got to try.*

Mark checked the Portal's menus. It was not possible to travel to the past during his current lifetime. His strength drained from his body and he sagged in his chair—his hope of saving his family,

TP 1000: The Bishops

torn from him.

He sat up straight. If he could not go back to Singapore after February 1975, what if he went back *before* he was born?

What would happen if everything had changed when he returned? To what would he return? His mind went back to everything he had done in the last six years. He would not have had the money to buy Keldthorpe farm and probably would not have returned to the UK. Mark did not care. He just wanted his family back.

After puzzling over how to get a warning to his parents, Mark decided to leave a letter with a law firm his father had sometimes used. They could deliver it to him a few days before the dinner dance. The solicitor might be reluctant to accept the letter, but Mark reckoned if he dangled enough cash in front of him, he would take it on.

But where to find the money he would need? Mark tried to buy 1970s Singapore currency on the internet but only managed to find two hundred and twenty-five dollars. It was not enough but he ordered the notes anyway and paid for courier charges. Then he remembered Mr Jones' gold bars, He checked the gold price in 1974 and a one-kilo bar would give him well over eleven thousand dollars... more than enough.

Mark planned his trip for February 1974. He needed a secluded location so selected an alley off Temple Street in Chinatown, Singapore, within walking distance of the law firm at People's Park Centre.

Mark spent several hours deciding how to word the letter to his father. He wanted to make sure it would not be taken for a prank, yet at the same time, he did not want to cause a panic. Remembering the family Bible and David's notes, he mentioned several anecdotes from it, and that this was not an elaborate practical joke. He finished with a final warning to his father—something terrible would happen if he went to his company's Dinner and Dance on the twenty-ninth of January, 2001. His mother was more than a bit superstitious, and when she read it, she would worry, and persuade his father not to attend.

By the time all the Singapore currency arrived, he had everything ready. Mark went to the sub-basement and set up the machine. He checked the settings three times before getting up the nerve to press the 'Initiate' key. The gateway opened halfway along the alley he had selected. At five-thirty in the morning, as he had hoped, it was deserted.

Holding the Portal, Mark took a deep breath and walked through. He shuddered at the slight clinging resistance—like pushing through a stiff cobweb—and stepped into the alley. He stood motionless and let his heart stop pounding. That one step had taken Mark from a cool ten-degree centigrade to a humid twenty-five degrees. The business suit he was wearing was more suited to England's weather than the tropics and his shirt was already sticking to him. It struck him where, and when, he was, and looked around in amazement. *The bloody thing really worked.*

He closed the gateway and put the device in the pilot case holding the gold ingot. Now he needed to kill time until the shops opened around ten o'clock, and find somewhere cool to wait. He walked to a coffee shop on Mosque Street, sat under the overhead fan, and ordered breakfast in fluent Malay. It had been a couple of years since he had been in Singapore and eaten *Nasi Lemak*. His mouth watered at the aroma of rich, creamy rice cooked in coconut milk. He crunched on the deep-fried anchovies slathered with the spicy-sweet chili sambal, the tart shrimp paste and fresh chili making his tongue tingle. He washed it down with frothy, freshly brewed milky tea.

TP 1000: The Bishops

After another glass of tea, he wandered to the shopping centre and luxuriated in the air conditioning. When the shops opened, Mark approached a goldsmith shop advertising gold bars for sale. Overcoming the goldsmith's initial reluctance to buy a one-kilo bar stretched Mark's patience. After an hour of arguing and haggling, and insisting on cash, he and the shop owner agreed on eleven thousand dollars. Pocketing the money he walked over to the solicitor's office, introduced himself, and asked for the senior partner.

'Mr Low, I realise this may seem a strange request, I wish you to keep this letter and have it delivered on the twenty-fourth of January, 2001.'

The plump solicitor's eyes widened. 'Mr Bishop, this is most unusual. I'm not sure whether we can accommodate your request. You are asking us to keep this document for twenty-six years.'

'It's a wager George and I have. I'm prepared to pay handsomely for this service.' Mark took out the wad of one thousand dollar notes. 'Would ten thousand dollars be sufficient?'

Mr Low stared at the money for no more than five seconds. 'Ah, I believe it will be more than adequate, sir.'

Mark handed Mr Low the sealed envelope addressed to Mr and Mrs George Bishop at the house his father would buy in Siglap Road in 1998. Mr Low called a clerk to draw up a document detailing Mark's instructions. Once signed and witnessed, Mark handed over the money.

Excited, Mark left. He wanted to return straightaway, but the streets bustled with people; he needed to find a secluded location. There was a spot in the Botanic Gardens, on the Jungle Walk, which would be ideal. After the taxi dropped him off, he headed in to the rainforest and stepped off the path towards a banyan tree; it was more than extensive enough to hide him. Standing in a pile of decaying leaves behind the tree, he opened the gateway. The device had automatically reset the destination to the original departure point and the date and the time to one hour after departure. This was a pre-programmed default control to prevent manual errors to avoid arriving before he had left. When the gateway opened, Mark rushed through.

Mark put the Portal in its drawer, closed the bookcase and headed upstairs. His heart sank when he saw he was in the same house he had built. He heard Jenny humming in the kitchen. If his plan had worked she should not be here. When he entered his study, he froze. Everything was the same. The urns still on the mantelpiece. It had not worked.

He checked the internet, found the law firm's current phone number and sat to figure out what had gone wrong. After hours of anguish, he called the law firm in the evening. The receptionist put him through to Mr Low, and Mark, barely controlling his anger, reminded him of the letter he had left with them and asked whether it had been delivered.

'Mr Bishop, I am so sorry. We tried contacting you, but we didn't have a forwarding address.'

He explained an intern had been given the old accounts to handle. Ten days before the letter was to have been sent, the intern had resigned and gone back to Malaysia. The letter lay in the archives until a new intern found it on sixth of August and posted it immediately.

'Unfortunately, it was returned by the postal service with the note 'Not known at this address'.'

The sixth of August was a month after Mark had sold the house and eight days after he had left Singapore for London. Mr Low offered a full refund but Mark slammed down the receiver.

Angry, frustrated and depressed, he sat in his study for hours. All the grief he had suffered after the accident rose up... it was like losing them all again.

TP 1000: The Bishops

Sitting in his study all night, Mark worked through his bitterness and pain. Early morning, he went to the basement and checked the Portal's menus. Under 'Paradoxes', Mark read the section on the *Novikov Self-Consistency Principle*. It stated, *if an event exists which would give rise to a paradox, or to any change to the past, then the probability of that event occurring is zero.* Visits from trained Tempus personnel to various eras did create local ripples in the time-space continuum; apparently these were minor enough to be smoothed out with the passage of time.

He was left with the heart-breaking conclusion he could not change the past. He had to accept he would never see his parents again, nor watch his sister grow up. He had now mourned them twice.

Brushing aside tears, he needed to determine what to do with the device. With a thousand years to choose from, *where to start?*

There was such a rich tapestry of history. The signing of the *Magna Carta*. He could meet *Leonardo da Vinci*, and learn who really posed for the *Mona Lisa*. And *Machu Picchu*... what was its real purpose? A royal site, a religious or pilgrimage centre? His mind buzzed with possibilities. Cold practicality reared its head. God knows what trouble he would get into in Machu Picchu in the 1400s.

Mark looked at the untidy desk where he worked on his stamp collection. He could even pop in to a post office on the sixth of May, 1840 and buy a whole sheet of Penny Blacks. Then he remembered his comment to Pauline about the early postal service. To find those answers he would have to live there and get to know the people involved. The genealogical chart hanging on the wall gave him another idea. He would have to travel to the 1500s to find Henry Bishop and work backwards through each generation. But that meant long term visits through a period of massive social change, wars and rebellion.

He had better stick to Victorian England, at least he had a lot of information on this era and Pauline's knowledge of Victorian life would be invaluable. Problem was, how to gain her interest and support—and not scare her off?

Mark retrieved an old map of York from his grandfather's map collection. He calculated the coordinates for a small courtyard off High Petergate and came up with a scheme on how to tell her about his time machine.

They would both need early Nineteenth-Century-style clothes. Mark held a long phone conversation with Pauline's friend, Julie, and spent a couple of hours on the internet. He ordered several sets of clothes and accessories. Now he needed money. He was sure, with Mr Harrison's help, he could buy sufficient for this one trip. Now that was settled, he was filled with relief, mixed with trepidation.

Monday, he focussed on his business plan. After the latest power failure, upgrading the bio-gas generator and solar power systems was his first priority. Most of his plans required time or specialist staff to implement and he decided building the hydroponics complex should be next on his list.

Mark contacted the relevant companies and arranged for site visits. In the afternoon he drove to York where Mr Harrison greeted him with a vigorous handshake.

'I was just about to call you, Mr Bishop. I have checked with the various authorities and am pleased to report none of the items were stolen and have the revised estimate for the collection.' Mr Harrison passed him a sheet of paper. 'Here is an itemised list, it comes to £285,000 in total.'

'That's unbelievable. I'm still waiting to hear from John Prentis. If there are no problems, I'll be looking to sell most of it, but that wasn't the reason I came. I want to buy some early Nineteenth

TP 1000: The Bishops

Century currency.'

Mr Harrison recommended a coin dealer nearby and accompanied him to make the introductions.

Using Jones' money, Mark proceeded to buy late Eighteenth and early Nineteenth Century copper and silver coins and a couple of gold sovereigns. His patience was tested overriding the coin dealer's protests over their quality, and whether suitable to form the basis for a rare coin collection. Mark was not interested in collecting—he intended to spend them.

In the evening, Pauline called. He told her of Mr Harrison's new estimate. He certainly was not about to mention his failed trip to Singapore, nor his plans for them to visit Nineteenth Century York. Not yet, anyway.

'Fantastic! Did you hear from your solicitor yet?'

'Not yet. Hopefully I'll hear something soon.' Hoping to distract her further he added, 'I'll also be transferring money from Singapore to the farm account.'

'When it's transferred let me know. I'll redo the financials for you.'

He hung up and leaned back, smiling. He was glad Bradley had come to his senses and sent Pauline. She not only knew her business but was also someone with whom he could actually have a conversation and share ideas; something lacking in his life recently.

After days of site visits, and Bill's complaints of turning the farm into a building site again, John called.

'Everything's settled. By the terms of Mr Jones' will, the sale of the house contents was restricted to specific items. Your find would be included in the remaining contents of the farmhouse and surrounding farm buildings. So, since Mr Harrison has confirmed none of it is stolen, it's all yours. Congratulations.'

Mark called Mr Harrison and asked him to sell everything, except for three specific items. He checked the newspaper and called to break the news to Pauline.

'That's wonderful news.'

'I want to celebrate. Would you like to go to a show and dinner this Friday?'

'Er... are you sure?'

'Absolutely. I've been breaking my back around here lately and this gives me a chance for a night on the town. Plus, you're the co-finder, we should celebrate together. Please, say yes?'

'What did you have in mind?'

'There's *Jim Cartwright's* play *'Two'* on at the York Theatre Royal, and for dinner, French, Italian or Asian. Your choice.'

'Er... French.'

'Great. I'll make reservations then, and call to confirm what time I'll pick you up.'

As soon as Pauline put down the phone, her feeling of euphoria quickly changed to anxiety, and wondered if this was such a good idea. She called Julie.

'Go for it!' Julie sounded ecstatic.

'Alright for you to say, but I've got butterflies the size of bats flying around my insides. What if this is another mistake?'

'I've met this one, remember, and he couldn't be more different than *that* bastard. Relax, and let him set the pace.'

'Things *have* been a bit different since we came back from our trip to Leeds. I'm not sure what to think.'

'Don't think! *That's* your problem. Go and enjoy a night out.'

TP 1000: The Bishops

Talking to Julie helped a little, but Pauline did not know what she would say to her mother, or, more to the point, what her mother would say to her.

While Pauline talked to Julie, Mark called the theatre and restaurant and made reservations. He secured dress circle seats in the middle of row C; nice and central. Mark took the Spanish crucifix and Victorian butterfly brooch, and drove to York to have them cleaned up.

At the restaurant, Mark talked about the play. Pauline remembered how, at the end, the husband spilled out the feelings he had kept pent inside for so long over the death of their son. How this confession had finally freed them of the tension and pain that had built up and damaged their relationship. The secret *she* was keeping threatened whatever was growing between her and Mark, but the shame persisted—even after five years. How could she tell him the truth?

'I'm sorry, what did you say?' Pauline asked, her 'wool gathering' had made her miss what Mark had said.

'I said you should see Harrogate Theatre after the renovations. It's fantastic; they've done a marvellous job.'

'Sorry, I was... er... thinking about all the jewellery we had found.' She concentrated on her pan-roasted duck breasts with sherry and honey sauce.

Pauline ate the last rich creamy mouthful of her chocolate mousse and sighed, contented. 'That was a fantastic meal, thank you.'

Mark grinned. 'Now, close your eyes, I've a surprise for you.'

'What are you up to?' Her sense of contentment changed to apprehension. She did not like surprises.

'Come on, humour me.'

Closing her eyes, she heard Mark stand and felt him lift her hair. 'What are you doing?'

'Hush, wait a minute.'

She felt something put around her neck. Cold metal on her chest.

'Okay, you can look now.'

She saw the silver crucifix shining. 'Mark, you can't. It's... but...' she stuttered.

'I must say it does look beautiful on you, and the emeralds really *do* match your eyes.'

Pauline was speechless.

'I take it you like it?' Mark asked, with an enormous smile on his face.

'It's... Mark, you... I...'

'Since you haven't said anything coherent for the last couple of minutes, it's settled. Just smile and say thank you. I believe that's the correct expression when receiving a gift.'

'You are too much. Of course I like it, it's fantastic, but...'

'No buts, it's yours now, so stop arguing, and enjoy.'

'You are the most aggravating man I have *ever* met,' Pauline retorted, not sure whether to be angry or overjoyed.

'Your eyes really *do* shine when you get angry, you know.'

Between the shock of getting the crucifix, and growing exasperation, she was thoroughly confused. She did not know *what* to think, and his grinning like a Cheshire cat did not help at all.

They drove back chatting about the secret room, Mr Jones and his jewellery. It was midnight when they pulled up at Pauline's house.

TP 1000: The Bishops

As she stepped out of the car, she tripped. Mark caught her, their faces inches apart. He leaned down and Pauline closed her eyes. He gently kissed her. Hesitance changed to passion and her hands moved along his arms until wrapped around his neck and she sank in to his embrace. Mark gently broke away, staring at her. Pauline stood for a moment, closed her eyes again, and moved back in to his arms. They held each other, not speaking, not moving—enjoying the close contact.

For Pauline, it was as if five years of repressed emotions had finally burst free, cauterising an old open wound. For Mark, it was an end to loneliness, and having someone with whom he could let his guard down at last.

'You had better get inside, before your mother comes out,' Mark advised, softly.

She sprang from his arms. 'Oh! Oh yes.'

'Don't worry, we can go as slowly as you wish.'

'What are we going to do now?' Pauline whispered.

'Take it one day at a time and see where it goes.' Mark responded gently.

'Thank you. You don't know how much that means to me.'

'Want to go for a ride up the fell tomorrow?'

'Sounds good. Princess hasn't been out much lately.'

'Good. Tomorrow morning around eleven alright?'

'Fine. Thank you for a wonderful evening. I don't know how to thank you for this.' Pauline held the crucifix up.

'My pleasure, believe me. Seeing your face light up was thanks enough.'

They saw the lights come on in her mother's bedroom.

'I'd better go,' she dashed into the house.

Mark drove home happier than he could remember.

Chapter 6
Saturday, 27th May 2006

Mark and Lucky arrived in the farmyard as Pauline rode in on Princess. Lucky's head came up and almost jerked the reins out of Mark's hands. The two horses put their heads together and blew into each other's nostrils.

Mark grinned at Pauline who fidgeted in the saddle. 'At least they like each other.'

They rode along farm tracks and country lanes, between hedgerows of blooming hawthorn and occasional red campion with its delicate pink flowers. They stopped at an old byre high on the hillside, dismounted and looked across the valley.

Pauline turned to Mark, 'Why did you buy this farm? I mean, you hadn't done any farming before, had you? And why here in Yorkshire?'

'No, I hadn't. I quit my mining job because of an argument over all the pollution; contaminated rivers and children suffering all kinds of illnesses. I'd had enough. After my family's accident I came back here and visited my cousin, David. He mentioned how the family used to be farmers ages ago, and that got me thinking...

how it would be much better to create; grow something, rather than destroy.'

'Your family were farmers? Where? When?'

'Farmers from way back, in *Cumberland*. In 1935, the family moved to Yorkshire and worked in the coal mines. That is until my father, an engineer, ended up as Vice President of Operations for an oil-rig company. Then there's me. I was born in Doncaster, so Yorkshire is my home really, but I've lived overseas since I was two years old. Started as a mines engineer and now a farmer. Full cycle, really! At least I didn't end up hung as a horse thief, like one of my ancestors.'

She grinned mischievously. 'Horse thief! What other skeletons are lurking in your family closet?'

Marked grinned back. 'Two mysteries and one scandal. My six-time great aunt Mary's only mention was being born on eighteenth of August, 1747, apparently she eloped. A scandalous generation—Mary was twin sister to the horse thief. Then there's my three-time great uncle James, same name as the horse thief, who disappeared in 1837.

He was a *very* successful gambler; a bit too successful, if you get my meaning. Also a poacher... deer, rabbits and a neighbour's fourteen year old daughter. He left her pregnant after raping her. The real black sheep of the family. The girl committed suicide and the family have never used the name James again.'

'Horse thief, poacher, gambler and rapist. I wonder if it's safe to be out here with you!'

'Since great-great whatever Uncle James, everyone's been quite law-abiding, believe me.'

'What's the other mystery?'

'Same family as the black sheep. Must have been a really screwed-up lot. James had an elder brother, John. Apparently he was a bit of renegade and headed off to America in 1849 to join the California Gold Rush. He returned to Cumberland in 1854 but died in a pub brawl a month later, just before he was supposed to be married.'

'As far as I know we have no colourful characters in my family. Farmers as long as anyone knows.'

Mark took her in his arms. 'I'm more than happy with the results.'

Time was suspended for Pauline; she had not felt this sensuous in years. She clung to him when they stopped kissing.

'Slowly, remember.' Mark said, softly. 'Let's ride back and have lunch.'

Taking their time, they rode back, holding hands until near the farm.

Mark left for a few minutes while Jenny cleared the dishes and chatted with Pauline.

Coming back, he held out a black velvet box. 'Jenny, I forgot to tell you. John cleared up everything about the jewellery, so here's the brooch you admired.'

'Mr Bishop, I couldn't...' Jenny took a step back.

'Yes you can, Miss Grainger has accepted the crucifix, the least you can do is accept this.'

Her voice broke as she admired the brooch. 'Oh, Mr Bishop, it's beautiful, I don't know what to say.'

'Thanks is enough, believe me.'

Jenny turned towards the kitchen, her eyes glistening.

'I need to ride back before it gets dark,' Pauline told him.

'Look, why don't you leave Princess here? She can stable with Lucky. It will save time in future.'

TP 1000: The Bishops

'That's not a bad idea.'

'Come on then. Let's get her settled in her new home and I'll drive you back.'

Mark dropped her at her home and drove off before Pauline's mother came out.

He arrived back at the farm in time to take delivery of a large parcel. Mark spent the next couple of hours in the basement trying on his Regency merchant's clothes and hanging Pauline's dress in a cupboard.

The following weekend a brewing storm cancelled their plans for horse riding.

'I've a video I want you to see.' Mark told Pauline and led her to the study. Switching on his laptop he ran the video he had taken the first time he had used the time machine. Pauline sat puzzled as she watched the screen. She saw Mark move around a strange room, when a flickering light appeared in mid-air. Alarmed, she turned to Mark. 'What... what's that... that *thing*?'

'Patience. Watch.'

She was stunned into silence when the light resolved into a clear view of Buckingham Palace. It was so different. No high ornamental fence and gates, no red-coated guards with busbies at the entrance, and no Victoria Memorial. It reminded her of an engraving she had seen, but this was live, and in colour; people were walking around dressed in early Victorian fashion and horse-drawn carriages passing by. The view closed and she watched him doing something on a computer keyboard. She turned to him and before she could speak, 'Wait. There's more.'

At first she could not identify the scene, then gasped when she recognised the old

London Bridge. She was stunned at the height of the buildings along the bridge, and the River Thames churning as it passed through the narrow arches. The crowds and variety of carts and carriages mesmerised her.

'Where did you get these? It's... it's...' she stammered, when the video stopped. Her mind spun. She had only seen these views in old paintings. This was sharp and clear—like looking through a window, or watching a silent movie, in colour.

'Come on, I'll show you the real surprise. It's in the basement.'

'What's going on?' She was unable to control the shakiness in her voice.

He smiled. 'If I tell you, it's not a surprise, is it? Patience is a virtue.'

After what she had just seen she was more than a little nervous about what was coming next.

Mark switched on the lights in the secret room, closed the bookcase door and told Pauline to close her eyes. A few seconds later she heard a faint grinding noise.

'You can open your eyes now.'

'What the...' she exclaimed, and moved to look through the new opening at the staircase.

'Our Mr Jones built another room down there.'

Pauline was astonished when she descended the stairs. 'So this is your surprise, but what's it got to do with those videos?'

'This is not the surprise.' He pointed at what appeared to be a metal cage with baking foil fastened to it. 'It's in there.'

'What's that?'

'It's a Faraday cage. It excludes electrostatic and electromagnetic fields.'

'English, please?'

'It blocks out electrical signals. Doomsday preppers use them to protect electronics in case of a nuclear explosion,' he explained. 'Check the signal on your phone and check it again when we're

TP 1000: The Bishops

inside.'

She looked. There was a strong signal.

'Now for the *real* surprise.' Mark led her inside the cage and closed the door. Pauline checked her phone—no signal.

She watched him take the silver coloured metal box she had seen on the video from the wooden cabinet and walk back to the table. 'This is it.' He opened the Portal and logged in.

'What is it? A computer?'

'That's what I thought at first. I've studied this a lot and believe me, it's definitely *not* a computer. Let me show you.' He touched a menu item on the screen. 'Read this.'

The more she saw, the more confused she became, especially when she read 'Time range: 1000 with -150 year safety margin'. She looked blankly at Mark.

'Now read this.' He pulled up the 'Warnings' screen. It was divided in to nuclear, natural, geographic and personal. Mark selected nuclear and showed her an entry under the heading 'Blocked era. 2240 to 2365 - nuclear reactor fallout after ice-slip'.

She stared at Mark. 'That's... that's over three hundred years from now.'

'There's more.' He changed the screen. The heading was 'Natural Disasters' with three sub-categories, volcanic eruptions, earthquakes and solar flares. Choosing volcanic eruptions, he told her to read.

The first entry was Santorini in BC1450. She scrolled through the screen; Vesuvius 79AD and other eruptions all the way through Mt St. Helens in 1980. She stopped when she read Eyjafjallajökull on fourteenth of April, 2010 and Mount Merapi on twenty-fifth of October, 2010.

'Those eruptions haven't happened yet.' Pauline started to feel scared.

'This thing is a time machine,'

Anger was her usual reaction to fear. 'It's a what? Is this some kind of joke?'

'Now you know why I showed you those videos first. If I had told you I'd found a time machine, would you have believed me? You'd have me put in a padded room. I have trouble believing any of it myself and I've been going through this stuff for days. He passed her the notebook they had found earlier. 'Remember this last entry?'

She read it and looked at him quizzically. 'Yes, you wondered how he could know the results in advance.'

'Well, I've checked entries in another notebook. I've even won money on the recent results I found. Now I've seen this,' he pointed at the device, 'all I could come up with is Mr Jones was from the future and landed here with all this information.'

'But... but... time travel is impossible!'

'If you had asked me a month ago, I'd have agreed with you. I moved a lot of his files to my study, they provide more evidence that he knew what was going to happen. It's as if it was historical fact for him.'

'This is unbelievable! What are you going to do with it?'

He explained his plans to visit Victorian England in 1839 and fill in all the postal history gaps from when the *Penny Post* started.

'You want to visit 1839? Is it safe?'

'Not visit, live there. I've already made one trip and I'm fine.'

Pauline's eyes bulged. 'You did *what*? Are you crazy?'

'It was the only way to find out for sure if it worked.'

'This is incredible. But what if you do something that changes history? What if you saved someone's life who was supposed to die, or somebody died who was supposed to live?'

'Apparently, that's not possible.'

Mark related his visit to Singapore and Pauline saw the grief etched on his face before he cleared his throat. 'According to what

I read on the machine afterwards, if you attempt to do something which would give rise to any change to the past whatsoever, something would occur to prevent it from happening. It's called the Novikov self-consistency principle.'

She did not know what to think or say. She looked at Mark; he was smiling from ear-to-ear.

'Want to go shopping in 1835?'

She could not help it... she burst out laughing. There was something so ridiculous about planning a shopping trip a hundred and seventy years in to the past.

'And I'm supposed to walk down the streets in jeans, sweater and riding boots?' she answered, still laughing.

'Ah! I've already thought of that.' He pointed to a cupboard in the corner. 'Have a look in there.'

Wondering what he was up to now, she opened the cupboard. Hanging there, she saw a Georgian period lemon organza and satin dress, with matching bonnet and purse. On the bottom of the cupboard stood a pair of lady's boots, and leaning in the corner, a parasol.

'What are these? Where did they come from?' She turned to him and asked warily, 'How do you know they'll fit?'

'They will. I called Julie to tell her I wanted to buy a dress for you and she kindly gave me a full set of measurements—*most* impressive by the way.'

'She did what? I'll strangle her, I promise,' she snarled. 'As for you...'

'As you said, you can't go in jeans and T-shirt, can you?'

'How come you're so sure I would agree?' she said, glaring at him.

'I've come to know you very well over the last four months. You're decisive, determined and obsessed with Victorian history. Plus, of course, there's my irresistible charm.'

'Irresistible charm? You wish! But you're right, this *is*

something I can't resist... and *nothing* to do with any charm business either!' She glared harder.

'So, when do you want to take our first trip?'

'It's actually real, isn't it? I'm not having some kind of dream, am I?'

'Oh, it's real, believe me.' He looked at her expectantly. 'We can pop over this afternoon, spend a few hours sightseeing, do a bit of shopping and be back here one hour after leaving. How about it?'

Chapter 7
Saturday, 10th June 2006

'Shit. Shit. Shit!'

Pauline muttered and cursed as she struggled with the corset and tried to button the Victorian period dress on her own. Mark had suggested, for privacy, she change inside the Faraday cage. She had appreciated the offer until she found out how cramped it was. It afforded scant room for manoeuvring, and trying to tie the laces of the leather boots led to another stream of expletives.

She came out of her 'dressing room' fidgeting with her dress collar and gave Mark a look daring him to laugh or make a comment. 'Now I know why Victorian women had maids to help them dress. So, where are we going?'

Her eyes narrowed at the faint chuckle as Mark bent over the machine's keyboard. 'High Petergate, near Bootham Bar. I've set the date for Monday, third of August, 1835.'

'Why there?'

'I have a detailed map of York from that time and was able to calculate coordinates pretty accurately'

Mark rotated the view through the gateway. They watched a woman chase two scruffy boys up three shallow stone steps into a dingy house, leaving the area deserted. Although Mark had showed her the videos, it was still strange to watch the scene unfold.

Mark nodded towards the gateway. 'Nervous?'

Pauline gulped and tried to ignore the icy feeling in her stomach. 'Nervous doesn't come close.'

They walked toward the gateway, suspended an inch above the floor and the grimy grey courtyard ahead. Pauline bit her lip, grasped Mark's hand in her sweaty palm and stepped into 1835. She stifled a shriek at the clinging cobweb effect. 'Ugh! What was that?'

'Sorry. I forgot to warn you. It is a bit unsettling.'

She pursed her lips and pinched his arm. 'Any other little surprises you *forgot* to tell me?'

Pauline turned to look back at the gateway. A faint distortion hung in the air, like a heat haze. She could see the courtyard through it, but no sign of the basement they had stood in only seconds before. Pauline examined her surroundings while Mark shut off the machine and put it in his leather backpack designed after the mail pouches used by Eighteenth Century post boys.

It was dark in the courtyard. The three-storey buildings, only twenty feet apart, blocked much of the light from the overcast sky. Narrow windows stared blankly at her. One or two had washing draped over the windowsills, others had poles sticking out, holding larger, shapeless garments hanging in the still air.

TP 1000: The Bishops

'This way.' Mark took her arm and pointed to the wet, uneven cobblestones. 'Walk slowly, I'll make sure you don't slip.'

Walking near to the narrow drain running along the centre of the cobblestones, Pauline held her hand over her mouth and nose and tried not to gag. Unfortunately, only light passed through the gateway, not sound and smells. A miasma assaulted their senses, from what, Pauline did not want to know. She had read about the poor sanitary standards in this era, but this was much worse than she had expected.

Mark passed her his handkerchief to keep out the ammoniacal stench of urine. 'Sorry, I didn't know it would be this bad.'

Entry on to High Petergate amazed her; the overhanging second floors of the half-timbered buildings, the overcast sky and the crowded street made the road claustrophobic. Pauline unconsciously pulled her shawl around her in the cold breeze, mesmerised by everything around her. A sign showing a painted candle swung from one shop front, next to which was another advertising itself a 'Saddlery and Bootmakers'.

She shuddered at the sight of the butchers further down the road. Along the shop front, whole pigs and piglets, alongside rabbits and geese, hung by rope from wooden beams extending into the street. The butcher, wearing a bloody smock, stood behind the display, wielding an axe to cut a piglet in to smaller portions. Her stomach went queasy when the butcher picked a leg and other small joints off the filthy street, and dropped them in with the rest of the meat for sale.

She hardly noticed Mark guiding her around the horse dung and the rotting fruit and vegetables fallen from delivery carts. Although familiar with the Yorkshire dialect, she overheard several expressions with which she was not familiar. What did 'Nanty-narking'[1] mean and who were the 'Three wise men of Gotham'[2]? Pauline doubted it had

---

[1] **Nanty narking** (*Tavern*, 1800 onto 1840) 'Great fun' (*See* Egan's *Life in London*)

[2] **Three wise men of Gotham** (*Peoples'*) Meaning that they were not wise. Generally applied to a trio of male fools. In the reign of Henry VIII, a law was passed by the magistracy of Westham, for the purpose of preventing unauthorised persons from setting ' *nettes, pottes, and annoyances*', or in

anything to with *Bruce Wayne* and *Batman*. It was so different from what she had imagined, yet somehow, much more real.

Mark interrupted her musing. 'Here we are.'

Pauline was puzzled. *A toy shop? Why a toy shop?*

The middle-aged proprietor, his longish hair brushed to give a slightly tangled appearance, and sporting bushy sideburns extending well below the ears, stood behind the counter. 'Good morning sir, madam, and how may I be of assistance?'

'I am looking for a suitable gift for my God-daughter's twelfth birthday,' Mark replied, with a faint smile at Pauline.

'If I may, allow me to show these to you and your wife.'

Mark turned to Pauline and raised one eyebrow. Pauline had her hand over her mouth, trying hard not to giggle.

The shopkeeper took a couple of dolls encased in glass-fronted wooden boxes from a shelf and placed them in front of Pauline then removed them from their cases.

'Madam, these are wonderfully crafted, all the way from the Continent. This one is a carved wooden doll. The wig is real hair, the head and torso carved in one piece with legs jointed at hips and knees.' The man demonstrated how it was able to sit or stand. 'The other is a papier mâché doll; a kid body with wooden arms and legs. Her clothing is well made, as you can see.'

While she examined them Mark wandered around the shop. Coming back to Pauline he asked, 'Have you decided yet, my dear?'

Pauline pointed at the wooden doll. 'This one will be perfect.'

'Anything else I may interest you in, sir... madam?'

'No, that will be all, thank you. How much do I owe you?'

'Fifteen shillings and six-pence, sir.'

Mark had the receipt made out to *Mark Bishop Esquire, Leyburn,*

---

anywise taking fish within the privilege of the march of Pevensey. Upon the proceedings, which was held at Gotham, near Pevensey, the facetious Andrew Borde, a native of that town, founded his *Merrie Tales of the Wise Men of Gotham*.

and took the doll with him. Outside the shop, Pauline squeezed Mark's arm in excitement. 'That was unbelievable,' she whispered.

'Did you see all the toys? Wooden sail boats, hoops, Noah's Arks with pairs of hand-carved animals. There was a beautiful rocking horse, and a selection of children's story books.' Mark pointed at a shop across the street. 'There's an apothecary; we can buy some perfume to put on your handkerchief.'

The aroma of floral scents, stringent medicinal herbs and spices was welcome after the street smells. Pauline asked to see a selection of perfumes and the proprietor took out several striking cut-glass and porcelain bottles from a display case. While Pauline was testing them, Mark examined the neatly ordered shelves. He selected a few items and placed them on the counter next to the perfume bottle Pauline had chosen. Mark paid ten shillings and sixpence for an oval shaped cut-glass scent bottle of Lily perfume, with a screw-top silver lid and his own purchases.

Leaving the shop a small raggedly dressed boy, no older than eight or nine, ran past, chased by three men.

The apothecary who had followed them to the door spoke up. 'Probably another pickpocket. Most likely he'll be transported when they catch him.'

Pauline had read about transportation; people received sentences from seven years up to life in Australia for the pettiest of crimes—the theft of a handkerchief, or just for being poor.

After the hue and cry had passed they walked towards Low Petergate and Pauline asked, 'What did you buy?'

'A box of cocaine tooth drops, a bottle of laudanum, guaranteed to ease coughing, diarrhoea and pain and a bottle of heroin-based cough mixture, guaranteed to cure bronchitis.'

Pauline stopped, her eyes widened. 'Are you out of your mind? They're Class 'A' drugs.'

With what Pauline could only call a 'shit-eating' grin, Mark laughed. 'I couldn't resist it. It's unbelievable what they use for medicine.'

Pauline shook her head and jerked him back in to motion.

Mark bought a rose from a grey-haired woman; she wore a threadbare shawl and sat on a step, resting a large basket of flowers on her lap. Standing next to her was a small boy, selling apples from a wicker basket tied around his neck. He gave her a silver half-crown to pay for the penny rose and told her to keep the change. He walked away and gave the rose to Pauline, leaving the old lady open-mouthed.

The sky darkened with the threat of rain. They quickened their pace towards the Minster.

Facing the South Transept, Pauline spent a moment admiring the elaborate carving of the gable framing the Rose Window. Mark held her arm and walked to the north side to reach their departure point. A secluded alcove by the Chapter House, in a corner with the North Transept, made an ideal place to activate the time device.

When the view cleared to show the basement, Pauline stepped through first, but when Mark had one leg through he heard a shriek. He looked around and saw a woman pointing at him, screaming her head off. He raced through, shut down the gateway and leaned on the table.

'We'll have to be careful in future. God knows what stories will be, or were, going around about people disappearing in thin air.'

Before he could calm himself, Pauline wrapped her arms around him and took the rest of his breath away with a fervent kiss.

Mark caught his breath. 'Wow! If that's what's waiting every time we come back, let's go back now.'

After the Portal was back in the Faraday cage, she hugged him again. 'That was fantastic, I still don't believe it. I must be dreaming.

Ouch! What was that for?' She winced and rubbed her backside.

'Just to prove you're not dreaming,' he replied with a smirk. 'Now let's change before anyone starts to miss us.'

Back in the study, Mark placed their purchases on the table and Pauline started giggling.

'What's funny?'

'Your *wife!*' She started giggling again.

'Well, it was a natural assumption.'

'I suppose so, but still...' Pauline felt her face and neck flush with heat and she blushed remembering the kiss she had given him in the basement.

To distract herself from Mark's gaze, Pauline examined the doll and cleared her throat. 'Have you any idea what this is worth? I saw a similar one on an auction website for six thousand Euros.'

'I know. I checked before we left, I'm going to keep it as a souvenir.'

While they talked, Pauline managed to compose herself and looked directly at him. 'So what are you going to do with that machine?'

'Learn what life was like in those days. You've seen how different things are, were... whatever, from what you read in books. So many changes took place in science, medicine, engineering and social reforms during Victoria's reign; the lives of the British people were completely changed.'

She caught his excitement. 'Yes! The first photographs, steamships, the Tube in London, electric lighting. You're right, it's an incredible chance to see it first-hand and learn what it was *really* like. It was when the Industrial Revolution spread globally.'

'And don't forget, the first postage stamps in 1840. I could go there and fill in all the postal history gaps from when the Penny Post started. Even buy a sheet of Penny Blacks on the first day of issue.'

Pauline did not try to hide her amusement. 'So, you're going to pop back and forth to fill up your stamp collection.'

'Not pop around. I intend to live there.'

Wide-eyed and open-mouthed, she tried to wrap her mind around the implications.

'It's the only way to find out what life was really like. Day trips won't tell me that.'

'I... I suppose not.' Pauline tried to come to grasp with the idea of actually *living* in the 1840s. 'How long are you planning on being there?'

'At least a couple or three years, from the pre-Four Penny Post in 1839 right to the early Penny Reds around 1842.'

'Three years! You want us to live in the past for *three years*?'

'Us? But I thought—'Mark replied, copying Pauline's earlier wide-eyed expression.

Pauline put her fists on her hips. 'You don't expect me to stay behind and let you have all the fun, do you?'

'But... you're...'

Pauline's eyes narrowed and she moved so close to him, Mark had to back up a step. 'If you say a woman...' she warned. 'So, it's alright for you to go swanning around enjoying yourself, but poor helpless little me can't handle it. Is that what you're saying?'

'No, no... I mean, women had such restricted lives in those days, and—'

'We'll figure it out.' Her tone of voice brooked no argument. 'I'm not going to be left behind, and that's that.' She poked him on the chest to emphasise her last three words.

'Okay, okay.' Mark raised his hands in surrender and chuckled. 'There's lots of planning to do before either of us goes anywhere. We've plenty of time to work something out, the past will still be there.'

'Alright, but don't forget, we're in this together.' Pauline looked at her watch, it was six o'clock. 'I'd better be getting home. We will discuss this later. I'm taking mum to see her sister in Darlington tomorrow and will be busy with other clients most of the week. I'll be back on Thursday and I'll bring my books and all my notes.'

'Great. I'll try and figure out how we can pull this off.'

Pauline walked to her car, not trying to hide her self-satisfied smile from Mark. Driving home, doubts and fears rose in her mind. She had just agreed, no, she had insisted on living in the past for months at a time. *What have I gotten myself into?*

Mark shook his head, and watched Pauline drive away. *Damn! I got my toes stomped that time.*

Back in his study, the memory of her kiss came back and awoke emotions he had never expected to feel again. Touching his bruised lip, he was sure there was more to the kiss than just excitement.

After all the hours they had spent together, arguing, laughing, while developing the business plan, it seemed he had known her for much longer than four months. She was smart, great company, good looking, and pretty damn forthright. *I'd better figure out how we're going to travel together or get stomped on again.*

First of all, he needed to work out the more practical aspects of living in the 1840s. Such as, where to live and how to pay for it? And transport; how to travel around? They could hardly walk everywhere. He went to bed hoping some ideas came to him in morning.

The next day, after morning milking, Mark left everything to Bill and Frank while he worked in his study. He was determined to have a few concrete ideas before Pauline next came. He knew one way to make money, but even with all Mr Jones' gold bars, it would not be enough—not to sustain them for three years, anyway.

He spent hours searching the internet for prices of everything he could think of; cost of food, clothing and luxury items, plus sanitary conditions, housing and salaries. He found the living conditions of most Victorians unappealing, to say the least. Presenting himself as a wealthy merchant seemed the best option; he could hardly aspire to nobility. He made a detailed list of goods to sell to sustain a comfortable life. The problem was how to transport them in sufficient quantity to make it worthwhile. He needed a wagon; this could not only transport goods, but also Pauline and himself. No matter how good a rider she was, he did not reckon riding side saddle would appeal to her.

It was midnight when Mark found what he was looking for from a wagonette break. With walls and roof added, back doors and benches with storage space underneath, a modified wagonette could serve not only as a goods vehicle, but also a novel carriage. The wagon manufacturers told him it would take three months to modify a standard wagon. The old byre overlooking the farm would be the perfect place to keep the wagon, and three months was plenty of time to clean it out and get it ready. Mark also ordered appropriate tack for Lucky; his western saddle would most definitely rise eyebrows.

He burst out laughing at what Bill would say when he told him why he wanted the byre cleaning out.

'Sorry I'm a bit late, we had a staff meeting this morning,' Pauline told Mark when she arrived at the farm at eleven. She pointed to the car's back seat. 'Help me with these boxes.'

'This is all your stuff on Victorian England?' he asked, looking at six boxes of books and a pile of files in her car.

'Yes, this should help us figure things out. So, have you come up with any ideas?'

While they unpacked the boxes, Mark explained all the research he had done. 'Before we decide on any long stays, we'll need money. I reckon on taking a leaf out of Mr Jones' book and bet on horse races, since I know the results already. But it won't be enough for me to live on for three years.'

Pauline held a thick heavy book menacingly, and Mark backtracked. 'I mean *us*, for the long term. I can sell most of Mr Jones' gold, but first they need recasting—Twentieth Century gold bars will raise questions. I've ordered graphite moulds to make smaller bars in that fume cabinet. But, I'll also need a regular source of income.'

'Why do you have to sell the gold? Surely you can earn enough money on horse races and make a killing on the gold in a few years?'

'A few blocks of mint Penny Blacks, *Twopenny Blues* and half-a-dozen first day covers will be worth more than all those gold bars. Why bother?'

She was stunned. She had not fully understood the

implications of buying the first ever stamps on the actual first day of issue.

'But that doesn't explain the gold though.'

'I'd have to make a lot of trips to horse races to afford a decent place to live, establish a credible background and identity. That takes time... and money. So, with a few horse racing trips and the money from the gold, I can open a bank account and keep the rest for collateral. The money and gold will give us a certain social status. Don't forget, the tax man doesn't know about Mr Jones' gold. Instead of paying taxes on it, I might as well use it there.'

This made Pauline uncomfortable. Legally, she knew they should report it, and he would have to sell most of it to pay taxes. However, the prospect of living in the past overcame her scruples.

They placed her books and files in the bookcase and sat on the couch. Pauline turned to Mark. 'So what's your cover story? You can hardly pose as a farmer.'

'I thought I'd establish a small business. A merchant of luxury goods—perfumes and spices, all of which were in demand, and not bulky. Might lose a bit of money, but we're not going there to make a fortune anyway.'

'Sez he, looking at buying a million-pounds worth of stamps for fifty pence,' she said, grinning widely at him.

This led to a lively conversation, each frequently interrupting the other, discussing possible trade items. Pauline made an interesting suggestion, 'Why not sell soap? The lye soap they used was strong enough to take your skin off. You can buy packets of regular soap in the supermarket cheaply enough... it should sell like hotcakes.'

'Hey, not a bad idea. Modern perfumed moisturising soap. I bet I could get a good price for them.'

'So where do you plan on us living?'

'Chesterfield, mid-1839 before the introduction of the *Uniform*

TP 1000: The Bishops

Penny Post. I've been there a few times over the years, and have a lot of research material on the area from my grandfather's postal history collection—maps and several reference books. Also, the town centre, especially the Shambles, hasn't changed all that much, in layout at least.' He smiled smugly at her. 'I can even track down that village postmaster I told you about, and find out how the postal service worked.'

Pauline frowned. 'What about the problem of fitting in, socially?'

'I'll say I've lived and travelled widely in the Far East and pose as a merchant who dabbles in natural philosophy. This would help explain any idiosyncrasies and hopefully, it'll cover up any mistakes.'

'Surely we can't disappear for three years though?'

Mark placed his hand on hers. 'Don't panic. We can do it a bit at a time. Live there for a couple of months and pop back here an hour after we left. After a rest we can be back in Chesterfield an hour after we left there. If we're careful, no-one will even notice.'

'I hadn't thought of that.' Pauline noticed the pressure from his hands, but did not pull away.

'It'll be like having two lives, but aging at the same rate. We may end up celebrating two birthdays a year. Won't that be fun?' Mark japed.

Pauline's eyes widened and she gasped. 'Three years here, three years there, I'll be thirty-three when everyone here believes I'm only thirty.'

Mark burst out laughing. 'Here we're planning on how to live a hundred and seventy years in the past and that's all you're worried about?'

Pauline huffed indignantly, then smiled at how ridiculous her worries were.

Chapter 8
Friday, 14th July, 2006

Mark reviewed all the applications for the farm specialists' positions he had received and held phone interviews with the most likely candidates. By the end of the day he had whittled the list down to five candidates—three for the hydroponic work and two for the outdoor work—and arranged face-to-face interviews in two weeks time.

Mark stretched and thought more about travelling to Nineteenth Century Chesterfield. He needed a video camera. He remembered the spy camera used in the *James Bond* movies he had watched in the eighties. By dinner time, he had ordered an easily concealed buttonhole camera, memory cards and nine volt battery clips to power it.

Pauline drove up early Saturday morning, and after breakfast they went to Mark's study.

'I figure I need to take a couple of trips to the horse races to collect some cash then two solo visits to Chesterfield to organise things before we go together,' Mark told her.

TP 1000: The Bishops

'How many short trips?'

'The 1837 and 1838 Derby races, then Sharp's in London to sell the gold bars. I've ordered the moulds already, and when they arrive, I can recast those ingots. Then it's off to Chesterfield to set up a business.'

'How are you going to get around? You can't walk everywhere.'

'I'll ride Lucky. I can hardly drive the *Jag* can I? We can go for a ride as we usually do and stop at the byre. I can depart from there. Let's face it, it'll be tricky getting Lucky down to the basement.'

'Be serious, will you.' Pauline glowered at him. 'And what am I supposed to do while you're away?'

'Come to my study.'

He took one of Mr Jones' journals from his safe room. 'This is Jones' first journal. Read it and see what you can find out about him.'

At the byre, Mark changed for his first trip to the races. He set the device for the Old London Road, for eight o'clock on Thursday twenty-fifth of May, 1837. Pauline held Lucky's and Princess' reins, concerned about what dangers he might encounter.

'Don't look so worried,' Mark assured her when he saw the expression on Pauline's face.

'Okay, but be careful.'

'Don't worry, I'll be back for lunch.' After a quick kiss, he took the reins and led Lucky to the Portal gateway. The horse balked at the strange sticky sensation, and Mark had to pull him through. He closed the gateway, placed the device in his backpack and mounted, letting Lucky canter along the empty dirt road. Approaching what would be Tattenham Corner Road, he slowed Lucky to a walk when he encountered people walking, riding, and others in gig carts. At the race track, for the Epsom Derby, Mark found a bunch of boys looking after horses and paid sixpence to care for Lucky.

The crowds grew, and he kept one hand tightly gripping the backpack containing the Portal. Mark placed half-a-dozen bets, one at 45-to-1 early in the day, the rest at 40-to-1 odds, all on *Phosphorus*, with different bookmakers around the course. Phosphorous had sustained an injury a few days earlier and *Rat-trap* was now the 6-to-4 favourite.

The huge crowd had to be cleared from the course and after another short delay the race was under way. A colt named *Pocket Hercules* took the lead with Phosphorus in third. The pace was fast, most of the runners struggling well before the turn into the straight. By this point Phosphorus and the second favourite *Caravan* had moved up to dispute the lead. The two colts pulled clear of the rest of the field and raced side-by-side. The closing stages was a magnificent contest echoed by the screaming and shouting from the crowd.

Although Mark knew the results, it was still exciting, and he yelled along with the other spectators as Phosphorous gained the advantage inside the final furlong. He beat Caravan by a head, the pair six lengths clear of the field. Mark was elated, although many spectators cursed and grumbled at the favourite coming in third.

Mark collected on all his bets, except one. He spotted the errant bookie, with two brawny minders carrying a sign 'Charlie Cattermole, Bookmaker', heading towards the exit. Mark pushed through the crowd and intercepted him. 'Going somewhere?'

The short pudgy man stumbled to a halt, his top hat tipping over his brow. The bodyguard not carrying the sign grabbed Mark's lapel. Mark took a step back and in seconds the burly bodyguard was on the floor in a wrist lock.

Mark ignored the spectators gathered around and held out a slip of paper with his right hand.

'Here's the marker with your name. I believe you owe me twenty guineas.'

Charlie looked at the growing, grumbling crowd, sweat beading his forehead. He reluctantly dug into his pouch and handed over the money.

With a final twist, Mark released the bodyguard, leaving him on his knees holding his hand. He tipped his hat at the bookie and walked to the exit. Leaving the race grounds, he tossed the boy looking after Lucky a shilling. Before he could mount, the boy shouted "Hey guvnor" and Mark looked around. The lad was pointing at the bookie's two hefty bodyguards approaching, each holding a cudgel. 'Better gerrout o' 'ere, mister.'

Mark did not need the warning. He had already mounted and with a gentle kick to the ribs, Lucky bounded forward. Looking back, he saw the two men waving their clubs at him, and the urchin bent over laughing.

Clear of the crowds, Mark let Lucky have his head. After half-a-mile, they approached a small copse. Mark slowed, dismounted and led the horse into the woods. Hidden from the road, he opened the gateway back to 2006.

At the byre, Pauline yelped and dropped the journal when Mark and Lucky appeared. 'You gave me a shock. That damn thing should have a bell or something.' She picked up the book and asked, 'How long were you gone?'

'Half a day. I bought a beer and had a cheese sandwich in my bag, but I'm starving now. Let me change and eat, then we can count the spoils.'

Later, in Mark's study, they counted out two-hundred and sixty pounds and ten shillings in winnings.

'I can get one thousand three hundred pounds for the gold and with these winnings I have enough for Chesterfield and can forget about the other race.'

'So how was it?' Pauline asked.

Mark described the spectators, noise and the race. When he mentioned the altercation with the bookie, she gasped. 'I told you to be careful. You could have been hurt and stuck there.'

'There were too many people around, and when I left, they didn't seem too happy with Charlie. I agree though, I do need to take precautions for future trips.'

Mark headed to his safe room and came back with a white sleeveless garment and a large knife.

Pauline pointed at the knife. 'Where did you get that?'

'When I was in Africa there was always the risk of getting lost in the rain forest, so they issued us survival kits. The knife was the most critical item.' Mark pulled it out if its leather sheath and checked the ten-inch blade with serrated upper edge. 'This should scare off any would-be muggers.'

'And that... vest, or whatever it is?'

'Ah, well, there was bandit activity where I worked. Not only did I have survival training, I was taught to use heavy weapons. The company also issued these fitted bullet proof vests. Since it was fitted, they let me keep it when I left. So... what did you find out about our Mr Jones?'

Pauline sat up straight, clearly excited. 'It's unbelievable. For one thing his real name was Nicholas Olafson and he was, or will be, born in 2495. He was thirty years old when he arrived. His first entry is dated ninth of January, 1945, and describes his arrival, five days earlier, during a V2 attack in East London. He detailed how he survived his first few months in London and took a new identity as John Alan Taylor. It stops at VE Day in May 1945.'

She went on... 'When he tried to activate the Portal device to return to his own time, he was locked out. The message on the screen read 'Password and User Name not accepted'. No matter what he tried, he could not gain access.' She turned to Mark, her voice dropping to almost in a whisper. 'Can you imagine what went through his mind knowing he couldn't go home? It must have been terrible.'

They sat in silence for a moment; Mark put his arm around her and kissed her forehead. 'Tomorrow you can read some more. I want to know how he ended up owning this farm, and when he built the second basement.'

'Okay, but I've got to go now, I promised to take my mother shopping this afternoon. I'll come tomorrow around nine.'

The next day Pauline read the second journal while Mark was busy around the farm.

'So what else have you found out about Nicholas?' he asked, in the afternoon.

'This journal runs from May 1945 to December 1946. It didn't have much information on his day-to-day life, except he rented a room from an old couple in Whitechapel and paid his rent in cash and black market eggs and meat. Nicholas still had some kind of computer he could use. He called it a Universal Library. He bet on horse races and used the money to buy food, clothes, a motorcycle and petrol, also through the black market. After that, it was a lot of tables; horse race results, land and house prices, stock market, including gold trends and currency exchange rates.'

'There's over forty journals, it's going to take time to wade through them all. Let's concentrate on planning for these Chesterfield trips.'

'One other thing. Since he was thirty years old when he arrived in 1945, he would have been almost ninety years old when he died.'

'What? He looked barely fifty.' Mark dropped onto a bale of hay. He stared at Pauline. 'How is that possible?'

'It doesn't say much but it does mention 'the Treatment' he received. Apparently some kind of disease prevention procedure which extended the normal life span and prevented him from aging at the normal rate.'

Monday, and the graphite crucibles arrived. Mark disappeared to the second basement and started melting and recasting the ingots in the fume cabinet. By the weekend, he had fifty-three half-pound bars.

Mark was raring to go. His new camera was firmly attached to his coat, and spare memory cards and battery packs in his bag. The leather backpack also carried twenty pounds of gold bars packed in pockets in the cotton lining. After this trip was over, he could open a bank account with fifteen-hundred pounds and use the rest for spending. He was keeping six and a half pounds of gold for future collateral.

Pauline did not share Mark's enthusiasm. Mark was carrying more wealth than most people in those days would earn in a lifetime. 'Mugging was rife in those days, and you'll be carrying a fortune. If anyone finds out...'

'Don't worry. I'm only going there to sell the gold, nothing

TP 1000: The Bishops

else.' Mark put his hands on her shoulders and looked straight into her eyes. 'I promise not to go wandering around, and I'll take cabs everywhere, okay?'

Mark turned away and took out the Portal. He set the coordinates to a wooded part of Hyde Park near Cumberland Gate for seven o'clock on Thursday, twenty-eighth of February, 1839. Before he pressed the 'Initiate' key, he held Pauline tightly and nuzzled her hair. 'I'll be back in an hour's time.' He stepped away and smiled. 'Make sure you keep some hot tea for me.'

Mark put his thumb on the pad, pressed the key and looked out on sparkling white grass; the trees obscured by morning mist. The park was deserted—he stepped through. He shivered at the sudden change in temperature and gave thanks for his thermal underwear. Settling his backpack, with the device securely stowed inside, he headed through the park, the grass crackling underfoot. By the time he arrived at Oxford Street, his nose and ears had gone numb. Hailing a cab, his first destination was to *Matthey's* in Hatton Garden to assay his gold and obtain proof of its purity. He sat back to enjoy the ride but his enjoyment was short-lived. He swayed and bounced on the seat as the cab rattled over the cobblestone roads, and the frequent jerking and jostling as the driver avoided other vehicles was, to say the least, unpleasant—not to mention the strong smell of horse dung and urine.

The noise from the congested streets was incredible; he wished he had brought ear plugs. The cacophony generated by street vendors trying to out shout their competitors, and the rumble of carriages and wagons would have made it impossible to have had a conversation. Mark turned to face the street, hoping the camera caught the passing scenes. He spotted a knife grinder and several costermongers selling fruit and vegetables. Alongside newspapers sellers stood young boys selling matchsticks, shouting *'Lucifers,*

Lucifers' at the top of their voices. He even saw a milkmaid, carrying a wooden yoke over her shoulders, supporting heavy looking milk-pails.

Mark was relieved when they stopped at seventy-nine Hatton Garden. After paying the cabbie and tipping him another shilling, Mark nodded to the doorman and entered the Assay Office. He was met by a neat, middle-aged gentleman, sombrely dressed in a dark suit and waistcoat.

Mark introduced himself and explained he had gold bars to be assayed and needed proof of their purity—the clerk looked down his nose despite Mark's appearance and manner. That is, until Mark took out the forty gold bars. The clerk's attitude changed dramatically and an elderly gentleman, dressed in frock-coat and striped trousers, was called.

'Mr Holmes, is it? How may I be of service?'

Mark presented his business card from a silver card holder he had bought along with high quality embossed cards, from York. Simple in design, only his assumed name, Michael Holmes, underneath which was printed, 'Dealer in Luxury Goods from the Far East'.

'I need confirmation of the purity of this gold from Dubai; I was assured your establishment was the most reliable.'

'Certainly Mr Holmes. This will require a few hours. May I offer you refreshments in the meantime?'

'That would be most welcome, particularly on such a cold day.'

Mark was escorted to a lounge and offered coffee and *Banbury cake*. With thanks, he settled and took out his notebook and pencil, and wrote up his observations to supplement the video. After several hours, the older gentleman returned.

'Mr Holmes, the gold has a remarkable purity, ninety-nine point two percent. We have stamped an assay mark on each bar and here is a letter of confirmation.'

Mark examined one of the bars—it had .992 stamped on it above the assay mark. He paid two shillings for each bar and asked, 'I am here for a few days on personal business. Could you recommend a good hotel, preferably near to Sharps?'

'Anderton's on Fleet Street, sir. Excellent service, if I may say, with many good coffee houses nearby.'

Mark left with profuse farewells and the doorman, tipped with half-a-crown, quickly found him another hansom to travel to Anderton's. It was already dark when he alighted and he wrinkled his nose at the odour of human excrement blowing from the direction of the Thames; he shuddered to think how bad it would be in summer.

He booked a private room and arranged for dinner. His hands and face darkened by the pervasive soot laden air, he had a thorough wash and a spare shirt ironed for sixpence. Pauline need not have worried about him wandering around. Between the filth on the streets and the stench in the air, he was more than happy to stay in the hotel. He enjoyed a dinner of roast lamb, baked potatoes and peas, with a fine wine, all for seven shillings then went to bed early. The next morning he hailed a cab to Sharp's, and presenting his card, sold his gold for one-thousand, three-hundred and sixty pounds in *Bank of England* notes, gold sovereigns and smaller coins.

'Time to go home,' he murmured. Outside in the icy wind, he asked the doorman to hail a cab to Anderton's. Fifteen shillings later and few half-crown tips, he was in a cab to St. James' Park. Much as he would have loved to have walked the streets, it was too cold for sightseeing. He entered the park by the gate at Buckingham Palace. The cold weather was evidently keeping people away and he headed for a wooded area on the southern boundary. Once certain the coast was clear, he opened the gateway and stepped through.

'So, how did it go?' Pauline asked, pouring him a mug of tea. She frowned at his dark grey coat. 'What are all those black marks?'

He looked down. 'Soot—I thought Mexico City was bad, London was worse. Otherwise it was a good trip although too damn cold to go anywhere, even with thermal underwear. The cab jolted so much I'm not sure how good the videos will be. I need a shower and something to eat but we can watch them later.'

She pointed to the filing cabinets. 'While you were away, I looked through those files. Did you know there's a whole set of files on UK weather from 1950 all the way to 2015?'

'What?'

'This winter is going to be fairly mild, by the way, although there'll be more rain than usual. Lots of really useful stuff—details of temperature, rain and snowfall. It's going to be very helpful planning the farm work. My dad used to complain all the time about the *Met* forecasts.'

Back in the study, Mark showed her the money... 'Now we're all set for Chesterfield.'

'I've been reading and calculating, and a small house with two servants will cost us a hundred and fifty pounds a year.'

'I'm sure we can do better than that. We have over fifteen-hundred already plus the gold, and I can always win more at the races. You never know, business may be good and I can show a profit.'

'I hadn't expected it to be so crowded and noisy,' Pauline exclaimed after watching the videos.

'It was worse being there, and the smell coming off the river was disgusting. Chesterfield should be better. It's a rural town, only five or six-thousand people.'

'All those street sellers and traffic, it looked like a madhouse.'

'I'd liked to have done some sightseeing, but February in any century is miserable, and it really was freezing cold. Maybe, when we're living there, we can take the train and spend a few days having a look around.'

'After seeing that, I'm not sure I want to go.'

'You fancy coming over for a ride tomorrow?' Mark asked, hopefully.

'Sorry, I promised to take my mum out.'

'That's okay. I can start buying my trade goods.'

Pauline's phone rang and the furrows on her brow deepened as she listened.

'Nothing wrong is there?'

'My aunt in Darlington has had a fall. My mum asked me to drive her over to help out until my cousin can come. I'll spend the night and come back in the morning.'

'If there's anything I can do, let me know. Call me when you arrive.'

Pauline gave him a quick kiss and headed home. After she left, Mark reviewed the list of goods they had compiled and added another item.

That evening she called and said her mother could not cope on her own, and she would stay until Tuesday when her cousin arrived.

Chapter 9
Sunday, 25th June, 2006

Next morning, after leading the cows to fresh grazing, Mark drove to the shopping centre in Darlington. By lunchtime, he had a case of regular hand soap and two-dozen scented ones, along with a bottle of twelve-year old double malt Scotch whisky. He was not sure how long he would be in Chesterfield, but reckoned he deserved to have something decent to drink in the evenings.

Later, he contacted a factory in Thailand and ordered twenty, six-metre long pieces of high quality Thai silk, all in different colours. After placing the order, he called an Indian merchant in Singapore recommended by Malik and placed an order for a kilo each of cinnamon sticks, cinnamon powder, cloves, nutmeg, and cardamom seeds, plus a kilo each of four different types of black and green Chinese tea.

Now to figure out where to store all the purchases. If business took off in Chesterfield, he would need a proper storage area. Since the byre was his departure point, he could modify it for storage, and it would be easy to load the wagon there as well. *How to explain it to everyone else at the farm?* Maybe Pauline would have some ideas.

Mark had finished checking the milk tanks next morning when Pauline called. Between the sobbing and hiccoughs, he gathered her house had been burgled.

'I'll be there in fifteen minutes.'

When he arrived, Pauline rushed in to his arms.

'I'm sorry. I didn't know who else to call.' Her tears splashed his shirt.

Once he had her calmed down, he asked her neighbour to take her inside while he spoke to the police. They told him the break-in had happened early that morning. The burglars had jimmied the back door, wrecked the house, cut up all Pauline's clothes, and spray painted *SLUT* on the walls. Nothing appeared to have been stolen, just smashed.

The house was obviously unfit to live in, even the mattresses and bedlinen had been slashed. Since Pauline was incapable of making any decisions or statements at present, Mark told the officer they could contact her at his farm. He called Jenny and bundled Pauline and her luggage into his car. Jenny was waiting when they arrived and whisked a shaken Pauline upstairs.

Figuring Pauline was in good hands, Mark called his security company, then her friend Julie. An hour later, Pauline came downstairs.

'Who would do something like this?' she cried. 'I can't stay there.'

'You're staying here and that's final,' Mark ordered. 'I've called Julie and a shopping trip will soon fix the clothing situation.' He told her he had made arrangements to install a security system in her house.

'But...'

Mark over-ruled her objections. 'No buts! It's settled. Now call your office, tell them what's happened and you're taking some time off, George will be here around one o'clock to sort out a security system.'

'I can't afford that,' Pauline exclaimed.

'Yes you can. We found the money and the other stuff together, so half of it is yours anyway.'

George joined them at lunch and gave his recommendations.

'Motion sensors, CCTV cameras at the two entrances to the house and...'

Pauline's face paled. 'No cameras in the house. None. None at all,' she shouted.

Mark wondered what the problem with cameras was, but saw no point upsetting her any further.

They soon sorted out what was needed. The back door would be repaired today and George's men would come on Wednesday to install everything else, including new front and back doors.

'Everything will be operational by Saturday. I'll give you a call when it's all tested,' George told Pauline, then left.

She called her mother and told her about the burglary, and that she was staying at the farm. After her mother recovered from the shock she was soon dropping none-too-subtle hints about Mark's bachelorhood; this did not help Pauline sort out her feelings about the burglary, or Mark, one little bit.

After Pauline had lodged a formal police report the next day, Mark drove her straight to Julie's flat.

'Julie, I'm putting you in charge. Make sure she replaces

everything, and buy some things for yourself as well,' Mark commanded and passed her a thick envelope. 'Take this,' all the while ignoring Pauline's protests.

Julie opened the envelope and gasped. 'What's this?'

'About five thousand. Should be enough to buy a pair of shoes or two,' he replied. 'Ow!' he yelped when Pauline punched his arm.

'That's the money you found, isn't it? I told you, you can't spend it like this.'

'Nonsense! Miss Parker will help, won't you?'

'Oh! Yes... sure...' Julie stammered.

'Done then,' Mark told Pauline, 'I'll pick you up around four o'clock Saturday.' He gave Julie a peck on the cheek and Pauline a long passionate kiss, leaving her stunned and breathless.

'See you Saturday.' Mark grinned and headed for the door, leaving both women speechless, for very different reasons.

Julie was the first to recover her voice. 'Wow! What have you two been up to? You've been holding out on me.'

'That is the most insufferable, arrogant, irritating ...*man* I have ever met.'

'He didn't look insufferable a minute ago,' Julie replied. 'Sit down! *You* have a lot of explaining to do.'

Pauline told her almost everything. The long hours working on the business plan, the secret room and the jewellery, but no mention of the second basement or the TP1000. She told Julie about their date in York, how he had given her the crucifix, and about the horse rides they had shared. Finally, she described coming back to a wrecked home and Mark insisting she stay at his farm.

'At last!' Julie exulted.

'It's nothing like that. For Heaven's sake, I only met him in March, and he's *still* my client.'

'Then what's all this money? And that kiss?' Julie replied, with a smug grin. 'I don't get kissed by *my* clients.'

Pauline muttered and glared at her friend. 'He's so different from when I first met him. He's considerate and caring, and you should see how passionate he gets talking about his ideas.'

'Oh! I'm sure his ideas are *very* passionate,' Julie replied, with an evil grin.

'Not like that!' she yelled, her reddened cheeks giving lie to her protests and she stormed towards the door. 'Come on, I have shopping to do.'

Three days of whirlwind retail therapy followed and, four large *Samsonite* suitcases later, Pauline had replaced all her missing clothing.

Saturday morning, Pauline started packing while Julie went to visit a client. When she returned, she told Pauline they had more shopping to do. Mark had texted to buy jeans and T-shirts, since Pauline needed to dress appropriately to stay at the farm.

'Okay, but I'm not going to be milking any damn cows!' Pauline muttered.

'There was a lovely milkmaid's outfit yesterday at *Ann Summers*, we could go and pick one up.' Julie laughed at the look on Pauline's face and ducked the cushion thrown at her.

'Come on then, I want to finish packing before he gets here,' Pauline grumbled.

When Mark arrived, four suitcases and a trolley bag sat waiting for him to put in his car.

'Any money left?' he asked, grinning at the two women.

Julie chimed up. 'About seven hundred pounds.'

'Hang on to it, I'm sure you two can think of something to do with it next time she's here.'

Back at the farm, Mark carried all the luggage to her room and left Pauline to put it away. Over dinner, he told her George had called and they could go to check the security system tomorrow.

George was waiting when they arrived at Pauline's house. He handed over the new keys and explained how the security system worked, and how to set and disable the alarms.

'Miss Grainger, one of my lads will be over every three months to inspect it. Mark, I'll come on Friday to install *your* new system.'

'Come on, let's see if everything meets with your approval.'

In to the living room, the first thing Pauline noticed was her parents' wedding photographs on the mantelpiece had been replaced.

Mark saw her staring. 'I found the photo frames smashed on the floor, so I had the photos reprinted and bought new frames for you.'

She did not know what to say, and her eyes moistened. She thought she has lost them forever.

'Come on, let's check the rest of the house.'

Upstairs, the bedrooms had been cleaned and walls repainted.

'I figured you'd want to choose your own mattresses, pillows and bedsheets. We can shop for them this afternoon.'

'Mark, you shouldn't, really.'

'Well you're paying for it. I'm cutting it from your share of the spoils. I cleaned up the torn clothes in here, and let Mary, Jenny's summer helper, sort out your mother's room. I didn't mind handling *your* underwear, but your mother's... no way!'

She grabbed him and gave him a long, arousing kiss.

'Thank you. You *are* impossible, and wonderful, to help like this.'

'My pleasure. Now let's get something to eat and shop for mattresses, bedsheets and so-on and head back to the farm.'

Sitting in the living room later, Pauline asked 'Why's George coming tomorrow? Don't you already have a security system?'

'He's upgrading it with new high-definition miniaturised cameras and putting additional ones around the farm.'

He noticed Pauline go pale and look around the room frantically.

'What's the matter? What's wrong?'

Her lips trembled. 'Where are those cameras? Where are they?' she demanded.

'There are only two in the house, and they're both in the safe room,' Mark explained, starting to look worried. 'What's the matter?'

Her look of panic slowly disappeared.

'What is it sweetheart, please?'

She closed her eyes, she took a few deep breaths, then stared at Mark. 'I have something to tell you. Something only Julie knows about.'

She lowered her head and stared at the floor. 'After I graduated, I took a job in London and met this man. He was thirty years old, mature and charming. Before long we started living together.' Her voice was barely audible. 'One day, I'd worked late and took the next day off. While I was cleaning, I went to put the bedsheets in an empty closet in the spare bedroom. The shelves were narrow and when I tried to push the sheets in, a panel at the back fell out.'

She wrapped her arms around her knees. 'There were racks of monitors showing views of the bedroom, living room and bathroom and a stack of DVDs with my name on them. I threw them in a suitcase, along with my clothes, and took a train to Julie's.'

A tear glistened on her cheek and Mark put his hand on hers.

TP 1000: The Bishops

Julie had put my phone on silent so we didn't hear his calls. When she checked the voicemail next morning, it was full of obscenities. He threatened to send copies of the films to my family and people at work, unless I returned the DVDs; Julie convinced me to call the police.

'When they searched his apartment they found more films of other girls, a bottle of the date drug *GHB* (gamma hydroxybutyric) and four-grams of cocaine. I had to testify at the trial and he was sentenced to seven years jail. I quit my job and moved in with Julie. Now you know everything. I'm so ashamed.' Her shoulders shook as she sobbed.

He put his arm around her; she tried to pull away, but he held her close to his chest until she stopped struggling.

'You've no reason to be ashamed,' he retorted. 'None at all.'

'What if he comes after me when he gets out?' she whispered, 'He said he would get even with me after the judge sentenced him. He lost his job. His photo was plastered all over the papers. He'll never be able get a decent job again. Maybe he sent someone to trash my house.'

'Don't worry, if that 'son of a bitch' comes anywhere near you, he'll find his balls decorating the barn door.' Mark stated, angrily. 'Now why don't you go to bed? I'll have Jenny make you a hot cocoa.'

Mark stayed in the living room. The wanton vandalism at Pauline's home bothered him, it seemed personal. *What kind of person would do something like that? And the way the guy had taken advantage of her... was it all connected as Pauline thought?* It was late before he went to bed.

When Pauline came downstairs for breakfast, her red-rimmed eyes told Mark she had had a restless night.

'Look, I have those interviews today, why don't you take it easy? Maybe relax in the living room, read a book or watch TV?'

'Can I sit in on the interviews? I'd prefer to stay busy, if it's alright with you.'

'Let me show you their resumes.'

Christopher Chan arrived at the farm promptly at nine o'clock in a battered old '92 *Volkswagen Beetle*. Chris was a foot shorter than Mark, baby-faced and a little on the chubby side. Every time he looked at Pauline, he blushed and stuttered. However, he changed when Mark showed him his plans for a two-acre hydroponic complex and asked for his opinion. Chris became animated and asked numerous questions. He made useful suggestions for different climate sections and sketched out his ideas for Mark. He said certain plants, like mango, lemongrass and cardamom flourished in a tropical climate, while parsley and fennel grew better in temperate conditions. His words tripped over themselves when describing potential experiments with different growth solutions and lighting to improve yield. Both Mark and Pauline were impressed.

The second candidate, David Baker, drove up in a flashy bright red sports car, an hour late. When asked his thoughts on Mark's plans, he said they looked okay and showed general disinterest in the whole project. The third candidate was a no-show, and when Mark called him, his reply was 'Sorry mate, decided not to bother'.

'Christopher is the obvious choice,' Pauline surmised. 'The other... all he was interested in was how much he'd be paid, and where the nearest pubs are.'

'Got to agree with you. Chris is perfect for what we're trying to do here.'

Mark called the hydroponics firm and faxed over Chris' sketches. They agreed to the changes and would send a new estimate in two days' time.

Not wanting to remind Pauline about the burglary, Mark explained his ideas for the byre.

'A riding stop...' she suggested. 'Once you're producing cheese, ice-cream and honey, you need to attract visitors, so add in a riding trail, with a rest stop at the byre for which you'll need a storeroom. You've a couple of good trails up to the fells from there. Signpost the routes and you're set.'

'Not a bad idea. How to explain the wagon, though?'

'Put in a picnic area and you can use the wagon to transport children. Maybe we can get Bill to be the park ranger.'

Mark doubled over when he imagined what Bill would have to say to that.

The first candidate next morning seemed suitable, but when Mark mentioned beekeeping, he said he could not take the job because of a severe allergy to bee stings.

Anthony 'call me Tony' Matthews, arrived on an old 1966 *Yamaha* motorbike with a 1946 sidecar. He was taller than Mark, skinny as a rake, and with a mop of red hair and a weather-beaten face, despite being only twenty-four years old.

Mark showed him a map of his farm and surrounding land, explained what he wanted to achieve, and asked for suggestions. Tony bombarded them with recommendations; terracing, reforesting the fell-sides using native trees like rowan, oak and alder, leaky dams using fallen trees, and more.

'That area provides a different habitat.' He pointed at the western edge of the map. 'It looks a bit marshier than you have near the beck. You could even create a wetland area there.'

Unfortunately, the stream he was pointing to was on neighbouring land and Mark said he could not afford more land at present, even if Jamie Sinclair, the owner, wanted to sell.

Mark asked him why he wanted this job.

'I really want an outdoor job,' he pleaded. 'I know the lab work is important and I'm good at it, but being junior, I'm always stuck with it. I never get the chance to do field work.'

Tony related how he spent every spare weekend travelling around the countryside recording the plants present in each location, taking soil samples and other measurements; checking back every few weeks to note any changes.

When Pauline mentioned beekeeping, Tony pointed to a spot north-east of the farm he highlighted as ideal. 'You say you've planted wildflowers there, near that stream. Perfect location—you could easily put twenty hives there. If you start now, you could be harvesting honey by summer next year.'

It was obvious he was a real environment fanatic, and the ideal person for the job. Mark mentioned the salary he was offering, and free accommodation in the three-bedroom cottage Mark stayed in while extending the farmhouse.

'That's very generous, believe me. But what I really want is to be part of the conservation and environmental work you are planning,' Tony replied.

'When can you start?'

'Monday next week, if that's alright with you.'

Mark shook his hand. 'It's a deal. I'll have all the paperwork ready. See you Monday.'

After Tony's motorbike roared away, Mark and Pauline adjourned to the living room. Mark rubbed his hands together. 'You know, with Chris and Tony on board I really feel optimistic about the farm's future.'

'Well, there's still going to be a lot of work before you start to show a profit.'

'Yes, but the important thing is we've made a start.'

Chapter 10
Wednesday, 5th July, 2006

The police arrived at the farm the next morning and Pauline and Mark met them in the living room.

'Miss Grainger, all we've been able to find out to date is that a tall man, dressed in black leathers, was seen riding a motorbike away from your house. He was picked up on a traffic camera, but we couldn't identify him,' the sergeant told her. 'In your report you said the only person you thought might have done this was a Steven Alan Johnstone, but he was in jail? Well, we checked. He was released last month.'

Pauline grasped Mark's hand. 'He was sentenced to seven years. How come he's out early?'

'Apparently he got time off for good behaviour.'

'I knew he'd come after me, I knew it,' she whispered.

Mark put his arm around her. 'Well, the police know about him now. He won't be able to show his face around here for a while, isn't that right, officer?'

'That's correct, sir. All local forces have been alerted that he's wanted for questioning.'

After the police left, Pauline received a call.

'I have to get back to work. Mr Bradley will make a fuss if I take any more time off.'

'Okay, but you're staying at the farm until they catch this guy. I will drive you there and back each day. I don't want you alone on those lanes.'

Tears appeared in her eyes. 'I thought it was all over. Now he's back to spoil everything.'

'He's not going to spoil anything,' Mark retorted.

Sunday evening, Mark and Pauline went over their research on Chesterfield. They waded through maps, lists of banks and inns, names and locations of solicitor and local shopkeepers. And, from the online newspaper archives they studied, the events Mark would be expected to know about.

'I'm sure when I'm there, there will be a lot *not* covered by all this.'

'So, when are you going to make the first trip?'

'Let me get Tony settled in first. I've a contractor coming in tomorrow to erect shelves, a small kitchenette and fix double doors in the byre so the wagon can fit through.'

'What did Bill say when you told him?' she asked, with a mischievous smile.

Mark looked disappointed. 'Not much actually. He just shook his head and walked away muttering to himself.'

Tony arrived at seven on Monday morning and Mark soon had him established in the cottage. He asked for large scale maps to plot the different habitats and environments around the farm, and armed with five six-inch to one-mile maps, he disappeared for the rest of the day. He settled in to a routine... an early breakfast, collect a packed lunch from Jenny and disappear until dinner time. Friday, Mark went to the cottage to check on what progress he had made. The maps had been stuck on the living room wall, annotated and coloured coded.

Tony pointed to a large stream coming off the fell. 'Did you know there are some old terraces along there? They haven't been maintained, but can be recut and reinforced. Best to have it done before winter.'

Mark told him to go ahead.

On Saturday, Mark packed his saddlebags with spices, tea and spare clothes. He wrapped the silk in oilskin, and secured it behind his saddle. When Lucky saw Mark changing, he snorted and started prancing.

Mark grinned. 'Looks like he knows we're going on a trip.'

Pauline huffed in exasperation at his casual attitude. 'Never mind him, are you sure you have everything you'll need,'

'Treble-checked. Anyway, I can always pop back if there's something I've forgotten.'

'Now you be careful. Don't get into any trouble, and try to keep a low profile.'

'Opening a bank account, starting a business and renting a house is not exactly low profile,' he replied, and set the Portal for seven in the morning, Friday first of March, 1839. 'I'll only be gone an hour. Make yourself comfortable and I'll see you in three weeks.' he joked, and gave her a long kiss. He led Lucky through the gateway and waved to Pauline before shutting it down. He could not see her, but knew she could see him.

Coming out at Brierley Wood, a sparsely settled area six miles north-west of Chesterfield, Mark rode through Whittington, and reached Market Square at nine o'clock. The Angel Inn, a coaching inn, had stables and decent rooms; it was also a good place to observe the mail coaches coming and going. Early March was a quiet period for travellers and he negotiated a price of fifteen shillings a week for a room, including breakfast and stabling for Lucky. The innkeeper made it very clear that any other meals and services would be extra and 'paid for directly'. A porter took the oilskin roll and his Western-style saddlebags earning more than a few strange looks. He carried the backpack himself; he was not letting it out of his sight.

After lunch, he switched on his camera and went for a stroll. He checked locations of grocers, drapers and milliners, visiting a few to gauge retail prices. The town centre layout was not that much different from the Chesterfield he knew back in the Twenty-First Century, and although dusty, it was not as crowded, filthy or noisy as London.

Mark was woken at two o'clock in the morning by the *London Mail* coach stopping briefly at the inn. Once it left, he went back to bed only to be woken again by the noise as the market set up. After breakfast, and lots of coffee, he made his way over to the stalls. Walking back towards the inn he saw the Sheffield bound coach pull in, and promised himself he would make that trip before he left.

He skipped lunch to watch the afternoon mails coming and going and made a short video of each coach. The crowds thinned, and the market stall owners started packing up around five o'clock. A slight drizzle started and he headed back to the inn for something hot to eat and drink. Back in his room, he wrote his notes in pencil. *What I wouldn't give for a good old BIC ballpoint.*

The next day was Sunday. Mark walked to the Church of St Mary and All Saints, commonly known as the Crooked Spire, then roamed along Knifesmithgate. The video of the people and the clothes they wore would fascinate Pauline. After dinner, he went to check out the local night life. The gas lights, his bullet proof vest and survival knife made him confident of his safety. Even with his backpack, he was certain he could handle any trouble.

It was pretty rowdy around Market Square thanks to a gang of navvies from the railway enjoying a night off. He gave them a wide berth and made his way back to his inn. Passing an alley, he heard shouting and saw two drunks accosting someone. Not hesitating, he struck one hard across the back of the neck. The other turned and swung a knife wildly. Mark stepped back, brought out his own knife and crouched in a fighting stance. The drunk took one look at the ten-inch serrated blade and ran. Mark helped the other on his way with a few well-placed kicks.

He helped the victim to his feet, and learned he lived nearby on Low Pavement. The short, middle-aged man was shaken and insisted Mark come to his house.

'The least I can do is offer refreshments after your assistance.'

The maid brought a decanter of brandy and two glasses to the parlour. To Mark, it was pretty harsh, and he immediately spotted another potential market.

'I am sorry, I have not introduced myself properly, John Marshall, Attorney.'

Mark presented his business card. 'Michael Holmes, pleased to make your acquaintance, sir. I arrived yesterday morning having rode down from York. I am looking to find a place to live and start a business. Somewhere quiet, London is too noisy for my liking.'

'Luxury items,' Marshal replied, looking at Mark's card. 'Interesting. There could be several opportunities here, and in Sheffield. If you do not like the big cities, Chesterfield should suit. I personally could not imagine living in London. I hear that a million people live there, can you imagine that? Those navvies rarely come to town thanks to the Hussars stationed here. They usually visit Staveley on Sundays and cause all their trouble out there.'

TP 1000: The Bishops

'I assure you, crime is a much bigger problem in London.'

Mark, told Marshall he sourced his merchandise from India and the Far East. 'This looks like a good place for business. The railway will soon be here and there is a good road network to Derby, Manchester and Sheffield.'

'Do you have samples of your goods?'

'They are back in my room at the Angel Inn, but I believe I have something with me.' He opened his bag and took out a small bar of scented soap. 'Mayhap you would accept this and have your wife pass an honest opinion.'

The soft silky surface and delicate rose scent impressed Mark's host. 'If your other samples are of this quality, I am certain you will have no problem finding customers. I may be of assistance in helping you contact local business men.'

'That would be most useful. First I need to open a bank account and find a house to lease. Perchance you could recommend a good bank to me.'

'I bank at the *Scarsdale and High Peak Bank*, and know the manager personally. We can meet tomorrow and I will introduce you myself. I have also heard of a lady in Brampton wishing to lease her house, you may be interested.'

'Thank you. That is most kind. Shall we meet at The Angel for breakfast tomorrow? I can show you my samples afterwards.'

'An excellent idea. Will eight o'clock suit?'

'Yes sir, I will meet you there in the morning. Now I must beg your leave.'

Mr Marshall, still fingering the soap, escorted Mark to the door.

Marshall was punctual and Mark paid for breakfast. An attorney would be useful in many ways; it had been a lucky break meeting him last night. Breakfast finished, Mark unrolled the silk and showed him two luxurious quilted silk dressing gowns he had brought.

His visitor was amazed. 'Mr Holmes, I assure you there is nothing around here to match this quality.' Marshall observed the condition of the spices was excellent. Lastly Mark showed him the long curly leaved *Oolong* tea.

'You will notice the fragrant flavour. I also have black teas from China and Ceylon.'

'Mr Holmes, these will find a ready market among the gentry. My wife was most impressed with the soap. She wishes me to obtain more. It will be quite the social coup for her.'

'It will be my pleasure. Now as to the bank, where is it located?'

'Allow me to escort you and introduce you to the manager.'

At the bank, Mark produced a thick roll of Bank of England notes and two large purses of gold sovereigns to astonished looks from the bank manager and Mr Marshall.

'One thousand, five hundred pounds. Do you have a vault where I could keep some gold bars?'

'Yes sir. Exactly how much gold are you considering?' The bank manager tried valiantly to retain his composure as Mark took out thirteen ingots.

'Six pounds, seven and a half troy ounces,' he replied calmly. Mark had had plenty of experience with people impressed by his wealth in the Twenty-First Century. His deposit, the equivalent of a hundred thousand pounds in 2006, and the sight of the gold bars caused a dramatic change in the bank staffs' attitude. He had always detested obsequiousness but hid his distaste as this would benefit him in becoming established locally.

With the bank manager's well wishes, he left with his receipt and bank passbook; Mr Marshall asking him to join him for lunch, at his expense.

Mark insisted on paying for the wine. 'I insist, the least I can do after all your help.'

'Mr Holmes, may I ask a personal question?'

'Of course.'

'That knife, where is it from? I have never seen its kind before.'

'It is modelled on those used by the American frontiersmen. It is a formidable weapon.'

'It most certainly is. Those ruffians wanted nothing to do with it. You are a remarkable young man, I must say. Now, if you could give me a few days, I am certain I can obtain some introductions to our merchants, and shall start immediate enquiries regarding the house in Brampton.'

'Most gracious. I also need to lease warehouse space for my goods if opportunities arise. May I retain you as an attorney for my business transactions, and the service of a clerk from time to time?'

'Assuredly. I know a merchant who will gladly lease some of his warehouse space, and my own clerk would be at your service, for a small remuneration, when needed.'

'Thank you, most kind,' Mark responded politely. 'May I also impose a little further and ask for a recommendation to a good boot maker and tailor. By circumstance, I carried few spare clothes with me.'

'By all means. William Bollington, a tailor on Vicar Lane, and Joseph Bonington at the New Square is an excellent boot and shoe maker. I am certain they can meet your requirements.'

'Thank you. It was an auspicious day when we met.'

'No thanks are necessary, none at all. Without your help I would have been robbed and maybe killed. It is I who is in your debt, sir. Please bide a day or two while I make enquiries. As soon as I have any news I will leave a message for you.'

Mark made appointments with the two tradesmen for the next morning and found a stationer on Low Pavement to buy writing paper, ink, pens and wax for seals. Back at the inn, he took Lucky from the stables and let him have a good run at the race track on

Newbold Common. The rest of the day was spent practicing with the steel nib pens. He finally managed to write three letters to himself care-of the Angel Inn, using different fictitious names. The letters commented on the range and prices of goods at the Market, the punctuality of the mail coaches and the disturbances caused by the railway navvies on Sundays.

Tuesday morning, he went to be fitted for clothes, riding boots and shoes. The total cost was ten guineas, with delivery in ten days. With little else to do, he rode Lucky over to Staveley and posted a letter with the receiver, making sure there was a clear number four written on the outer sheet, acknowledging the four-penny payment. He had lunch at the Devonshire Arms and headed back to Chesterfield. A Mr Baker, local grocer, was waiting for him to enquire about his tea samples. Within an hour Mark had negotiated the price for fifty pounds of Chinese black tea and five pounds each of cloves, nutmeg and cardamom. Mark was delighted at his first deal which, hopefully, would help him establish a viable business.

The next day he posted a letter from Clown. He was delighted at finding the elusive post office at Richard Revill's tailor's shop in Back Lane and used a whole memory card on the visit. He left another letter with Henry White, the carrier in Barlborough.

Friday morning, after stabling Lucky, the landlord handed him a note asking him to come to Mr Marshall's regarding the house for lease. Marshall informed him the house at Brampton was available. The owner, a widow, was leaving to live in Oxford with her daughter, and wanted to lease the house, fully furnished for a Midsummer lease.

'Mrs Houghton's house comes with five acres of pasture and gardens, separate stables and carriage house,' Mr Marshall told him. 'The house has a parlour, dining room, drawing room and study on the ground floor. There are three bedrooms and changing rooms on the first floor and servant quarters in the attic. Below-stairs has the usual kitchen, scullery, pantry, larder, a small laundry room and a separate dairy room.'

Mark was pleased to hear something was available so soon. The house was bigger than he had planned on, and he was not sure how Pauline would feel about running such a large house with all the servants it needed. It was outside the town limits, but an easy three mile ride.

'May I ask you to negotiate with the lady in question on my behalf while I am away?'

'It will be my pleasure. When will you be returning?'

'The middle of April. Mr Marshall, you have been most helpful.'

'It was a pleasure, and, may I say, I feel it a duty after you saved me that night.'

Mark was kept busy with merchants coming to visit, placing orders. He had managed to sell nearly all his merchandise and secure advance orders for tea, spices and silk, and even obtained a reference for a silk merchant in Sheffield. He bought a ledger from the stationer and kept clear accounts, having each merchant witness the order details. During a short trip to Sheffield to meet the silk merchant, he found a beautiful wooden jewellery and toiletry box for Pauline.

Mark visited the merchant with storage space near the River Hipper. The area comprised a few warehouses, clusters of small houses and two pubs, one of which was opposite the warehouse. When he left, he heard a man called out. 'Hey, Jamie, yer ratbag, thought I'd forget that half sovereign you owe after yer went darn to Nottingham, did yer?'

Mark ignored him and walked towards Lucky.

'Where'd yer thieve yer coat from? Ignorin' yer old mates now yer well clobbered are yer? Well it won't save yer from a good bashin'.'

Mark looked around. A scruffy hulk was crossing the road brandishing a cudgel.

Mark reached under his coat for his survival knife.

'Hey! You're not Jamie.'

Relieved he was not the actual target, Mark nevertheless held his knife ready. 'Who is this Jamie person?'

'Sorry, guv'nor, sorry. Yer the spitting image of James Bishop. Meant no offence, none at all.'

Mark was shocked to hear his own family name, then remembered his family history.

'Tell me about this fellow,' Mark returned his knife to its sheath.

'Well sur, he showed up last year, then a couple o' months ago said he was headed of t' Nottingham. A sharp, yer know, loses small bets but allus wins the big 'uns, if yer know what I mean. Fancies 'isself a bit of a ladies man. Allus tryin' t' impress the dollymops, not that they're intrested in 'owt but his silver.'

The remarkable resemblance—a gambler and womaniser. This must be his James Bishop, the one who had raped that young girl.

He was stunned, not sure what to do. He left the man without another word, mounted Lucky and rode back to the Angel.

The next day Mark returned from his morning ride to find two gentlemen waiting for him. The older one introduced himself as Sir Reginald Barker then his son, Bartholomew. Sir Reginald had heard of the silk robes from Mr Marshall and gladly paid five guineas for each. Sir Reginald asked if he had any for ladies, but the ones Mark had bought were far too immodest for this day and age and he had given them to Pauline and Julie. He asked Sir Reginald to join him in a drink; the double malt impressed Sir Reginald with its smoothness and Mark assured him he would bring more on his return.

'I gather from Mr Marshall you are looking to lease the

TP 1000: The Bishops

Houghton place over in Brampton?' Sir Reginald asked. 'I knew the colonel well. His wife is most anxious to move to Oxford, you know. I'll mention your name when I visit her next.'

'That is most kind, Sir Reginald.'

'Please, don't mention it. I look forward to our meeting when you return.'

This was a great opportunity for Pauline to meet the upper gentry and have some kind of social life. It was also a potential market for the brandies and whiskies he intended to bring in future.

The day before he left, he rode over to Brampton to have a look at the house. It was a large two storey building, with a wall along the roadside and a dilapidated greenhouse off to one side. Five cows grazing in the neighbouring field explained the dairy room.

Mark was glad to be leaving; it had been taxing minding his 'P's and Q's'. Living conditions had proved to be better than he had expected, but he was not sure how Pauline would adapt. At least she would have a proper house and not have to stay at an inn. He paid his bill and made sure the stable hands received a good tip. He made good time back to Brierley Woods, and once hidden from sight, he turned off the road. Once the gateway opened he led Lucky through.

Chapter 11
Saturday, 15th July, 2006

Mark closed the gateway, put the Portal in his backpack and gave Pauline a big hug and kiss. 'Boy, am I glad to see you. You are a sight for sore eyes.'

'How long were you gone?' She patted Lucky who was pushing in, wanting a bit of fussing himself.

'Nineteen days altogether.'

'This will take some getting used to. I've been sat here an hour, but it's been nearly three weeks for you.'

'Come on, let me change, and I'll tell you all about it. I used all the memory cards. When we go, we'll have to bring a lot more cards and batteries. Oh! I have a present for you in my saddlebags, hang on a minute.'

She unwrapped the parcel and gasped when she opened the mother of pearl inlay lid. Inside sat glass perfume bottles, powder bottles with silver-plated lids and a range of silver-plated accessories.

'You can fill the bottles and jars with your own make-up and stuff. You do *not* want to buy local cosmetics, believe me. They used mercury and lead.'

'Oh, Mark. This is beautiful.' This was followed by a long passionate kiss.

Mark regained his breath. 'My pleasure, believe me.'

Pauline grabbed his hand. 'Come on, change, and let's get back to the farm.'

After stabling their horses, they went straight to Mark's study where he stacked the memory cards on the table. 'I'll download these onto the computer, that way they'll be easier to watch. There's twenty-four hours of video altogether, you're not going to finish today.'

'You'll never believe this, I might have found one of my ancestors,' Mark told Pauline while he transferred the videos to his computer.

Pauline's eyes went wide with shock. 'What? Who?'

'Remember the black sheep of my family?'

'The rapist? The one who disappeared?'

'Yeah. Apparently, up to a couple of months ago, he was living in Chesterfield, before he moved to Nottingham. I was even mistaken for him.'

'What are you going to do?'

'I don't know.' Mark paused and stared out the window. 'Damn! I wanted to find out more about my ancestors, but I never thought about actually meeting any of them.' Mark rubbed the back of his neck. 'Especially not this one.'

'Well, he may never show up and it won't be a problem.'

'That's true.' He stood after downloading the last memory card. 'Anyway, start with videos ten and twelve. They're the ones on the house I'm looking at leasing.'

An hour later Pauline turned to Mark, biting her lip. 'That's a *big* house. How many servants are there?'

'Not sure. Financially, we'll be okay with all the money in the bank and all the orders I've taken. We can easily afford their salaries.'

Pauline gave him a dirty look. 'Alright for you, I'll be the one who has to deal with them.'

'I'm sure you'll manage,' Mark quipped and dodged away from her swinging arm.

Sunday, Pauline spent the whole day watching the recordings. After she had watched the first one, she yelled at Mark, 'You promised to stay out of trouble.'

'I did! Marshall was the one in trouble.'

'You... second day and you get in a fight.'

'What was I supposed to do? Leave the poor man to be robbed and beaten?'

'I suppose not, but you do seem to attract trouble.'

'Well, I'll leave you to it, I have work to do. I'll pop in from time to time.'

In the afternoon, he saw her watching the meeting with Sir Reginald. 'We may receive invitations and get a better idea how the gentry lived. At least it will give you a social life.'

Pauline smiled sweetly. 'Well, in that case, I'll need more clothes, won't I?'

Mark groaned but a glimmer of humour was evident in his eyes. 'I'll show you the website and you can order your own. Charge my account... I'll cut it from your share after I sell the jewellery.' He beat his retreat before she could react.

When Mark picked her up from work on Wednesday, he told her the contractors had started work on the greenhouses. The extra solar panels had already been installed on the barn and storage sheds. 'Next Tuesday they'll come in to upgrade the biogas system; once it's all connected, there'll be plenty of heating for the greenhouses.'

'Things are starting to look good,' Pauline replied.

'Yeah. Poor old Bill has been walking around like he's bitten a lemon. He doesn't think much to all the disruption. Says it upsets the cows.' Mark laughed. 'I reckon it upsets him a lot more than the cows.'

At the weekend, Mark drove Pauline to her aunt's house despite her objections she would be safe driving herself. Sitting in her aunt's parlour, he was amused by the admiring glances, sly comments and hints he received from Mrs Grainger and her sister, Lily. Pauline, however, fidgeted and appeared to be in some discomfort.

After an hour, Mark managed to escape the two predatory old ladies. 'Sorry ladies, I have to get back to the farm. Miss Grainger, I will pick you up tomorrow evening. Around seven be alright?'

Sunday evening, he parked back in front of her aunt's house and Pauline's mother came out. 'Mr Bishop, please come in, Pauline will be ready in a moment.' She herded Mark into the living room. 'You have time for a cup of tea?'

Pauline rushed in, 'Mum, Mr Bishop and I need to be off before it gets too dark.' She sounded exasperated, which puzzled Mark. He knew she and her mother were close, especially after Pauline's father had died.

Diplomatically Mark agreed, 'Yes, a good idea. Maybe another time?'

As they drove off, Pauline waved to her mother, sat back and let out a long sigh.

'Nothing wrong, I hope,' Mark asked, gently. 'Seemed a bit tense back there.'

'Sorry about that. My mum and aunt have been on all weekend, nagging me about grandchildren, and settling down, and getting married,' she replied grumpily.

Laughing, Mark jested, 'Not in that order, I trust.'

Realising *exactly* what she had said, she started chuckling. 'Thanks, I needed that. Those two have been giving me the third-degree.'

Monday, after dropping Pauline at work, Mark went to help Tony with the terracing project—driving new stakes along the old terrace line, fitting the retaining logs, and backfilling with soil. The terraces covered both banks of the beck, considerably more extensive than he had imagined. After four days of backbreaking work, the security alarm next to Mark's bed woke him at two o'clock in the morning. He checked the monitor, and saw a man running away from the biogas dome. He rushed outside and heard the dogs yelping and howling and a motorbike racing down the road. The intruder had come prepared... he had used a pepper spray on the dogs to make his getaway.

Bill came out at the commotion. 'What's all t' racket?'

'Someone tried to break in and Max and Fritz chased him off. Call the police while I see to them—the bastard sprayed them with something.'

George's people had already alerted the police and, by the time Bill called, they were already on their way. When they arrived, everybody was awake and Jenny was making tea.

Mark explained what had happened and took the policemen to the site. They noticed fresh drops of blood and a strong petrol odour. A crowbar and five bottles lay next to the gate, one of which had broken and was the source of the smell. The bag contained a screwdriver, hammer and three different sized crescent wrenches.

Bill looked closely at the evidence left behind. 'Looks like one o' t' dogs gave 'im summat to remember. Good job too, them bottles are full o' petrol.'

'We'll have a forensics team over here later,' the officer informed Mark. 'We would like to see your security tapes, please.'

Mark replayed the tapes in his office. They saw a man wearing a black leather jacket and a motorbike helmet approaching the fence around the biogas storage holder. He took the crowbar and glass bottles out of a bag and started to break open the lock. They saw Max and Fritz come hurtling around a corner and Max latch onto the man's left calf; the dog let go when sprayed in the face. The intruder knocked over the bottles when he sprayed Fritz, who came up a second or two later. When he turned to run, the camera caught a clear view of his face. Another camera caught the motorbike leaving and the number plate.

'Bloody 'ell!' Bill exclaimed. 'If he'd damaged t' gas holder, the whole bloody lot could 'a blown up. There's o'er ten-thousand cubic feet o' gas in there.'

Mark pointed at the screen. 'Yeah, but did you notice he came from the direction of new generator house,'

'Better go and check on it.' With that, Bill headed out.

They found the housings for the lubricating system and alternator had been removed and sand poured in. The generator was wrecked.

'Mr Bishop, I will need a copy of those recordings for evidence.' The sergeant then asked if Mark recognised the man. 'Never seen him before in my life.' Mark turned to Bill.

'Complete stranger to me an 'all.'

Pauline's leaned over Mark and her face had paled. 'That's Steven!' she cried.

'You mean the guy you knew in London?'

'Yes. That's him. He must have found out I was staying here.'

After questioning Pauline, the sergeant asked her and Mark to come down to the station later and make a formal report.

After Mark escorted the police to their car, he found Pauline sat in the office. She raised her drawn face to him when he came in. 'I'm so sorry. It's all my fault.'

'What are you talking about?' Mark asked.

'Steven... the generator. It's all my fault. If I wasn't living here, none of this would have happened. I'd better not stay here anymore.'

Mark's stomach jumped to his throat and he froze. 'No! No, you can't,' he shouted. 'I mean... you'll be a sitting duck on your own.'

'I knew you would be angry, I'd better leave. ' She walked to the door.

Mark gently took her arm and turned her towards him. 'Yes, I am angry, but not with you. I'm pissed off at the 'son of a bitch' who tried to blow up my farm.' His voice softened and he pulled her to his chest. 'But never with you.' He kissed her hair. 'I don't want you to leave. I'll keep you safe, I promise.'

Pauline relaxed and put her arms around his waist.

'It's four-thirty, why don't you grab a few hours' sleep. I'll drive you to the police station in the morning, then drop you off at work.'

'You can't keep driving me to work. I need my car to visit clients.'

Mark stared at her for a moment. 'Okay, but I'm following you there and back. He won't know your client schedule, but I'm sure that bastard knows you travel between the farm and your office.'

She squeezed his waist. 'Alright. Goodnight.'

They made their statements to the police and Mark followed her to Richmond.

As Pauline headed for the office door Mark grasped her arm. 'Don't leave the building, you hear. Have someone bring your lunch for you. I'll be back at five.'

'Stop fussing.'

'That guy is crazy. I don't want you taking any risks, okay?'

A quick kiss and Mark drove away.

George was waiting when he returned to the farm. Installing cameras to monitor all the farm buildings, plus a security fence around the generator building would cost Mark another fifteen thousand pounds, plus additional monthly monitoring charges. The news from the generator contractor was not good either; although covered by insurance, they needed two months to repair and re-install it.

By the time Mark drove to meet Pauline, he was ready to pull his hair out. He decided not to tell her about the extra security costs, she was feeling bad enough already. No sense making it worse.

Pauline was subdued over dinner. Mark put his hand on her. 'Don't worry about that bastard. The police are on the lookout for him now. He's likely miles away from here already.'

Pauline shook her head. 'It's not that, it's my boss. I forgot to call to say I would be late. He called me into his office before I left. I explained what had happened but he got angry. He said this was the third time I had taken urgent leave and I was spending too much time on your account and not enough on my other clients.'

Mark's face flushed. 'Why, that sorry excuse for a...'

'What upsets me most is I've not been neglecting my other clients,' she clenched her fists as she spoke. 'I reckon it was Rosemary, his secretary, who stirred him up. She's always been jealous, and now I'm living here, she had to have a go.'

'What she got to be jealous about?'

'I joined the company early last year and have already been promoted past others who've been there longer, including her fiancé.'

'I know all about office politics. Had to listen to my dad moan for hours about all the backstabbing in his own company. Look, why don't you visit your mother this weekend? No point moping around here. I've a lot to sort out, and Saturday, I need to go to York for the final arrangements for the jewellery auction. I can drop you off on my way there.'

Pauline grinned at him. 'You're chicken! You're just using it as an excuse not to be grilled by my mother and aunt again.'

'Guilty as charged. Especially when it comes to potential mothers-in-law.'

'What mother-in-law? Where did that come from?'

'Something about grandchildren, settling down and marriage, remember?' He smirked. 'I don't mind trying for the first part,' he said, with a straight face. 'Not sure about the last bit though,' he mumbled. 'Ouch! What was that for?' rubbing his arm where she had slapped him.

'You can get those ideas out of your head. We're not *trying* for anything.' she replied hotly, and stormed upstairs, leaving Mark sniggering.

On reaching the farm on Friday evening, Pauline slammed her passenger door shut and stormed into the house.

TP 1000: The Bishops

'What's the matter? Your boss been on at you again?' Mark asked.

'No, it's Rosemary. She was talking to her fiancé in the next cubicle, saying how some people can ignore professional ethics and get away with it. She went on and on about how personal relationships can bias a proper accountant's judgement. If she stirs up the boss again, I could be disciplined, and you may end up with a new tax advisor.'

'Like Hell I will!' Mark's jaw tightened. 'I already warned Bradley, if he sends some idiot here again I'm changing companies.'

'It's been horrible. Everyone is scared of her. They have all been ignoring me as if I was a leper or something,' Pauline was twisting her fingers into knots. 'If she goes running to Mr Bradley again and he takes it to head office, I could lose my job.'

'That's not going to happen. Trust me.' Mark held her shoulders. 'Go and freshen up. We can talk after dinner.'

Hoping to distract her from her worries, Mark asked, 'I know you were raised on a farm, but how come you know so much about sustainable farming?'

'After I left London to stay with Julie, I enrolled in a part-time farming management course and took a distance learning program on hydroponics. I figured it would help my dad back at the farm. When he was sick, I came back here and took this job. My farming background and my courses meant I was given all the farming accounts and why I've been promoted.'

'Ah! That explains a lot. No wonder your suggestions are so detailed.'

Mark dropped her at her aunt's house the next morning, and drove off before her mother could pounce on him. At Harrison's shop he finalised the auction details. It was scheduled for the end of August and had already attracted several enquiries from overseas buyers.

'It's a pity you kept the crucifix and ear rings, those would have increased the overall sale price dramatically,' Mr Harrison told him. 'But you should still realise two-hundred thousand after commission and costs.'

After taxes he would have a hundred and forty thousand to share with Pauline. This additional income would offset his recent losses and expenses, although it would not compensate for the delays.

In the afternoon, the police called Mark. The motorbike, which had been stolen from Reading, had been founded dumped behind a hedge near Bilton, outside Hull. CCTV footage at the ferry terminal showed Steven had boarded a ferry to Rotterdam and the police had contacted the Netherland authorities.

This was good news. If Steven was in Europe, he would not be bothering them for a while.

Driving back from Darlington with Pauline, he told her what the police had said.

'He speaks fluent German and has several friends there. He often boasted no-one knew he was British. I'd better let the police know, he may be going there,' Pauline took out her phone. 'I'll feel a lot better when I know he's behind bars again.'

After dinner, Pauline said she needed an early night. 'I cannot afford to be late. It will only give Rosemary more ammunition.'

Mark sat in the living room after she left. Pauline still blamed herself for what Steven had done, and Mark did not want to cause her any trouble at work. What would he do if she lost her job and blamed him? He went to bed, his stomach in knots.

Chapter 12
Monday, 31st July, 2006

When Mark returned from Richmond the next day, a VW was parked in front of the farmhouse. *Damn, I forgot all about Chris coming today.* In the house, he heard Jenny's voice coming from the dining room, and found Chris being fussed over by his housekeeper while having breakfast.

Chris jumped up when he saw Mark.

Mark smiled. 'Sit down. When you're finished I'll show you the cottage.'

Mark sat and helped himself to a cup of coffee. 'I'm afraid there's been a problem in getting the hydroponics centre ready.' Mark explained the sabotage had delayed getting heating and electricity connected to the greenhouses.

'That's terrible. Have they caught whoever did it?'

'Not yet. But at least they know who it was. Anyway, it's going to be a couple of months before the new generator is running.'

'That's alright. If I can order some lab equipment and chemicals, and set up a temporary lab somewhere, I can start on water and soil analysis.'

Mark thought for a moment. 'We hardly use the workshop, you could use that for now. What equipment do you need?'

'I'll prepare a list for you.'

'Sounds good. I'll show you to the cottage. Afterwards we can drive around the farm.'

They took the utility vehicle to where Tony was working and Mark introduced them. It was not long before they were deep in conversation about the pros and cons of nutrient film versus deep flow techniques. When they started discussing the different types of nitrogen and cation exchange capacity, Mark shook his head and left them to it, telling Chris to have a list of laboratory equipment ready as soon as possible.

When Mark met Pauline outside her office, she was smiling.

'What are you so happy about,' he asked, glad at the change.

'Rosemary's on holiday for two weeks.'

Mark grinned back. 'Should make life a bit easier for a while.'

After dinner, Pauline told him they needed to have vaccinations against typhoid and cholera, and buy doxycycline tablets for their stay to Chesterfield.

'I kept my shots up to date after Africa,' Mark replied. 'What do we need doxycycline for?'

'Typhus. It's spread by fleas and lice; they had thousands of cases every year in the early 1840s. Also, I'm going to start taking first aid courses, we'll probably need them at some time or another.'

'Well, I did plenty of that when working overseas but I reckon it would be a good idea to work out how to build a water purification system, Nineteenth Century style. That'll keep me busy.'

The next morning Chris brought his list. 'It's not necessary to order everything now, wait until the greenhouse is completed; though I do have to buy some equipment now to analyse the water.'

'What about bacteria? Can you test for them?'

'Yes I could...' Chris asked, looking puzzled.

Mark told him last year a farm nearby had lost four cows to neosporosis. The pregnant cows had aborted and been barren afterwards. 'I want to be sure there's nothing nasty in any of the farm ponds.'

'Not a problem. I will need count plates and an incubator. Let me check on costs.'

Later Chris handed Mark his revised list. 'The incubator is the most expensive piece of equipment and with everything else, comes to two thousand pounds. I've a friend who works at a laboratory supply company in Huddersfield, I'll check with him. Might even get a bit of discount.' Chris took the farm *Land Rover* to Huddersfield and when he returned, he and Tony spent their time setting up the temporary laboratory.

Friday lunch-time, Pauline's mother called her at work to say she was ready to come home. Her Aunt Lily could now manage on her own and her mother wanted to go back to her own home. Pauline was torn. She and Mark had become really close in the last six weeks, and true to his word, he had put her under no pressure at all. She called Mark to let him know and heard the disappointment in his voice.

The next morning, Mark drove her to Darlington. On the way back, no matter how much Pauline tried to interrupt, her mother regaled Mark with all the latest Grainger family history. Once they reached their home, Pauline explained the security system and showed her the house had been redecorated. Her mother became so profuse in her thanks for all his help, Pauline rushed him out of the house.

'I need to get my mother settled, I'll see you next weekend.'

'I'm going to miss having you around all the time, but family comes first.'

After he drove away, Pauline turned back to the house to listen to more of her mother's innuendos.

By Monday, Jenny had had enough of Mark's moping around and scolded him. 'Give 'er a call or go an' see 'er will yer? Either that, or find summat to keep yerself busy.'

Mark took the hint and contacted a few horse dealers. The wagon would be ready by month end and he needed horses to pull it, or be subjected to more of Bill's sarcastic comments.

The next morning Mark drove to Doncaster to inspect draft horses. He described the wagon he had ordered and weight, and explained it would be used on country lanes and farm tracks. On their recommendation, he bought two eight-year-old Belgian draft horses for eight thousand pounds to be delivered to the farm by the weekend.

When he returned, three large boxes had been delivered along with two wooden brass-bound steamer trunks—Pauline's clothes and their luggage had arrived. He took the boxes to his study and stored the trunks in his garage. He called Pauline to let her know; she sounded excited and said she would come on Saturday to try them.

Pauline arrived at the farmhouse followed by a horse transporter with Mark's two new horses, both chestnuts. Nellie stood at sixteen-and-a-half hands and Lizzie, half-a-hand shorter. Pauline followed as Mark took them to the pasture to meet Lucky and Princess. They saddled their horses and rode out to the byre. After checking it was cleaned out ready for the wagon and the alterations underway, he turned and took Pauline in his arms. 'I've missed you.' After they stopped kissing he asked, 'So how's work?'

'Great. I brought in two more clients. According to my boss, they had heard about me and want to be represented by the same company.' A wicked smile spread across her face. 'Rosemary is going to be so pissed off when she gets back to work on Monday.'

'Just goes to show, there's more than one way to skin a cat.'

'What do you mean?' When she saw his smug expression, her eyes narrowed. 'Did you have something to do with it?'

'I may have met a certain farm machinery supplier and restaurant owner and told them how much tax rebate I received and how much lower my future taxes are thanks to you.'

Pauline doubled over laughing. 'I love it!'

'Thought you would. Now let's get back and you can try on your new clothes.'

They rode back to farm admiring the splashes of colour the red clover made in the fields and clusters of dark purple elderberries in the hedgerow.

Back at the farm, Mark was an attentive audience of one for a two-hour fashion show as Pauline tried on each dress in turn. The magenta, amber, dark chocolate and creamy-white colours she had selected matched her skin tone perfectly.

The next day Pauline took her mother to visit Lily. She later called Mark to say her aunt was planning to move to her daughter's in Scotland. Pauline's mother was upset; her sister was the only family living nearby and she wanted to offer to let her live with them, but they only had two bedrooms.

When the byre alterations were nearly completed, Mark ordered more silk from the Thai silk factory and spices from the same Indian merchant. A trip to Darlington bought soap, natural oils and half-a-dozen bottles of brandy and malt whisky.

Mowing the fields, and baling and storing the silage for fodder during winter kept Mark busy. He hardly saw Pauline. When the crates of silk and spices arrived he took an afternoon break to use the trailer to transport them to the byre while everyone was busy in the fields.

Near the end of August, the jewellery auction saw extremely competitive bidding for the earlier Mughal pieces. The prices realised for a gold Mughal turban ornament inset with emeralds and rubies, and a gold necklace embellished with pearls and sapphires, pushed Mark's return to a hundred and sixty thousand. Pauline was staggered when he gave her a cheque.

The wagon was delivered just after August Bank Holiday. Frank helped him harness the horses and Mark spent the next three days driving along the farm lanes and up and down to the byre. On Saturday morning, Mark was ready for his second trip. He harnessed the two mares, changed clothes and set the coordinates. He gave Pauline a kiss and pulled on the halter when the two mares balked at the gateway. Lucky, used to it now, walked through unaided.

He tied Lucky to the back of the wagon and headed towards Chesterfield as it was getting light. By the time he arrived, he and the wagon were as dusty as if they had travelled all the way from York. Mark offloaded all the boxes at the warehouse and drove to the Angel. His modified wagon received a lot of attention; they had never seen anything like it before.

With spring, more customers were stopping at the inn. The innkeeper had increased his rates and now asked Mark for two pounds, ten shillings a week for a room, stabling and feed for three horses and storage for the wagon. Tipping the stable hands, he left them examining the wagon and went to his room. He carried his backpack, while the porter brought the small portmanteau with his clothes. He ordered a basin of hot water, and after freshening up, Mark headed to Marshall's.

Mr Marshall greeted him warmly and said he had good news regarding the house, also several merchants had been asking to meet him. Agreeing on a shilling a week, Mark handed over his ledger and asked Marshall's clerk to send notes to the merchants listed, and one to Sir Reginald to tell him he was back and waited on his convenience.

'Now, Brampton House,' Mr Marshall declared. 'Mrs Houghton was most pleased to find a tenant so quickly. I'll arrange a visit to finalise the arrangements. She is asking a hundred and fifty pounds per year but is concerned regarding her servants. Will you be taking them all? She is taking her lady's maid and cook with her, however, she cannot accommodate the others at her daughter's home. Their combined salaries are two hundred and ten pounds per annum plus livery and allowances for tea, sugar and beer. Here is a list with names, wages, and references.'

'Well, I would need to meet them first, of course, although if Mrs Houghton has provided good references I foresee no problem. I do want to arrange a cook before I return.'

'I'm certain something can be arranged.'

'Much obliged, now I'll head back to the Angel, it's been a long journey.'

Over the next few days, Mark made his deliveries and had sufficient supplies on hand to sell.

Marshall's clerk came during breakfast and told Mark the appointment to meet Mrs Houghton was for twenty-ninth April. At the chemist, *Claughton & Bettison*, on Market Place, he secured orders for the natural oils he had brought, with promises to bring aniseed and ginger oils on his next visit.

Mark loaded a new battery and card into the camera for his visit to Houghton House. He and Marshall presented their cards to the footman who escorted them to the parlour. Mrs Houghton appeared with her daughter, Mrs Cantrell, and the lady's maid, Miss Thompson. Mrs Houghton was a handsome woman of about fifty years old, her daughter clearly a younger version. Mark and Mr Marshall rose from their chairs and after introductions, the ladies sat.

'Please sit, gentlemen. Mr Holmes, Sir Reginald told me you are recently returned to England after extensive travels abroad.'

'Quite correct, Mrs Houghton.'

'I am given to understand from Mr Marshall you now wish to settle down. I assume your wife will be accompanying you? I could not consider leasing to anyone except a married couple.'

'My wife. Ah, yes, that is correct.' Mark's scalp prickled. *This was going to take some explaining when he returned.*

Mrs Cantrell, showed obvious interest when he mentioned his wife.

'Your wife, may I ask her name?' the daughter asked.

The maid entered with tea. Mark's mind was racing. He had committed himself now, no choice but to put his head on the block.

'Er... Pauline, ma'am,' he replied. *She is going to kill me!*

'Pauline. That is an unusual name. Where does it come from?'

'Her grandmother was from Corinth in Greece where *Saint Paul* visited, so her mother named her Pauline.'

'You came from York, I am told. I presume your wife is currently residing there?'

'Er... yes, ma'am. We recently married and have rented furnished rooms, however, she desires a proper home.'

The small talk that followed helped Mark regain his composure. He learned Mrs Cantrell's husband was a major in the Thirty-Third Regiment, the First Yorkshire West Riding, and Mrs Houghton's late husband had been a colonel in the same regiment. The ladies' conversation became more informal and after fifteen minutes, Mrs Houghton broached the subject of leasing the house and the fate of the servants.

Mark assured her, the terms of the lease were acceptable, and asked about the greenhouse. 'I would like to cultivate some exotic plants. Would you have any objections to my restoring the greenhouse for that purpose?'

'How fascinating. Not at all, Mr Holmes, not at all.'

With regard to the staff, Mark agreed that with Mrs Houghton's references, he and his wife would gladly keep all the staff. This gave him the opportunity to raise hiring a new cook.

Mrs Houghton addressed the footman. 'Palmer, please call Mrs Compton.' She turned back to Mark. 'Our housekeeper will be able to recommend a suitable cook, I am certain. Naturally, your wife will require a lady's maid-companion. We have a distant cousin with a niece seeking such a position. She is both well-educated and mannered, I assure you.'

Mark had not considered this, and remembered Pauline's swearing when she tried on Victorian clothes. He reckoned she would welcome one—to keep up appearances, if nothing else.

The housekeeper arrived; a tall middle-aged looking woman with a definite no-nonsense air. Mrs Compton said she knew of a cook looking for another position, and would arrange for references.

'My wife will have the final decision on the female staff, of course, hardly my place,' Mark explained.

'Quite understandable, Mr Holmes,' Mrs Houghton agreed. 'Now allow my footman to show you the house and grounds. Mr Marshall can draw up the necessary papers.'

Recognising a dismissal when he heard one, he politely bid them farewell and followed the footman. Starting on the top floor, he had a thorough tour of the house, recording his conversation with each of the servants. Surprised, he noticed 'modern' earth toilets encased in wooden cabinets in a small room attached to the bedrooms; apparently, the Houghton's were progressive in their sanitary habits. In the well-ordered kitchen, he noted a *Kitchener* stove with oven, hot plate and boiler for water.

When Mark asked the source of the water, the footman pointed to a pump outside and six rain barrels. While inspecting the pump, he surreptitiously took a water sample in a small glass bottle. The scullery had a stone floor with wooden slats for the scullery maid, Mary, to stand on. She was fifteen-years-old, her hands red from being in water most of the time. Pauline was right, they had to work out a way to introduce modern household products.

TP 1000: The Bishops

Outside, Mark met the gardener, groom, stable boy, and cowman, and was pleased with the condition of the stables and cowshed. He asked the gardener, Robert Witcombe, why the greenhouse was in such poor repair. He said the mistress had not kept it up after the master passed and Mark told him he would have it restored. After the tour, they asked the footman to bid good-day again on their behalf.

Back in Chesterfield, Marshall explained the arrangements for coal and deliveries with current tradesmen would be continued unless Mark wished otherwise. He would prepare a full listing of the house contents with the footman and housekeeper and details of deliveries by Mark's return.

Marshall sent the references for the cook and lady's maid later in the afternoon. Mark agreed to hire the cook, a Mrs Humphries, and took the lady's maid references to show Pauline. While trying to work out how to handle Pauline's reaction when she saw the video, he realised the answer was obvious.

On Sunday, twelfth of May, Mark took a two-day coach and train trip to the Epsom Derby, where, on the Wednesday he placed bets on *Bloomsbury* at twenty-five to one odds. Quickly collecting his two hundred and fifty pounds in winnings before the official objection over Bloomsbury's pedigree was announced, he took the coach to London, to *Palmer's* in Newgate Street. He left owning a *Gould's 'Larger Improved Compound Microscope'*, a silver *Stanhope* lens and beautiful set of fifty prepared glass slides mounted in a mahogany case. These would help cement his cover as a natural philosopher. In the morning he took the six o'clock Leeds coach. He secured an inside seat and after two days, Mark gratefully descended at the Angel in Chesterfield. On arrival, his first priority was a long relaxing soak in a hot bath, for which he gladly paid half-a-crown.

Refreshed, he deposited his winnings and visited Mr Marshall who told him the lease papers would be ready for signing on his return.

When Mark arrived in the byre, he quickly changed, and led Lucky to the paddock. After he showered and had lunch, Mark downloaded the videos.

'The ones with my visit to Houghton House are on number fourteen,' Mark told Pauline. 'I'll go fetch coffee.'

When Mark returned, Pauline shot out of her chair, her body rigid.

'How could you tell them I was your wife?' Pauline screamed. 'The shopkeeper in York was one thing, but this...'

'Listen to me first,' he said, hands upraised. 'I've been racking my brains trying to figure out how to manage to be together while we're there. Each trip will last for a month or two. You realise that means we will be living together in the same house with all those servants around?'

'Oh,' she murmured. '*Oh!*' She blushed deep red, then declared vehemently 'I will not be left behind, not when it's starting to get interesting. We have to find a way.'

'I do have a solution, if you're agreeable.'

'What?' she snapped.

'I've always thought the best solution is usually the simplest.' He paused.

'Well get on with it.' She was becoming exasperated at his casual attitude.

'The answer's easy really—surprised I didn't think of it before. Solves your office politics problem, us living together in Chesterfield and should also make your mother and aunt happy.' He paused again.

'Will... you... get... on with it?'

'Bill can more than handle the day-to-day running of the farm and planning for a year ahead, and Chris and Tony have great plans for the future. The trouble is, none of us have the skills and knowledge to pull it together.'

'So what do you want me to do?' Pauline was confused at the apparent change in subject. 'You want me to find someone for you?'

'In a manner of speaking. To solve the first of the problems... I want you to come and work for me... full-time.'

'What? You can't be serious?'

'I've never been more serious in my life. I can offer you fifteen percent more than you're getting now, and better benefits.'

Pauline dropped back in the chair.

'Of course, it doesn't solve the other two problems.'

'And what's your solution?' she asked, still stunned at his offer.

Mark took a long breath. 'Oh, that's easy. If we were married, we could live together...'

'Married?' holding her hands to her mouth, she could not believe what she was hearing. 'Married?' She continued to stare at him.

'You're repeating yourself, you know. Can you say something different?'

He sat quietly letting her digest the idea.

Her eyes narrowed. 'If that was a proposal, it was the most unromantic one I ever heard.'

Mark sat and watched her.

'You are the most impossible, annoying and down-right

irritating man I have ever known,' she declared, then giggled. 'Yes! Yes, yes, yes.'

'Now I can give you this...' He took out a one-carat diamond solitaire ring and knelt on one knee. 'Pauline Grainger, will you marry me and make my life complete?'

'Oh yes!' she whispered; her eyes sparkled when he put it on her finger. 'It's beautiful.'

'It was my mother's and I know with all my heart she would want you to have it.'

She wrapped her arms around him and kissed him until both were breathless.

Mark recovered first and asked, 'Who do we tell first? Your mother, or Julie?'

'My mother!' she squealed.

'Let's break the news to Jenny, or she'll never forgive me, then we can ask for your mother's approval.'

She laughed. 'Approval? She's been waiting twenty-seven years for this. And Julie... she's been trying to get us on a honeymoon since she first met you—wedding or not.'

They left Jenny with a triumphant smile on her face and tears in her eyes.

Chapter 13
Saturday, 2nd September, 2006

Her mother rushed to call her sister, Lily; Pauline called Julie. The shriek from her phone was all the answer they needed, setting them both laughing. Mark could make out 'bridesmaid', and 'dresses' before she hung up.

Pauline chuckled. 'She'll be here soon.'

Pauline's mother had finished calling everyone she knew when Julie burst in.

'Congratulations!' she yelled, and hugged Pauline. She took one long look at Mark and gave him a bear hug. 'When's the wedding?' she demanded.

Pauline burst out laughing at Julie's exuberance. 'Hold on, he only asked me a few hours ago. We haven't had time to discuss it yet.'

'Pauline, if it's alright with your mother, I want us to be married as soon as possible. I don't want you to get away now I've found you.'

'I'm so happy, I wouldn't mind if you got married tomorrow,' her mother remarked, coming back in the room.

'Mum, are you sure?'

'I can see you're both happy and that's all that matters. I just wish your Dad was here to give you away.' Her eyes teared with happiness and regret.

'I'll leave you ladies to talk, I have things to do and plans to make.' With that, Mark left for the farm.

Mark spent the rest of the day on the phone finding a venue and, thanks to a cancellation, was lucky to book Bolton Castle, Leyburn for twenty-first of October. He called a friend at the Registrar of Marriages to arrange the paperwork and confirm the date. It only took a few more phone calls to contact all his friends.

Jimmy, his closest friend scolded him. 'You are going to be in such deep trouble. Meifen is going to be so pissed with you, you know, giving her only a few weeks' notice. She's going to be wearing out her credit cards making new clothes. The least you can do is send us a photograph.'

At Pauline's home in the evening, he told them he had secured a wedding venue and fixed the date. 'We need to finalise the paperwork and meet with the Registrar and we're all set.' He passed Julie a cheque for twenty thousand pounds and said he would pay for the venue and honeymoon; Julie, Pauline and her mother stood speechless.

'I know I have the most beautiful bride. Julie, I want to prove it to the whole world.'

Pauline grabbed his head and gave him a long ardent kiss.

'Good job the wedding's soon,' her mother murmured, getting her voice back. Blushing, Pauline let go while Mark kept grinning.

'The Castle Hall holds a hundred and twenty seated guests, I have a dozen and the rest are for you. Will that be alright with you, Mrs Grainger?'

TP 1000: The Bishops

'Yes... yes, that'll be fine,' she stammered.

'Okay, I'll leave you all to it, I've got to run,' he kissed Pauline so thoroughly she could not say a word. He headed for the door to leave and called out, 'See you later.'

'He is still the most irritating man I have ever known!' Pauline muttered. She quickly calculated and started to panic. The wedding was only seven weeks away.

When Pauline told her boss she was resigning and getting married he was not pleased, but her colleagues were truly happy for her. Even the office bitch, Rosemary, managed a weak smile when she congratulated Pauline.

Pauline, with a great sense of relief, figured office politics was now a thing of the past. She called Mark around two o'clock to tell him her last day would be twenty-ninth of September. They agreed she would start work at the farm after the honeymoon.

After work she drove to the farm and scolded him for giving such a big cheque.

'Nonsense. I want our wedding day to be one you'll always remember,' he declared, then, with a shameless expression, 'I also intend to make the honeymoon pretty memorable.'

'You... Julie was already convinced we're sleeping together, it took me all weekend to convince her otherwise.'

'I already promised you, we'll wait, and I *do* intend it to be memorable. Anticipation of pleasure is, in itself, a very considerable pleasure.'

Pauline grinned. 'So, it's going to be pleasurable, is it?'

'Definitely!' Mark kissed her fiercely.

When they came up for breath, he was nuzzling her ear and gently stroking her breast.

'Enough! I made a promise. We *will* wait!' he murmured softly and pulled away.

When her breathing was back to normal, she asked, 'So, where are we going on the honeymoon?'

'Ahah! That's a surprise.'

'Come on... give me a hint.'

'Sorry, you'll have to wait and see. Anticipation, remember.'

'Oh! You want anticipation do you?' She pushed him on the couch and started kissing him, running her hands over his chest. Down and down... then rubbing him through his jeans until she felt him harden—she stopped. Jumping off the couch, she ran out giggling, leaving Mark rampant and frustrated.

'You minx!' he called as he chased after her.

In the corridor he almost knocked Jenny over. She said Bill was looking for him, abruptly stopping whatever he had planned, much to Pauline's amusement.

Mark returned to the house an hour later. 'You know your mother wants your aunt to move to Richmond? You can stay here if you like. Heaven knows there's plenty of rooms, and your aunt can be settled-in that much sooner.'

'I can't do that. The whole village will be talking!'

'They've more than likely been gossiping anyway. After we're married you'll be living here anyway.'

'I'll talk to my mother and see what she says.'

Pauline's mother had no objections at all and they arranged for Lily to move in on Saturday. Between packing and moving her suitcases to the farm after work and spending all weekend helping her mother and aunt get organised, Pauline was too busy to be sad about leaving home. Sunday night, her bedroom at the farm resembled a warehouse, stacked high with bags and boxes.

'It'll take me days to sort all those out,' she complained to Mark.

'I'm sure Jenny won't mind helping, she's been clucking around like a hen with a solitary chick.' He grinned at her. 'When's Julie coming over?'

'Next weekend. She is organising a wedding planner. We still have to choose my wedding dress and the bridesmaids' dresses, arrange fittings... there's so much to do,' she wailed.

After Julie left Sunday afternoon, Mark asked Pauline. 'How's everything going?'

'Wedding dress selected and being made, and Julie is sorting out the menu details with the caterers at Bolton Castle. Mum's driving me crazy over the invitations and Julie is having fits with the florist. The flowers for decorations are fine, but she's not happy with the bouquets.'

'Don't worry, I have another surprise for you. Wait a few days before the wedding.'

'Now what are you up to?'

'Don't worry, it will be a nice surprise, I promise, just wait and see,' he announced with an annoying grin.

'What is it? What have you done now?'

'Just something to make our wedding special,' he told her sincerely.

'Okay, keep your secrets.' she grumbled. She knew he would not tell her, and he *knew* she hated surprises.

Monday evening, Mark told Pauline he would take another trip to Chesterfield to settle the lease on Houghton House after he restocked the byre. He wanted everything ready for when they made their first trip together after the wedding.

'I know you're busy at weekends with your mother and Julie. You concentrate on your wedding plans.'

After Pauline left for work the next day, Mark placed his orders to Thailand and Singapore and made a few a trips to the supermarket.

When his order arrived, Pauline was in Leeds with Julie. He called her and told her he would be making his trip on Saturday.

'I have a dress fitting, I can't cancel it.'

'Don't worry. You carry on, I'll call you soon as I'm back.'

'Make sure you do. Call me before you leave and when you get back... and stay out of trouble this time. If you don't call, I'll...'

'My, what a fierce little bride I have.'

'You'll find out how fierce if you're late, believe me!'

He arrived back in Chesterfield on the twenty-fifth of June, and after arranging deliveries, he and Marshall settled the papers for leasing the house. He told the attorney he would return at the end of July with his wife. Mark transferred the money to pay the lease for one year and for Mr Marshall's services, and made arrangements for the servants' salaries and provisions until he returned. He asked Marshall to inform Mrs Houghton to arrange for the lady's maid to arrive in early August.

He did not take any orders, the wagon would be loaded with luggage when he returned. He would make a few trips after they settled in the house. It had been a hectic trip–at least he had a few months to rest before the next trip.

He called Pauline when he entered the byre. 'Everything is settled. We can travel once you've recovered from the honeymoon,' he joked.

'Ha! Sez you. We'll see who needs to recover.'

Mark laughed. 'See you Monday.'

Chapter 14
Saturday, 7th October 2006

Julie took leave and moved to the farm two weeks before the wedding and Pauline's mother and aunt visited every day. Mark's few attempts to talk to Pauline were met by complaints of how much still had to be done, how little time they had... and it was all *his* fault. Luckily, harvesting the maize and preparing it for winter fodder, and two cows calving kept him out of the way.

Chris and Tony were not so fortunate. They had managed to hide out on the fells or in the greenhouse, but the weekend before the wedding, Julie swooped on them like a hawk. She had them provide a taxi service for the other bridesmaids between their hotel, the farm and Bolton Castle and running errands to and from the various suppliers.

Mark's routine was disrupted by Jimmy and his family's arrival; Meifen approached Pauline, leaving Jimmy to handle the twins.

Taking Pauline's hands in hers, she said, in her soft, slightly accented voice, 'I am Meifen, Jimmy's wife. You must be Pauline. I am very angry with Mark, he has told us so little of you.'

Pauline smiled and tried not to stare at this tall elegant oval faced beauty. Although the same height with the same black hair, Meifen's was straight in contrast to Pauline's slightly wavy look.

'Thank you, I'm very glad to meet Mark's friends at last. I know he and your husband are close friends.'

Jimmy interrupted. 'Not that close apparently. He kept *you* a secret.'

When Jenny came out, Jimmy put the girls down and gave Jenny a hug and twirled her around, no mean feat considering her bulk.

'Jenny, my darling, I couldn't keep away any longer,' he gave her a resounding kiss. 'If I wasn't happily married I'd give your Bill a run for his money.'

'Gerraway with yer. I bet yer say that to all the girls.'

Pauline's eye's almost popped out her head when Jenny blushed and giggled.

'These are my daughters. This is Jia Zhu,' Meifen announced introducing the taller one. She put her hand on the marginally shorter child's head, 'And this is Jia Lin.'

Both girls shook hands politely, and retreated to grasp their mother's coat.

'They are tired from the journey.'

'Just wait until they have had some sleep and get to know you. They won't be so quiet then, believe me,' Jimmy added, with a broad grin. 'Mark, you bum, aren't you going to introduce me to your beautiful bride-to-be that you have told me nothing about?'

'Er... Jimmy, meet Pauline Grainger, my fiancée.'

'Miss Grainger, I'm Jimmy Chen. *Very* pleased to meet you. The photos he sent do not do you justice. You are positively gorgeous.'

Pauline blushed at the flagrant compliment and saw Meifen smile and roll her eyes, clearly used to Jimmy's antics.

Having regained her composure, Jenny interrupted. 'Enough

standing around, your rooms are ready and I'm sure you are hungry.' She and Pauline ushered Meifen and the twins to their rooms while Mark and Jimmy carried the luggage.

That evening Mark presented Meifen with the Mughal earrings. Jimmy was fascinated by Mark's story of how they had found the jewellery and insisted on seeing the room. Mark showed him the first room—there was no way he was going to show the second basement and its secrets.

It only took a couple of days for the girls to come out of their shell. They had never been on a farm before. Mark took them on wagon rides and let them play in the fallen leaves which lay like golden-brown snowdrifts across the country lanes. They helped feed the newborn calves and when Mark gave them handfuls of grain to feed the chickens, they shrieked with laughter as the hens swarmed them.

Three days before the wedding, they had a brief rehearsal. Afterwards, Pauline gazed around the room where she would become Mark's wife and tried to imagine what the room would have looked like when *Mary, Queen of Scots* was imprisoned there in 1568.

They would stand underneath the same oak rafters, before a stone archway. Behind and to her right, a roaring log fire blazed in a huge stone fireplace. In the Great Chamber, the caterers had arranged the tables and chairs for the reception. White rose centre pieces sat on each table with larger floral decorations rested behind the table holding the cake. Bright flags and tapestries hung on the white plastered walls alongside crossed spears.

She could not imagine a more romantic setting for Mark and herself to commit themselves to each other.

When they returned to the farm, a huge package addressed to Pauline had arrived. She opened it and gaped at one-hundred orchid stems. The note said:-

Cattleya Paulina, named for a beautiful Bride by a loving Groom

'He's named them for me,' she whispered.

Julie gasped. 'They're beautiful! Got to call the florist,' she rushed off and left Pauline, her mother, and aunt goggling at a mass of golden-yellow flowers.

Pauline went in search of her fiancé and found him in his study with Jimmy.

She ran across the room shouting 'Thank you, thank you, thank you,' and pounced. Her mouth melded into his, and a second later he responded; his tongue sending a rush of flames coursing through her body.

'Ahem. Can you two wait a couple more days?'

Pauline sat on Mark's lap, face flushed. 'You have to see those fantastic orchids,' she said to Jimmy and turned to gaze into Mark's eyes. 'And this wonderful man had them named after me.'

Mark gasped for breath. 'Glad you like them.'

'I do, I do. Have to run, still a lot to sort out.' She gave Mark a peck on the cheek and rushed out as quickly as she had come in.

Jimmy looked at Mark. 'I hope you've been working out, otherwise you're not going to survive the honeymoon.'

The weather was clear and bright as the guests started to arrive at the castle. Upstairs, Julie and the bridesmaids, all Pauline's college friends who Julie had tracked down, made final adjustments to their iris-blue satin and chiffon dresses and admired their miniature versions of Pauline's bouquet. Amidst the controlled chaos, Meifen, in a deep red, floor length embroidered cheongsam, calmly organised her daughters and ensured the baskets of rose petals stayed out of their reach.

Pauline adjusted her veil and looked at herself in the full-length mirror. The wedding dress, a cathedral train gown in ivory silk, had hand-sewn *Swarovski* flowers resting upon French lace. She had borrowed her mother's silver locket with photos of her parents on their wedding day, her grandmother's veil as her 'old' and the florist had braided blue irises with the golden orchids and white roses for her bouquet. Her choice for 'new' was Mark's wedding gift; a pair of pearl and diamond drop earrings.

She turned at a knock on the door and Julie poked her head around. 'Are you ready for the photographer?' she asked and walked in. 'Oh, Pauline, you look fabulous.'

'You think so?' Pauline replied with a nervous smile.

'Let me call him.'

The camera man entered with her mother. All he could say was 'Wow!" over and over as he looked at his camera monitor. After he left, Pauline was alone with her mother.

Pauline's mother's eyes glistened. 'I do wish your dad was here, you look like a fairy-tale princess.'

A lump formed in Pauline's throat and she held back her own tears. 'I wish he was here too, Mum.'

She thought of Mark with no family at all. No matter how much she missed her father, she still had a large family here today to help her celebrate.

Julie burst in before they both broke down. 'You ready? Time to go.'

One last glance in the mirror and Pauline followed her mother with Julie holding her train.

After the bridesmaids adjusted the ten-foot long train, Pauline took a deep breath and stepped in to the Solar on her uncle's arm. She looked towards the arch where Mark and Jimmy, his best man, both in black herringbone morning suits, stood. When she took her first step on the red rose petals Jimmy's daughters had scattered before her, *Mendelssohn's 'Wedding March'* started to play. She saw Mark turn, his mouth open. A moment later Jimmy nudged him and whispered something in his ear.

The ceremony was a blur. Her hands trembled when she put the gold band onto Mark's finger and barely managed a demure 'I do' at the appropriate time. When Mark lifted her veil, her green eyes caught his grey ones, then he bent and kissed her. In that moment, all her fears faded and drifted away like smoke.

As they turned to leave for the photography session, the local choir, led by a tenor, rose up and sang *Julio Iglesias' 'Can't help Falling in Love'*, bringing more tears from some of the guests.. Outside, ten white doves flew into the clear blue autumn sky as confetti poured down on the wedding party. Pauline was having the most wonderful day of her life.

Jimmy's speech after lunch included many of their escapades, much to the guests' amusement and Mark's embarrassment. Then came a poignant moment when he mentioned Mark's family. He said he knew they were here in spirit and blessed this marriage.

'To the Bride and Groom. May they live in happiness all their long lives, and may they be blessed with ten beautiful children.'

Julie had had the caterers entwine the golden Paulinas orchids with fragrant *Papa Meiland* dark red roses to cascade between each of the tiers of the ivory iced cake studded with tiny gold roses. Mark and Pauline cut the cake with an engraved longsword to cheers and congratulations. When they visited each table, accepting the guests' well wishes, Meifen hugged Pauline and presented her with a deep-green jade pendant, the same shade as Pauline's eyes, carved with the Chinese character for beauty.

Before she left for her honeymoon Pauline tossed her bouquet for the unmarried women. Julie outleapt everyone else and gave a victory punch when she caught it. She turned triumphantly to her fiancé, Hugh, and yelled, 'Watch out, buster. You're next.'

A *Rolls Royce Phantom* drove them to Leeds airport where a private jet, courtesy of Jimmy, was waiting for them.

'Where are we going?' Pauline asked for the tenth time. 'You still haven't told me.'

'Patience is not one of your virtues, is it? Just give me your passport and wait and see. By now Jimmy will have told the guests where we're going and *you'll* find out soon enough.' This left Pauline fuming.

An hour into the flight, the pilot came and said they would be landing soon. Pauline looked out the window and recognised the approach to *Charles de Gaulle Airport* and Paris, her favourite city. A limousine drove them to *Prince de Galles Hotel* and after checking-in, a porter escorted them to the Mosaic Suite.

'Alone at last,' he sighed.

'Mark, this is wonderful,' she exclaimed admiring the Art Deco furniture. 'Everything today has been perfect. It's like a dream I don't want to wake from.'

'As long as you're happy. That's all I wish for.'

'Happy doesn't come close to describing how I feel. Come here,' she commanded with a lascivious smirk. 'Let me show you.'

An hour later, both sated, Pauline moved on top and gently kissed him. 'Thank you. For everything,' she whispered.

'I don't know about you, but I'm starving! If I'm going to survive the next week I need to eat.'

'Beast!' she hit him with a pillow. 'You enjoyed it as much as I did.'

'If I'm going to *enjoy* any more, I need food. Take a shower while I order something to eat.'

After ordering, he joined her under the hot water and proved himself a liar by making gentle love to her again. While eating, he asked her what she wanted to do. She smiled and placed her hand on his groin.

'Not that! God, you're insatiable.'

'I've six years to make up for.'

'Not in one week! I meant sightseeing... going for a walk... having dinner somewhere...'

They walked along the Seine, visited Notre Dame and looked at antiques and old books at the stalls by the river side. They had a portrait drawn by an artist near the Basilique du Sacré-Cœur, with Montmartre and the rest of Paris in the background. They ate crepes along the Champs Elysee and sat for quiet lunches in small cafes. The rest of their time was spent making love. Mark amazed and delighted her with his imaginative use of the furniture in the suite.

The days passed in a haze of passion and romance and both had regrets when the time came to board the jet to Leeds. A limousine dropped them home to a warm welcome from Bill, Jenny, friends and family. In Mark's bedroom, where she realised she would be sleeping from now on, she examined the room closely, especially the enormous grand king-size bed.

'Why are there so many mirrors in here? You have them everywhere.'

Mark groaned and told her to blame Jimmy. He said he had barely managed to stop the installation of a large mirror on the ceiling. When the implications hit her, a hot flush rushed to her loins.

'Why are your eyes shining? What are you thinking about?' Mark asked, with a sly grin.

'Nothing!' she retorted. 'Nothing at all! Now stop being nosey and let me unpack.'

Mark woke the next morning to Pauline slowly kissing his chest and working downwards. He stopped breathing.

'That was for being so wonderful... sweet... kind... adorable... charming and... passionate.' She punctuated each word with another long kiss.

Lifting her over him, he whispered, 'Now I'll show you what the mirrors are for.'

Over a late breakfast, Pauline asked what Jimmy had said to him when the wedding started.

'He told me to close my mouth and stop drooling.'

Frank came in, interrupting their laughter and trying hard to suppress a grin.

'Mister Mark, need to tell yer summat. While yer were away, Lucky covered Princess, there weren't no stoppin' him.'

Mark and Pauline stared at each other.

'Thanks Frank, you couldn't have done anything, anyway. Looks like we'll soon have a Mustang—Arabian crossbreed.'

After Frank left, Pauline started laughing again. 'Looks like Lucky got lucky, and *he* waited until after the wedding as well.'

Mark and Pauline spent the next month buying supplies for their joint trip, including Victorian-style luggage labels for authenticity. They filled the shelves in the byre with everything they could think of to sell and make life more comfortable in 1839.

When Mark pointed out Victorian ladies' favourite pastime appeared to be sewing and embroidery, Pauline threw a fit—she could not sew a stitch.

'I suggest you start learning,' Mark told her unhelpfully.

'Easy for you to say. Do you know they made their own clothes from scratch?'

He laughed at her outrage. 'Well, you need to find a socially suitable pastime.'

'I'll write a book or something, but *no sewing!* You'll just have to pay for all my clothes at a dressmakers,' she replied, and stuck her tongue out at him.

Mark laughed. 'Good job you have a rich husband then. Actually, that's not a bad idea. You can introduce natural *safe* products, a 'Woman's Guide to Cosmetics'. We found plenty on the internet.'

Pauline tried formulations they could prepare themselves for natural cosmetics, household cleaners and disinfectants. Mark had a recipe book of their favourite dishes and one titled 'Household Products and Remedies' printed and bound in leather.

The day before they left, Mark parked the utility vehicle at the byre. The sky, barely tinged with the red and yellow dawn of the last day of November, greeted Mark as he rode through the morning mist leading Nellie and Lizzie. He harnessed them to the wagon and drove back to the house to fetch Pauline. An hour later it was twenty-sixth of July, 1839 and Mark was driving the wagon along Brockwell Lane towards Houghton House.

Pauline tensed when she saw all the servants waiting outside the house; someone must have seen them coming down the drive.

'It's okay, they're probably more nervous than you are. Relax, and try to be a lady,' Mark whispered. Pauline restrained herself from giving her husband a thump on the arm.

They stopped at the front door and John, the footman, helped Pauline descend, then introduced the new cook and other staff; the cook's, Mrs Humphries, rotund shape evidence of her culinary skills. Pauline recognised the others from Mark's video and meeting them in person gave her a better idea of their personalities. While the footman and groom carried their luggage indoors, Mrs Compton led them to the parlour, followed by the two maids.

'Sir, ma'am, would you care for tea while Elsie prepares your rooms?'

'Splendid idea,' Mark answered, giving Pauline time to gain her bearings. Betty left to prepare the tea and Elsie went to their rooms.

When Mrs Compton took Pauline upstairs where Elsie was waiting, Mark left to check on the horses. Pauline and the maid started to unpack her trunks and Mrs Compton left to arrange a light lunch.

Asked about her background, Elsie replied, 'Bin with Missis Houghton since I was thirteen, ma'am,' her eyes cast down and hands folded in front of her as she spoke. Pauline was in a quandary. *How to retain the staffs' respect and at the same time find out more about them?* She decided on a direct approach.

'Elsie, your references are excellent, but I prefer to find out about the people who work for me myself. Thus, I know what to expect of them, and they, of my husband and myself.' Her voice softened. 'My husband is used to caring for himself. I, however, need your help. Let us unpack and learn more about each other.'

'Yes, ma'am.' Elsie replied, obviously more relaxed.

Pauline saw the maid was dazzled by the rich colours of her satins and silks, and lingered as she unpacked Pauline's toiletry box. Elsie took a set of clothes for pressing and returned with hot water. Pauline suppressed a grin when Elsie's mouth gaped at the scent and the amount of lather from the soap.

Betty returned with the freshly pressed clothes and Elsie helped Pauline dress and arrange her hair. As they left the changing room, Mark returned and Elsie left.

'How's it going?' he asked softly. They needed to be careful what they said with all the servants around; they were likely already gossiping about their new master and mistress.

'Alright, I guess. Elsie was real nervous at first, but she's okay now. Trying to tread the line between propriety and friendliness is tricky.'

'Give it time, we just arrived. You'll be fine,' he reassured her and was about to give her a kiss when there was a knock on the door. Mark answered and Mrs Compton came in to say lunch was ready.

In the dining room, John and Betty served cold cuts, a rich carrot soup, followed by apple tarts and coffee. After lunch, Mark unpacked with John's help while Pauline asked Mrs Compton to show her the house, starting with the servants' rooms. Pauline made it clear she expected a high standard of cleanliness and neatness; disease could easily spread in unhygienic conditions.

A thorough inspection from the neat and cramped servants' attic rooms and through the bedrooms on the first floor, satisfied Pauline. The drawing room was more of a family room with a small walnut desk in one corner, comfortable chairs and couch, and several small side tables covered in knick-knacks. In the study, a small bookcase stood behind a beautiful wooden desk. The large sturdy safe in the corner would ensure the Portal was safe. They had brought a lot of beeswax and scented candles with them for lighting which she handed over to the housekeeper for storage.

Below stairs, she inspected the scullery and kitchen, as well as the larder and pantry, thoroughly. Noting the large tubs, wooden dollys, a mangle and *Sheila Maid* in the laundry, she gave silent thanks for electricity, washing machines and tumble driers.

Back in the parlour, Pauline told Mrs Compton and Mrs Humphries she was pleased, and wanted to interview each servant privately to better understand their skills and experience. She addressed the cook. 'Mr Holmes has developed a taste for exotic foreign food in his travels. I have the recipes and any herbs or spices necessary for their preparation.'

The cook was delighted at the chance to add new dishes to her repertoire.

Pauline provided Mrs Compton a bar of soap for each member of staff. She said the recipe was her husband's and provided protection against disease. Actually it was a commercial scented antibacterial soap. Pauline told Mrs Compton she would pass her money to ensure each servant had new livery, and new Sunday best. 'Mr Holmes and I expect clean and well-dressed servants at all times.'

After Mark and Pauline retired to their rooms, the servants met in the servants' hall.

'Good for us, I say,' the cook exhorted. 'They could've been real nasty. I say we don't have 'owt to complain abart.'

'The master's bringin' in 'undredweight of sugar for ar allowance an' first rate tea, same as wot he sells them merchants. Right generous, I tell yer. Not cheap stuff like before,' the footman added. 'Fine clothes, good manners and I 'eard he's a tough 'un an all. 'E took down 'alf-a-dozen thugs what were attacking that Mr Marshall.'

'It were only two o' them railway navvies,' corrected the cook. 'Frightened the daylights out of 'em is what I 'eard from 'innkeeper's wife at the Angel.'

'I saw that knife when I 'elped him unpack. Wicked looking thing it is, no wonder they run off. Still an' all, 'e seems a right gentleman, much better than Sir Francis' lot when they stayed here last Michaelmas. Fetch this, fetch that, wouldn't even look at yer, and the vale[3] would a' done a miser proud.'

'True enough,' agreed Mrs Compton. 'The candles the mistress gave me are far better than what we 'ad before. No smoke an' real clear light. I reckon we can put up with a few odd ideas.'

'You should 'ave seen the lovely dresses madam 'as. Real fine silk, much grander than Mrs Houghton's... an' that fancy toiletry

---

[3] Vales (*Soc., 18 cent.*). Presents to servants. Still used in old houses.

box...' Elsie said dreamily. 'The smells were real nice.'

'Cook sez she's givin' us all a bar of soap each month. Summat abart keeping disease off,' Ada, the kitchen helper, added, a bit sceptical. Betty added, 'They'll be scented an' all.'

'New livery and a set of Sunday clothes, and not even year-end. Never 'eard o' that afore,' Alfred, the groom, reminded them.

'Madam was real interested in wot we used to clean with, sez she has summat better what won't make yer 'ands sore either,' Mary the scullery maid remarked.

All in all, the servants gave their new employers a tentative seal of approval.

Meanwhile, Pauline and Mark finished making love for the first in 1839.

'Must be a name for it, I suppose 'honeymoon' works, even though it's a hundred-and-seventy years before we were married,' Mark murmured, holding Pauline closely.

'Mmm...' she answered, moaning softly. 'Doesn't matter what it's called, come here, you think too much.' She proceeded to take Mark's mind of semantics... or anything else.

Chapter 15
Saturday, 27th July 1839

Mark woke early, stretched and heard one of the maids bringing hot water. After washing at the sink, he dressed, woke Pauline and called Elsie to help her dress.

Mark strolled over to the stables and Alfred came over to ask if he was going riding.

'Later, when I visit my attorney,' Mark told him and fed carrots to the horses. 'I need to talk to Robert about repairing the greenhouse.'

'Right you are, sir.'

Robert was pleased when the new master asked him to arrange repairs and new glass for the greenhouse. He would now have work worthy of a proper gardener instead of merely growing vegetables for the table.

At breakfast John gave Pauline a letter from Mrs Houghton. It was a brief introduction for Miss Penelope Wright, and informed her Miss Wright would be arriving in Chesterfield on Wednesday, seventh of August at three in the afternoon, aboard the Champion mail coach from Manchester.

'We'll go and pick her up, it will give you the chance to see the town,' Mark told Pauline.

'Mrs Compton, please ensure her room is ready.' Pauline asked.

'Certainly, ma'am. Miss Wright can have the same room Miss Thompson had; the small one next to your own.'

'Now I wish to talk to Mrs Humphries. Ask her to meet me in the parlour. Afterwards we can discuss the household accounts.'

Mrs Compton went off to call the cook.

Pauline held out her recipe book. 'Mrs Humphries I am entrusting you with this. You may copy any recipe you wish. I will come to the kitchen later to give you the spices and review the supplies in the larder and pantry.'

'Thank you, ma'am. I'll take good care of it.'

While Pauline was discussing recipes and checking the household accounts, Mark headed for Marshall's office. He had the clerk send notes to the merchants and shopkeepers listed in his ledger to let them know he would be available for business in the afternoons at Houghton House.

'Several merchants have been enquiring about your return. Your merchandise has generated a great deal of interest,' the attorney told him.

'I anticipate bringing in more goods in future, can you negotiate extra warehouse space for me, double what I have now?'

'Not a problem at all, Mr Holmes.'

'Thank you, now I need to visit the bank. I bid you good day and look forward to meeting again soon.'

At the bank, his payments for sales from Mark's last trip had been deposited. The one thousand, six hundred pounds in his account made him and Pauline financially secure. With more horse races to come and the increase in business, they could focus on learning about life in this era.

Monday morning, Mark drove his wagon to Sheffield and returned with a large two hundred and ten gallon barrel bought from a brewery and steel pipe from a steelworks. Although the water sample analysis had shown no coliform bacteria, it would still need filtering with water purification tablets added to be really safe.

He erected the barrel on stone blocks by the water pump and, with the gardener's help, placed layers of gravel, sand, charcoal and water purification granules inside. Once he had connected the pipes between the pump and the top of the barrel, any pump water would be filtered. He could now be confident drinking the water, especially after it had been boiled.

When he had finished, he saw the staff's suspicious looks and took a sample of water from the pond in the cows' pasture. He set up his microscope and mounted the pond water between two glass slides and called the staff to his study. It was cheating, but once they saw the paramecium and amoeba swimming around, they used the water filtration system religiously.

Mark and Pauline waited at the Old Star Inn for the coach to arrive. Mrs Houghton's letter had told them Penelope Wright was twenty-three years old and been raised by her aunt and uncle in Manchester after having been orphaned at twelve.

Penelope disembarked from the coach. Pauline thought her attractive as she moved gracefully towards her. She was two inches shorter than herself, slim, with dark golden hair and startling pale blue eyes. After Penelope tipped the coachman half-a-crown,

Alfred took her small trunk to the wagon and Pauline introduced herself. 'You must be tired and hungry. We will go straight to the house where you can rest and have some refreshments.'

'Thank you,' she replied shyly, 'the chance to change and rest will be most welcome.'

Mark helped Pauline board the wagon and Alfred aided Penelope. Mark hopped in front and turned to the women. 'Let's be off then.'

Alfred took the trunk inside and Pauline led Penelope into the house where Mrs Compton waited. 'Ma'am, I will have Elsie assist Miss Wright in her unpacking after tea.'

While having tea, Pauline asked Penelope about her interests and was startled when she mentioned archery and natural history.

'I used to come here years ago, Mrs Houghton's daughters had archery butts behind the stables.'

'I haven't seen them, I have had little opportunity yet to look around,' Pauline replied.

'We can always resurrect them, if you wish Miss Wright. It will be useful exercise and I haven't drawn a bow in years,' Mark said, startling Pauline. 'It's something I picked up in Singapore.'

Pauline wondered what other skills he had forgotten to mention. It was time to have another little chat with her husband.

After dinner, Penelope noticed the framed European and Asian butterflies and insects Mark had hung in the study as part of his cover.

'Oh, those are wonderful, I have only seen them in books,' she exclaimed.

'Yes, you mentioned you were interested in natural history. What other interests do you have?' Mark asked, with honest curiosity.

'Beside entomology, botany, music and embroidery of course,' she remarked, the latter much to Pauline's dismay, and Mark's barely concealed amusement.

'You may find my recent experiments interesting. I have a Gould's microscope and his 'Companion to the Microscope' which you may use if you wish.'

'That will be most interesting. I must confess my fascination with such topics has been a hindrance to my prospects, and it is gratifying to meet someone who shares my interests.'

'Well, we will have plenty of time to talk once you are settled in,' Pauline told her, upset that an active, inquisitive mind should be a hindrance to anyone.

'When were you going to tell me about the archery, then?' she asked, as they lay in bed.

'It's one of the things I learned along with knife and sword-fighting.'

'Regular one-man army, aren't we?' she replied, snuggling closer and kissing his neck.

'Now the servants are using the filtered water, it's time to show them how to pasteurise the milk. I'm sure Penelope will be interested.'

'Never mind Penelope, keep your mind over here,' she rubbed her hand down his chest, 'and just to make sure...'

Any thoughts Mark had about experiments were forgotten for the next hour.

The next day, Pauline and Penelope explored the house grounds and found the archery butts in a dilapidated condition. Pauline asked Mark to restore them then drive to Derby to buy suitable bows and arrows. Two days later she was getting archery lessons from Penelope and Mark.

Mark decided it was time to introduce pasteurisation. The process would not be invented until 1865, but tuberculosis and salmonella poisoning were not something he wanted to risk. Besides, he *really* missed fresh cream in his morning coffee.

Mark substituted shallow glass dishes for petri dishes and used clear gelatine for the nutrient. He added a few drops of raw milk on the gelatine and scratched its surface then left it uncovered for two days.

When he showed the staff the growths, he explained these could cause illness. After having seen what swam in the pond water, they were convinced and Mark proceeded to show them how to pasteurise the milk.

Not having stainless steel pans, he had bought large tin copper pots. Pauline and Penelope watched him heat the milk, controlling the temperature with a thermometer and removing the pan from the stove occasionally. After thirty minutes he put the pot in the stone sink full of ice water. Once at four degrees centigrade, he had Mary pour the milk into sterilised glass bottles and store them in the ice room.

'I want all the milk treated this way from now,' Mark told the kitchen staff. 'There will be less chance of diarrhoea. I want you to use it for making cheese and butter also.'

Penelope was fascinated, and *very* curious; she had never heard or read of this technique before.

The servants did not know what to make of the master's ideas. However, they considered madam's hand soaps, detergent and oven cleaners almost miraculous. When the material for their new livery and Sunday clothes arrived, they decided they could quite happily live with the master's quirks. Mrs Compton and Mrs Wright were just as pleased now they had ample funds to buy the best supplies and produce.

Pauline was amazed at Penelope's intelligence. She had immediately understood the process behind Mark's cultures and quickly grasped the principles of microscopic organisms causing illnesses. When the filtration system was explained, she was delighted at such a simple idea.

After a month, Pauline and Mark had settled in to their respective routines. After breakfast, Mark took Lucky for a ride while Pauline discussed the day's menu with Mrs Humphries and reviewed the household accounts with Mrs Compton.

In the afternoons, when raining, she and Penelope sat in the drawing room. Pauline would write in her journal and Penelope would read from the small library or embroider. Otherwise, Pauline practiced her archery skills. To Pauline's surprise, she became proficient under Penelope's tutelage, so much so, she told Mark she wanted archery butts erecting when they returned home.

After an impromptu competition, which Pauline barely lost to Penelope, she lay next to Mark. 'This archery business is good exercise, but I miss riding Princess.'

Mark chuckled. 'I'm glad you have something you enjoy. Penelope's influence is rubbing off. You're definitely becoming more lady-like.'

'I'll give you lady-like,' and promptly started to demonstrate some most unlady-like abilities.

Penelope lay in bed blushing at the sounds coming from their bedroom. She speculated, with their nightly and often early morning unions, if all she had been taught was correct, they were undoubtedly both strong and healthy, and showed no signs of debilitation, which was said to be a result of such over-indulgence. Her employers were causing her to question many pre-conceived ideas.

Mark rode out to various villages and posted letters to himself from everywhere within fifteen miles. He took videos of the mail coaches arriving at various towns, the gig-carts used to send mail from small villages, and wrote extensive notes on timings and the people involved. After a month, Mark had started on a second volume of notes. These were going to be the most comprehensive study of the rural postal service ever written.

In October, Penelope caught a cold and Pauline insisted she rest in her room. There was little privacy with Penelope around all the time, and they had to be careful what they said in front of her. Now they had the chance to talk freely.

Mark had been thinking about his business plan—his biggest hurdle was money. Expanding on what he had already started was straightforward, the problem was paying for it. They talked about Nicholas' files. Based on them, Mark could reliably invest in gold, currency and property, but he would have to wait years before he would have a meaningful return.

Mark decided when they returned, to have Chris and Tony draft budgets for their respective projects, so he would know how much he needed.

Pauline cuddled up to Mark one night in bed. 'It's strange no-one came for Nicholas.'

'Under the 'Warning' section, 1945 to 1964 was a banned era due to atmospheric nuclear tests. His people couldn't travel to those times even if they knew he was here.'

Pauline sat up. 'That's why he wanted to go to California. To find those Tempus people to take him home.'

'Well, after all this time, it's unlikely anyone will come now. We'll probably never meet anyone from the future,' Mark replied, pulling her back next to him. 'Unlike the people here who already have and don't know it.'

TP 1000: The Bishops

During the heavy autumn rain, Pauline taught Mrs Humphries Asian and Italian dishes. They made batches of pasta by hand, and once dried, had it stored in the pantry. Mark soon enjoyed the results of these cooking classes with spaghetti and meatballs, vegetable samosa, tandoori and butter chicken, baked tom yum chicken and green curry. Mrs Humphries was fascinated by these dishes and could not wait to prepare them for guests.

As the weather turned colder, getting out of bed on to a freezing cold floor was torture. Mark vowed to bring rugs back on his next trip. Later they sat in Mark's study and Pauline complained, 'I wish I could have a real shower, just turn on the taps and soak under the hot water. I can't bear to keep asking Elsie or Betty to bring up buckets of water to have a hot bath. They start work at six in the morning and are not finished until ten.'

'Only another month we'll be home and you can soak as long as you like.'

The study door was not closed and Penelope overheard them. *What did they mean 'back home'? What home? Where? And what was a 'tap' and how could you possibly get hot water by turning it?* This was most peculiar and some of the words and expressions she had heard were very strange indeed. *What was 'Murphy's law'?* She had never heard of it. *And 'okay' and 'gobsmacked' were outlandish, almost a different language.*

After nearly four months Mark and Pauline were ready to go home. The weather was becoming colder still, and in the poor heating, not even the prospect of learning how Christmas was celebrated appealed to them. Mark planned to leave after the uniform Fourpenny Post started on fifth of December; now they had to come up with a reason to leave for a couple of months.

'I'll ride to York and send a letter to you ostensibly from your family inviting you to stay with them for Christmas,' Mark suggested. 'Being newlyweds everyone should accept that.'

'What about Penelope? She'll expect to follow.'

'Tell her your family house is too small and ask her to stay here.'

Mark announced he was going on a trip and would be back in five days. The journey took him two days each way. He spent a day and a night in York and posted the letter before leaving; it should be at Houghton House before he returned.

When Pauline received the letter, she showed it to Penelope and apologised she would not be able to follow, she had such a large family there would be no room. Penelope accepted this calmly and helped Pauline to pack her clothes. When Mark arrived, he pretended surprise and agreed to the trip. He placated Penelope by giving her access to his microscope and showed her how to prepare slides—he figured with her curiosity she would be more than occupied in their absence.

Mark spent most of the beginning of December riding from village to village and town to town, posting letters to himself either at Houghton House or Marshall's office. Mark stored them all in the safe with their journals.

Mark had made arrangements with Marshall for the servants' salaries and expenses, and before they left, Pauline distributed a generous bonus for each of the staff.

Their first night back at the farm, Mark heard Pauline cursing in the bathroom. She stormed out. 'Damn all that rich food. I've gained three kilos.'

TP 1000: The Bishops

'Sounds like it's time to set up the basement gym.'

Besides getting herself back in shape, Mark showed Pauline basic Taekwondo moves. He also taught her self-defence techniques using a rolled-up magazine, an umbrella and pencils. Pauline's favourite was the 'rock-in-a-sock'; she could take the weighted sock out of her pocket and hit the practice dummy in the face or wrist with bone-breaking force in less than three seconds.

It took them a fortnight to adjust to their normal routines, although Bill did remark Mark was sometimes 'talkin' funny'. Mark and Pauline sat in the office with Chris and Tony; Mark outlined their plans for the farm and needed to know how much it was going to cost.

'Tony, I want you to work on plans to develop a berry plantation—strawberries, raspberries and blackberries to use for natural flavours in the ice-cream. Then I want you to work out what it's going to cost to have eighteen more beehives. Work out a budget for each project and pass it to Pauline.'

He turned to Chris. 'I want you to work out new designs and budget for two more acres of greenhouses and how we can improve productivity.'

'Vertical stacking will do that. We'll need better lighting, advanced nutrient feed system and—'

Mark interrupted. Once Chris started they would be here all day. 'That's fine. Look into tropical fruit crops—mangoes, bananas, papaya; fruit we can use for ice-cream flavourings and sell to shops and supermarkets. Work on the designs and a tentative budget and pass it back to me when ready.'

After they left, Mark told Pauline, 'What I need is more land. I'll have a chat with Bill and see what he has to say.'

Mark rested for two more weeks before he made another trip. He arrived in York on seventh of January, 1840 and stayed at the York Tavern, right next to the Post Office. For four days, he wrote and posted letters to Houghton House, Marshall's office and a couple care-of the Angel Inn. By the time he returned to Chesterfield, there would be a good collection of letters covering the end of the Fourpenny Post and beginning of the Penny Post waiting for him.

Pauline's mother and aunt came to the farm two days before Christmas, and Julie and Hugh arrived on Christmas Eve. Mark, Tony and Chris had spent days decorating, using holly from the farm and stringing lights outside and on an eight-foot high fir tree. They had had a great crop of mistletoe and Mark made strategic use of it around the house.

When Pauline left their bedroom Mark took advantage of a big clump of mistletoe above the door. Both were oblivious to Julie standing behind them until she coughed and said sweetly, 'Can't you two wait until after breakfast?'

Pauline blushed. Mark grinned and greeted Julie with a hearty 'Merry Christmas!'

Laughing, Julie grabbed Pauline's arm and raced downstairs. Spotting the piles of presents under the tree, and giggling like school girls, they started searching for theirs.

'Hold it, you two,' Pauline's mother commanded. 'Wait 'till everybody's here.'

Jenny and Pauline's mother cooked a traditional Christmas lunch. Turkey with stuffing and cranberry sauce, honey glazed ham, golden roast potatoes, honey glazed carrots, Brussel sprouts and roasted parsnips. The plum pudding had thick brandy sauce and Mark made sure there was plenty of mulled wine and home-made apple cider.

TP 1000: The Bishops

After the New Year, Mark studied Chris' and Tony's budgets. He would need half a million pounds to fully develop his expansion plans. To buy another two hundred acre of land and more cattle was going to cost him close to a million pounds. *Where am I going to find that kind of money?*

Pauline pestered Mark until he built the archery butts. Behind the byre, he added a wooden store for the bows and arrows, and wooden stands for the target bosses and faces.

Once the basement flooring was completed, Mark installed exercise machines at one end with a dojo mat covering half the rest of the floor; now Pauline could exercise and he could practice his Taekwondo.

In the middle of March, Mark returned from rolling the field to prepare for spring, to find Pauline talking to a stranger.

'Mark, this is Mr Novak. He's a birdwatcher and wants permission to establish a hide on the fell.'

The stranger shook Mark's hand and said in a very precise voice, 'Mr Bishop, Victor Novak. I was told in the village you owned the land up there. As your wife said, I want to camp and build a hide to observe the birds when they come back in spring. I have heard there was a sighting recently of a little bustard in the area and want to photograph it.'

Mark studied the tanned stranger—he was the same height and build as himself, with dark yellow hair and intense pale blue eyes, almost colourless. He was certainly dressed for the part... red anorak, corduroy trousers, hiking boots with a pair of high-power *Zeiss* binoculars hung around his neck.

'I don't have any problem with that. You should avoid the flower meadow though, we're planning new beehives soon and they are likely to be irritated.'

'Thank you for the warning. I will let you know where I will be once I am set up. I have rented a small apartment in Richmond, but will be spending most of my time up there,' Victor waved his hand towards the hillside.

'Seems a bit aloof,' Mark remarked after Victor had left. 'Never seen the fascination in birdwatching myself. Takes all kinds I suppose.'

At the end of the month the byre was stocked and the wagon loaded. Mark set the Portal and they made their way back to Houghton House.

Chapter 16
Friday, 14th February, 1840

Heavy rain and a cold biting wind was waiting for them on the other side of the gateway. On their arrival at Houghton House, Penelope rushed out and almost dragged Pauline inside.

'Ma'am, you are soaked to the skin, no telling what kind of chills you could take.' Penelope stripped Pauline to her underclothes, wrapped her in a blanket and towelled her hair.

'I'll be fine, but a nice cup of hot tea with honey would be most welcome.'

'I will make one for you right away, now stay wrapped up and warm in front of the fire.' Penelope left, giving Pauline time to get her wits back.

Penelope fussed for several days—pneumonia in 1840, with no antibiotics, was a deadly illness.

When Mark received a dinner invitation from Sir Reginald, Pauline panicked. Although now comfortable with Penelope and the servants, this would be her first encounter with the upper gentry.

James and John looked splendid in their new livery as they drove the hired *Brougham* to Sir Reginald's. Besides Sir Reginald, his wife and two daughters, Amelia and Florence, were two other couples, friends of Sir Reginald's—Sir Paul Markland, and Henry Miller, a leading attorney from Sheffield, and their respective wives.

Sir Reginald proffered his hand. 'Mr Holmes, pleasure to meet you again.'

'May I present my wife? Mrs Holmes, Sir Reginald Barker.'

Pauline curtseyed elegantly, having practiced for hours in her room.

'Allow me to introduce you to the other ladies.'

'Sir Reginald, it is customary in the East to bring a gift when invited to someone's home,' he presented a bottle of French brandy and another of double malt whisky. 'My wife has selected some gifts for Lady Barker and your daughters, if I may send the footman to the coach for them?'

'Sir, that is most generous of you.'

When John presented the packages, all the ladies were astonished at the quality and rich colours of the silks Pauline had selected.

While the ladies admired the delicate fabric, the men's conversation centred on Mark's travels, until the butler announced dinner. After a fine seven course meal, accompanied by good wines, the ladies adjourned to the drawing room while the men sampled the brandy. Sir Paul and Mr Miller wanted to know if Mark could obtain some more for them.

'Gentlemen, don't badger our guest,' Sir Reginald joked. 'Now what are your plans now you have settled at Houghton House?'

Mark explained he was still establishing his business, but wanted to live a quiet life after years of travel and told of his hopes to grow tropical fruit and plants.

'Splendid! Grow quite a few blooms, myself, you know,' Henry Miller boasted. 'You must come and see them. I'm certain my wife will enjoy the opportunity to meet with your wife again.'

'Let us join the ladies, shall we?' Sir Reginald announced.

'Mr Holmes, thank you for your gifts. The silk is absolutely beautiful,' Lady Barker gushed.

'Thank you, ma'am, I am pleased you find them acceptable.'

'Mr Holmes, I detect from the gleam in my daughters' eyes, I will soon be ordering more,' commented Sir Reginald.

'Yes sir, life will not be worth living until my wife also has some,' added Sir Paul.

Later, in bed, Mark told Pauline, 'Looks like you made quite a social coup today, sweetheart.'

'Amelia and Florence were so excited over the thought of new dresses, a trip for more was all they could talk about. Looks like retail therapy is alive and well in 1840.'

A few days later, Penelope followed Pauline and the ladies from Sir Reginald's to Mark's warehouse to select material and visit the dressmaker. They were all suitably escorted by grooms and footmen as the area where Mark's warehouse was situated was not the most salubrious of neighbourhoods.

Penelope was amazed at the luxuries in storage; chests of bohea black tea and the finest sugar she had seen, costing at least fifty shillings per hundredweight and the price increasing rapidly. The variety of colours of the silks, satins and linens amazed Pauline's guests; rich reds, emerald-green and varied shades of blue and yellow—colours they had never seen before.

As they left, Amelia Barker remarked, 'Is that Mr Holmes over there?'

Pauline looked across the street and saw a man leaving a public house. He had the same build as Mark, maybe slightly shorter, but when he turned, she was astounded. He could be Mark's twin except for his long hair and enormous sideburns. On closer scrutiny, his clothes looked worn and a few years out of fashion.

'My husband does *not* have such facial hair or such shabby clothes.'

The man saw them looking, smirked and raised his hat.

'Scoundrel!' declared Lady Barker and they mounted their carriages to return to Houghton House.

Once her visitors had left, Pauline recounted the meeting to Mark. 'It was like seeing your twin. It was incredible,' she exclaimed.

'Sounds as if James has decided to return to Chesterfield. I think I'll go and find out more about my dear uncle.'

'Now you be careful. That area is disreputable to say the least, and he looked like he belonged there.'

The following day Mark visited the pub where Pauline had seen his double. The man behind the bar glanced up as he entered. 'Morning, James, yer looking a right nob.' When Mark moved closer, the barman yelled, 'Hey, you're not 'im.'

'Who is this James person?' Mark replied haughtily.

'Meant no offence, none at all, guv'nor. I thought you was James Bishop.'

'My name is Holmes. Tell me about this person whom I supposedly resemble.' Mark slipped a sovereign onto the bar counter and stared at the barkeeper.

'I want no trouble, I mind me own business,' looking avariciously at the coin

Mark loomed over him. 'Just tell me what you know.'

The barman gulped. 'Well sur, 'e come back last month. Said 'e'd bin darn in Nottingham or Newark or somewhere like that. Was in 'ere last night winnin' at cards as usual and left with one o' the lasses to 'is room somewhere in t' Shambles.'

Mark started to hatch a plan.

'You have not seen me, I have not been here, you understand?' He placed another sovereign on the bar top.

The coins disappeared like magic. 'Mum's the word, guv'nor.'

'I want to know everything about him, and I will pay well. But, I do not advise trying to cross me.' Mark drew his knife from under his coat.

The barman's face paled. 'Ye Gods! I want no trouble. 'E'll 'ear nowt from me, 'onest-to-God 'e won't.'

'You can send a note to me at Houghton House in Brampton when you have any information. I bid you good-day.'

'That 'son-of-a-bitch' is going to pay. I don't care about him cheating at cards, but raping that girl and causing her to hang herself...' he told Pauline when he returned.

'But what can you do?'

'I know the girl's father's name, William Wilson, and where he lived, from my cousin's notes. I'll write and send a cheque for him to travel here. He's not going to get away with what he did, family or not.' Mark penned a letter straight after dinner.

A few days later, Penelope showed Pauline a book on palaeontology and Mark suggested a trip to look for fossils. Saturday dawned clear and warm for March and Mark drove them to Matlock Bath and stopped near the Heights of Abraham for a brief picnic. They walked to the foot of the cliffs where they found fossil gastropods, ammonites and large crystals of fluorite.

Ferns grew thickly in the shade of the cliffs along with tree-like mosses on the damp rock face. Although mostly fox-tail feather-moss, on one limestone face Mark spied a different species. Narrower leaves with very coarsely-toothed tips, the branches further apart than the common type. He found more just beyond the water's edge of a stream running toward the River Derwent. He collected samples still attached to the rocks and back at the house placed them in the ornamental pond behind the house. Mark was certain it was the Derbyshire feather-moss. In the Twenty-First Century it grew on a single square yard of stony riverbed in the Peak District—the only known example in the whole world.

After dinner Penelope overheard them talking through the partly open door of the family room.

'When we're back, I'll put the moss by the beck and

hopefully it'll grow; Tony and Chris will go wild.'

Penelope was confused. *Why were they so thrilled at a simple moss? Who were Tony and Chris and why would they 'go wild'? Were they savages or uncivilised? What did they mean by when they 'get back'? Where were they going?*

Six weeks into their stay, everything was going smoothly until Ada slipped carrying a pan of hot water and broke her arm. Penelope was astonished at how decisively Pauline took control.

After gently moving her hands over the arm and observing the bruising and swelling Pauline proclaimed, 'It is a simple fracture, and the burns are not severe.'

She bathed Ada's scalded hand in cold water, applied cream and lightly bandaged it. While she secured splints on the arm, Pauline sent James to purchase some plaster of Paris.

Pauline made a smooth paste with the plaster in which she soaked bandages. With the staff staring in amazement, Pauline wrapped them around Ada's arm over a layer of wool padding. When the bandages dried, the arm was completely immobilised.

'Mrs Compton, please hire a new kitchen maid as soon as possible. She may remain on the staff after Ada recovers,' Pauline told the housekeeper firmly.

'Ada, I will examine the dressings daily and no work for at least four weeks. You will still be paid in full, but I insist you follow my instructions to the letter. Mrs Compton, Mrs Humphries I expect you to ensure she does just that.'

Penelope was astounded, she had never seen or heard of a plaster cast before; its simplicity and effectiveness was incredible. *Where had she obtained her medical knowledge?*

When Penelope asked her later, Pauline realised she had blundered. She hummed and hawed before saying Mr Holmes had taught her... Penelope was faced with another puzzle. They had knowledge she had never heard of or read about, they used strange expressions between themselves, and the frequent mention of 'back home' she kept hearing confused her.

Whenever Pauline examined Ada's arm, she also spent time observing the servants, amazed at how so little went to waste. Just about everything was recycled; clothes were used for one purpose after another until they ended their life on the compost heap; food was converted to leftovers, fed to the chickens or sold to the 'wash man' who sold it to pig farms. Tea leaves and old coffee grounds were used to clean the floors; even chicken feathers were sterilised in the oven and used for pillows and mattresses. To everyone's astonishment, especially Fanny, the new kitchen helper, Ada's arm healed perfectly. From then on, every small complaint and ailment was brought to Pauline.

Penelope was puzzled at some of the remedies she prescribed—she did not know Mark and Pauline had brought a large range of over-the-counter medicines in pillboxes and apothecary bottles. *Benadryl*, *Robitussin* and *Paracetamol* tablets to treat cough and colds, and *Milk of Magnesia* for Mrs Humphries' indigestion and heartburn.

On May Day, the temperature rose to eighty-two degrees. Pauline told everyone it was their first wedding anniversary and they had decided to go for a picnic, giving them the excuse to be away for a few hours alone. She was surprised by Penelope's reaction.

'That is so romantic, and Mr Holmes is, if I may be so bold, a very vigorous man,' she blushed deeply. 'Please, do not worry about me, I have my embroidery and will be quite occupied.'

Pauline realised what the blush, along with the reference to vigour meant—their walls were not as thick as she thought and she wondered how many disturbed nights Penelope had had in the next bedroom. Mark, naturally, laughed at her discomfort.

'Come on. Let's get ready for our *romantic* picnic.'

Mrs Humphries handed them a hamper of cold food with a bottle of white wine and a knowing smile. Mark packed a rug and the hamper in the wagon and headed along Chatsworth Road towards Baslow to activate the Portal. After a picnic in the byre, Mark restocked the wagon before they returned to 1840.

The following day, after their usual morning horizontal gymnastics, Pauline dropped the bottle containing her birth control pills. Mixed with broken and powdered glass, they were unusable. Not at all interested in celibacy, they would need to be careful from now on.

Mark was in Chesterfield post office the minute they opened on the sixth of May to buy the world's first postage stamps. He bought a hundred and twenty Penny Blacks for ten shillings. He separated the stamps with a pair of scissors—stamps would not be perforated until the 1850s—and spent the rest of the day riding around the area posting letters he had prepared. He kept two corner blocks of eight, one with the plate number, and another strip of twelve from the upper row showing the instructions on how to use them.

Having post office-fresh Penny Blacks in their hands was so unbelievable, they celebrated most of the night. They forgot about Penelope next door, or birth control. Two days later Mark was out again posting letters with the Twopenny Blue stamps, with extra penny black stamps on deliberately overweight letters.

Pauline now had an active social life, entertaining, paying visits with Penelope and going shopping with the other wives she had met. Her own journal was becoming a detailed social study of the different classes of people in this era. During a visit with Lady Barker and her daughters to a local Brampton school, she learned attendance was poor. She determined this was due either to the children having to work or because the families could not afford the fees. Mark agreed to donate funds, providing it would be anonymous, to educate ten local children and provide supplies of writing and reading material.

William Wilson arrived on the afternoon coach from Manchester and Mark drove him to Houghton House. Obviously uncomfortable at Houghton House, the thought of making James Bishop pay overcame William's nerves.

'Mr Holmes, I must admit, I gorra a shock when I saw yer earlier. Yer look just like him.'

'Mr Wilson, I have had my own problems being mistaken for him. When I discovered what grief he has caused you, I thought it only right he received justice.'

'He has to pay for wor 'e did to my Elsie. You said in your

TP 1000: The Bishops

letter you had a plan?'

Mark outlined his idea to catch James cheating at cards. Mark had asked Mr Marshall earlier to contact and obtain a deposition from the authorities in Carlisle. Once arrested, he could also be charged with the rape.

Thanks to the barman, Mark learned James would be at a big card game the following Saturday night in the back room of the Rose and Crown. James looked astonished when Mark walked in.

'I had heard I had a double and wished to ascertain if it was true,' Mark drawled. 'Ah! You enjoy a game of chance. Do you have any objections if I join?'

'Not at all,' James replied, overcoming his shock.

Throughout the game, Mark deliberately lost. After an hour of play he bid the stakes up until there were ten sovereigns in the pot—a large sum for everyone at the table except himself.

Mark spoke quietly and slowly. 'Gentlemen, a moment of your time. I seem to have a defective card here.' He showed the other players an ace slightly longer than the rest of the cards.

'They've bin shaved!' a prosperous farmer declared and turned to James. 'This is your deck, ain't it?'

James shot out of his chair, overturned the table and drew a six-inch boning knife. People scattered and the room went quiet. James thrust at Mark, who turned, grabbed James' wrist and broke his arm against the bar. A strong oblique kick precisely to the outside of James' knee resulted in a piercing scream.

Mark calmly adjusted his coat. 'I believe it is time to call the constable, gentlemen.'

With abundant witnesses Mark had acted in self-defence against a card cheat, the police hauled James away, ignoring his cries of pain.

With Mark and the other witnesses' testimonies, and the depositions from Carlisle, James Bishop was found guilty of cheating at cards, poaching, attempted murder and the rape of Elsie Wilson, giving her cause to take her own life. He was sentenced to Transportation for life.

The judge remarked after sentencing, 'I have been lenient in view of your injuries, which you have only yourself to blame after attacking Mr Holmes.'

Mr Wilson shook Mark's hand after the trial. 'Mr Homes, I canna thank yer enough. At least my Elsie can rest in peace now.'

'I am sure not all Bishops are evil like this one. Do not blame the rest of the family for James' transgressions.'

Pauline was so proud of him. Her appreciation of her husband resulted in another disturbed night for Penelope. The next month, Mark heard James had died aboard the hulks where he was imprisoned while awaiting transport to Australia.

'You know, it was always a bit of a mystery what happened to James. David had numerous notes on his searches but didn't find anything. Never even thought about checking court records here—why would I?' Mark told Pauline after he heard James' fate.

'Well, that's one mystery solved anyway. At least you know what happened, even if no-one else does.'

Near the end of June, Pauline entered Mark's study while he was writing in his journal.

'What are you so happy about?' he asked, seeing the brilliant smile on her face.

'I have some news for you. Why don't you put that ink away, I wouldn't want you to spill any,' she replied calmly.

She sat next to Mark and reminded him of how they had celebrated buying all those Penny Blacks, and that she was not taking birth control pills.

Mark's face changed. 'You mean... you're... we...' He stared, temporarily speechless.

'Yes, you're going to be a daddy.' she then struggled for breath as he hugged and kissed her.

'This is fantastic! When did you find out?'

'I've missed two periods and been feeling nauseous at the oddest times, I think I'm about two months gone. It must have been that night we bought the first Penny Blacks.' She smiled impishly. 'We *were* rather busy for most of it, remember,'

'We have to go back. You need a proper check-up,' Mark told her.

'I'm fine really. I'm not showing yet and thank God I've not had morning-sickness. We can leave in a few days' time.'

After the weekend, Pauline told Penelope she and her husband were making a short visit to the school in Brampton and there was no need for her to follow. Penelope was struggling to understand her employers. Most of the time they acted like any other wealthy gentry, but sometimes were so different from anyone she had ever known. Their scientific and medical knowledge was quite amazing. This sudden decision to go without her baffled her even more.

Mark drove past the school and pulled in to a heavily wooded area half-a-mile past the Robin Hood Inn and opened a gateway.

On their way back to the farm, they saw Victor's bright red anorak on the fell above the byre. Mark shook his head. 'I still don't get the fascination of camping out in all weathers just to get a photo of a bird.'

'We'll have to be careful around Penelope, I'm sure she's getting suspicious,' Pauline mentioned, after dinner. 'She asks a lot of questions and I've been struggling to give her plausible answers.'

'She has a true scientist's mind; inquisitive and analytical. Damn smart really and could go far here—back there, she hasn't a chance.'

Chapter 17
Monday, 2nd April 2007

The doctor confirmed she was approximately eight weeks pregnant, the baby due in early November. Pauline's mother and aunt fussed over her when they broke the news, both smiling and crying at the same time. Leaving them planning what baby clothes to knit, they returned home where Jenny cried and laughed as much as Pauline's own mother.

Riding prohibited, Mark took Pauline on walks around the farm. This gave him the chance to set the Derbyshire feather-moss in an isolated part of the beck above the wildflower meadows, a brilliant riot of purple, red and yellow against the lush green of the grass. Bright green shoots of maize poked through in the fields and the orchards were a beautiful sight with cows grazing under branches laden with clouds of apple blossom. For further exercise, Pauline continued her archery practice with Mark, and partook in gentle workouts in the basement gym until her baby bump and backache stopped her.

Victor became a familiar sight with his binoculars and camera. They met him several times waiting patiently to photograph birds coming to feed on the elderberries in the hedgerows. Mark told Victor he had installed owl boxes around the farm and invited him to photograph the owls nesting there.

As autumn approached, breathlessness and back ache forced Pauline to restrict herself to short walks around the farm. Coming back from her usual trip to watch Princess and the other horses and look in on the new born calves, she slipped on a patch of manure.

Before she hit the ground, Victor caught her. Back on her feet, she cried out when she put weight on her ankle.

'I will take you to the house,' he offered, and with no apparent effort, lifted her in his arms and carried her across the yard. Jenny saw them coming through the kitchen window and rushed out.

'Pauline, what happened?'

'I'm fine, thanks to Mr Novak. I slipped and turned my ankle.'

Victor carried her to the living room while Jenny took an icepack from the kitchen. Victor elevated her foot and wrapped the pack around her ankle.

'You should be alright now, Mrs Bishop it is only a slight sprain; if the swelling becomes worse you should get an x-ray.'

'Mr Novak, thank you so much,' Pauline held her stomach. 'If you hadn't been there the baby could have been hurt.' Tears welled in her eyes at the thought.

'Well, I will make a move now—'

'Oh, please stay for lunch, it's the least I can do to thank you.'

Mark burst in the room and knelt next to his wife. 'Are you alright? What happened?'

'I slipped and twisted my ankle. Luckily, Mr Novak prevented me from falling.'

Mark turned to Victor and shook his hand with profuse

thanks for his help.

'I invited Mr Novak to stay for lunch but he seems reluctant to accept.'

Mark turned to Victor, 'You *must* stay. I'm sure a good home cooked meal is not something you normally have camping out on the hillside.'

Victor appeared uncomfortable but accepted.

Mark and Pauline tried to draw him out, but he spoke only briefly about his birdwatching and when asked any personal questions, led the conversation to Mark's environmental projects.

'Not the best conversationalist, was he?' Mark commented after Victor had left. 'Still I'm glad he was there.'

'He's damn strong. He carried me all the way back to the farmhouse, and that's no mean feat now.'

Mark was surprised. 'He doesn't look that strong, must be all the outdoor living.'

Pauline used crutches until her ankle could bear her weight and three weeks later she was back to waddling slowly around the farmyard.

Two weeks before Pauline was due to give birth, Bill called them to the stables. They arrived as Princess foaled a beautiful dark-grey colt; Pauline promptly naming him Nicholas. Within an hour he was nursing, and Pauline spent most days wrapped in warm clothes, watching him trot and run after Princess.

Saturday, Julie took up residence at the farm and early next morning Pauline went in to labour. Mark drove her to the hospital, and Julie went to bring Pauline's mother. On the afternoon on eighth of November, after fifteen hours of labour, which Mark found almost as exhausting as Pauline, not-so-little Penelope Elizabeth was born, weighing eight pounds and fifteen ounces.

Penny, as everyone was already calling her, latched on to Pauline's breast as fast as Mark had when they were first married.

Everyone in Pauline's family and the farm attended the christening. Mark had even invited the reticent Victor. Jimmy and Meifen had flown over and he and Julie agreed to be Godparents. Penny was well behaved until Meifen gave her a sterling silver locket with a letter 'P' in crushed diamonds in the centre. She immediately tried to push it in her mouth, yelling at the top of her voice when it was taken away.

'I'd better get my figure back before we return to Houghton House.' Pauline mused one morning, 'but I'm dreading having to leave Penny.'

Mark tried to console her. 'At least she won't notice we've been away, it'll only be half a day for her,'

Pauline wanted to return to help run the farm, especially with the greenhouse now producing decent crops of tomato, lettuce, and strawberries. They had found a ready market with local grocers and had started negotiating a contract with a nearby supermarket. Mark and Tony had added six more hives and next year they wanted to add another dozen. The honey they harvested was sold to a local grocer, and Mark hoped, with more hives, to expand the market.

They agreed to hire a nursemaid, and with the salary and conditions Mark was offering, Melanie Thompson was soon looking after Penny. Pauline continued to breast feed and intended to do so for a few more months. Pauline now had time for riding and regular sessions in the gym so she soon regained her figure.

Hiring Melanie also gave them the time to plan their next trip to

Chesterfield; they had decided they would find an excuse to leave after a couple more trips. Mark could undertake short trips later to collect the other stamps he wanted. Pauline was upset at the thought of having to tell everyone at the house they would be leaving, but the idea of not seeing Penny for a month or more at a time made the decision easier.

The weekend after Easter, Pauline stocked the fridge with a day's breast milk and on a misty Sunday morning, they headed for the byre.

'Was everything alright at the school?' Penelope asked, when they returned.

'Er... yes it was,' Pauline replied, remembering in time the excuse she had given almost a year ago.

As Penelope helped Pauline undress for bed, she was shocked when she noticed Pauline's larger breast size and what appeared to be faint stretch marks on her abdomen—it was as if she had recently given birth. Of all the anomalies so far, this was the strangest. The next morning she heard them talking about taking 'antiques back' with them, and that phrase, 'going back' again. *Where* were they going?

After their regular afternoon archery session, Pauline went to Mark's study while Penelope ironed Pauline's dress for dinner. As Penelope tidied the room, a piece of stiff paper fell out of a book on the bedside table. Picking it up, she froze. It was a picture, in clear brilliant colour. There was an oriental man and a blonde-haired woman standing in front of a church, both wearing strange clothes. The blonde woman's skirt was so short it actually showed her knees. Between them were Mr and Mrs Holmes, smiling, and holding a baby.

Penelope could not wait any longer, she had to say something.

As if called, Pauline came in to change. Penelope held out the photograph with a look of complete bewilderment on her face... Pauline stared back at her.

'Please, do not be angry, but I *have* to know. What is this?' Penelope pleaded. 'When you came back from the school yesterday, you looked as if you had given birth, yet you were only away for a few hours, and this picture of you and Mr Holmes holding a baby. What does it all mean?'

Taking Penelope to the study, she passed Mark the photograph of Penny's christening.

'Penelope found this when cleaning our room.'

'Damn! I forgot to lock it away. Miss Wright, please sit down,' Mark requested kindly. 'We have a lot to talk about. Why don't you start by asking all the questions I am sure you have and we will try to explain?'

Penelope's voice quivered. 'Please, I do not want to cause any trouble.'

'There'll be no trouble. *Please*, sit down,' Pauline replied, in a reassuring tone.

Penelope sat, twisting her fingers into knots, and related all the oddities she had noticed. Pauline's sudden changes in hair length and loss of weight last year; their amazing knowledge of medicine—the cast on Ada's arm and the remarkable nostrums given to the staff. Various mannerisms, phrases and ways of talking. Embarrassed, she told them of overhearing their conversations when they mentioned people called Tony and Chris, and the remark about 'when we get back' and 'taking antiques' with them. Finally the colour picture.

'Who is this baby? Who are Chris and Tony? Where are you going back to?' She was clearly exasperated. 'Your knowledge of science and medicine is unheard of, and this picture is beyond comprehension.'

TP 1000: The Bishops

'Mark, we have to tell her the truth. I told you she was getting suspicious so I checked all the census records and directories I could find, even the ones in Nicholas' files. In the 1841 census, there is no mention of a Penelope Wright, but I did find a mention in the census for 2011 of a Penelope Wright living in Leyburn yet no mention in the 2001 census. By the way, there was no mention of a Mr and Mrs Michael Holmes either.' She hesitated, and after a quick glance at Penelope, 'I think we are meant to take her with us.'

Penelope's lips trembled at all this talk of records from the future and taking her somewhere. Mark noticed how pale she had gone and poured her a glass of brandy, and then poured two more; he figured they would need it.

'Miss Wright, the answer to all your questions is actually quite simple. The problem is you are going to find it difficult to believe,' he told her calmly. 'We are not from here, that is, not from 1840, I mean England in this time era...' He looked flushed and took a stiff drink.

Pauline decided to get it over with and deal with the consequences. 'What he is *trying* to say,' she said with a smile for Mark, 'is we are from the future... the year 2008 to be precise, one-hundred and sixty-eight years from now.'

To Penelope's credit she did not faint. She took a long draught of the brandy and choked. When she regained her breath, Mark took up the explanation.

'I know this sounds unbelievable, but I can prove we are definitely *not* from the here and now, however, I want you to swear you will tell no-one what we discuss.'

'Tell someone?' Penelope squeaked. 'Who is going to believe me? I will be sent to an asylum.' Her curiosity started to overcome her fear. 'But you said you were from 2008, can you travel to your future as well?'

'No, the person who had this time travel device before us left detailed records all the way to 2025; I checked them, that's all. The device can only travel to the past from a specific date,' Pauline explained.

Mark and Pauline related how they had found the Portal and how they had been as amazed as she was now.

'Now I'll try to answer your questions.' Pauline told her. 'Chris and Tony are two men who work on our farm in Yorkshire and the baby *is* ours. She was, or will be, born on ninth of November in 2008, and her name is Penelope Elizabeth Bishop, our real surname.'

'Penelope! Surely, you didn't name her after me?'

'Not quite. You know we are interested in these new postage labels, we call them Penny Blacks. Since we believe she was conceived on the day they were issued, I wanted to call her Penny, and decided on Penelope, but everyone is calling her Penny already.'

'This is all too fantastic,' she whispered.

'When we went back last time, we were there for nearly a year. We stayed until after I gave birth four months ago. However, only a few hours passed for you here.'

'Penelope, I'll be returning soon to collect more merchandise. I would like you to come with us, for a short trip, and prove what we are saying,' Mark proposed.

'You want me to travel to the future?' She paled even further and her hands shook.

'Just a short trip, no longer than an hour or two. I promise you, it is quite safe.'

After a minute of hesitation, Penelope agreed 'Alright. When?'

Three days later, at seven in the morning, they drove the wagon to Walton Woods. Penelope shrieked when she saw the gateway appear and Pauline put her arm around her. Mark led the horses through and Penelope held the guard rail in a death grip.

While Mark loaded the wagonette, Pauline showed her the farm below.

'That's where we live.'

Penelope was speechless. It was not the sunny day she had left behind, but a cold one with mist over the fields and rain clouds in the sky. She stared at the farm, fields and surrounding hills. Her attention was drawn by a strange noise and saw a red machine travelling at high speed along a road near the farm.

'What is *that*?'

'An automobile, I will explain it all back at the house,' Pauline replied. 'There's a lot you need to learn.'

'Come on, ladies, time to return. I've changed the settings for a few hours after we left to allow for a trip to Chesterfield.'

Penelope was still in a daze when she entered Houghton House and saw the clock. It was already five o'clock, but she had only been gone for three hours.

Over the following weeks, they explained all the changes that would take place over the next hundred and seventy years—population increases, transport, scientific discoveries, wars and social life. Penelope went through every imaginable emotion, from wonder to amazement, horror to confusion. Most amazing to her personally was when she learned Pauline had graduated from university. This filled her with a longing for the same opportunity, denied to her in Victorian society.

Pauline held long talks with Penelope of life in the Twenty-First Century, particularly the opportunities for women, which Penelope scarcely believed possible.

'Penelope, I need to go back and see my daughter, but I *promise* you, we will be back in a few hours and we'll bring books which will help explain our time better.'

After they changed, they walked into the main room of the byre and stopped. Victor was standing near the door, pointing a strange looking gun at them.

'Victor, what are you doing?' Mark demanded.

'Don't move any closer. I will not hesitate to use this. Cooperate and hand over the Portal and no one will be hurt,'

Mark tried to buy time. 'What in Hell are talking about?'

'Do not try to fool me. I have been tracking you. I know you have Nicholas Olafson's Portal. It is poetic justice really, Nicholas was one of the team that tracked me down and had me locked up.'

'How do I know you won't hurt us?'

'Once I have it, I have no reason to harm you. All I want is the Portal.'

'How did you find us?' Pauline asked.

'If you had screened the Portal when you used it, as you do when it is not in use, I would never have been able to find you. It emits a signal when activated and a gateway opens. A screen does not stop it opening, it only stops the signal being detected,'

'If you have been watching us for so long, why wait until now?'

'There are no more signals after today, and do you know why?' he said with a smirk. 'Because I will take it from you, properly screen it and leave this Godforsaken place. Enough talking. Now, hand it over.'

While Victor's attention was on Pauline, Mark had sidled away from her and nearer to Victor. He slowly took the back pack off his shoulder and threw it, yelling for Pauline to run.

Pauline rushed to the archery store, took her bow and a quiver of hunting arrows and hid in the trees next to the byre.

Pauline saw Victor drag Mark outside; there was blood on Mark's arm—her face set and she bared her teeth. No one was going to hurt her husband. She notched an arrow and heard her name called. Victor was holding Mark around the neck and looking at the boulders in front of the byre.

'I will not hesitate to kill him, *and* your daughter, if you don't come out.'

He turned in her direction and at thirty yards she could not miss. The arrow hit Victor in the chest. Seconds later another sprouted next to it—both straight through the heart.

Pauline came over, another arrow notched. 'You bastard! Nobody threatens my family,' she screamed, standing over his body, her bow drawn back.

Mark got to his feet. 'Sweetheart, relax, he's not going to threaten anyone anymore. Help me get a blanket and drag him inside, before somebody comes.'

Once they had the body inside, Pauline checked Mark's wound.

'His gun went off when the back pack hit him—just a graze, that's all.'

'Let me clean it up.'

Afterwards Mark covered the blood stains outside with soil; the rain that threatened would wash away any other signs.

'Now we have to get rid of him,' Mark explained. 'There's no way we can explain a body from the future—or any other body come to that.'

Pauline nodded... adrenaline had kept her going so far but now shock set in. Her eyes glazed and her body started to shake. Mark made her sit and wrapped her in a blanket. He put his arm around her and they drank the hot sweet tea he had made. Mark tried to figure out what he was going to do with the body. When he saw his backpack on the floor, he knew exactly how to hide it.

One of Mark's ancestors had died at the Battle of Ancrum Moor in 1545 and from his studies of the battle, he knew deep marshes flanked either side of the battlefield. They made an ideal disposal site. He checked his laptop for the coordinates and set the Portal for late February 1545. He dragged Victor's body into one of the stalls, stripped him and wrapped him back in the blanket. He carried the burden through the gateway and dumped the body in the marsh, throwing the blood-stained blanket further in to the mire.

'If anyone finds him they'll think he was killed in the battle,' he told Pauline. 'I can burn the rest of his stuff in the furnace, then there'll be no trace of the bastard left.'

Pauline took a deep breath and shakily got to her feet. Mark cleaned up, took her to the farm and put her to bed.

'Don't leave,' Pauline begged in a broken voice.

'I'll put his rucksack and gun in the safe room and be right back.'

He met Jenny and told her Pauline had a fever and was staying in bed. He would bring her meals to their room.

He stayed with her all day and held her when she cried out in her sleep.

While Pauline nursed Penny the next day, Mark talked about the attack. 'From everything I've read on the Portal and in Nicholas' journals, the Temporal Research Council, or Tempus as Nicholas calls it, is for historical and economic research. Victor, if that was his real name, must have been a criminal who wanted one for his own purposes.'

TP 1000: The Bishops

Mark inspected the rucksack and besides money and clothes, found a map with the farm clearly marked and a notebook with the names of everyone at the farm. He examined a four-inch square box with a collapsible antenna, which felt like neither metal nor plastic, and a strange looking *iPhone*. Maybe one of these was what Nicholas called a 'Universal Library', but without a thumbprint and password they had no way of accessing it. That afternoon Mark burned the rucksack and all the clothes in the furnace; the gun and electronic devices, he put inside the Faraday cage.

When the police arrived a few days later and asked if Mark had seen the missing bird watcher, he told them he had last seen him two weeks before and told them where to find his campsite. He mentioned he had invited him a couple of times for hot meals, but knew nothing more about him.

For the next few weeks, Pauline was withdrawn and spent all her time with Penny, comforting herself with her daughter's presence. Mark stayed with her as much as he could and held her during her nightmares.

As she recovered and the nightmares faded, Pauline wanted to get back to work. Melanie was doing a great job of looking after Penny and they had the time to discuss what would be most useful to prepare Penelope for the Twenty-First Century. They bought text books, magazines and a selection of clothes and cosmetics.

After what Mark had learned from Victor, he called the architects to build an extension to the byre with fine aluminium mesh embedded in floor, ceiling and walls and a wooden door with more mesh fitted behind decorative panels. The room was now one large Faraday cage. He also built a portable one from copper mesh to take with them; CCTV and intrusion alarms linked to motion sensors, ensured they would not be surprised again.

On thirteenth of December, Mark loaded the wagon, harnessed the horses and drove the utility vehicle back to fetch Pauline and the trunk for Penelope. They drove through the gateway, reassured no signals could now be detected.

Chapter 18
Tuesday, 30th June 1840

Giving Penelope no time to ask questions, they tutored her using the textbooks they had brought. She devoured every lesson, studying under candlelight until she fell asleep at the desk. Now Penelope knew their secret, Pauline and Mark went home every weekend. Each time they left, Penelope had her nose buried in a book and barely noticed their absence.

Penelope was normally compliant in her studies of Twenty-First Century life, but when Pauline asked her to try the modern clothes she rebelled.

'I cannot wear these. They are... indecent!' she cried, when Pauline showed her lace underwear and tried to get her into a pair of jeans, T-shirt and trainers.

'You saw those magazines, this is what we all wear.' Pauline bullied her to put them on, and to Penelope's absolute horror, called Mark, who looked approvingly at the change.

'No-one will believe you are not from our time,' he reassured her.

Blushing a brilliant shade of red, she tried to smile, then Pauline shooed him out. Pauline forced her to try the clothes every day, but she still blushed whenever she wore the tight T-shirt and snug jeans.

Pauline held long discussions with her on social life and especially equal rights.

'You mean you have your own money?' Penelope blurted. 'It doesn't belong to Mr Holmes?'

'It does *not*!' Pauline replied, and explained she had her own salary and bank account.

'But that's impossible. The law does not allow a married woman to manage money. The husband controls everything.'

'Like Hell he does!' she retorted, and called Mark.

When he understood the problem, he laughed. 'Penelope, *believe me*, everything my wife owns is hers, nothing to do with me. She even pays her own taxes.'

'Trust me,' Pauline added. 'Women have *rights* where we come from. We're not yet fully equal on pay, but we're getting there,' she smirked at Mark, who beat a hasty retreat.

More than the advances in science and technology, this was the hardest concept for Penelope to grasp.

After watching Penelope study day and night for three months, Mark decided to check her progress with GCSE past papers. He was astounded when she scored between fifty and sixty percent in most subjects, over seventy in French and Ancient History, barely failing Maths and Physics.

'She's a bloody genius,' Mark told Pauline after rechecking the answers. 'With proper tuition she'd ace everything.'

Penelope asked if this meant she could go to university.

'No problem.' Mark replied. 'I will arrange for you to take the exams privately, and afterwards study for the advanced courses. At this rate you could apply to university in a couple of years.'

'But how would I pay for it?' she asked whilst biting her lips. 'Everything is expensive there and I have so little money. How would I earn my keep?'

Pauline could not help laughing. Mark explained he would support her and pay for her education.

'I *cannot* accept your charity,' she declared, firmly. 'I want to be able to support myself.'

'Good for you,' Pauline replied. 'You know those postage labels we are collecting, if you buy some at the post office, we will arrange their sale and you will have more than enough to support yourself, believe me.'

'They are valuable in the future?' she asked. When Mark told her how much they were worth, she was lost for words.

'What about this? Is this valuable?' She took a letter from her dress pocket. It was from a friend in Manchester with a Twopenny Blue stamp neatly cancelled on eighth of May 1840, the first day of usage, with a Chesterfield receiving handstamp for ninth of May.

'Penelope, I can very likely obtain two-hundred thousand pounds for this, and with a few unused Penny Blacks, you'd easily have half-a-million. You would be an independently wealthy woman.'

This was unimaginable to Penelope. She had lived all her life on the suffrage of others, only since working for Pauline had she had her own money. She was more determined than ever to succeed—her dream, one she had secretly longed for all her adult life, was within her grasp.

Once they figured Penelope was as knowledgeable as possible, it was time to give her a practical education.

When they emerged in 2009, Pauline reminded her of the cover story they had concocted. 'Remember, you've known me since 2001 when I lived in London. You dropped out of school to care for your parents. You have a passion for early Nineteenth Century British history, that's how we became friends and I invited you to come and stay with us after your parents died.'

'I... I understand,' she replied, apprehensive at what lay ahead and *very* embarrassed wearing what she considered to be thoroughly shameful clothes.

'And don't forget here I am Pauline Bishop, not Mrs Holmes or ma'am.'

Penelope's face flushed at the thought of such informality, but she took a deep breath, determined to face this future world and realise her dream.

Mark drove them to the farmhouse in the utility vehicle, bundled them into his Jaguar and headed for Darlington.

Penelope slowly eased her vice-like hold on the armrest. The fastest she had ever travelled before was on a train at seventeen miles-per-hour. This was *much* faster.

'How... how fast are we travelling?'

'About seventy miles an hour,' Mark answered.

She gripped the arm rest even tighter.

The constant stream of fast-moving vehicles was bewildering, and the smell of petrol fumes on a short walk in Darlington made her nauseous.

'Everything will be alright, you'll see,' Pauline told her, and held Penelope's hand on the journey back to the farm.

Jenny thought they had just returned from the railway station and brought tea to the living room. Pauline was showing Penelope how to use the TV remote when Mark came in after carrying Penelope's portmanteau to her room.

'Room's ready. Why don't you take Penelope to freshen up, then we can tour the farm.'

After thorough instructions on how to use the shower, Pauline said they would meet her in the TV room when she was ready.

Penelope reappeared wearing, in her opinion, the most modest clothes she had. A knee length tweed skirt, blouse, sweater and coat.

Pauline introduced people as they met them around the farm and Mark tried to explain his conservancy projects and what he wished to achieve.

'Because of poor land and environmental management, many species are endangered or extinct,' Mark explained. 'You remember the fern we found in Matlock? Well, now, there is only one small patch left in the whole world; that's why I brought it back here.'

Tony, usually brash and talkative was tongue-tied when introduced to Penelope. 'P-p-pleased to meet you, er... Miss er... Miss Wright.'

Penelope seemed just as affected by the encounter and lowered her eyes and blushed a deep red when she shook his hand.

Mark and Pauline stared.

Mark broke the impasse. 'We'll head back to the house now.'

'Yes... yes, of course... right,' Tony stammered while not taking his eyes of Penelope and hastily let go of her hand.

Pauline and Penelope spent the next day with Penny in the nursery; Penelope delighted to meet and play with her namesake. Over the following days Penelope began to relax and asked many questions, except when she met Tony. Whenever he showed up to discuss something with Mark, which seemed to be much more frequent than usual, Penelope blushed and fidgeted while Tony became lost for words.

Electricity, and everything powered by it, was a constant wonder to Penelope—lights, telephones, television, cameras and stereo. Once Pauline showed her how to use the computer, Penelope spent as much time as possible on the internet. When she had had the kitchen and laundry appliances explained, she thought them fantastic inventions; she now understood Pauline's concern for the servants at Houghton House.

Shortly after they had returned, Mark called a friend who was an identity theft security expert. After searching the online UK Grave Records, Mark found a Penelope Wright who had been born on the nineteenth of November, same as their Penelope, and died in 1984, a few months old. He contacted the General Register Office and said he was researching his family tree and purchased a copy of the certificate. Once in his possession, he successfully applied for a National Insurance card using a letter of employment from Keldthorpe Farm. By the middle of February, Penelope had a completely authentic identity.

When Mark told her he had made arrangements for her to take the GCSE exams in May, almost nothing could drag her from her studies. Mark helped her with Maths, Physics and Geography, Pauline with Modern English, and Tony with Chemistry and Biology; he also helped her perform practicals in the lab. When Pauline went to check on how Penelope was doing, she wondered how, and what, she was learning. She and Tony both seemed unable to communicate without a lot of stammering and blushes.

Mark caught her reading the 1482 copy of *Islamic Medicine* by *Ibn Zuhr* and *Ibn Rushid* he had found, and registered her to take Latin. Pauline did manage to drag her outside for a few hours a week for archery practice and to teach her to ride a horse. She took a lot of persuading to mount one of the draft horses—she considered riding astride *most* unladylike.

When Penelope's collection of stamps and the first day cover were put up for auction, she was staggered when she received the cheque for four hundred and twenty-eight thousand pounds. Pauline took her straight to the bank and helped her open an account.

'Now you're all set. Let me introduce you to retail therapy.'

In Harrogate, Penelope was amazed at the number and variety of shops, but what astonished her most was the people's clothes. She considered the mid-thigh skirts and tight shorts worn by several young women outrageous.

At *H&M*'s, Penelope goggled at the variety of clothing while Pauline led her on a frenzied few hours choosing and trying a whole range of clothes. Penelope balked when Pauline suggested trying some lingerie. 'Ma'am! I cannot wear that!'

Pauline eventually persuaded Penelope that the negligée was *not* obscene, making her buy one in a lace transparent mesh.

'No one is going to see you in it—unless you want them to,' she half-joked, to horrified looks from Penelope. 'Relax, if we women want to feel sensuous, that's our business.'

Putting their shopping in the car, Pauline took her along James Street. At *Waterstones* bookstore, Penelope found Paradise. She bought so many books they struggled to carry them and Pauline had to drag her out with promises to come again.

'You wait here, I'll pick you up. We can't carry all these,' Pauline told her, leaving her waiting on the pavement. This was the first time she had been alone, but she was so distracted by the books displayed in the shop window, she was totally unafraid, and completely oblivious to the admiring stares from the men walking by.

Penelope chattered the whole return journey about the bookstore and the shops they had visited. 'Can I buy a car and come again?' she asked, excitedly.

'You have to have a driving licence, I'm sure Mark can arrange something.'

Mark saw them staggering under an enormous number of boxes and bags and helped carry them to Penelope's room.

'I see you enjoyed yourselves.'

His exhausted wife groaned. 'Penelope quickly learned how to use her debit card, believe me.'

Penelope was as ready as she could be when Mark and Pauline drove her to her first exam in May. Although nervous, excitement was her dominant emotion—she was taking the first step to achieving her dreams.

After five months, Penelope was becoming accustomed to modern life, with only occasional minor culture shocks and a few inadvertent slips when she called Pauline 'Mrs Holmes'. Lifts and other scientific marvels she could handle as technological advances, but social changes, such as public kissing, were something else altogether. After her last exam in June, Mark suggested a day trip to Scarborough.

Following lunch at the *Grand Hotel*, they walked along the beach. Penelope was aghast when she saw young women in miniscule bikinis and men in swimming shorts. This was the first time she had ever seen an almost naked man; her face was aflame and she did not know where to look.

The following morning, Tony rushed in to the house yelling and hollering. Penelope was the first person he saw and was shocked and amazed when he hugged and kissed her.

'What's all t'fuss?' Bill exclaimed.

'You've got to see this. It's fantastic. Unbelievable,' Tony blurted. He grabbed Penelope by the hand and dragged her to the beck while everyone followed.

Tony was almost incoherent, 'It's a Derbyshire feather-moss. They are nearly extinct,' he cried.

Chris called his old professor and soon Mark had to restrict access to the site to protect the plants.

Waiting for her results, Penelope started taking driving lessons twice a day with Pauline and Mark, and passed her test the first time. Mark advised her to buy her own house in Leyburn as a future investment. Leaving her money in the bank at a half percent interest was a waste of time; she could rent it out and stay at the farm. With her own house and newly purchased *Mini*, she felt independent and in control, but also apprehensive about going back to 1840, even for a short time. How could she accept the restrictions on her life she had accepted as the norm before? More troubling for her were thoughts of Tony and the way he had kissed her.

Penelope was so excited on results day, Pauline offered to drive her. Penelope had scored A-star or A in everything except for B's in Physics and Mathematics and was embarrassed with all the attention she received, especially from Tony. Although used to the public displays of affection between Mark and Pauline, she had never had a man's attention so focussed on her personally.

Penelope told Pauline she wanted to study archaeology.

'Why archaeology?'

'I come from the past, so it was either history or archaeology. I chose archaeology because it allows me to discover how people lived and find and handle artefacts that were important to them.'

They selected History, Geography, Biology and Chemistry along with General Studies and Latin, which was almost her second language, as her A-level subjects.

Before Penelope buried herself in the text books she had bought, Mark said they should go back to Houghton House. Penelope was distraught; she did not want to go back. She wanted to study. Pauline explained if she studied while at Houghton House, she would actually gain extra study time.

Pauline and Penelope both groused over cutting and dressing their hair in Victorian fashion and applying make-up so they looked as they were when they ostensibly left for their drive. Penelope felt strange and uncomfortable wearing her Victorian dresses again after the freedom of movement modern clothes afforded. When they arrived at Houghton House, it was disconcerting when she realised she was eight months older, but for everyone here only six hours had passed.

Penelope thought about her future life in the Twenty-First Century and wanted a reminder of her past. Decision made, she approached Pauline to suggest they open a museum and she would help run it. She outlined her idea for a typical Victorian kitchen with cooking demonstrations using Victorian utensils and methods. Mannequins wearing typical Victorian clothes could be additional exhibits.

TP 1000: The Bishops

Mark still had money in Singapore, not enough for his main projects, but enough for this. Then he remembered how much Penelope had earned from the sale of her stamps. He could do the same when he returned and easily have enough for all his plans. He agreed it would be a good idea and later, could be an adjunct to a future farm shop and provide valuable publicity.

They decided on a replica kitchen, larder and pantry, living room and an exhibition area with several display cabinets. Penelope prepared a list of everything they would need, then dove back into her books. Mark ordered a Kitchener stove from *Flavel*'s and Pauline bought a complete set of kitchen utensils from Chesterfield as well as typical clothes worn by the different classes and occupations. Several trips to Sheffield added hallmarked silver candlesticks, cutlery, silver-plated tableware and ornaments, salt cellars and snuff boxes. Mark even found a silver Georgian tea set he planned on keeping at the house.

Business picked up and, with winnings from horse races, Mark soon had over five thousand pounds in his account. It would have been more, but they entertained quite often. Pauline had to drag Penelope from her books to accompany her on visits and was soon involved with social causes. Pauline made an arrangement with a member of the Board of Guardians of the Chesterfield Union of parishes to hire women to make embroidered cushion covers for the future farm shop, paying them a shilling a week and another sixpence for each cushion completed. She also talked to the master of the work-house on Newbold Road. He agreed to allow suitable residents to engage in paid work, for which the work-house would allow the women to keep tuppence from the shilling Pauline was offering, but agreed to them keeping the sixpence. Pauline was not pleased with this arrangement, but she knew from her own research this was common practice to offset the costs of maintaining the work-house.

Pauline was updating her journal one morning when Penelope remarked, 'Mr Matthews is exceptionally passionate about his work, isn't he?'

'That's why we hired him,' Pauline answered, not paying much attention while she concentrated on her writing.

'Could we go and collect another rare plant? I know where to look and he was so excited when he found the fern—it would please him so much,'

Pauline looked up and saw Penelope was blushing.

'Penelope! Are you *sweet* on him?'

'I mean... he is, well...'

Pauline put her pen down. She was now *very* interested in the direction this conversation was going.

'You *are* attracted to him, aren't you?' Pauline exclaimed.

Penelope's face was now burning.

'Well, what are you going to do about it?'

'Me? Do what?' she yelped. After a pause her face fell. 'He would not be interested in someone like me.'

'Don't be stupid!' Pauline scolded her. 'I've seen you two together and he's besotted.'

This led to some crucial lessons for Penelope on dealing with men; a subject on which she was totally clueless.

'This is all so confusing,' she moaned. 'A relationship needs honesty, but I cannot tell him who I really am, or where I come from, can I?'

'That *is* difficult,' Pauline agreed, and remembered her own confession to Mark. 'I think it's time we talked to my husband.'

'I cannot tell Mr Bishop. He will think I'm wanton,' she cried.

'No he won't! But, we do need to talk to him about the way things are between you and Tony, *especially* your concerns about being honest with him.'

In the evening they cornered Mark in his study. Pauline explained Penelope's dilemma and eventually, after much discussion, they decided to collect an extinct plant and tell Tony where it had come from. Mark thought this the best way to gain his cooperation and ensure his secrecy.

Penelope showed Mark and Pauline drawings of plants in her journal. Mark saw one of a fungus, the wavy webcap, and knew it had become extinct in England before the end of the Nineteenth Century.

When asked about it, she said, 'Oh that is *Cortinarius cumatilis*, it has a lovely violet cap. I saw it on Saturday twelfth of June, 1824, when mama and papa took me on a picnic in a wooded area not far from here.'

Pauline shook her head. Penelope must have been only eight years old and could even remember the date.

Later when they were all sat in the living room, Pauline asked Penelope how she remembered where all those plants were located and she told her she could remember most things after reading or seeing something.

'Even after reading it once?' Pauline exclaimed.

'Yes, I usually remember everything I read, I just have a bit of trouble with some of the long chemical names,' looking puzzled at the expressions on their faces.

Mark and Pauline just stared at each other, not only did she have a genius IQ, she also had an eidetic memory, or something like it.

A few days later Mark drove them to the location Penelope remembered and found the fungus growing on fallen branches near the edge of the woods. Mark told her they would wait until just before they went back to collect specimens.

Mark and Pauline planned a trip to London for more museum exhibits, but Penelope refused to leave her studies. Taking trains and coaches, they arrived after a miserable and uncomfortable journey and secured rooms with attendance at the *Clarendon* on

Bond Street. They bought clocks, glass and silver plated bottles and jars, salt and pepper shakers, napkin rings and many items of jewellery, all to be delivered to his warehouse.

'Good job there are more races to come,' Mark told Pauline on the way back to Chesterfield. 'We've spent over two thousand pounds.'

'It has to be spent on something, the money's no use at home. The museum's collection is as good a place as any,' Pauline replied.

After they disembarked from the coach in Chesterfield, Mark had his wagon brought from the stables. They were ready to go home; the journey had been tiring and uncomfortable to say the least. As they passed the turn to Walton Mill, Pauline saw a group of men harassing a couple of girls.

'Mark! Stop! Look over there.' she yelled.

Mark turned to where she was pointing. 'That's Fanny and Grace! I'll put a stop to this.' With a grim expression he turned the wagonette towards the group of men.

When the four men saw the wagonette coming they spread out a little, giving Fanny and Grace a chance to run towards Mark and Pauline.

'Wha' we got 'ere, then?' one of the men shouted.

A huge brute of a man, much bigger than Mark and the obvious ring-leader, pushed to the front of the men. 'Yer spoilin' t'fun and we don't take that from nobody, mister.'

'And what do you think you can do about it?' Mark replied, slipping off his coat.

Three of the four men headed toward Mark, while one, a skinny ruffian, his leering smile showing black rotting teeth, headed toward the women by the wagonette.

'I'll keep the li'l ladies company while yer deal with 'im,' he laughed.

'Fanny, Grace, are you alright? Have you been hurt?' Pauline asked, noticing their torn clothes. Both of them obviously shaken and scared, shook their heads.

'Alright, then, stand behind me, please, while Mr Holmes and I deal with these scoundrels.'

The young women ran behind the wagonette and Pauline reached into her dress pocket for her favourite weapon—her rock, now replaced by a steel ball, in a sock, and smiled as the man approached her. He grinned lustfully as he reached for her. 'That's right me darlin'. Just wait a bit an' we can all 'ave some fun.'

Peering around the front of the wagonette, Fanny saw Mrs Holmes take a white bag out of her pocket. Her hand blurred as the man reached for her and within seconds he was lying on the ground with blood streaming down his face. Fanny heard a scream and saw two of the other men lying on the ground, one not moving and the other holding his groin.

When the ring-leader pulled a knife, Mr Holmes stood relaxed.

Fanny heard him taunt the last man. 'Well, what are you waiting for? Is a big boy like you scared?' She saw him smirk at his attacker, whose face turned red and lunged. All of a sudden the big man was on the ground with Mr Holmes throwing the knife away. She had not even seen him move!

'Had enough yet, or do you want some more?' she heard Mr Holmes ask, quite calmly.

She saw the rage on the man's face as he rushed towards Mr Holmes, then he was flying through the air landing four feet away with a loud gasp as the air was driven from his lungs.

Grace and Fanny cowered behind the wagonette and heard Mr Holmes say, 'Mrs Holmes, would you pass me the rope under the front seat, please?'

Peering out they saw their mistress pass the rope to her husband who tied the four men together in such a way that the more they struggled, the tighter the rope around their necks became.

'They're not going anywhere for a while,' they heard Mr Holmes remark.

'Girls, you can come out now,' Pauline told them both. 'Now what were you doing here in the first place? Should you not be working?'

'Ma'am, sir, we went to visit me mum just down t'road,' Fanny explained. 'She's bin poorly an' Mrs Compton gave us leave t' go an' visit. Then them men stopped us and said such awful things an' started pulling on our dresses.'

'Alright then, sit in the back seat and we will take you home. They will not be bothering you again.'

'Once we are back at the house, I'll ride into town and bring back the constables,' Mark told them, as he turned the wagonette back to the main road.

In a few minutes they arrived at Houghton House to see Mrs Compton waiting at the top of the steps.

'Mrs Compton, good morning. How are you?' Pauline asked as Fanny and Grace clambered down.

'Fanny, Grace. What have you been up to?' the housekeeper scolded, staring at their dishevelled clothing.

'Absolutely nothing!' Mark answered, helping Pauline down. 'On their way home from Fanny's mother, they were assaulted by a gang of ruffians. Luckily we came by and put a stop to it. They are a little shaken, but not harmed.'

'Now let us see these girls are settled, while Mr Holmes goes to bring the constables,' Pauline added.

On their return, Penelope bombarded them with questions about amino acids in organic chemistry and how they related to those in her biology texts about DNA.

'I'll be glad to get back, then she can ask the 'lab-rats' all these questions,' Mark told Pauline, referring to Chris and Tony. 'I tell you, she's gone way past me.'

Penelope was also anxious to get back, she needed to start the biology and chemistry practical work. In some ways, Pauline felt sorry for Tony and Chris, her tutors for lab work. Penelope's single-minded pursuit of going to university was frightening, and exhausting for anyone she believed could help her achieve it.

Two weeks later, Mark appeared in the local magistrate's court. Three of the four men had previous criminal histories as evidenced by the constable producing certificates of numerous convictions for assault and robbery. After hearing the testimony of Fanny and Grace, and Mark's detailed account of the encounter, the magistrate pronounced his verdict.

Seven years Transportation for two of the men while the ringleader, still nursing cracked ribs, was sentenced to fifteen years. The youngest one, twenty years old and with no previous convictions, received one year in the county gaol and a flogging.

After sentencing, the magistrate, smiled and addressed Mark. 'Mr Holmes, the court thanks you for your aid in bringing these criminals to justice. This is the second time you have appeared before us after performing this service. At least, this time, the defendants were able to walk.'

That last comment raised raucous laughter from the courtroom and a dignified bow from Mark.

Pauline found their regular day trips back to visit Penny most unsatisfactory. Penny had started to walk and although Pauline was not missing her development, this trip had still been tough.

Mark explained to the staff they would be visiting Pauline's family in York again for three months, but he would return occasionally because of his business. Mark made arrangements for their wages and allowances with Mr Marshall and gave Mrs Compton more than adequate funds for any emergencies.

The day before they left, Mark rode to the woods and collected a log with several fungi attached.

Chapter 19
Wednesday, 30th September 2009

Once through the gateway, Mark called Tony's mobile phone and asked him to come up to the byre. When he arrived, he was surprised to see them all in period clothes. 'Why are you all dressed like that?'

Penelope passed him the log. He examined the fungus carefully, then forgot all about their strange garb and yelled, 'Where did you find these?'

Mark looked calmly at Tony. 'We went to collect them. Not to worry, there's plenty more left.'

Tony's voice cracked. 'What do you mean you went to collect it? These are *Cortinarius cumatilis*. They became extinct here in the 1860s.' He stared back and forth between them. 'What's going on?'

'I'll explain everything back at the farm after we've changed.'

They all went to the basement, and Mark opened the two concealed doors and led them downstairs—Tony was bewildered. Mark activated the TP1000 and let him read through the same screens he had shown Pauline over three years ago.

'You mean... this... this thing... it actually *works?*' he stammered.

'Sure does. This is how we found the Derbyshire Fern, the fungus,' Mark paused, '...and Penelope.'

Tony could only stare at her. 'You mean... she's...'

'We went to 1840 to collect Penny Blacks and brought back a real life Penny as well,' Pauline quipped cheerfully.

Tony collapsed on a chair his face ashen and Penelope wrapped her arms around him.

'Anthony, we could not tell anyone, please try to understand,' she explained with an anxious look on her face. 'But I had to let you know who I really am.'

'You're from 1840?'

'I was born in Salford on nineteenth of November, 1815, and met Mr and Mrs Bishop in 1839 when I went to Chesterfield as Mrs Holm... I mean Pauline's lady's maid.'

'She found out about our secret and we brought her back with us,' Mark clarified.

He explained how Pauline had researched the census data for 1811 and 2011 and found Penelope's name in Leyburn.

'But where did *that* come from?' he asked, pointing to the TP1000 and clutching Penelope, who did not appear to want to let go either.

Mark revealed how they had found it, the trips they had made, and a brief outline of what they had done on those trips.

'That's how we found these extinct plants,' Pauline reminded him. 'Penelope has a journal from when she was young which has descriptions and drawings of some extinct or endangered plants, so we went to collect one and bring it back.'

'You realise the amount of trust we are placing in you, showing you all this?' Mark added.

'Oh! Absolutely. Not only can this be used to bring back these plants, but it also brought me Penelope,' Tony smiled broadly at her, making her eyes shine.

Penelope's voice quavered a little. 'Anthony, I did not want us to have any secrets. I have become to like you, very much, and I wanted you to know the truth.'

'Penelope, its fine. It's okay. It doesn't alter how I feel about you, or anything,' and stared in to her eyes.

The kiss that followed started getting steamy and Pauline coughed and amusement bubbled in her voice. 'Ahem, can you save this for later?'

Penelope jumped away, her face crimson with embarrassment.

'Tony, we have videos of these trips you can watch,' Mark informed him, 'but have I your word you will not breath a word of this to anyone? I know it's a lot to ask, but I'm sure you understand the risk if this is not used properly.'

'Mr Bishop... Mark, you have my word. If nothing else, it brought Penelope here and that's the best thing that's ever happened to me,' he agreed and looked at Penelope, whose eyes glistened with a brilliant smile on her face.

'Come on, you two love-birds, let's go look at those videos. Then you can study Penelope's journals,' Pauline told them.

After celebrating Penny's first birthday, Pauline organised one for Penelope. She was twenty-four years old according to 1800s reckoning but with the time spent in 2009 actually twenty-five, which agreed with her birth certificate. Pauline told her not to think about it too much and enjoy herself.

Penelope was overwhelmed at having a special dinner in her honour. She had never had a birthday party before. The exuberant

Happy Birthday song was a custom she had never experienced and was barely able to control her tears. Her politeness, charm, curiosity and good looks had made her popular with everyone. Tony gave her a vintage silver pendant with a large teardrop topaz. She had never received such a gift before in her life and when he kissed her in front of everybody, she blushed a bright cherry-red.

However, soon enough, she was back to her single-minded focus on her studies and her and Tony's budding romance now progressed glacially.

Mark explained to Pauline his idea to obtain the money to go ahead with their plans for the farm. 'I know this wealthy Japanese collector personally. He's outbid me in auctions more times than I care to think about. If I put together a rare combination of stamps on a couple of envelopes, add in a few choice mint blocks and first day covers, he'll not be able to resist them and happily pay a couple of million. Problem is going to be authentication; Makoto won't part with that kind of money without extensive testing.'

'So how are you going to get around it,' Pauline asked, astonished at Mark's audacity.

'I'll just have to travel back, hide everything, return here and collect them. Problem is, where to hide them that's going to be safe for such a long time.'

'How about somewhere on our farm?'

'It has to be somewhere that won't change or be developed.'

'How about the byre? It's certainly old enough.'

'Good idea. I'll need to check and see for myself, though.'

TP 1000: The Bishops

That afternoon, they set up the Portal to view the byre every ten years, starting from first of December, 1841. Their first view of the building was a ruin; the western wall and roof had collapsed but the eastern wall was mostly intact. Rotating the gateway towards the farm site, there was no sign of habitation, only a pile of stones where the farmhouse would be. There was no significant change until 1940, when they saw the byre rebuilt pretty much how it was at present, but no sign of a farmhouse.

Mark had to skip past the atmospheric nuclear testing period to 1970 where they saw the byre, still in good condition, and the original two-storey farm Nicholas had bought.

'Well, that's not a problem. I'll make a trip to post the letters to myself, head back to receive them, then travel to the byre in 1840 and bury them inside. Let's go and have a look.'

The floor was covered in large flagstones, except along the eastern wall where smaller ones had been laid.

'I can easily lift those. I can bury them underneath and dig them up when I'm back.'

Two days later, Mark went back to Houghton House. He collected matching mint blocks of six of each of the first two plates of Penny Blacks and the Twopenny Blues with marginal instructions. He added one of his first day covers with a pair of Penny Blacks to sweeten the pot.

He rode Lucky to Sheffield and wrote two letters. One on a *Mulready* sheet with additional enclosed sheets purportedly from a merchant in Sheffield making enquiries on the possible supply of spices. He attached a pair of Penny Blacks to pay for the extra weight.

The other letter was from another fictitious correspondent containing a lengthy diatribe against *Edward Oxford*'s recent attempted assassination of Queen Victoria and her husband. The letter, plus a copy of the *Derbyshire Courier* from his safe dated thirteenth of June 1840 regarding the assassination attempt, made a heavy package. Mark affixed two Penny Blacks and a block of four of the Twopenny Blue stamps on the outer sheet and posted them. Mark then bought a small ornamental brass trinket box and rode back to Chesterfield.

To preserve everything from damp, he enclosed the stamps in a layer of paper and waxed cotton and sealed the edges of the box with wax. He wrapped it with a layer of canvas, then oilskin, secured with strong twine. Mark travelled back to his farm and prepared for his trip to bury the box.

Mark exited on the Richmond road. At the byre, it was evident no one had been there in ages. Clearing the floor, he prised up the small corner stones with a crowbar and dug a hole large enough to bury the box. Replacing the flagstones, he covered them with broken roof tiles and other debris. Making sure he had left nothing behind, he returned to his present time where Pauline waited for him.

Mark held the excavated parcel. 'The outer wrapping are a bit water-stained. Let's go to my study and see if this worked.' The box was corroded, but the contents were in pristine condition. The next day, he sent the stamps and envelopes for authentication.

Nicholas' journals clearly stated the coming winter would bring heavy snowfalls and very low temperatures. Mark had duly prepared for it, causing Bill to ask why he was so concerned. All Mark would say was he did not want to be caught out.

That evening Mark confided in Pauline. 'The first snowfall is due on seventeenth of December. Then it gets really bad by fifth of January, with temperatures dropping below zero—*Fahrenheit*, We'll have to stock up the freezers, in case we're cut off.'

The first snow fell right on schedule; the snow-blower Mark had bought was busy clearing the snow while he and Frank gritted and salted the access roads to allow the tankers to collect the milk. Mark was not about to throw away a couple of days of milk.

Christmas was another new experience for Penelope. When Pauline dragged her to Richmond for Christmas shopping, she was astonished at the crowds and asked Pauline who the fat bearded man was in the red coat. Pauline gaped at her and remembered the modern version of Christmas did not appear in England until the mid-Nineteenth Century. Pauline gave her a lengthy explanation of modern Christmas traditions, including Christmas crackers and cards and it was often a week-long holiday for many people.

Penelope watched Mark, Chris and Tony decorate the house and Christmas tree. They hung mistletoe and holly, the only decorations she was used to seeing at Christmas, all around the house. On Christmas Day, she was embarrassed watching Mark and Pauline kissing under the mistletoe. She was more embarrassed when Tony caught her standing underneath a bunch hung near the dining room.

When Mark received the certificate of authenticity for his stamps, he emailed scanned copies of the items and the certificates to the Japanese philatelist, and the price he was asking. Three days later, Makoto agreed to meet Mark in London at the weekend. Mark explained why he wanted to sell these items and after examining them and the original certificates, Makoto arranged a transfer of two million pounds to Mark's London account.

Back at the farm, Mark informed Tony and Chris to review their initial budgets and get back to him with revised estimates. He also wanted to prepare the ground for planting, bring in more beehives and start construction of the museum, farm shop and ice cream plant when the weather improved in March. Although he had the funds to fulfil his and Pauline's plans, Bill had not yet found any land nearby for sale.

Mark was updating his family tree with what happened to James Bishop when Penelope came in to ask a question on geography.

'What is that?' she asked pointing to the elaborate chart on the desk.

'My family tree, I've been adding James Bishop's story to it,' he replied.

'How far back does it go?'

'To Henry Bishop, born in 1513; I've been trying to find out more about his parents. All I know is his father was William and lived in Crofthead, near Netherby in Cumberland.'

'That is *so* strange.' Penelope remarked. 'I remember my great-grandpapa saying he lived in Netherby before moving to Liverpool. We went to visit him and great-grandmama often when we lived in Prescot. My great-grandparents were so happy and always shared a smile, as if they had a big secret. Great-grandmama said I reminded her of her mother. When I asked about her mother, it was the only time I saw her looking sad. Mama took me out to play so I would not bother her with any more questions.

'Later, grandmama Amelia told me my great-grandparents' families had been against their marriage and they had run away to Gretna Green. Afterwards they moved to Liverpool where great-grandpapa worked in a friend's shop, repairing clocks. I thought it so romantic, but also very sad, as both of them were estranged from their families.'

'What was your great-grandmother's name?' Mark asked.

'Mary. No-one ever mentioned her maiden name.'

'Do you know when and where she was born?'

'Eighteenth of August, 1747. I remember because Papa said she died only three days before her seventy-sixth birthday in 1823. Great-grandpapa died three months later, Mama said it was because he could not live without her. Great-grandmama Mary must have lived near Netherby as she told me she and great-grandpapa used to be neighbours.'

As Pauline was reading to Penny before bedtime, Mark sat staring into space. When she finished the story, she and Melanie put her to bed, leaving Mark brooding in the living room.

'What's up with you tonight?' Pauline asked him when she returned. 'You were miles away. You usually joke around while we're reading,'

'I've been thinking on what Penelope said about her family this morning.'

'What about them?'

'Her great-grandmother's name was Mary and she was born on the same day as my great-great whatever aunt Mary, and my family lived only a mile or so away from where her great-grandfather came from, and she *did* say they were neighbours before eloping.'

Pauline was startled. 'You don't think Penelope is descended from your great-aunt, do you?'

'It's a Hell of a coincidence if not, but there's one sure way to find out, isn't there?'

'What! You're not going there are you?' Pauline screeched.

'Why not? If Penelope is my six-time great-aunt, she really will be Penny's 'Aunty Penny' won't she?'

'What are you going to tell Penelope?'

'Nothing. Not until I know for sure. The videos will prove it one way or the other. Anyway, it won't be for a while, there's lots of research I need to do before I even think of going.'

The architects designed the museum based on layouts of the kitchen and parlour at Houghton House and others from the internet. With Penelope's help, they finalised the plans, and building started in March. Mark made several solo trips back to Chesterfield to check on his business and bring back more exhibits for the museum.

'We'll need to hire extra help when the museum and farm shop are running,' Pauline informed Mark. 'The museum will be ready by the end of summer and neither me nor Penelope will be able to run it full-time. We'll need people for the farm shop and ice-cream factory as well.'

'Once construction is well underway we can start advertising,' Mark replied.

By the middle of April, Mark had completed his research on the 1760s. From what he had learned, the only place with any decent accommodation was in Carlisle, but this was a good seven or eight hours riding back and forth to Crofthead. He bought a large amount of period copper and silver coins, gold guinea and two-guinea pieces and ordered appropriate clothes made from wool and hessian.

Once Mark began to change, Lucky started prancing.

'Looks like someone is happy,' Pauline said, rubbing Lucky's face and scratching his ears.

Then she saw Mark wearing a three cornered hat. His hair, which he had allowed to grow for the last few months, was clubbed back with a black ribbon, Pauline was soon doubled over with laughter.

'What's so funny?'

Gasping to get her breath back, 'You. With a pony-tail. And that hat! It makes you look like something out of the *Pirates of the Caribbean*.'

'I'll have you know this is the height of fashion, my lady,' he replied haughtily. 'At least it's better than wearing a damn wig.'

'Oh! I'd love to see that.' She doubled over again.

'Not a chance, this is bad enough. Now if you're quite finished, I'd like to get this over with.'

Barely controlling herself, she nodded.

Mark opened a gateway near a wooded area on the Netherby Road, a mile west of Crofthead, and went through into a mild summer morning in July 1767.

He planned on staying only long enough to identify his own ancestors and find out if they were also Penelope's—once satisfied either way, he would travel back. Lucky trotted along the dirt road and within minutes Mark saw a small farm house with a heavy-set young man standing at the gate.

'A good day to you, young sir. May I have a moment of your time? I am looking for an inn to stay, mayhap you could give me directions?'

'Need to talk to me da, he's at 'hoose. Ar'll ca 'im,' the young man ran towards the farm house.

A few minutes later, an elderly farmer came out followed by the youngster.

'Good day, sir. My name is Michael Holmes from York and I am looking for a decent inn to stay at for a few days. Could you give me directions to such an establishment?'

'Nowt aroun' 'ere for a gent like yoursen 'till Carlisle, an' that's a good ways away.' The old farmer looked curiously at Mark. 'What yer be doin' in these parts?'

'I am an historian writing about the families loyal to King George in the area.'

'Well then, if yer really wantin' to know abart loyal families yer can abide wi' us for a while, none more loyal than my family.'

'Most kind sir, much obliged, May I know your name?'

'John, John Bishop, this 'ere's one o' me sons. Yer can make do in me sons' room.'

Bingo! He had lucked out and found his family straight away.

'You must let me recompense you for board and lodging at least. Will a guinea a week be sufficient?'

'Very generous, sur, very generous indeed, we do orright, but coin's kinda scarce. Come along and we'll get yon 'orse stabled.'

Once Lucky was settled, they went inside. The farm house was stone with a slate roof, living, dining and kitchen all one room and two bedrooms. Over a tankard of ale John asked, 'Yer say yer name be Holmes?'

'Yes sir, from York.'

'Yer look a lot like me Uncle John who were kilt by them papist Jacobites in forty-five.'

Mark studied John's wife, Anne, as she brought bread and cheese and went back to the fire to stir a large pot. She did look like Penelope, her yellow hair had a few grey streaks but her eyes were the same startling cornflower blue. Mary, the daughter, resembled Penelope even more, with rich golden hair and the same blue eyes.

Chapter 20
July, 1767

Sitting with John over a mug of ale in the evenings, Mark learned about his ancestors.

'I have all the birth dates an' such, I'll show you.'

John returned from the bedroom holding a very familiar book. It was the family Bible he had found in his cousin's effects.

'Me da, Edward, started it in 1740 and there's a list of 'is brothers and sisters; I've updated it to include me own children. 'N' if yer wantin' to find out any more, yer can visit the kirk o'er at Netherby.'

Mark had found John's recitals of family history back to Henry Bishop in the 1500s fascinating; when John and his son went out tending the sheep, he wrote up their conversations and drafted a rough family tree going back to his thirteen-time grandfather Henry. It was this Henry who was the first yeoman farmer, granted deed to the land in 1542 after the battle of Solway Moss.

He heard how his great-something Uncle John was killed in the Siege of Carlisle by the Jacobites, and how the plague had struck following the sack of the same city in 1745 by the

Roundheads. Two of his ancestors, Luke and Elsie, twin sister of his own direct ancestor Edward, had died in that outbreak. Farm accidents, childbirth, and disease seemed to have ended the lives of quite a few of the others.

At the end of his first week, Mark was writing his notes when James, the elder son who he had not yet met, showed up. He was a slimmer version of his father, with the same red-brown hair as Mark. Although the eldest, it was apparent he was not interested in farming. His father clearly disapproved of him, but politeness prevented any family arguments in front of a guest.

Early the next morning, after a breakfast of piping hot oat porridge, bread, honey and cheese, and a mug of ale, Mark rode over to the church to see their records. He was now convinced he and Penelope were related. After he checked the church records, he would look for the Wrights' farm. The records helped fill in details back to his thirteenth generation ancestors. After thanking the rector with a few coins, he visited Longtown and had lunch at the Graham Arms inn.

Nearing the farm he saw Mary talking intently with a young man near the side of the road. He reached into his coat to activate his camera.

'Good day, Miss Mary.'

She spun around and the lad stood defensively in front of her.

'Aren't you going introduce me to this young man?'

'Mr Holmes, sur, please sur, dinna say owt to my pa, 'e'll skin me,' she cried.

'Miss Mary, it is none of my business. Now, will you introduce me?'

'William Wright, sir.' The lad answered. As Mark suspected,

this was the man Mary would elope with. 'Mary's da dinna approve of us meeting, sir, and it'll go badly for 'er if 'e found out.'

'Please sur, you willna say owt, please?' Mary pleaded

'Miss Mary, as I said, it is really none of my business, however, the next time you decide to tryst, I recommend you not do so in plain sight of the road,' he tipped his hat and rode on to the farm.

Over the next few days, Mark recorded more family anecdotes from John, and about life in the Eighteenth Century. He also learned of the family feud between the Bishops and Wrights going back three generations over a question of some missing sheep, and still simmering.

'Sheep stealers, they are, nowt but! Might be good Royalists, but still sheep stealers, none the less,' was about the politest comment John Bishop made and Mark diplomatically changed the subject.

He assumed the Wrights were saying the same thing, making things impossible for the young couple.

He rode to Netherby and found the Wright's farm. They were tenant farmers, not freeholders like the Bishops, and from the look of the farm, not as prosperous either. Thomas Wright met him at the farm gate and invited him in once he explained his purpose. Over mugs of ale, Mark learned more of the Wright family tree and duly recorded it for Penelope. He also learned Thomas Wright's side of the family feud and after a lengthy tirade understood why William and Mary had had no choice but to elope.

Leaving the farm, he met a terrified looking William.

'Do not worry, young William, I said nothing to your father,' Mark assured him. 'However, I do sympathise with your plight and if I can help in any way, please let me know.'

'Thankee, sir. It's that arl feud, and neither of 'em know wot really 'appened, anyroad. Mary and me want to be betrothed but our families are so set agen it. Dinna see wot anybody can do t' 'elp.'

'I'm sure something will turn up.'

After he stabled Lucky, he heard John senior shouting and the thwack of something, or someone, being struck. A moment later James burst out of the door, ran across the yard and down the road.

'Feckless! Yer no use to man nor beast,' John shouted from the doorway holding his leather belt, then saw Mark standing there.

'My apologies, sir, I 'eard from a neighbour how the young divvy's bin poachin' an' selling grouse t' butchers in Longtown. He'll ger isself 'ung, 'e will.'

'I am sorry to hear that, Mr Bishop. I can talk to him if you wish.'

'I thank you, sir, but lad's allus bin trouble. I only fear the worst now.'

Anne's family lived a few miles away in Moat and Mark made a few visits, adding more to the family history and a few more branches to Penelope's and his mutual family tree. By the end of July, he had a wealth of notes and several hours of video; he decided to visit Carlisle before heading home.

Returning from the privy that night, he saw Mary hurrying towards the road. Thankfully it was a waning moon and by staying next to the hedgerows he remained unseen. He followed her to where she turned off into a small copse half way to Netherby. Working his way slowly through the trees, he spotted Mary and William embracing.

'Now, what do you two think you are doing?' he announced, causing both of them to spin around.

'Mr Holmes! Sir, what are you doing here?' Mary squeaked.

'More to the point, I think, is what you two are doing here,' as if he did not know from the two cloth wrapped bundles next to them. However, he had *not* expected to witness them actually eloping.

Young William gave Mark a defiant look, somewhat tempered by fear. 'Mr Holmes, sir, we're goin' to Gretna to be married and lead our own lives, we canna be t'gether 'ere.'

'Sur, tis 'only way we can be t'gether, our families' dinna understand. Are yer goin' to stop us?' she asked, in heartrending tone.

'And after you are married, how are you going to live? William, how will you support your wife?'

'We'll be goin' to me friend's place in Liverpool; 'E can find me a job, there.'

'How do you plan on getting there? It's about a hundred and forty miles from here and the roads are none too safe. How much money do you have?'

'A whole sovereign, sir,' William announced, proudly showed Mark the coin.

Mark said a silent prayer to whomever the patron saint of fools and teenagers was—he was dealing with both. Well, they *did* elope, *and* manage to end up living in Liverpool.

Mary gazed at Mark with tears in her eyes. 'We canna bear to be apart any more, sur.' William put his arm around her to console her.

'Here are two guineas, I want you to meet me at the Red Lion in Carlisle two days after you are married; I will see what I can do.'

'Yer willna tell our families?' William asked, staring goggle-eyed at Mark.

'It is six hours to dawn and Gretna is over five miles away. You had better be there and married before the hue and cry starts here.'

They stood there, frozen.

'GO! Don't waste any more time. Meet me in Carlisle in two days' time,' he ordered and walked away through the woods. He did not sleep for a long time; he knew from Penelope they had successfully eloped to Liverpool, but was still worried his involvement might change everything.

He was woken by shouting and cursing. When he left his room, he walked into a scene from Bedlam. John senior was stomping around the room, banging his fist on the table and yelling at the top of his voice. Anne was bent over the table sobbing and John junior stood by the door looking poleaxed.

'Mr Holmes, our Mary has run away.' John told him. 'It'll be yon damned Wright boy, I know it. Good riddance, I say, 'er and 'er worthless brother. Ungrateful whelps. Now I only have one child, young John here.'

Anne sobbed louder.

Mark knew that John junior would never marry and John senior would have one more son, William, in 1768, from whom Mark was descended. Much as he wanted to console Anne with this news, he bit his tongue.

'Mr Bishop, I had intended to leave for Carlisle on the morrow, but I can leave today. If you wish to lodge a complaint with the Sherriff, I can carry it for you.'

'I'm grateful, sir and ashamed yer should see me family this way.'

'No sir, not at all. The least I can do for all your hospitality.'

'Mr Holmes, yer must eat summat before you go. I'd be shamed if yer left wi'out,' He nodded to Anne who wiped her tears and went to prepare breakfast.

After packing his belongings, Mark said his farewells and headed towards the road when he heard Anne call him.

'Sir, dinna report 'em, please sir,' she pleaded in a desperate whisper. 'It's all due to the stupid feud m' husband and that Thomas Wright keep chewing o'er. They're good bairns and tis 'only way for 'em to be 'appy,' her voice quivering as she passed him a bundle of food for his journey.

'Mrs Bishop, they will be well. I cannot say how I know—trust and believe me.' He turned Lucky and headed towards Carlisle.

Booking a room for three nights, he described William and Mary to the innkeeper, saying to inform him immediately they arrived. While waiting, Mark toured Carlisle, recording sights of interest, and writing in his room.

The innkeeper brought the young newlyweds carrying their small bundle of clothes to him two days later, during breakfast, and he ordered a meal for them.

'Have you thought any more about what you are going to do?' he asked.

'Willy and me still want to go to Liverpool. His friend's a watchmaker and will help him find work.' Mary explained, much more sure of herself than three days ago.

'I be verra good a' fixin' things, real deft wi' me 'ands,' William added.

'How do you plan on getting there?'

'We'll walk and get lifts when we can. As long as we're together, we'll manage.' Mary replied with a confidence that made Mark wince.

Young love! Bloody bulletproof!

'I have a better idea. There's a coach to Liverpool in the morning, it will have you there in four days.'

'We canna afford a coach.' William exclaimed.

'I can. I will book you a room for the night and arrange for your passage as soon as we finish our meal.'

'Mr Holmes, why would yer 'elp us like this?' Mary asked, stunned at this turn of events.

'Miss Bishop, apologies, Mrs Wright,' he said and watched Mary's face glow. 'Let us just say I know what it is like to live a life of emptiness and suddenly find the one person who can fill that emptiness and make life worth living again. Now, let me arrange a room for you. Newlyweds should have some privacy, don't you think?'

Mary's face went a brilliant crimson, as bright a colour as he had ever seen on Penelope, making the family resemblance even more obvious.

Mark arranged their passage on the morning coach, paying the agent extra for the short notice and ensuring inside seats. After he passed William the vouchers, he took them shopping. He bought a good coat for William and a long golden-brown woollen shawl for Mary.

The next morning at breakfast, Mary blushed every time she looked at William, who grinned back as though he had won the lottery.

Amused at their innocence, he broke into their reverie. 'I have a gift for you to help you on the journey and make a start in Liverpool.' He passed a leather pouch to William. 'There's ten guineas in gold. Now, you must swear *never* to tell *anyone* of my involvement.'

'Mr Holmes, sir, I dinna ken what to say. You have my word,' William answered, staring dumbfounded at the pouch in his hand.

'Oh sur, I canna believe it. Yes! Yes, I swear,' Mary agreed, astonished at their good fortune, her eyes brimming with tears.

'Good, then it is *our* secret. Now let us be on our way.'

Four hours after the coach left, Mark lodged John Bishop's complaint with the Sherriff. He collected Lucky from the stables and rode toward Scotch Gate and the road to Longtown. Reaching the gate, he spotted young James, obviously drunk, with a prostitute holding him upright.

Mark shook his head. 'Nothing to be done there.'

He rode through the gate, over the wooden Eden and Priest Beck bridges, past the Guard House and let Lucky stretch himself for a mile before pulling over. Mark let him cool off, then led him to a small coppice and went home.

'How was it? Did you find out if you and Penelope are related?' Pauline asked, after he shut off the Portal.

'Oh yes! Have I got something to show you? First I need a long hot shower, clean clothes and hot breakfast with *lots* of coffee. I never want ale for breakfast ever again.'

Later Mark listened to Penny recount how she had spent the morning with her pony, Magic, riding in the paddock trailed by Nicholas. She was growing in to a very inquisitive child with a rapidly growing vocabulary, and he noticed Penelope's influence in her formal and correct way of speaking. When Melanie came to take her to her lessons, Mark went to the study where he downloaded the videos. While Pauline watched them, Mark drafted a much more detailed, and complex, family tree.

'So Penelope *is* your great-great something aunt, this is so weird. I can't wait to see her face when she's sees all her relatives.'

'Yeah. She really is Aunty Penny. Anyway, the last three discs are the interesting ones.'

She glared at him, suspicious of his apparent innocent demeanour. 'Why? What's on them?'

'It's getting late. We can finish them tomorrow,' Mark replied.

'Oh no you don't. You'll either tell me what's on those videos or we'll sit here all night watching them.'

He chuckled and started the next video, while Pauline fumed. 'You really *don't* have any patience, do you?'

'Oh... my... God! You helped them elope,' she yelled, after watching the scene in the woods.

'Not really,' he mumbled, looking uncomfortable. 'They'd already eloped. We knew they made it to Liverpool, I just... made it a bit easier that's all.'

'What a load of... That's pure sophistry.'

'What was I supposed to do?' he pleaded. 'They hadn't a clue!'

A few minutes later, 'You had a cheek telling Anne they'd be alright.'

'I had to tell her *something*, the poor woman was at her wit's end.'

'That's another thing,' she glared fiercely at him. 'How could you tell John you would deliver his complaint to the Sherriff?'

'I didn't say *when*.'

'You're *so* damn sneaky. What other help did you give them? Come on, own up. I know that look, you're hiding something.'

'It's all on the videos, but there's a couple more hours and it's eleven o'clock already.'

'You're not putting this off.'

She played the next video and the arrival of William and Mary at the inn.

'Oh Mark!' she said with tears in her eyes when she heard him tell Mary about his life before and after meeting Pauline. 'I don't know what to say.'

She pounced on him and proved the saying 'actions speak

louder than words'.

'How about 'let's go to bed?' It's midnight already.' Mark croaked, catching his breath

'Stop it. No bed for you until I've seen them all.'

After watching him embarrass Mary arranging their private room, she stared at Mark as he bought their coach tickets and took them shopping. She chuckled as she watched the last video of them over breakfast the next day. 'Looks like they enjoyed their wedding night.'

A few moments later she gasped, 'You gave them how much?'

'I tell you, they were clueless. If they'd tried to walk to Liverpool, God knows what would have happened,' he protested.

'So *you* were the reason they made a life for themselves in Liverpool.'

'What could I do? We know it happened, all I did was... facilitate a little bit.'

She smiled sweetly at him. 'You are just a big sentimental softie,' and chuckled. 'I don't know what Penelope is going to say when she sees this. She's going to flip, I still feel sorry for Anne, she never knew her daughter was safe and sound and had a good life,' Pauline said, wistfully.

'I've been thinking about that.'

'What are you planning now?' she said, distrustful of the look on his face.

'Well, if I popped back for a day to let her know Mary was happily married and about the twins she gave birth to, it would give her some peace of mind.'

'You're hopeless! I never knew you were such a romantic.'

'If we ever get to bed, I'll show you how romantic I can be.'

Later Pauline showed him how she made his life worth living

and Mark showed her more passion than romance, but she was not complaining.

He rode up to the Bishop's farm—this time it was September, 1769. He called out and Anne came to the door. She had aged in the two years since his last visit.

'It's Mr Holmes, ain't it?' she said, startled at seeing him again. 'Well this is a surprise. Wha' brings yer back around 'ere agen?'

'Good day, Mrs Bishop. I am staying with a friend in Bewcastle and came to visit as I was nearby.'

'Please come in, m' husband and son are at the cattle fair in Carlisle, but they'll be back in a few hours. You'll be staying the night?'

'My apologies, I have to be back by nightfall. I came to pass on news of your daughter.'

'Mary? My li'l girl? What's 'appened to her?' she asked, going pale.

'Please, Mrs Bishop, there is nothing to fear. She is well, happily married to William and living in Lancashire, and a few months ago gave birth to twins; a boy, Christopher and a girl who she named Anne after you.'

'Oh Mr Holmes, that's wonderful news.' Tears of joy cascaded down her beaming face. 'Thank you, thank you so much. My husband will not allow 'er name t' be spoke in 'house, and I've been ever so worried.'

'I felt it only right you should know.'

He spent the next half-hour reassuring her Mary and William were really alright. He also learned James had never been home since the night his father had beaten him and the Sherriff was looking for him for poaching and horse stealing; John senior had turned into a hard and taciturn man.

'I must be off now. I am glad to have had this opportunity to bring this news.'

'Mr Holmes, God bless you. I miss her and pray for her every day. You have made an old woman verra happy, Thank you.'

Shortly, after a tearful farewell, Mark headed along the road and home to Pauline.

Over the following week, he finished the family tree and prepared two sets printed on large heavy-weight paper; both showed photographs of the people he had met, their homes and inset maps of where they lived. Mark then edited the videos onto four, three-hour DVDs.

Penelope had spent the last two days with a study group in York. The next morning when she parked her car, Penny pounced.

'Aunty Penny, Aunty Penny, look what I can do?' she yelled and promptly started turning clumsy cartwheels, whooping each time she was upside-down. Penelope had been trying hard to teach her to be a proper lady, obviously with little success. Mark and Pauline came out to see what the ruckus was and saw Penny hugging Penelope who was saying, 'Penelope that is *not* the proper behaviour for a young lady.'

'I don't want to be a lady. I want to be like Mummy.'

Mark's loud guffaw earning him a bruised arm from his wife.

TP 1000: The Bishops

After unpacking, Penelope went in search of Tony and was not seen again until evening. Penny usually had impeccable table manners thanks to Penelope's efforts, however, in her excitement she chattered all through dinner recounting every minute detail of what had happened around the farm while Penelope had been away. Once Penny was in bed, Mark and Pauline discussed how best to tell Penelope about her family.

Chapter 21

Friday, 1ˢᵗ May 2010

Before Penelope went to hunt for Tony, Pauline led her to the study saying they had a surprise for her.

Mark handed her a large roll of paper. 'Penelope, I've made this for you.'

Unrolling the extensive genealogical table, she looked confused, 'But this is your family tree.'

'And *yours*... you're my three-time great-aunt.'

She stared at Mark with a look of shock and bewilderment.

'Remember when you told me about your great-grandmother, I suspected she was my six-time great-aunt Mary, so I went back to 1767 to find out. Look at this,' he pointed to a photograph of Mary.

'That's my great grandmama! She's younger here, but her eyes, her smile; they are exactly as I remember.'

'Here's another surprise,' Pauline told her switching on the TV.

Penelope sat mesmerised as she 'met' both her Wright and

Bishop ancestors. When the video finished she sat in stunned silence, tears scoring her make-up.

'The next two are all of Anne's relatives, but I think you should watch the last one first.'

'Are you alright, Penelope?' Pauline asked, worried at Penelope's expression.

'Oh, oh yes! That was wonderful. Thank you, thank you,' she replied, smiling through her tears.

'Are you ready for the next one?' Mark asked, gently

'Yes! Yes, please.'

When she saw William and Mary being confronted by Mark in the woods and heard his offer to help them, tears spilled down her face. She sobbed when she heard Anne's plaintive plea not to report them. She smiled watching Mary and William having breakfast and Mary's embarrassment when Mark booked them a private room, and her face lit up with joy when she heard Mark's offer of booking a coach and paying their passage.

'That's the shawl she always wore!' she exclaimed watching Mary try the shawl on in the shop. 'I never saw her without it. She would stroke it all the time with a secret smile and great-grandpapa William would look at her with the same smile.'

She gasped when Mark gave William the purse of sovereigns and heard them both promise to keep everything secret. She turned to Mark and gave him a huge hug and a kiss. 'Mr Bishop... Mark, I do not have the words to thank you. Without your aid they may have never have arrived safely in Liverpool. They kept their oath, you know. No-one in the family ever heard the full story, nor why the shawl was so special to her, and now *I* know.'

She hugged and kissed him again, then turned to Pauline. They clung to each other, both of them crying. Mark's eye glistened and he paused the DVD player.

'Can I call you 'Aunty Penny'?' Mark asked, making both

women laugh so much they collapsed on the couch. 'There's a little more, and I think you'll really want to watch the last part.'

Penelope was silent when she saw her great-uncle James with the prostitute and then stunned as the video jumped to Anne greeting Mark on his second visit. More tears escaped when she heard Anne bless Mark, and her lips quivered when she heard Anne's husband would not mention his daughter's name and the Sherriff had a warrant out for James' arrest. At the end, her face broke out in to a brilliant smile and looked at Mark and Pauline.

'I am glad she knew they were alright, I only wish great-grandmama knew how happy her mother was for her.'

'Do you know where they lived in 1770? I could always go back and let her know,' Mark offered.

'I know where they lived when we visited, but they sold the shop in 1815 and no-one said where it was,' she replied.

'Do you know William's friend's name or where he had his shop?'

'No. I don't, I'm sorry.'

'Well I can't go back to the 1820s. I'm only a couple of months older, but it'll be over fifty years for them and I can't afford to risk meeting you there either, can I?'

'I understand,' she replied mournfully. 'But I thank you and may God bless you for helping them and making her mother happy. I do not know how I will ever be able to repay you. If not for you... I may never have been born,' she cried, and hugged him tightly.

He downloaded all the original videos to Penelope's laptop so she could watch them whenever she wanted. When he finished, they heard Penny plonking away on the piano.

Mark looked towards the door a moment, then turned to Penelope. 'Aunty Penny, looks like your great-great whatever niece needs a few more lessons!'

Mark showed Penelope the family Bible and pointed out her great-grandmother's name.

Wanting to give Penelope some closure, he researched clockmakers and shops in Liverpool, the first census in 1801 giving him several names to follow-up on, but when he went to Liverpool in 1770 he found no-one who knew William Wright. He made several visits, but, with a population of thirty-four thousand and growing rapidly, he never did find William's shop.

In order to catalogue everything for the museum opening, Pauline and Penelope interviewed candidates for the curator post. They both agreed on Andrea Jensen, a tall, attractive, athletic—looking woman with impressive qualifications and experience at private museums in Europe. Penelope was especially fascinated by her depth of knowledge of the Victorian era. She was willing to relocate and Pauline helped her find a two-bedroom caravan to rent near Leyburn.

Construction on the farm shop was well underway thanks to Mark offering a generous bonus for completion by the end of July. As the date neared, Chris worked well in to the night tending his new crops of fruit and vegetables which were to be sold in the shop. Mark decided it was time Chris had an assistant and, with his help, placed advertisements in newspapers and appropriate journals.

'Chris, where are we on the assistant for the lab and greenhouses?' Mark asked when he and Pauline went to visit the greenhouse.

Chris shuffled his feet and looked anywhere but at Pauline. 'We have a few candidates, but the best is a woman.'

'And that is a problem?' Pauline asked, tartly. She knew Chris' shyness around women; he still tended to stammer when around herself or Penelope.

'No... not... not at all,' he stammered, alarmed at her tone. 'There are three bedrooms in the cottage, she could stay in the one with the attached bathroom, Tony and I can share the other one. It's just there's a lot of heavy work sometimes, not sure whether she can cope, that's all.'

'Well, interview them and make sure you're clear on the work involved. Show them around the greenhouses, lab *and* the cottage, so there's no doubt what's expected.'

Naomi Griffiths, Chris' assistant showed up at the farm in a twenty-year-old *Morris Minor*. A petite young woman, with light-brown hair and hazel eyes, she was eager to start her new job. Chris and Tony helped move her luggage to her room before taking her on a tour of the farm. Although interested in the environmental developments, she was fascinated by the laboratory and plans for the greenhouse. Chris overcame his bashfulness when Naomi described experiments she had performed using a mix of red and blue light to increase growth rate with markedly reduced power consumption. When Pauline went to invite Naomi to dinner she found her in the greenhouse. She and Chris, who was showing no signs of his usual self-consciousness, were absorbed in calculating how many LED lights they needed and barely acknowledged her presence.

Once Penelope's exams finished, Mark suggested they all have a break and take Tony on his first trip to Houghton House. At the weekend they gathered at the byre and Mark opened a gateway.

At Houghton House, John met them and carried their luggage to their rooms.

'Mrs Compton, this gentleman is Mr Anthony Matthews, Miss Wright's fiancé. He will be staying with us for a while,' Pauline explained.

'Certainly, ma'am. Elsie will have Mr Matthew's room ready in a little while.'

After settling in, Mark took Tony on a tour of the house and grounds. 'Some of the wildflowers around here are rare and endangered back home—corn buttercups, wild cornflower and Shepherd's-needle. We can take some back, but I can't have them keep popping up around the farm every time.'

'Put them in the greenhouse. Once they're thriving we can introduce them to their natural habitats all over Britain,' Tony suggested.

With the men outside, Penelope and Pauline closeted themselves in the parlour.

'How could you say Anthony is my fiancé?' Penelope wailed.

'We have to explain why he's here, and if anyone sees you two together, it will be a satisfactory explanation. Now stop worrying and go along with it.'

Mark took Tony to Chesterfield and Sheffield to collect more items for the museum and a trip to the Peak District secured two more endangered plants. 'A lot of endangered plants are not from around here. We will have to make separate trips later to collect them,' Mark told him.

Pauline took up her social activities again, visiting and being visited by the ladies she knew, especially those wanting to know more about Tony. After the latest visitors had left, Penelope voiced a concern to Pauline. 'This is very difficult for me. I do not like lying and Anthony has not mentioned anything about marriage at all.'

'I'm sure he will before much longer. Now stop worrying, will you?'

Tony and Penelope managed to find some time alone when he suggested they go shopping in Chesterfield, but Penelope asked to visit Baslow instead. They stopped in a secluded wooded area after the Robin Hood Inn. In the heat of their passion she let her inhibitions slip and allowed Tony to unfasten the front of her dress and kiss the prizes he found. When they returned a few hours later, Pauline noticed her hair was not its usual tidy self.

'What were you two doing for so long?' she asked, smiling.

The resultant bright glow on Penelope's cheeks caused her to laugh. 'What *were* you doing?'

When Penelope explained what had happened, Pauline was shocked.

'You mean you let him... Penelope, are you sure about this? Your upbringing... and... everything?'

In a prim and proper tone, despite her blazing cheeks she said, 'Oh yes. But we will wait until our wedding night for consummation.'

Pauline proceeded to have a detailed 'birds and bees' chat with Penelope.

'That's enough for now,' she declared. She was embarrassed at having to give such intimate advice to an adult; she had not expected to have this type of conversation until Penny was much older.

Pauline changed the subject to a problem that had been bothering her. 'Now you live in the Twenty-First Century I'm sure you do not want to return here.'

'I could not live here again, and I have to stay at the farm to be with Anthony.'

They decided to tell the staff Penelope would not be returning and worked out a plan to train Elsie as her replacement.

When Pauline told Elsie, she was delighted, especially with an increase in wages to twenty-five pounds per year. Pauline intended Elsie fit into her new role as soon as possible and she and Penelope started to teach her the proper etiquette when visiting gentry. Finding she had only the rudiments of reading and writing, Penelope enforced a strict regime to improve her literary skills, using the newspaper to not only improve her reading but also bring her up to date on what was happening in the world outside Houghton House. When Pauline took her to Chesterfield and bought her appropriate clothes, Elsie thought she was in Heaven. It was the first time she had ever had new clothes which were not livery.

Pauline also taught Elsie basic first aid such as handling simple strains and sprains, scalds, small cuts and wounds. Since Penelope was all too busy with Tony, Elsie followed Pauline when she visited her friends' homes and gradually adjusted to her new role.

In November, Elsie had the opportunity to apply her newly gained knowledge. The Barker sisters visited Pauline on returning from the 'season' in London. Amelia, although now twenty years old, was still her flighty and exuberant self. Demonstrating some recently learned dance steps, she slipped and fell. Elsie sprang in to action; she had the swollen ankle wrapped with an ice-pack and the leg elevated and when the swelling subsided, she bandaged it so it would bear her weight. Her sister Florence thanked Elsie profusely and a few days later Lady Barker expressed her thanks with a beautiful piece of printed cotton, enough to make a dress for her day off.

A week before Christmas, Mark told the staff they planned a trip to York to meet Tony's family and would return at the end of January.

As soon as the gateway opened, Tony and Penelope rushed through to put the new plants in the greenhouse. Once alone, Pauline told Mark about her little 'chat' with Penelope.

'Tony's not the only one who'll be interested in the results of that conversation. You can show me tonight, in detail.'

The next day, Mark and Tony installed the Kitchener stove and the complex network of flues and chimneys controlling the heat to the different parts of the range. Mark had obtained a permit to use a coal-fired oven and a fireplace in the parlour by installing scrubbers to remove all the pollutants. Andrea had already dressed the mannequins and Penelope helped her arrange the display cabinets of honey-coloured Brampton pottery, Georgian and Victorian tableware.

Once Mark and Tony finished with the stove, Penelope

mercilessly directed them to organise the kitchen and drawing room furniture.

'God! My back is killing me.' Tony told Mark. 'Doesn't she ever take a break?'

'Get used to it. Once she starts on one her passions, there's no letting up. You've seen what's she's like with her studies.'

That weekend, Julie drove over and presented some marketing ideas. She had photo-shopped the Paulinas onto mugs, and showed them preserved in acrylic, all with the farm name written underneath.

'These are brilliant! I was wondering about the whole marketing aspect and you've just solved it!' Mark told Julie. 'We can register this as our logo and have it on all our products.'
'What made you think of it?' Pauline asked.

'There were so many people asking about the wedding bouquets, it just made sense.'

Mark shamelessly called in favours. Several newspaper articles and an on-site interview with the local TV channel ensured the museum and farm shop opened with a fanfare. The Paulinas brand jams and condiments, honey, ice cream and yoghurt sold quickly and the fresh strawberries and vegetables from Chris' greenhouses also proved popular. Chris had grown more of the Paulinas orchids and could hardly keep up with the demand. Even Hugh, Julie's fiancé, had got in on the act and his postcards of scenes around the farm sold as quickly as the mugs. Before the end of summer they were having visitors from all over Yorkshire.

Penelope's cooking demonstrations and handouts of typical Victorian recipes were a great success and attracted a lot of paying participants as well as free advertising from local newspaper articles. Among the many visitors were a group from York University. The professor in charge of the group, Dr. Susan Smith, had seen Mark's interview on television and brought ten of her first year archaeology students. She was astounded by the range of artefacts displayed and amazed at the authenticity of the kitchen and parlour. Penelope stunned the students when she changed into Victorian period costume and cooked a meal of mock turtle soup, roast duck with baked potatoes and vegetables followed by Marlborough pudding using Paulinas strawberry jam and apple sauce. All the time she prepared and cooked the meal, she gave a detailed explanation of the various utensils used and on display.

Penelope's A-level results provided another excuse for a party. She had scored A-star or A in everything except for a B in General Studies. Penelope was, however, disappointed. She had hoped for A's in all her subjects. Tony, persuaded her, with a little coaxing and a lot of kisses, the results were still fantastic and to make her day complete, he proposed.

He figured he had better do it before she started studying again, and since everyone was gathered together, this was as good a time as any. He went on one knee and simply asked, 'Penelope Wright, will you marry me?'

She nodded and whispered 'Yes' to great applause and an 'About time!' from Mark. Their lips were locked together for so long Pauline had to pry them apart so everyone could congratulate them.

Although she already owned a two-bedroom house in Leyburn, Penelope wanted a larger place to live when she married. She had collected several more Penny Blacks and Twopenny Blues and when they went for auction, they realised more than enough to build her own house. She asked Mark if she could build it on the farm. Pauline thought it a great idea but Mark protested at her insistence on buying the land. Penelope was adamant and said it would be *her* home and *she* would pay for it... and the land, firmly silencing any further objections. Pauline was pleased she had assimilated so well, although Mark grumbled about bossy women.

When she turned to Tony and told him she wanted to build a Tudor style five-bedroom house, he was flabbergasted.

'*Five* bedrooms! There's only two of us.'

'After we are married, there will be more than two of us,' she answered, her face glowing like a scarlet sunset. Despite having lived in the Twenty-First Century for one-and-a-half years, her face still turned varied shades of red whenever discussions bordered on sexual matters.

A few days later Penelope received an unconditional offer for a place at York University. A separate letter from Dr Smith said she was looking forward to having Penelope on the course.

Once school started, except for weekends, visitors to the farm declined. Chris' fresh vegetables and fruit continued to be snapped up, and their half-litre tubs of 'velvet-smooth strawberry ice cream' were their best seller. The cool wet October weather meant everyone could relax and they decided to close the shop and museum Mondays and Thursdays for cleaning.

Mark and Pauline reckoned it was time for a final trip to Houghton House. They concocted a story about Mark's father and brother having died and Mark needing to return to Dover to run the small family estate and business. At the end of October, the wagon fully loaded with merchandise, Mark activated the Portal and drove to Houghton House.

Mark no sooner settled his accounts than he travelled to London for the final Penny Black plate—plate eleven, the rarest of them all. On fourth of February, 1841, he bought sixty stamps, posted letters and two days later was back in Chesterfield. He and Pauline celebrated the last Penny Blacks as they had celebrated the first—noisily and with exuberance.

Mr Marshall was shocked when Mark related his reason for leaving and offered his sincere condolences. He reminded Mark he had a Midsummer Lease and since it was past Christmas he could not give the customary six months' notice so Mark agreed to pay an additional six months' rent to Mrs Houghton. He asked the clerk to inform his customers he was leaving and would be selling his merchandise to the highest bidders.

The servants were in shock. Mark and Pauline tried to assuage their worries saying they would provide excellent references and a generous bonus before they left. Mark estimated by the time he sold all his merchandise, with the money he already had in the bank, he would have at least ten thousand pounds. Even after giving each of the servants a generous bonus Mark would still have over seven thousand pounds to spend on the museum and for future visits. Pauline still worried what their departure would mean to the staff. She had come to know each of them so well and was determined to find good openings for them if any wanted to leave.

Sir Reginald and Lady Barker, and Sir Paul visited as soon they heard of Mark's planned departure. Lady Barker, with Pauline's permission, asked Elsie if she would be Amelia and Florence's lady's maid. Amelia had a grown very fond of Elsie, and her sister had been telling everyone how she was such a marvel.

'Addicted' was a fair description of how Sir Paul felt about Mrs Humphries' Asian cooking and solved another of Pauline's worries when he came to a generous agreement with Mrs Humphries to work for him.

'I want to give each of the staff something personal, not just money,' Pauline told Mark.

A trip to Chesterfield bought silver pocket watches for the men and silver-mounted cameo brooches for the women. Pauline had brought large jars of moisturizing creams for the maids and kitchen staff and a wide selection of spices for Mrs Humphries. For John and Alfred, Mark took two bottles of his finest brandy for each of them from his warehouse. The four pots of Paulinas' orchids would delight Robert and ensure the envy of other gardeners.

Before their departure, Mark wrapped all his stamps and journals in waxed cotton and packed them in brass boxes. He sealed the boxes with wax and placed them in a sealed steel chest lined with oilskin and tightly packed with newspapers. He then wrapped the chest with canvas and oilskin as before.

At the byre, everything was unchanged. He pried up the flagstones in the north-east corner with a crowbar and started digging. Using a tripod, made from the timber lying around, he lowered the chest in to the four-foot deep hole he had dug. He replaced the flagstones, covered them with debris and returned to Houghton House.

Two days before they left, Mark handed out the bonuses. Everyone was overwhelmed—none of them had ever dreamt of having so much money and could not believe their good fortune. When Mark and Pauline distributed the personal gifts it was too much for some of the staff, and many a 'God Bless you m'am, sir' was said with tearful faces.

As she helped Pauline complete her packing the next day, Elsie could not stop weeping.

'I'm going to miss you, ma'am, I really will. If it weren't for you, I'd still be a housemaid,' she sobbed.

'Thank you, Elsie, I will miss you also. But I'm sure you will be happy with the Barkers'. They are nice girls and the whole family is fond of you.'

'I know, ma'am, but it won't be the same.' She rushed out as Mark came in.

'What's the matter with Elsie?'

'She's upset about our leaving, and I'm not doing so great either,' Pauline replied.

'Same with Robert, and the lads over at the stable,' he replied. 'It's to be expected, I suppose. Still we'll be gone by tomorrow and can get back to our normal lives again.'

'I suppose so.'

'Well I can think of something to take your mind off things,' he whispered in her ear as he leaned against her back and kneaded her breasts.

'You can wait until tonight. Elsie will be back soon and won't that be a sight for her to remember us by?'

That night, they forgot all about leaving as they made love, repeatedly, for the last time at Houghton House, not sleeping until early Saturday morning.

As Elsie was helping her dress the next morning, Pauline gave her the rest of her dresses and her 'Household Products and Remedies' book. Elsie started crying all over again.

After a sombre breakfast, Mark and Pauline drove off to more weeping and mournful cries of 'God Bless, ma'am', 'God Bless you sir' and 'Safe journey'.

Pauline joined the watery farewell. All the servants stood at the main gate and waved until the wagon was a mile down the road and out of sight.

Still snuffling, Pauline let Mark lead her back to the farmhouse.

After a shower and a quick breakfast, they sat in Mark's office and figured out a plan to 'find' the steel box, this time with witnesses.

'We already use the byre as a resting stop, how about we take it one step further and turn it into a proper refreshment stop?' Pauline suggested.

Mark agreed. 'That'll give me the excuse to dig up the flagstones to install drainage for sinks and so-on.'

Chapter 22

Monday, 1st November 2010

Monday morning, Mark called his architect, Charles Henderson, and arranged for him to come over the next day with his building contractor to inspect the byre. Mark showed them where he wanted to put in a bar counter to serve drinks, and the location of a sink in the south-east corner.

Richard Stone, the contractor studied the ground. 'It shouldn't be too difficult. The ground underneath may be rock hard but that's not a problem.'

Mark grabbed a crowbar. 'Let's see,' He raised the flagstones and Richard took the crowbar and poked at the ground to break it up and dug until he hit metal.

'Sounds like summat's buried down there.'

Mark tried to appear calm as he cleared the earth to expose dark grey canvas. 'Give me a hand and let's get this out.'

Once it was up, they all clustered around.

'Looks like it's been buried for ages. Wonder what's inside?'

TP 1000: The Bishops

Charles said.

'This needs doing properly. Help me take it back to the house,' Mark asked, and Richard helped him load the box onto the utility vehicle.

'Is it okay?' Pauline whispered, as she saw them carrying the box.

'Looks alright; we'll take it to my study and have a look.'

Mark's fingers trembled as he cut the twine and carefully unwrapped the cracked canvas and oilskin in his safe room. He pried the rusty chest open and took out the newspaper packing.

Charles saw the date. 'Bloody Hell! Twentieth of February, 1841.'

Mark unwrapped the stained cotton and took out the two corroded brass boxes.

Charles' and Richard's eyes looked ready to pop out. Mark scraped the wax off one box and unwrapped the bundles of journals. The leather bindings were slightly discoloured and the edges of the pages exhibited some foxing.

'What're them? Look like some sort o' diaries or summat,' Richard offered.

'They're likely journals, I'd guess,' Mark replied. 'Let's see what's in the other box.'

Mark took more care with the second box. He slowly unwrapped the cotton to expose the stamps and covers to find them just as he had left them a hundred and seventy years—or two weeks ago, whichever way you wanted to look at it.

'Let me photograph all this,' Mark told the two men

'What you reckon it's all worth, then?' Charles asked.

'No idea, some of those stamps may be expensive, but until I get an expert out here, there's no telling.'

Pauline was amazed at how her husband kept a straight face; he would have made a great actor, or con artist!

After extensive paper and ink analysis of the documents and envelopes, along with the witness statements and the dates on the newspapers, Mark's 'find' was authenticated. Experts now started arguing over its value. The lowest estimate Mark heard was 'in excess of twenty million pounds'. The historical value of the journals was priceless. They filled in many gaps in historians' knowledge of the early 1840s. Mark and Pauline scanned and posted them on the internet for anyone to read, providing invaluable research material.

Morning sickness struck two weeks after they returned and a check-up confirmed Pauline was pregnant again—Penny's third birthday was a cause for dual celebration.

They closed the shop for Christmas and New Year and Tony went to visit his parents. Andrea took the opportunity to do stocktaking and change some of the exhibits. Mark and Pauline arrived as she finished rearranging the collection of Georgian silverware and had started checking all the utensils in the kitchen.

'Hi Andrea, how're things going?' Pauline asked brightly, as she and Mark walked into the museum kitchen.

'Fine, Mrs Bishop, I am checking all the utensils. These knives need sharpening and the egg whisk gears are getting worn, but we have another in the store. The chimney needs cleaning also.'

Busy examining the utensils and deciding when to call the local chimney sweep, they did not notice a bearded man enter until he shoved Mark to the floor.

He stabbed Pauline and screamed, 'Take that, you bitch. You ruined everything.'

Before Mark could move, Andrea leapt past him, her movements a blur. By the time he managed to stand up, the attacker was unconscious on the ground and Andrea was standing over him talking on her phone.

A man and woman rushed in... the woman cut away Pauline's blouse and placed a patch across the heavily bleeding wound. She attached blue discs to Pauline's chest, temples and around the patch and looked at what appeared to be a large iPhone. She turned to the man standing next to her. 'Hans, there is kidney and spleen damage with internal haemorrhaging. Pulse one-fifty, racing, blood pressure eighty-over-fifty. We need to get her to a treatment centre immediately.'

Mark reached for his phone. 'I'll call an ambulance.'

He heard a hissing sound, looked up and saw the woman pressing a tube to Pauline's neck; her body went completely slack.

'What are you doing?' he yelled.

He tried to jump at the woman but was held tightly by Andrea. Mark, ninety kilos and fit from farm work and Taekwondo, could hardly move; Andrea was holding him as if he was a little boy.

A white-walled room with a group of people dressed in white wearing surgical masks appeared in the air. He froze—it was a gateway. *Who were these people?*

The woman who had injected Pauline turned to him, 'Do not worry; it's a 'Deepsleep' shot. It will slow her bodily functions and minimise the blood loss.'

'Nikita, let him go and carry her while Talia monitors,' the man called Hans ordered. 'Quickly now before anyone comes.' He turned to the man standing in the doorway. 'Sven, clean up after we've gone.'

Mark, numbed by what was happening, watched Andrea, Nikita, or whatever her name was, effortlessly lift Pauline and carry her through the gateway.

Hans took Mark's arm. 'Mr Bishop, quickly, your wife needs immediate treatment. She will never make it to one of your hospitals.'

Mark felt the familiar resistance as he followed and heard Talia explaining the extent of the injuries as they took her away on a medical trolley.

'Where are they taking her?' His distress over Pauline masked his astonishment at the turn of events.

'Not to worry, Mr Bishop,' Hans answered. 'They are taking her to the operating and treatment room. Come with me and you can see for yourself.'

Mark sat in an observation room and watched the medical team attach a drip and work on her wound and using those strange tubes several times. Four hours later, they wheeled her out and the man who had operated on his wife came in.

'Is she going to be alright?'

'Mr Bishop, I'm Doctor Harrison. Everything went perfectly. She and the twins are well. She is in the recovery room and will probably wake in thirty minutes,' he assured Mark and pointed to Hans. 'Major Walker will take you to her.'

Mark followed Hans, his mind a haze. *Twins?*

Mark sat at Pauline's bedside watching a nurse adjust her drip.

'Your wife will be awake soon and I will remove the drip. Is there anything I can get you? A drink perhaps?'

'No. No thank you. Are you sure she'll be alright?'

'All the injuries have been repaired and the lost blood has been replaced. She should be completely healed by tomorrow.'

'What?' he exclaimed. 'She was stabbed just a few hours ago.'

'Mr Bishop, this facility is the most advanced there is, believe me. See, she's starting to wake already. Major Walker, can you call the doctor, please?"

Mark stared as Pauline slowly awoke and stretch like a cat, as she did every morning.

'Darling, sweetheart, how do you feel?'

'Fine. Where am I?' she asked, looking around the room.

Before Mark could answer, the surgeon came in. 'Good afternoon Mrs Bishop, I'm Doctor Harrison. How are you feeling?'

'Pretty good actually. What happened?'

'Some guy stabbed you in the museum,' Mark said.

She clasped her hands to her stomach 'The baby! Is he alright?'

'Honey, that's *babies*. The doctor said you are carrying twins, and they are fine.'

'Twins!' she yelled and sat up.

'Yes, that's correct,' the doctor confirmed as he entered the room. 'But please, don't worry. Although your injuries were extensive, you and the babies are going to be alright. We had to bring you here for immediate treatment, you would not have made it to one of your hospitals.'

'What do you mean, 'One of my hospitals'? Where am I?'

'You are in the Medical Wing of the Temporal Research Headquarters.'

Pauline looked frantically at her husband. 'Tempus! Mark, what's going on? How did we get here?'

'It's okay, darling. I was shocked at first, but all I know, or care about, is that these people brought you here and saved your life.'

'After we stopped the bleeding and repaired the injuries, we administered a full Treatment to accelerate recovery,' the doctor told her.

'This Treatment, what is it?' Pauline asked, sharply.

'Essentially stem cell treatment, mitochondrial regeneration and adjustment to telomerase levels to counteract the shortening effect of cell replication on your telomeres, along with complete detoxification of your major organs,' Dr. Harrison explained. 'Besides accelerating the healing process and nerve regeneration, there are other beneficial effects. You will find you have greater strength, agility and improved reflexes in addition to virtual immunity from nearly all diseases, physical and neurological. You will see the full effects in about two weeks.'

Mark and Pauline gawked at each other.

'What about my babies? Will this affect them?' she asked.

'On the contrary,' he reassured her. 'In fact, it will boost their immune system tremendously giving them better protection against illnesses and allergies.'

'The Treatment you mentioned, is it the same as the Longevity Treatment?' Mark asked

'Yes, it is. How did you know?'

'So my wife has a much longer life expectancy now?' he asked, ignoring the question.

'Yes, in fact her biological age will be about twenty. She should live another eighty or ninety years barring accidents. More with booster treatments.'

Pauline's head shot up at hearing this. She stared open-mouthed then, her voice a whisper. 'You mean I could live to be a hundred and twenty years old?'

'That is correct.'

Pauline looked distressed. 'What about Mark?'

'Mrs Bishop, in view of our 'interference' in your natural life-span, I have been authorised to offer the Treatment to your husband.'

Mark turned to the doctor. 'When will you perform this Treatment?'

'We have scheduled it for the day after tomorrow. In the meantime, I will arrange your transfer to an apartment we have prepared for you.'

Pauline looked thoughtful. 'You said the full effects of this Treatment will kick-in in two weeks. Can you delay Mark's Treatment until then?'

'Whatever for?'

Mark, the nurse and doctor looked stunned.

'Weeell, you said I'd be much stronger and agile then. It'll be fun to be able to handle him like a baby for a while.'

Her mischievous look, caused a burst of laughter from everyone, especially Mark.

Pauline gasped when she walked in to the apartment. 'Andrea! Are you from Tempus as well?'

'She was the one who laid out the guy who tried to kill you. She also held me like I was a ninety-pound weakling while they treated you.'

'Mr Bishop, I apologise, but we needed to treat your wife as quickly as possible.'

'I'm not complaining, believe me. I'm glad you were there. But I would like to know *why* you and the others were there in the first place.' Mark's frustration and anger now overcame his initial shock and horror at the attack and finding himself at Tempus headquarters.

'Mr Bishop, Director Grogan will be here soon and will explain everything.'

The apartment was simply furnished with fitted cupboards on one wall, a large bed, table and chairs, and a couch by a large picture window showing a magnificent view of mountains and a lush tropical plain below. What appeared to be wardrobes or cupboards turned out to be doors to small cubicles. Nikita pushed on one and it folded back to reveal a small shelf and unfamiliar equipment. 'Would you care for something to eat or drink?'

'Yes, thank you,' replied Pauline, staring at this new space.

'Let me order for you.'

She pressed a touchpad screen and fifteen minutes later a musical chime sounded and Nikita removed two meals from a hatch. Large sirloin steaks, baked potatoes and steamed vegetables, a bowl of salad with blue cheese sauce and glasses of fruit juice. Pauline dived into her meal. Mark was amazed how she showed no discomfort. A few hours ago, she had been bleeding all over the museum floor.

The doorbell chimed and two men entered. One was an elderly Indian gentleman dressed in an Indian *Sherwani*, a dark blue knee-length jacket buttoned up to the *Nehru* collar. The other, fine featured with dark olive skin, wore a plain grey uniform.

'Mr and Mrs Bishop, I am Dr Anit Grogan, the Director of this facility,' said the older one. 'And this is Security Director, Colonel Ohuru I am sure you are very confused at the moment, but I will try to answer as many questions as I can.'

'Dr. Grogan, I know we're at Tempus and came here through a gateway, but what I want to know is why all your people were at my farm,' Mark said. 'Don't get me wrong, I'll be eternally grateful they were there, but *why* were they there in the first place?'

Shock was written all over Grogan's face. 'You know about gateways?'

'Yes, we do. But I want to know why your people were crawling all over my farm. I saw four of them—one even on my payroll,' he replied, looking at Nikita.

'Please, Mr Bishop, tell me how you learned about Portals and gateways? I'll answer any questions I can.'

Mark looked at Pauline, who nodded. 'Okay, fair enough. But let's start with what date this is?'

'Wednesday, fifteenth of May, 2535.'

After recovering from the shock of finding himself over five hundred years in the future, he related how he had found the

TP1000 and Nicolas' journals. He explained how Nicholas had died, and then told Grogan they had used it to travel to the 1840s for their own research.

'You said the name of the person who wrote those journals was Nicholas. Do you know his full name?'

'Nicholas Olafson.'

'Mr Bishop, thank you. We have been looking for him for over ten years.'

'How come you did not track the Portal opening before we screened it?' Mark asked.

'Yeah, like that other 'son-of-a-bitch' did.' Pauline added.

Grogan's eyes widened. 'You mean to say someone managed to track the Time Portal?'

'Yeah, about two years ago. He said he could detect each time one opened. That's how he claimed to have found us,' Mark told him.

'Each Portal does have its own signature, and *that* we can detect. We cannot, however, detect the actual location or date whenever a gateway is opened with any accuracy.'

'Well that bastard did, *and* threatened us and our daughter,' Pauline exclaimed hotly.

'You said this was two years ago in your time era? Colonel Ohuru, please call Major Walker, he will want to hear this.'

When Hans came, Grogan recounted what Mark had told him and Hans showed them an image of Victor Novak.

'That him, that's Victor. He's the bastard who shot my husband.'

'His real name is Jacob Reinhardt, he is a rogue Traveller. Do you know where he is now? We have been chasing him for years.'

'Well you needn't worry about him any longer, my wife made sure he won't bother anyone again.' Mark recounted the whole story. 'All his electronic devices and the gun are locked away back at my house. Now, answer *my* questions. Why were your people watching my family? Andrea has been working for me for six months so it's at least that long.'

Dr Grogan looked at Hans then back at the Bishops. 'Reinhardt escaped from prison in the Andaman Islands five years ago. After he received illegal Treatment in India—bone marrow replacement to alter his DNA and plastic surgery, he killed everyone involved. Luckily, we found the records and an image of him after surgery. Major Walker's team traced him to the home of a senior researcher, Hikoro Franklin in Cherbourg, in what you know as France.

'After Nicholas' disappearance, all Portals were retro-fitted with a beacon, so Reinhardt could not steal hers without being tracked. From central records, we discovered he downloaded a huge amount of data for northern England from 2006 to 2008. Shortly after, he used Hikoro's Portal to travel to a city called Durham in England on the first of April 2006. Hikoro died and her Portal was destroyed in an explosion and fire after he left. We despatched Major Walker's team to re-arrest him. They spent three years tracking him through northern England and a year ago found he had been living in Richmond posing as a birdwatcher. From newspaper archives, we learned his motorcycle and campsite had been found abandoned near your farm. Hacking into police records, we determined no trace of him had ever been found, despite extensive enquiries and numerous searches.'

Hans continued the story. 'He had always moved every few months before, but now he stayed over a year in this one area, often in primitive conditions. We found he showed particular interest in you, Mr Bishop, and your farm.'

'Due to Reinhardt's interest, he was observing you for over a year, by the way, we did some research on you both.' Grogan told them. 'We have since been trying to provide you and the other couple with protection and...'

'Hold it! Who else were you spying on?' Pauline demanded, in a tone Mark knew did not bode well.

'Mrs Bishop, I assure you, we were *not* spying and have not interfered in your lives in anyway. Not until now that is,' Grogan answered in an attempt to placate her. 'The other couple are Miss Wright and Mr Matthews.'

'You said you have been providing protection for us. Why would we need protection? And from who?'

'During our background checks, we determined you and some of your descendants, were of crucial importance to several critical events in the last five hundred years.'

Pauline choked and squeezed Mark's hand. 'What? You're joking?'

'I assure you it is quite true.'

Pauline was not satisfied. 'You have still not explained why we have been singled out for protection.'

'Since our foundation, there have been protests groups who believe we should not meddle with the past. Actually, all we do is observe the past to determine how certain decisions were made and problems developed that led to political, economic and environmental instability. This is solely to advise the World Council and avoid the same mistakes. Some of these groups have a violent agenda and we feared Reinhardt may been working with one of them in an attempt to disrupt our work through threatening or killing you. We did not know Reinhardt was after Nicholas' Portal.'

Mark and Pauline looked at each other in stunned silence. Mark recovered first. 'According to what I have read on Nicholas' Portal, that is impossible.'

'Yes, that is essentially true. However, theoretically, if a large enough disruption was in some way engineered, it may give rise to an alternate universe. Depending on when the disruption occurred, it could have dramatic repercussions in this timeline.'

'I see, so when we go back, we're going to have a Tempus team watching over us all the time?'

'I assure you, they will be most discrete,' Grogan hastened to say. 'Rotating teams were despatched to provide protection not only for yourselves, but for all the critical individuals throughout the last four hundred years or so.'

Pauline appeared mollified.

'In the meantime,' Grogan asked, 'maybe you can help us identify the person who attacked you? We have him in the Security Wing.'

Mark cracked his knuckles. 'I want to meet that bastard. Give me five minutes alone with him.'

Ohuru and Hans escorted them to the Security area. Through an observation window, Pauline saw a heavily bandaged, bearded man lying in bed with casts on his arm and leg and a vivid bruise on his jaw.

'He looks familiar,' said Pauline, then yelled, 'Wait a minute. That's Steven!'

'The one who sabotaged the generator?' Mark asked.

'I want to talk to him. Now!' she demanded in a tone brooking no opposition.

'That can be arranged. He is inside an electronic security shield, and with his injuries, quite immobile.'

Pauline smiled sweetly as she walked in to the room. 'Hello, Steven, long time no see. How've you been keeping? I must say you don't look so good.'

'You... how...' he stammered.

'How what? How come I'm still alive?'

'You bitch! I lost everything and I've been treated like a pariah. You ruined my whole life.'

'Oh, you managed that all on your own,' her voice hardened. 'You ruined my life for five years, and now you'll have to pay for trying to kill me.'

'Just you wait,' he shouted. 'I'll get my own back, just wait 'til I get out of here.'

'I am afraid that will not be possible,' Colonel Ohuru remarked. 'The Council has decided you are a serious threat to the Bishop family, and as such have sentenced you to the Andaman Penal Colony for the rest of your natural life.'

'You can't do that! What about a trial? You can't just lock me away,' Steven shouted.

'Too bad, Steven. You should have stopped when you were ahead. Anyway, you now get an all-expenses paid holiday in an Indian Ocean resort. Enjoy,' she said, and left him screaming and ranting.

'Feel better now?' Mark asked, when she came back.

A broad grin stretched across her face. 'Much better.'

'I didn't know you had such a mean streak.'

'Just you wait. If I *can* have your Treatment delayed, I'll show you what I'm really capable of!'

Back in their apartment, Pauline asked Hans why Steven was still in casts. He told her they reserved full bioengineered treatment for critical cases; a few fractures did not warrant such level of care.

'How badly was he injured,' Mark asked

'I am afraid Captain Istanov was a little enthusiastic,' Hans told them. 'He suffered a broken tibia, ulna, radius and collar bone, along with two fractured fingers and three ribs. He lost two teeth and his jaw was broken in to two places. We repaired his jaw in order to interrogate him.'

An embarrassed Nikita said, 'I'm afraid I lost my temper when I saw Mrs Bishop attacked right in front of me.'

Mark laughed. 'Remind me not to be late with your pay cheque.'

Chapter 23
Thursday, 15th May 2535

Pauline woke the next morning and smiled at Mark's tousled hair next to her. After her shower she nudged him awake. 'Come on sleepy head, time for to get up.'

After their breakfast, Dr Grogan entered.

'Mrs Bishop, how are you feeling?'

'Fine, thank you, but I'm dying to hear what you found out about us.'

'Yeah, me too,' Mark added.

'This may take some time,' advised Grogan. 'Would you agree to stay here for a while?'

'How long?' Pauline asked, already missing her daughter.

'Only until you have had time to adjust to the effects of the Treatment; no longer than two weeks.'

They looked at each other; Pauline nodded at Mark and said, 'Okay.'

'All I can tell you about these pivotal individuals is they were descended either from yourselves or Miss Wright and Mr

Matthews, or carried all *four* blood lines.'

'Surely we can't be the only families involved?' Mark asked.

'Certainly not,' Grogan replied. 'Many others interacted with your gene pool over the years, but genetic interactions between the descendants of the two families were the most common factor. An interesting fact is that during our research we found one more crucial bloodline; A specific line of Armstrong's, however, we have not been able to trace it any further back than mid-Fifteenth Century Scotland. Interactions between your two families and the Armstrong bloodline account for sixty-five percent of the pivotal persons in our history.'

'What can you tell us about these Portals?' Mark was intrigued to know more details.

'The Temporal Research Centre was founded on the work of twin brothers, Manfred and Simon Vesco, who were your direct descendants by the way, in 2400.' Grogan paused, apparently lost in thought. 'It's rather a strange story. Not the discoveries or invention of the first Portals, but about Simon, the first real Time Researcher. He was a gifted linguist and, in 2363, spent thirty years in Fifteenth Century Europe studying the social structure in Germany—when he finally returned, he wrote up his findings. They were extremely detailed with regard to social conditions and so-on, but said nothing of his own personal experiences. After submitting it to the Research Council, he withdrew from everyone, even his twin brother.'

'Do you know why?' Pauline was fascinated by the story.

'No. We assume it was a form of Timelag, a condition several subsequent travellers experienced. It is due either to too long in the past or from too many trips without allowing adequate time to adjust between them. Simon refused any further Treatment, which would have given him another thirty years of life, and died ten years later at the age of seventy-five.

TP 1000: The Bishops

'If Simon was my direct descendant, why was his surname Vesco and not Bishop?' Mark asked Dr Grogan.

'You need to understand the history of the last four hundred years. By 2105, many glaciers and most of Greenland's ice sheet had melted. The steady rise in sea level had already triggered a concerted effort to dramatically reduce the use of carbon-based fuels and large-scale regeneration of depleted forests in the Amazon, China and central Africa. Nearly all power generation by then was from nuclear or renewable sources. Sea level rise stabilised at six metres, although there was huge political and economic upset for many years.

Due to committed warming from existing greenhouse gases in the atmosphere, Himalayan glaciers effectively disappeared over the next fifty years. The main rivers in India, the Ganges, Indus and Brahmaputra along with the Mekong, Yangtze, Irrawaddy and Salween Rivers, which provided drinking water and irrigation for one point five billion people virtually dried up. The riots and refugee crisis that followed led to what are now called the Water Wars and devastated seven-million square kilometers of land. World economies eventually stabilised by the start of the Twenty-Third Century.

However, that's when the main disaster occurred. The key event was a deep magnitude-eight earthquake in 2211 along the western segment of the West Antarctic Rift line triggering a series of volcanic eruptions underneath the ice cap. This completely removed the West Antarctic ice cover. The sea level rose by fifteen metres over the next twenty years. Cities such as New York, London, Cairo and Shanghai were completely inundated and the Indian sub-continent and Asia suffered tremendous loss of life. Over this period, billions lost their life.'

Mark's and Pauline's ashen faces reflected their struggle to grasp the enormity of the disaster and level of destruction.

'Over thirteen million square kilometres of land was lost in all and the economic and social disruption was catastrophic,' Grogan said, shaking his head. 'Fourteen percent of the earth's land surface was now either underwater or uninhabitable. From the start of the Water Wars, it took the next hundred and fifty years to establish peace and stabilise world economies and politics. Seven main politico-economic blocs emerged from these wars with a few smaller ones in Asia—from these a World Council was formed in 2265.

Anyway, to answer your question, Mr Bishop, the wars involved tremendous religious conflict. Many people with names like Moor, Church, Aliyev, Lacroix and Bishop changed them because of the religious connotations.'

Grogan spent the rest of the day with them and answered as many questions as he could without giving away details.

'Mrs Bishop, it is getting late and you should rest. We can continue this tomorrow after Mr Bishop receives his Treatment.'

'Alright, thank you for being so frank with us.'

Mark stroked her stomach as they lay in bed that night. 'You know, in one way, Penny had a gestation period of about a hundred and sixty years,' Mark joked. 'How're we going to calculate this one? Five hundred?'

Pauline said, 'Nine months is long enough, thank you.'

She reached over and moved her hand tantalizingly down his chest until she found what she was searching for.

'Are you sure you're alright?' Mark asked.

'Let me show you,' she replied in a sultry voice.

'You realise we've been making love for almost seven hundred and seventy years in one place or another,' Mark murmured in her ear after he had recovered. 'Not that I'm complaining, mind you, but having a twenty-year-old in bed with me who is stronger than I am is definitely a challenge.'

'Well, after tomorrow, it won't be as challenging, so come here and let me enjoy it while I can.'

Hans took Mark for his Treatment and Pauline watched from the observation room as the nurses attached monitors to his body and a drip in his arm. They applied several high-pressure jet injectors to his neck and arm and after two hours, it was all over.

'The effects will be evident in about twelve hours,' Dr. Harrison told Mark.

Nikita/Andrea was waiting for them in their apartment. 'Director Grogan has been called away but will meet you in the evening. In the meantime would you like a tour of the facility?'

The facility was a huge multi-level complex built in to a mountain. The lowest floor was an engineering and power distribution complex; the next two floors accommodation, dining and recreation areas. The fourth level was dedicated to lecture rooms and what appeared to be a gymnasium. When they entered, Nikita pointed to a group of young men and women undergoing strenuous exercises.

'They are trainee security staff who will eventually undertake temporal security assignments. The training normally lasts for two years, most of it on avoiding temporal fluctuations. Nicholas Olafson's journals have been the subject of considerable interest in light of your untrained use of a Portal without causing any disturbances in the continuum.'

The upper four floors could only be accessed by security personnel. The first of these secure floors was the Medical and Security floor with an operating room, wards and rehabilitation rooms, including their own apartment. Nikita showed them the three Portal Chambers from where Travellers departed and returned—and the fourth one, not in use since Nicholas disappeared, but ready in case he returned. Nikita looked at the chamber with a sad expression. 'I suppose Chamber Three will be put back in use now we know Nicholas will not be returning.'

'Anyway, before each person travels, whether from here or a remote chamber, they have to connect their Portal and Universal Library to the central computer. This records their arrival and destination coordinates, time and dates; it also performs a backup of their UL before they leave and on return. Return journeys are automatically logged. One of the big questions we have is how you activated Nicholas' Portal without connecting it to the central computer.'

Offices, laboratories and workshops occupied the next two levels with the flight deck and hangers on the top floor. The engineer in Mark was fascinated by the Delta Wing aircraft design. They took a lift to the roof of the complex and emerged into bright sunlight and a tropical garden. Nikita led them past pavilions, fountains and a small lake to an observation deck. Rainbows marked where waterfalls cascaded down the mountain sides to the plains below where herds of buffalo, elephants, giraffe and a multitude of antelopes roamed.

'Where exactly are we?' Mark asked.

'In the foothills of the Udzungwa Mountains in what you call Tanzania. This site was selected for its remoteness and designed to have minimal impact on the local flora and fauna. Most of the facility is inside the mountain and powered by solar and hydroelectric energy.'

Later, Grogan quizzed them more on their use of the TP1000 and the trips they had made. 'I have no need to remind you not to tell anyone else of this.'

'A bit late I'm afraid,' Mark answered, with a rueful smile. 'Penelope and Tony have already made trips with us.'

The Director was astonished when Mark told him how they had brought Penelope from 1840 to their farm. And more amazed when he described the trips he and Tony had made to the 1700s to collect endangered and extinct plants.

'We knew from our background checks Miss Wright's credentials were false but never imagined her true origin. How you achieved that without causing major fluctuations to the time-stream is unbelievable. I must discuss this with the Temporal Council.'

The next evening, after a leisurely day in the rooftop garden, Dr. Grogan returned. 'Mr and Mrs Bishop, your accomplishments in time travel were a revelation to the Council. They have decided to offer Miss Wright and Mr Matthews the Treatment and to replace your TP1000 with a version which can be used by multiple users.'

'You want to give them the Longevity Treatment, why?' Mark was astonished, and Pauline speechless.

'We have done a more detailed background investigation and found some of their most significant accomplishments were achieved at a very late age. The only explanation we can deduce is they received the Treatment. After they have received it, all records will be sealed, as will our findings about yourselves and your descendants. We want no-one else to learn of your significance, for your own safety.'

'We will send Nikita and Hans with you. On your return here with Miss Wright and Mr Matthews, we will teach you all how to use the latest TP2000.'

'We can't just go and grab them,' Mark protested. 'We need to explain everything to them first, and Tony is not there at the moment anyway.'

'I understand, we have plenty of time,' Grogan chuckled at his weak joke.

That night they discovered their new abilities led to some very satisfying, and very long, love-making.

Speaking to Grogan at one of their regular meetings, Mark asked how the floods had affected Britain, particularly his farm.

'The whole east coast of England was badly impacted. I can arrange for Major Walker and Captain Istanov to fly you there if you wish. It is a seven hour flight and you can stay overnight at the Tempus base in Scotland and return the next day.'

Mark's mouth gaped. He had flown from Cape Town to London and that had taken twelve hours non-stop.

The next morning, they met their companion for the journey, Zahra Pembe, a technician transferring to the Scottish Tempus base. After three hours Mark asked how fast they were flying.

'Fourteen hundred kilometres per hour,' Zahra answered. 'We are almost at the Mediterranean coast. The Qattara Sea should be just below.'

He and Pauline stared incredulously out of the window at a huge body of water surrounded by miles and miles of forest where there should have been the Sahara desert.

'The Council had two tunnels driven from the Mediterranean to the Qattara Depression in 2388. Water flows through a hydro-electric plant generating three gigawatts of electricity before entering the Depression.'

'How big *is* it?' Pauline asked, barely able to grasp the scope of the project.

TP 1000: The Bishops

'Seventeen thousand square kilometres. After it filled, millions of trees were planted. It's really changed the weather down there.'

Three hours later, to the west, the sheer white chalk cliffs of Dover gleamed in the sunlight on their approach to the English coast. Hans slowed the aircraft and descended to five thousand feet—Mark and Pauline were numb as they beheld the devastation below. The Thames through central London was at least four kilometres wide. Tower Bridge stood isolated. Only the top of the two towers, and the four towers on the keep of the Tower of London rose above the water. The rooftops of Westminster Palace and the upper part of Big Ben were visible but there was no sign of Buckingham Palace.

Climbing, Hans flew north along what was now the east coast. Pauline noticed huge glistening towers clustered around towns and cities and asked what they were.

'Farms,' Zahra replied. 'The rising sea level not only flooded land but made ground water in many areas more saline. Famine was a real problem until the Corporation built these high-rise farms after the flood. Now they are everywhere, some of them one hundred storeys high. The Corporation is now the biggest natural food suppler in the eastern hemisphere.'

Fascinated, Mark turned to look at the unfamiliar view below and recognised where they were. Below was what used to be East Anglia, but the Wash was now a huge bay covered by hundreds of enormous wind turbines, with Cambridge and Peterborough now sea-side cities. Mark pointed out Lincoln Cathedral to Pauline; it sat at the southern end of a narrow island with Scunthorpe at the northern tip. A larger island to the east was all that was left of the Lincolnshire Wolds. To the west the A1 (M) was a coastal road.

'Look, there's York Minster.' Pauline pointed out the cathedral standing proudly on an island no more than half a kilometre across.

They stared awestruck at the immensity of the disaster. Subdued, they vainly attempted to absorb these overwhelming changes.

Slowing and descending to three thousand feet they had a clear view along Swaledale.

'There's our farm,' Pauline exclaimed.

Mark's attention was, however, riveted by the sight of an enormous geodesic dome and a tall glass tower to the east. The dome covered at least four acres and appeared to be over fifty meters high. 'What are those?' he asked.

'A biome and an experimental farm.' Zahra said. 'It is also the Corporation head-quarters. You'll see the main research centre when we arrive at Fort Augustus. Their research and technological advances helped develop the high-rise farms you saw earlier. Here, I have one their honey bars—they're delicious. Not only natural honey but there's sunflower and flax seeds, raisins and dried apricots.'

Mark examined the wrapper—it had their Paulinas logo on it. He looked at Pauline and could tell she was thinking the same thing... *did our family develop these?*

Hans' voice came over the intercom. 'Fasten your seatbelts, please. There is a storm over the mountains and we may experience turbulence.'

Skirting the Cairngorms, they descended and flew the length of Loch Ness on their approach to Fort Augustus.

Zahra pointed out of the window. 'Look over there. That's the Corporation research centre and their high rise farms. Its proper name is the Centre for Biodiversity and Sustainable Living.'

Mark and Pauline saw an enormous geodesic dome complex

south of the town, bigger than the one near their farm and five multi-storey buildings around it.

'And over on the other side of the loch you can see the entrance to their seed bank,'

Zahra indicated a stone and glass five-storey building half way up the mountain-side.

'It's the second biggest seed bank after the one in Svalbard. It goes a hundred metres into the granite and holds seeds for over twenty thousand plant species, five percent of which are endangered or extinct. Hydroelectric power is used to keep the seed bank at minus eighteen degrees.'

'What is this Corporation you keep mentioning?' Pauline asked.

Before she could answer, Nikita came and announced they would be landing in five minutes.

The Tempus base was a three-storey building, a ten minute drive in an electric car along the northern side of the loch. After they said farewell to Zahra, Hans and Nikita took them to an apartment identical to the one in Africa.

'What is this base used for?' Mark asked.

'It's one of five satellite bases in Europe and Africa,' Hans answered. 'It allows the hundred and twenty Researchers to travel to different eras from multiple locations.

'Avoids the traffic jams we encountered in the first few years after Tempus was founded.' Nikita joked. 'Each base has three Portal Chambers. These are in addition to a few personal chambers such as the one Hikoro had in her home.'

'Do they all travel alone, like Nicholas?'

'Since he was lost, all Researchers travel in pairs or teams of three, no matter how low a risk is assigned to the trip.'

After lunch, Nikita took them into Fort Augustus, now a bustling town of eight-thousand people catering mainly to the Corporation and Tempus staff, as well as occasional tourists. Walking around, Mark noted how warm it was. He had expected it to be about ten degrees, but this was more like twenty.

All along the streets stood rows of vending machines, selling everything imaginable from soft drinks, hot meals and ice-cream, to umbrellas and shoes.

As they strolled about, Pauline looked into one of the few shops she had seen and asked, 'Can we buy some souvenirs?'

'Not a problem. What do you like?'

She bought a blown glass pendant and matching earrings and a cute soft green Loch Ness monster wearing a tartan bonnet for Penny.

Nikita waved her Tempus identity card over a machine to pay for them.

Relaxing in the recreation lounge, Mark asked Nikita about the Corporation Zahra had mentioned; a fleeting look of annoyance crossed her face.

'It is a hydroponic and aeroponic agricultural company founded in the Twenty-Second Century. They built the main research centre here after the first flood when the Greenland ice cap melted. It designed and help construct multi-storey farms which greatly relieved the famine after the major flood in 2211.'

Before they could ask any more questions, Nikita said she had to help Hans check out their aircraft as they had an early start planned for the next day.

On the flight back, they were the only passengers and Hans and Nikita stayed in the cockpit leaving Mark and Pauline on their own.

'You get the feeling there's something about this Corporation they don't want us to know?' Pauline asked.

'Damn right.'

Back at headquarters, Grogan said Hans and Nikita had taken a few days to visit their families and Sven and Talia would escort them around.

Both Pauline's and Mark's curiosity was roused.

Five days later, Hans and Nikita took them back to the museum and Nikita, once more assuming her pseudonym of Andrea, continued her work in the kitchen as if nothing had happened.

Pauline and Mark met Penelope at the farmhouse. 'I have been looking all over for you. The University called and asked me to give a talk about the museum. I will stay to study and return the same day as Anthony,' she told them and rushed off. This effectively prevented them telling her about their recent trip.

Mark took Hans and Nikita to the basement and handed over Victor's equipment and showed them the journals.

Handling the box with the antenna, Hans explained, 'this is a Time-Space scanner, but it has been modified. This is how Reinhardt must have tracked the Portal signal. This will be invaluable. Thank you.'

Both showed their amazement at this underground room and

how effectively Nicholas had screened the Portal. Using a handheld scanner, Nikita ran it over every page of the journals and travelled back to pass everything to Director Grogan. When she returned, Mark showed them the screened room at the byre and the portable Faraday cage he used when travelling away from the byre.

Just before the New Year, Tony and Penelope returned and Mark called them to his office. Pauline pulled up her sweater to show the faint scar on her abdomen and explained when and how she had been wounded and their visit to the Temporal Research Headquarters.

Mark and Pauline spent hours describing what they had seen and about the Longevity Treatment being offered. Neither Tony nor Penelope could take it in at first. When they introduced Andrea as Nikita, they were convinced. Penelope, however, was reluctant to have the Treatment. She never missed Sunday services and her religious principles made her worry this may be interfering with God's plans. Mark explained Penelope's concerns to Hans to relay to the Temporal Council.

Penelope spent many hours with Penny and watched Pauline's baby bump start to show. She kept thinking about the rejuvenating effects

TP 1000: The Bishops

of the Longevity Treatment. She was twenty-six years old and if she could put off aging there would be more time to have all the children she wanted. After the Twelfth Night celebrations she agreed to have the Treatment. In the basement, Hans led them through the gateway where Director Grogan was waiting for them.

'Welcome to Temporal Research, Miss Wright, Mr Matthews, and welcome back to you too, Mr and Mrs Bishop. Let me escort you to your apartments. After you settle in we can talk.'

Nikita showed Tony and Penelope how to use the facilities in their rooms, and later they all met in Pauline's room.

'So how are you both feeling?' Pauline asked.

Penelope looked nervous. 'Alright I suppose. Andrea said our Treatment is planned for tomorrow morning and what to expect, but it is a little overwhelming.'

'It certainly is. One minute it's freezing and now we're in the Tropics,' Tony commented, looking out of the window. 'It's unbelievable.'

'Imagine how I felt,' Pauline said. 'Passing out in the museum and waking up in a hospital in the Twenty-Sixth Century. But by tomorrow evening you'll feel great, believe me.'

The next morning, Pauline and Mark waited in their apartment until Tony arrived and Penelope an hour later.

'They found a hormone disorder,' Penelope told them. 'Apparently it reduced my ovaries' ability to mature and release eggs, the doctor called it *Polycystic Ovary Syndrome*. The doctor said they have corrected the imbalance and there should be no problems now.' She turned to Tony with a calculating look.

When Grogan came to visit, Mark gave him Nicholas' passports and the model soldiers he had found to pass to his parents.

'These are the only photographs and personal items we have. I'm sure they would appreciate them.'

'They will be delighted. Thank you Mr Bishop.' He turned to Tony. 'You know, Nicholas is descended from you, Mr Matthews and Mr and Mrs Bishop, through his great-grandmother. Her name was Lara Matthews before she married Casper Vesco.'

Leaving Penelope and Tony flabbergasted, he turned to Mark. 'We have examined Nicholas' Portal and our technicians say a massive radiation burst disrupted time-space as he stepped through the gateway. We have traced it to the merging of two massive black holes. This was why Nicholas ended up in 1945 and caused all approved users to be locked out. The only way it could be activated was by a new user. Even if Nicholas took the risk and asked a stranger to log in, it would only have taken him to the past, not back here. Your TP2000 is also capable of being used without connecting it to the central computer, although it does have the tracking beacon we retrofitted after Nicholas' disappearance.'

Over the next two weeks, they learned how to use the new Portal and adjusted to the changes the Treatment brought. Besides sightseeing trips over the plains, Nikita showed them the library complex. Grogan's reason for Simon's withdrawal, and the appearance of this critical Armstrong branch, had intrigued Penelope and aroused her curiosity; so much so, she spent hours in the library until Tony was forced to drag her out.

The day after they returned to their own time, despite actually being thirty-three years and four months old, Pauline celebrated her thirty-second birthday. The highlight turned out to be Penelope and Tony announcing their plans to be married in April. Penelope said she wanted a simple wedding, but Pauline, Naomi and Julie had different ideas.

Chapter 24
Saturday, 13th March 2011

Mark and Pauline wanted Penelope to have a traditional Victorian wedding dress and what better way than have it made in the Nineteenth Century. When spring term ended, Mark whisked Pauline and Penelope back to York in 1846. After a month in the city, Penelope's gown, with its eight-foot train, was completed. The dressmaker used rich white and blue silk with pearl-beaded Nottingham lace across the bodice; the fingertip length veil made of the same beaded lace. The colours held special significance to Penelope. In Victorian tradition, they declared she had chosen her husband wisely and her love would always be true. When they returned, Penelope cut Tony off from any more erotic trysts. When Pauline asked her about this apparent change she quipped, 'Abstinence makes the heart grow fonder.'

On a crisp clear mid-April morning, Mark drove the bride to the church in the wagon. Repainted and decked out with loops and garlands of white hibiscus and violets, crowds gathered as they drove through the villages to the church. The four bridesmaids, all

Penelope's friends from university, arrived in a vintage Rolls Royce. Each wore different coloured pastel silk dresses, and resembled a cluster of wildflowers standing behind the bride.

Chris and Naomi had festooned the church with elaborate floral arrangements made with blooms from the greenhouse. The guests were met not only with brilliantly coloured decorations, but also the sweet scent of lilies of the valley, frangipani, magnolia and jasmine.

Penny had thrown a rare tantrum, determined to be involved in her 'Aunty Penny's' wedding. Not without many threats, she and Jimmy's two daughters, walked ahead of the bride, spreading a carpet of red rose petals. Tony, on hearing *Mendelsohn's Wedding March*, turned. Stunned at the sky-blue and white cloud of beauty standing in the doorway of the church, his mouth gaped open.

Penelope walked down the aisle on Mark's arm amid gasps of amazement from the guests at her gown and her stunning bouquet. Naomi had crafted a floral work of art from pink myrtle, a traditional Victorian bride's flower, white fragrant roses from Houghton House intertwined with flowing spikes of purple *Vanda coerulea* orchids.

Tony raised her veil and her sparkling blue eyes held him spellbound. Their prolonged kiss provoked Chris, his best man, to surreptitiously poke Tony in the ribs to let the guests leave. After a reception at the farm, Pauline could not stop grinning when she waved them off on their honeymoon. The illustrated *Kamasutra* and revealing nightwear she and Julie had slipped in Penelope's bag promised an interesting week for the newlyweds.

Shy and embarrassed on her first night, the next morning, Penelope recovered from the initial shock at the contents of Julie's book, and became fascinated by the possibilities. For the rest of the honeymoon she enthusiastically worked through it, page by page, with a dedication Tony hoped he would survive—even with his enhanced strength and stamina. Tony did however manage to cajole her to visit Hadrian's Wall fifty miles away; he figured if he could interest her in something archaeological, he might get some well-needed rest.

When the newlyweds returned to the farm, everyone watched Tony lift Penelope to carry her across the threshold of their house—and nearly drop her. The resultant ribald comments, particularly from Mark, caused Penelope's face to turn the brightest red they had ever seen. During the following month, Mark noted Tony did not appear to hike off to the fells as early as before his marriage.

After everyone settled back into their normal routines, Mark visited the greenhouse to check on the latest strawberry crop and overheard Chris and Tony talking.

'...and the Panama disease wiped out Gros Michel bananas in the 1950s. Now it's spreading to the Cavendish variety in Australasia,' Tony said.

'That's the danger of agricultural monoculture,' Chris replied. 'Just look at the Irish Potato Famine in 1845.'

'In my final year at university, I read a report by the *UN Food and Agriculture Organisation.*' Tony recounted 'It stated since the 1900s, seventy-five percent of agricultural crops have disappeared as farmers have abandoned varieties for single variety higher yielding crops. Today, three-quarters of the world's food is generated from only twelve plant species. Before long we'll have another famine.' Red-faced, Tony stood up. 'That's why seed banks are important. They conserve genetic diversity and help safeguard against disease. There's over thirty-thousand species in the *Kew Gardens' Millennium*

Seed Bank and the *Svalbard Seed Vault* can store four-and-a-half million seed samples.'

With the Portal, he and Tony could travel anywhere in the world over the last two-thousand years and collect native wild plant seeds, and extinct and endangered species for preservation. He broached the idea of building their own seed bank with Tony and Chris, and they roped in Naomi to help design one.

Their design included a fifty square metre cold room designed to hold twenty-five thousand collections— six thousand litres of seeds, and a ten square metre drying room. With humidity monitors, incubator-dryer and all the other equipment needed, it would cost one hundred thousand pounds. Solar panels on the building roof, plus the excess electricity they already generated, would supply more than enough power to maintain the required minus-eighteen degrees temperature.

Tony made lists of plant species, particularly those with agricultural and medicinal importance. 'Almost half a million square miles of rain forests have been lost in the last twenty years. That's like five times the size of Britain,' Tony told Mark. 'Deforestation started in the sixteen-hundreds, we'd have to travel back at least that far. God knows what plants have disappeared since then.'

Mark, knowing what would happen two hundred years from now, recognised how critical their efforts would be. He considered selling a few of his stamps a small price to pay. To be prepared, Mark enrolled Tony and Naomi in the September residential course on Seed Conservation Techniques at the Millennium Seed Bank.

In the middle of May, after a weekend of nausea and vomiting, Tony took Penelope to the clinic. On their return, Penelope rushed in the farm house, a beaming smile on her face and Tony trailing behind looking stunned. 'I'm pregnant!' she yelled, practically dancing in the hallway. 'The baby is due in October.'

In June, a convoy left the farm for Julie's wedding. After a simple wedding ceremony, everyone adjourned to a hotel for the reception. Before the speeches started, Mark, Chris and Tony slipped out and filled Hugh's car with balloons they had packed with rice, and Pauline, Naomi and Penelope hung sexy underwear from the car antenna and all over the back window.

When the newly married couple left to drive off for their honeymoon, Mark presented them with a hatpin each. Hugh removed the panties from the antenna. 'She won't be needing these for a while.' Amid the laughter, it produced an actual blush from his wife.

When Penelope broke the news she was carrying twins, reactions varied from joy and delight to dismay. Melanie, alone in the dismay faction at the thought of caring for five children, was relieved when Mark and Pauline told her they had decided to build a nursery wing on the house and Penelope would hire another nursemaid.

Four days after Penelope's housewarming party, Pauline's water broke. At seven o'clock the next morning, twenty-first of July, she gave birth to the twins. Edward, named after Mark's earliest known ancestor, was followed ten minutes later by George, named after Mark's and Pauline's fathers. Penny, delighted to have two baby brothers, helped Melanie as much as allowed.

When Joanna Porter, a plump motherly woman of forty-five arrived. Melanie showed her the normal routine and told her things were going to be busy soon when the next set of twins arrived.

When Julie came for the christening and saw Penny, the twins and Penelope's burgeoning stomach she was aghast. Rising above the congratulations, her voice carried across the room as she told Hugh, 'You're not getting any this week, so you can just tie a knot in it while we're staying at this damn hormone factory!'

Hugh's look of disappointment was greeted by laughter from Mark and a prod in the rib from Julie. Pauline's reminder that Julie was taking birth control pills, received a withering reply—she did not trust *anything* in this place.

Tony walked in to the soil lab while Chris and Mark discussed growing pineapples. 'She's got started on something again. Her study walls are plastered with maps and notes, and there's books all over the place. Every evening, once she's back from classes, she starts again. You won't believe it, but I have to *make* her go to bed at night.'

Mark and Chris doubled over laughing. Stories of Penelope's sexual awakening, and the rings around Tony's eyes in the first three months of their marriage had become legend.

'What's she up to?' Mark asked.

TP 1000: The Bishops

'No idea, but there's genealogical charts and maps from the English-Scottish border plastered everywhere. Every time I ask, she goes all cryptic. All I get is, 'the answer has to be here somewhere'. Answer to what she won't let on.'

At dinner, Mark related Penelope's latest mysterious fixation and Pauline decided to have a chat with her in the morning.

'In the Tempus library, I read Simon Vesco's report and have retyped it,' she told Pauline, who continued to be amazed at her eidetic memory. 'I do not believe that story about Timelag; there must have been another reason for his behaviour, a *very* personal one, and I want to know what it was.'

Penelope continued in her lecturing tone. 'Let me summarise. In his report, he states he used the name Simon Viscof. Apparently the Longevity Treatment leads to apparent agelessness, and with the phobia about witches at this time he spent twenty-seven years moving around Germany and Switzerland before ending up in the city of Sion. After only a couple of months, for no reason he mentions, in late 1427, he undertook a nine-month long journey through France and the Low Countries to Scotland; he finally settled near Langholm in the Scottish-English borderlands.'

Frustration crept into her voice. 'Why face all the dangers of travelling on foot and horseback, then a risky boat ride to Scotland? Why could he not pop back to the 2300s and reappear in Scotland? After two years there, and for no apparent reason, he returned to 2365 and cut himself off from everyone?

I have checked every record I can find for every town and village he mentioned,' she waved her arms at the piles of paper on her desk and maps on the wall. 'But there's nothing—nothing at all.' She turned to Pauline running her hands through her hair. 'You remember Grogan mentioned the

317

Armstrong line? Well, it started twenty years after Simon left; don't tell me that's a coincidence.'

'Well there's not much you can do, is there?'

'Yes, there is. I'm going to 1429 and find out for myself!'

'What? You can't be serious? Do you know how dangerous that could be?'

'Anthony can protect me.'

Pauline used the one argument she knew would make her listen. 'You are due in a few months' time. At least wait until you give birth, for the babies' sake. That way you have ample time to arrange clothes, money and so-on.'

'Tony, it was the only way I could stop her rushing off in to God knows what,' Pauline explained. 'You know what she's like better than anyone. If I hadn't reminded her about the babies, I don't know what she'd have done.'

'I suppose so. She's started studying the early and Middle Scots language and sewing clothes for us to go as travelling merchants. She even expects me to learn how to use a bloody *sword*.'

'Is she out of her mind?' Mark said, after Pauline told him of Penelope's latest obsession. After she explained Penelope's logic and her insistence on Tony learning to use a sword, Mark started musing.

'Well, she does have a point, about Simon anyway. I reckon she's stretching it a bit on the Armstrong link though.'

'Can you help Tony?

'Sure, no problem. Makes sense, and it gives me another

sparring partner. This'll be fun.'

'Fun! You have a weird sense of humour.'

He rubbed his hands together. 'We can start in the morning.'

Tony looked on his dismay as Mark selected weapons. 'Mark, I tell you, I'm useless at anything athletic. At school when choosing teams, guess who was always the last to be picked?'

'I think you might find things a bit different now,' he replied, balancing a German Sixteenth Century style side-sword and a medieval anelace[4]. 'Um... a bo-staff I think,' he murmured, clearly not paying much attention to Tony's complaints. He reached over to a rack of staffs on the wall. 'You should see Pauline with one of these.'

'What?'

Mark chuckled. 'Only knife and staff... plus her rock. She's pretty damn good with it too. Now, let's get started.'

After an hour of routine exercises and simple moves, Mark increased the pace and Tony matched him stroke for stroke.

'I told you, the Treatment makes a big difference.' Tony stared at the staff in his hands as if at an alien artefact. 'Pauline, let's show him it's done.'

The next ten minutes Tony and Penelope stood with their mouths gaping. The staffs blurred and the clacking as they struck sounded like a demented machine gun. Tony stood speechless

---

[4] An anelace, also called an anlace, is a medieval long dagger or a very short type of sword. An anelace was sharp on both sides and could be carried at the small of the back or girdle. Two anelaces could be used in a paired fighting style similar to using a sword and parrying dagger.

when they stopped; Mark and Pauline were not even breathing heavily, and neither had broken a sweat.

'Now for the sword and knife. We'll practice with each separately and then together,' Mark told him. 'If you ever have only one handy, you need to know how to use it. Using both together is a very different technique; still, lots of practice will fix that. With your new reflexes it won't take long for your muscles to learn and we have months to practice.'

Mark and Tony trained three times a week. From one week to the next, Tony's skill improved until—after more time, and bruises, than he wanted to admit—he could hold his own with Mark with both staff and sword. Penelope and Pauline popped in from time to time to watch the practice sessions and Pauline noticed the glint in Penelope's eyes when she saw her husband giving as good as he got. She figured Tony was in for a much more challenging workout when Penelope got him back to their house than he was having with Mark.

After this latest session, Pauline and Mark said they would go with them, Mark's reason being, two swords were better than one. Another reason was he did not trust Penelope to be discreet in her enquiries and they could end up in more trouble than they could handle.

Jamie Sinclair, from the neighbouring farm, visited the next day. 'I'm sixty-eight, kids all gone t'city t'work 'n these last two winters 'wife's arthritis played up summat fierce. I canna manage t'farm any more if we go through another winter like them last two, but we dinna want to live anywhere else. Bill told me yer looking for more land 'n yer've been a good neighbour, so I'm givin' yer first shout.'

Mark's shoulders drooped; saddened the old farmer had to sell up. After a little negotiating, Mark agreed to buy ninety-two acres of pasture land, twelve acres of hay fields, and thirty-five acres of woodland with sixteen acres of hillside. Jamie would keep ten acres and the farmhouse. In addition, Mark agreed to purchase fifty one-year and two-year old cows and five heifers.

Mark did not quibble over price and agreed on eight-hundred thousand pounds for the land and cattle and said he would contact a lawyer to finalise the arrangements and arrange payment. For Mark, it was the most depressing day since his cousin David had died.

'It's a damn shame he's had to sell up. His family have been farming for generations,' Mark told Bill and Pauline after Jamie had left.

'Yeah, a lot o' the old 'uns have left—costs going up, weather going haywire...' Bill shook his head in commiseration.

That evening, they tried to figure out what building work and new equipment would be necessary.

'Let's work out what we *need* first. If we set everything up properly right from the start, it'll pay off in the long run,' Mark told him.

'Wi' fifty more cows and ten heifers, we'll need to add another livestock shed and more milking space an' equipment.' Bill said. 'Plus another bulk milk cooling tank for the extra milk. The barn and silage area will need expanding an' all.'

Mark and Bill spent the next two days planning the construction they needed with no grumbles this time from Bill.

On twenty-ninth of October, Penelope went into labour. Tony's hands shook so badly Chris took his car keys and drove them to hospital. A few hours later Penelope gave birth to William and Mary named after her great grandparents; their copper-coloured hair leaving no doubt of their parentage. Back at the farm, streams of visitors made the nursery the most frequented place on the farm. Pauline's mother's face beamed on her daily visits. After five years she considered Penelope as much her own daughter as Pauline, and the twins, two more grandchildren to cuddle. Julie and Hugh arrived an hour after Jimmy and Meifen for the christening, leading to a boisterous and noisy week.

Near the end of December, Pauline received a call from an outraged Julie. 'There's something about your farm. I'm six weeks pregnant! We hadn't planned on children yet and it's all your fault!' she wailed.

Jimmy called Mark three hours later with identical news. Meifen and Jimmy, unlike Julie, were excited and overjoyed—the scans showed they would have a son at last. When Mark told him Julie's news, Jimmy joked it must be the water and Mark should bottle it and make a fortune.

Over Christmas, they decided that after Mark's birthday, they would try to find out what happened to Simon. Since accommodation would be a problem in the Scottish borderlands, Mark decided to bring it with them. He modified a four-wheeled cart, replacing the wheels with iron-tyred ones, to handle the rough terrain. Mark added insulated wooden walls and roof, and hung water barrels on the outside until it resembled a cross between a Romany caravan and old-west chuck wagon; cooking gear, provisions, bedding and clothes fitted in lockers. Mark reckoned his survival training should hold them in good stead for everything else. Tony trained on driving the wagon and Mark would ride alongside.

They exited the gateway on the ninth of May, 1429 near Fiddleton, seven miles north east of Langholm and made camp. Mark, in his usual systematic approach to problems, brought a map of the area around Langholm divided into what he called search areas.

'Simon mentioned he had a small farm and sold wool and sheep's milk cheese in Langholm.' Penelope told them. 'He did not mention its exact location, which in itself is suspicious.'

'Okay,' Mark said. 'All we have to do is track down every farm selling cheese in town—there can't be that many.'

They parked the wagon outside the town and Mark elected to stand guard while the others wandered in, ostensibly to buy fresh provisions, but mainly to give Penelope the opportunity to hone her accent. They decided to speak French amongst themselves and leave Penelope to do all the talking. Before Penelope left, Mark repeated the warning he had given several times already. 'Remember, don't ask direct questions. Gain their trust through gossip and see what you can discover.'

Pauline carried a knife in her belt and her trusted sock with a two-inch marble sphere in her dress pocket; Tony had his short sword and staff. Once accustomed to the accent and dialect, Penelope bought fresh vegetables, a few withered apples, butter and some cheese. The women she spoke to were less suspicious than the men—as another woman speaking their own dialect, she soon allayed any distrust they had towards a stranger. Unfortunately, the exact farm locations from where the cheeses came remained vague. Most people did not travel far from their homes and only had a general knowledge of the local geography. Penelope learned of six farms selling either goat or sheep cheese and heard of another three from visiting those farms over their next few trips.

By November 1429, and after six trips, they had eliminated seven leads and, in the process, bought several kilos of cheese, but still no news of Simon. With winter approaching they agreed to schedule their next trip for spring 1430. They had two more leads left, both in secluded valleys north-west of Langholm; Penelope was confident one was Simon's farm.

Chapter 25
Monday, 7th March 1430

Although Penelope had not uncovered anything about Simon Viscof, Simon had heard about these strangers. When Alex Armstrong told him they had returned, Simon walked in to Langholm to check them out for himself.

Simon easily spotted them; something in the way they walked and held themselves did not seem right—too self-assured and confident for strangers in a border town. A blonde woman spoke the local dialect and did all the bargaining at the market stalls. The others talked French among themselves, but a different French from what he usually heard in these parts... a strange group to find in Langholm.

After they boarded their wagon, he discreetly followed. When they set up camp, he waited until dusk and crept closer. They were speaking English—modern English. He moved closer.

'Penelope, how long are we going to stay around here? It's been two weeks already,' the red-haired man asked the woman who had done the bargaining.

The other man said, 'Penelope, let's go back home. We can

come again after we've had some rest.'

'Alright, but I mean to find Simon Vesco eventually. At least we know his farm must be out this way.'

Simon froze. He had called himself Viscof since he arrived in Magdeburg in 1400. *Who were these people and what did they want with him?*

Rumours had already started about his strength and medical knowledge, becoming more far-fetched with each retelling. He could not pull up roots again. His daughter was due to marry a Bruce next month and his son had started courting a local girl, plus Elsebeth had been sick recently. There had been few witch trials in Scotland to date, but if these strangers said anything... an accusation would be enough to destroy him and his family.

He raced over the hills and told his wife he had decided to go to New Castleton to buy another ram for his flock and would be back in a week. Elsebeth knew where he hid his gold, more than enough to keep her living well for a long time. Clement, now a strapping young man, could care for her and the farm. Simon packed his Portal and rode east over the hills. Once well away, he cut his palm and spread the blood on his saddle. He opened a gateway and, with one last look at the heather covered craggy hills he had started to call home, stepped back to 2365, leaving the horse to find its own way to his farm.

When Mark and the others arrived back in Longtown, the whole market was talking about Simon's disappearance.

'Penelope, you better try and find out what happened,' Mark said.

'Old Meg', selling pies from a shop front, happily regaled

Penelope with her fanciful thoughts on the subject, as did several other stall holders she knew. An hour later, and with a basket full of food they did not need, Penelope walked back to Mark, and whispered, 'Let us return to the caravan and sort out the facts from the rumours and gossip.'

Sat around their camp fire, Penelope repeated what she had heard. 'Discounting the weird and fantastic rumours I heard, Simon disappeared three days ago, just after we left.' She crossed her hands in front of her and slipped into full lecturing mode. 'A month ago, Simon rescued a young man trapped by a rockslide. The family had tried to move the slab of rock trapping his legs to no avail. When Simon appeared, he singlehandedly lifted the block himself while the family pulled the lad out. Not only that, he set the leg and carried him to his home; he and his wife cared for him giving him herbal medicines to help with the pain.'

'Yeah, well if that Treatment we received is anything to go by, he'd certainly be strong enough,' Tony added.

'Yes, well, apparently this was not the first time he had demonstrated medical knowledge, often with remarkable results. But, this show of strength amazed everyone and started all the wild rumours.'

'What rumours?' Mark asked.

'Witchcraft. I know they had witch trials in Europe a couple of years ago, but they did not start in Scotland until the Great Scottish Witch Hunt in 1597.'

'That may explain why Simon disappeared,' Mark remarked. 'He must have been spooked by all these rumours going around and decided to do a bunk before things got nasty.'

'Yes and we now know he had a wife and, according to one of the stall holders, two children as well,' Penelope told them.

'That is probably the reason he travelled overland through

France and the Low Countries to get to Scotland,' Mark added.

'But we were so close,' Penelope complained, and started making plans to visit Simon's family.

Mark persuaded her not to interfere. 'They are likely grieving and do not need a bunch of strangers showing up asking questions. Also, there may be consequences for Simon's family what with all these witchcraft rumours going round.'

Penelope, being Penelope, was not happy but finally agreed with Mark to revisit the area fifteen years from now. 'The rumours should have died down by then and we can find out what actually happened.'

'Alright,' Tony agreed. 'But can we visit in summer? I can't handle camping out in this cold weather much more.'

Before they returned to search for Simon's family, Penelope, in her usual meticulous way, checked their clothes to see if still suitable for 1445. They arrived in Langholm in mid-July and walked around the market. Penelope bought fresh bread, vegetables and fruit as an excuse to listen to the general talk and gossip. There was nothing about Simon's disappearance or any rumours of witchcraft.

By now they knew the rough location of Simon's farm, and Tony drove the wagon up to a small stone building with turf and thatch roof. Mark was surprised to see smoke coming from a stone chimney—none of the other places they had visited had one; he thought they were not constructed until the Sixteenth Century. Penelope sat next to Tony and saw a young woman with two boys tending a vegetable patch look up on their approach; she grabbed the children and ran into the house.

A tall broad shouldered man came to the doorway with a bow, arrow nocked and a quiver of arrows at this waist and called out in the broad local dialect, 'Where you headed, strangers?'

'We seem to be lost. We were headed for Moffat but have taken a wrong turn. It is getting late and we wondered if we can camp over there,' Penelope answered in the same dialect and pointed to a stream across from the farm house.

The man lowered the bow keeping it nocked. 'How many are ye?'

'Four of us; I am on the way to visit family with my husband and the other couple are here to provide companionship and escort.'

'Come oot where I can see ye all.'

Penelope called to Pauline and Mark in English to come to the front of the wagon and she nudged Tony to help her descend. Mark dismounted to help Pauline, keeping his hands away from his sword. Penelope introduced everyone and the man looked surprised.

'Ye be English!' he said in the same language. He stared at them for a moment. 'Ma name is Clement, Clement Viscof. Wha' brings an Englishman up here?' he said to Mark.

'As Mrs Matthews has stated, we are escorting her and her husband to visit her family in Moffat, and somehow took a wrong turn.'

At this, he called out, 'Meg, ye can come oot now with the bairns.' The young woman came to the door with the boys behind her. 'Yon is ma wife, Meg. The bairns are Jamie and Angus,' he pointed to the two red-haired boys standing in the doorway. 'Meg, these here travellers will be staying by yonder burn.'

'Thank you. We have our own provisions and will gladly share them.'

Penelope stepped forward and smiled at Meg. 'We have

fresh bread and some venison, and will gladly help prepare the evening meal.'

At this, Meg relaxed and chatted with Penelope who turned to Pauline. 'Let's fetch the food and we can cook inside.'

'While the women are preparing dinner is there anything we can do to help around here,' Mark asked and noticed a partly completed dry-stone wall next to the farm. 'Maybe we can help you finish the wall in return for your hospitality? The three of us could finish a lot quicker.'

'Verra generous of ye. I need to bring the sheep off the hills and have 'em safe afore winter.'

For the next two days Mark, Tony and Clement worked on the wall. The camaraderie from working together loosened Clement's tongue and Mark asked how long he had been farming.

'Ma pa started the farm when I was sixteen. We came over here from Sion in 1428. My pa helped Jamie Armstrong fight off an attack by them Johnston marauders and the Armstrongs let him settle here.'

'Where is your father now?' Mark asked, masking his excitement by setting another rock in the wall.

'When I was eighteen, he went to New Castleton to buy a new ram. Two days later, his horse came back with dried blood on t' saddle. Me and some o' the Armstrong lads searched for two weeks thinkin' he'd 'ad an accident but we found no trace o' him. We reckon he must have fallen in a gully, or been attacked.'

'And your father... What was he like?'

'His name was Simon, tall, like you, and verra strong. Had a gift for languages he did and taught me and my sister English and French besides the German we spoke. Built this house from a ruin and settled here. He started selling wool, meat and cheese in the market down at Langholm. Meg still sells the cheese to the shops there.'

'Where are your sister and your mother?'

'My sister, Katherine, married a Bruce a month after he disappeared and moved to Edinburgh. She died wi' her whole family six years ago in one o' the sicknesses they have o'er there.'

'And your mother?'

'She wasna' a strong woman an' just after my father disappeared, she foond she was carrying another bairn. 'Twas a hard birth and she couldna' care for young Donald, as she named him.

Jamie Armstrong and his wife Agnes had none o' their own and promised to raise him as an Armstrong. They moved oc'r toward Hawick. Havna' seen 'em since. When my ma heard aboot Katherine, 'twas more an' she could take an' she passed a few months later.'

In the evening at the wagon, Mark told the others what he had found out. 'Now we know why the Armstrong line is so important. It's a direct Viscof line starting with Simon's son Donald.'

Penelope seemed satisfied but puzzled over what had happened to the Viscofs; the name had apparently died out in the late Fifteenth Century.

Pauline remarked, 'What with clan rivalries, Reivers and clashes with the English, never mind disease, it's not surprising. A few other small borderland families died out as well.'

'Anyway, we can get on with our own lives now. There's a lot of work on the farm and seed bank to do,' Mark added. 'Plus, school holidays start next month and we can expect to be damn busy.'

Penelope stared at Tony's glum expression. 'What's the matter with you? We can now go back to our normal lives. I thought you would be happy.'

'I am. It's just that I spent months of nursing bruises to learn how to use this sword and staff and never got to use them.'

Mark laughed. 'Be glad you didn't. We might have started something we couldn't finish.'

They completed the wall the next day and Mark told Clement they would be leaving. 'We cannot delay any longer, we need to move on to Moffat.'

Clement gave them clear directions and said they should make it to Moffat in two days. They left some of their provisions, a sack of flour, a bag of salt and the balance of dried venison and fish, saying they could pick up more from farms they passed on their journey.

A week later, Mark had just returned from checking the bee hives with Tony when Ben Attwood, a cantankerous neighbour with a farm to the west, drove up in his battered old *Vauxhall Nova*.

'Ben, what brings you over?'

Blunt and to the point as always as Mark remembered, Ben told him, 'I heard Jamie Sinclair got a fair deal from yer on 'is farm. I'm wondering if yer want more land. I've thirty-odd acres bordering yours oe'r to t'west if yer interested. Can't afford to keep it goin' anymore. And I can sell some of me cows an' all.'

'Why don't we go inside and talk?' Mark led the way to his office. He knew from Nicholas' journals that farm land would go up in price and this was an opportunity to expand his farm holding he could not afford to miss. Problem was, how to pay for it?

After some dickering and poring over a map of the area, they agreed on six thousand pounds per acre for thirty-seven acres of good dairy pasture.

'Let me talk to my bank, Ben. Give me some time, will you? I promise I'll get back to you as soon as I can.'

After dinner and once the children were asleep, Mark discussed Ben's visit with Pauline. 'His land is exactly where I saw that biome when we flew over the farm in 2535. I don't want to sell any more of the stamp collection and I can hardly *discover* another stash of them, can I? I don't want to take on any more bank loans, either, if I can help it, but I have to have that land.'

'Pity you used all Nicholas' gold bars in Chesterfield. That would have solved your problem.'

Mark stared at her. 'Remember I told you about my great-something Uncle John, the one that took off to join the California Gold Rush?'

'Where are you going with this?'

Mark gave one of his annoying smiles. 'How about we get ahead of the rush and pick some up before anyone else?'

'What are you talking about?'

'The gold rush started around 1848. If we go to Sutter's Mill before *James Marshall* gets there, we can get first pick.'

Pauline's mouth gaped open. 'You... you want to go panning for gold? ...In California?'

'Why not? If we go a few years earlier, there'll be nobody there. Come on.' Mark grabbed her arm and pulled her to his study.

Mark set up his laptop and Pauline remarked, 'Must admit, we haven't been anywhere for a while. It's been five months since we were in 1430.'

'It'll be fun as well. Just the two of us. Penelope can't follow since she was still alive in 1836 and that would set up a weird paradox.'

After three hours of internet research, Mark had a map of the location, coordinates and had ordered a list of mining and survival equipment he would need. Mark leaned back and stretched. 'That should do it. Everything should be here in a couple of weeks. Then we can be the first of the *forty-niners*.'

'How many trips are you planning?'

'I reckon about five or six trips. Two trips per day with a day's rest between should be enough to find enough gold to pay old Ben. Especially with the metal detector we're taking.'

'So, soon as everything gets here, then?'

'Yes. Once we have the gold, I need to smelt it into bars and sell it. I want to settle this before Ben changes his mind and sells to someone else.'

By the third week of August, Mark had all the heavy, bulky equipment stored in the byre. He and Pauline tested the metal detector around the byre. All they found were a lot of rusty nails and some old bottle caps left by visitors, but they were now confident in its use.

Mark had decided to make the first trip on his own to pass the supplies through the gateway, then make all subsequent trips from the basement. It would look strange if they kept riding up to the byre twice a day. They had agreed they would arrive at dawn on the banks of the South Fork American River where James Marshall made his discovery, and leave at seven at night to travel back to 2012. After a few hours rest, they would make a second trip for the following day in 1836.

'Can you shoot?' Mark asked.

'I grew up on a farm, what do you think?' Pauline retorted. 'My dad taught me to use a shotgun and air-rifle as soon as I could hold them.'

'Well, I have two shotguns and ammunition, just in case. We'll head off tomorrow morning about eight o'clock. Wear jeans, hiking boots and pack plenty of work shirts and a hat, and a good waterproof sunblock. We'll arrive in summer, twentieth of June to be exact, and it could get up to forty degrees in the afternoon.'

Chapter 26
California, Monday 20th June, 1836

It was a drizzly morning as Mark drove to the byre. He activated the Portal and checked around for any animal or human activity before he carried the heavy supplies through. After everything was moved, he headed back to the farmhouse for breakfast with Pauline.

'Everything is set, once we've eaten, we can head off.'

In the basement, Mark checked the backpacks and the weapons they had left there the night before then set the same coordinates as before, but one hour later. He checked the site again, and they stepped through.

'I'll make a shelter for shade before we get started. We'll need it later.'

Mark cut down some saplings and made a lean-to shelter near the trees at the edge of river. Once satisfied it was sturdy enough, he and Pauline walked along the river bank.

Mark stopped, picked up something, grabbed Pauline and whirled her around. He put her down and, after fending off

Pauline's slaps to his arms, showed her what he had in his hand—a small gold nugget.

'You could have just showed me instead of swinging me around like a maniac.'

'Look there's more of them,' he pointed down, ignoring her protests.

They spent a busy hour scouring the river bank picking loose gold nuggets from off the ground.

Pauline examined the handful of gold they had collected. 'I didn't realise it would be this easy.'

'Well, the hard work is about to start if we want to find enough to pay for that land.'

Mark and Pauline took turns using the metal detector and, after a couple of hours slowly sweeping it across the sand and gravel, they selected two spots indicating good concentrations of metal. Mark took some samples of the sand from each spot, and in the washing pan detected the distinctive colour they were looking for. He set up the sluice, shovelled sand into the hopper, and baled water from the river to wash the sand onto to the expanded metal screen and raised metal bars to trap the larger gold pieces. The underlying mat would catch the really fine material. After about an hour or so, they had several more small nuggets and flakes of gold.

'We need to dig down deeper. The heavier gold will settle near the bedrock,' he told Pauline as they took as short break. 'I'll dig, you check for signs of gold.'

Mark dug a trench about five feet deep and three feet wide, slowly extending it away from the river bank. Pauline pointed at a yellow streak in the hole. 'Look there! To your left, near the bottom.'

Scooping out the soil, Mark went to the river to pan it. There was gold dust and flakes but also a nugget, water worn, but about two ounces.

Mark looked at the plastic tubes he kept the gold in. 'If this keeps up we won't have to make too many trips at all. We must have at least twenty ounces already.'

'It's getting really hot, my shirt is stuck to me. Let's take a break and eat,' Pauline suggested and went to the river to wash her face and neck. 'Good job you said to bring sunblock, I don't burn easily, but it's scorching out here.'

'Drink more water, it's easy to dehydrate in this heat, especially as there is little wind around. I brought two gallons, so don't worry.' Mark advised, and took a long drink himself.

After lunch, they made sure all their wrappings were collected to take back with them. Pauline continued to scoop the earth Mark had dug from the hole onto the sluice's hopper, while Mark poured the river water. Once the baffles were full, they panned the fine material at the river edge. By six o'clock they had filled another plastic container.

Mark stood and stretched. 'This is damn tiring. Let's tidy up here and go home.'

'I need a shower,' Pauline grumbled as they stored their gear.

'Same here. Leave your backpack and we'll sneak upstairs, while Jenny is busy in the kitchen.'

After they cleaned up, they had a quick lunch and went to sleep. Seven hours later, after dinner, they were back to the basement. They arrived back at the same location on the twenty-first of June, 1836. While Pauline checked the rest of the sandbank, Mark continued sluicing the dirt from the hole. By the end of the day they had another eleven ounces in small nuggets and flakes.

'You know we've been up for fourteen hours here and twenty-two there, I need a good sleep,' Pauline told Mark as they lay in bed.

'Jenny will be thinking we're on a second honeymoon all the time we've spent in here, but I'm too damn beat to make her thoughts reality,' Mark told her.

'Good, because I'm too exhausted to be interested!'

Mark sat up looking more alert. 'You mean that if you weren't exhausted you would be?

'No! I'm going to sleep. Goodnight!'

The next day, they were very successful and collected sixty-one ounces of gold, several small nuggets, and a lot of flakes and dust.

After dinner, Mark told Pauline that they had collected eighty-two ounces altogether, worth about one-hundred and fifty-thousand US dollars at the current exchange rate.

'Another day like that and we'll call it quits. I didn't realise how tough this would be... and *we* have the advantage of knowing exactly where to look. The metal detector saves a lot of time as well. The old prospectors dug it out with their knives and fingers and used crude panning techniques. I don't think they even had proper sluices,' he explained.

The next morning, nothing seemed to have been disturbed. Mark started sluicing more sand and gravel while Pauline slowly walked across the sandbank with the shotgun over her shoulder.

He spun around at a yell from Pauline, She was about a hundred yards away and bending over the gravel bank. He quickly rushed across carrying his shotgun.

'What's the matter?' he asked, concern evident in his voice.

Pauline just held out her hand and there was a large rounded water-worn irregular shaped nugget, roughly four inches long, two inches wide and about an inch thick.

'That must be seventy or eighty ounces at least! We can definitely wrap up after this trip.'

As they sat having lunch, they could not stop talking about her find. Then... Mark heard a noise from across the river and grabbed the shotgun.

He saw a small group of Native American Indians coming out of the trees. They froze as soon as they saw Mark; the women pushed the children back in to the tree cover as two men raised their bows. They all stared at each other, then Mark passed the gun to Pauline to hold and took a step forward with his arms out and palms up. The Indians slowly lowered their bows and moved to the river bank. Mark motioned them to cross over and mimed eating. The two men talked to each other and the taller one waded across.

Mark took a beef sandwich, tore it in two, bit into one half and offered the other. After taking a bite, the man said something in a language Mark did not understand, then spoke in broken Spanish.

'Elsu,' the man said, and pointed to his chest, then pointed his thumb at Mark.

'Mark,'

'Why here? No hunting no...' Elsu said something Mark did not understand, then pointed at Pauline. 'Woman safe, no harm. Peace?'

'Peace,' Mark then pointed across the river. 'Your family is safe. Come, eat. My woman can meet your women.' Mark gestured to Pauline to stand next to him.

'Is that Spanish?' Pauline asked, softly, 'Do you understand what he's saying?'

'Yes. This area was part of Mexico in this time, so Elsu here must have had some contact with Mexicans and picked up a bit of the language. Take out the oranges you brought and those chocolate bars... and that sling bag in my backpack.'

Elsu waved and shouted at the other man; the rest of the group came out of the trees and crossed the river. Both men were taller than Mark; Elsu was well over six feet and the other only a little shorter. Both had long hair bound back with a leather strap. They were well built, wearing just skin loincloths and had shell ornaments in their pierced ears and nose. As the women and children came across, she noticed the men and women all had three lines tattooed from their chin down their chest to the stomach. The women were about five and a half feet tall, quite stocky and wore only loincloths, naked from the waist up. While one of the bigger children had a loincloth like the men, the other two boys were naked. Most of them wore deer skin moccasins while the two men had knee-high deer-hide boots.

They all sat outside Mark's shelter and the Indian women took out some berries from the beautifully woven baskets they had placed on the ground. They offered them to Pauline, who peeled an orange and offered them the rest. Pauline ate the mixture of raspberries, cherries and another fruit with a subtle honey and elderflower aroma and a sweet, tart taste and looked similar to the raspberries. When the native women bit into the oranges there were big smiles on their faces as the juice ran down their chins. Mark unwrapped a chocolate bar, broke off a piece, put it in his mouth and passed the bar to the two men. Elsu broke into a huge smile when he tasted it and passed the chocolate to the others—big smiles broke out all over, especially on the children.

'Looks like *Cadbury's* is a favourite here as well; pass me another bar,' he told Pauline. He unwrapped it and gave it to Elsu.

Elsu pointed to the other man. 'Honon, brother. Son of father.' Then he pointed at one of the women who looked to be no more than sixteen, 'Huyana, my woman.'

Honon then pointed at the other woman. 'Malila.'

'Pauline,' Mark told them, indicating his wife.

Elsu told Mark that only he spoke Spanish and asked what they were doing here. When Mark showed him some of the gold dust and flakes they had found, they all started laughing. Elsu pointed at the gold, 'Not good, no eat, not make arrow,' and showed him the crude iron arrow heads he had.

'Must have got them from the Mexicans. I don't think they did much metal work themselves, if any,' Mark murmured to Pauline while he examined the arrow heads.

Mark explained to the two men that white men like the yellow metal and used it for ornaments, pointing to Pauline's gold ear studs and his own signet ring.

'You like? We find.' Elsu turned and said something to the children. They quickly ran off down the sandbank and started searching through the gravel and sand.

'Thank you. Take this gift,' Mark passed the cotton sling bag, which had a beaded border and beaded design of a bird on it, to Elsu, who passed it to his wife. Her smile showed her obvious delight.

Mark learned they were a small family group of Miwoks, travelling to hunt for deer and forage for berries and whatever else they could collect. They had come to the river to rest and fish, and their village was about a three-day walk southwest of where they were, in another valley.

The children came running back, shouting and laughing with several small nuggets on a piece of bark, at least seven ounces. To their delight, Mark gave them some more chocolate and they ran off to find more. Mark suddenly laughed at something Elsu said and looked at Pauline. His replies were met with grins and more comments.

'What did he say?' Pauline asked.

'He wanted to know how many children we have—he said you had good hips and can bear many boys,' he told her with a straight face. 'I told them we had two boys staying in another place with your mother. Then he said you were a strong woman, a good woman and would make many strong boys.'

Pauline was speechless and blushed heavily, causing the two Miwok men to laugh again. Mark explained to Elsu they would be leaving soon and would leave the shelter behind for them. While they talked about fishing, hunting and about where each other lived, the children kept coming back bringing the gold they had found. Mark was so impressed when they brought back several large nuggets, he gave Elsu a spare plain stainless steel knife and an unwrapped chocolate bar to each child.

'You good man, she strong woman. We go find fish. Come back at sunrise.' He grasped Mark's arm and called to the others. They gathered all their baskets and goods and started heading down river as Mark and Pauline waved to them.

Once they were sure the Miwoks were not coming back, they sorted the obviously modern tools and equipment in to one pile and checked the site making sure it was cleaned up. They left the shelter, a roll of strong twine, fruit and some energy bars, taking off all the wrappings first to take back with them. They wrapped all the food in a cotton bandana and rewrapped it in a spare wool shirt. After opening the gateway, they passed everything into the basement. Just before they walked through, Mark left his axe on top of the pile.

It was ten o'clock in the morning when they crept out of the basement. After three hours in 2012, another eleven hours in 1836 and, with the prospecting and stress of meeting the Miwoks, they were both completely worn out. Back in Mark's study after they had cleaned up, they sat on the couch and Mark told Pauline they had just over three hundred ounces worth over three-hundred and thirty-thousand pounds. 'That's more than I needed, but I'm not complaining. I wonder what Elsu will think when he comes back. There'll be no tracks, it will be like we just disappeared in to thin air.'

'We did, when you think about it. You know you took a risk giving away your knife and axe. Stainless steel wasn't invented then. Won't that create an anomaly?'

'Can't! If it would, the Novikov Principle would have kicked in and prevented it happening somehow.'

'Any idea what those berries were Huyana gave me. They were like raspberries, but not.'

'Not sure, I'll have to look them up.'

'Do it now! I want you to find out and start growing them in the greenhouse. They'd make excellent jam.'

'Mark groaned and stood up, grumbling. 'Bloody slave driver.'

Half an hour later Mark told her, 'They're thimbleberries and native to western North America. If I can get some rhizome segments I can grow them in the greenhouse and then plant them outside; they will be good for the bees as well.'

Mark looked at her with a sly grin. 'Talking about Huyana, seems you made a bit of a conquest with Elsu.'

She blushed and laughed. 'I'm not sure how I feel about his

crack about my hips.'

'Having children was obviously important to them. His wife has three, the youngest, a daughter, was back in their village with her grandparents. Remember he said you were strong and would be able to have many more strong boys.'

'More children! We've got three already!' She sputtered so much Mark could not help but laugh.

'You should see your face.'

'It's not funny. You men are all the same. One-track minds!' she retorted.

A knock on the door silenced them both. Jenny popped her head around the door to say lunch was ready, looking intently at Pauline. 'Is everythin' awright?'

'Everything's fine, Jenny. I was just telling her a bawdy story about Jimmy that's all.'

'Nowt would surprise me abart 'im. Don't get me wrong, 'e's a lovely man an' all, but a bit on t' wild side, if yer ask me.' She sniffed and left.

They took it easy the rest of the day and after the children were asleep, Pauline asked, 'How are you going to sell all this?'

'Selling the gold as it is will take too long. I'll have to melt it all down into bars again. Problem is nobody will touch unmarked gold bars. They'll be considered blacklisted DRC Congo gold.'

'So how are you going to get around it?'

'What if good old Uncle John bequeathed the gold to his ancestors?'

Pauline gawped. 'Eh?'

'What if he snuck back to England with the gold, made it in to bars and had them all assayed back in the 1850s? Then, what if he left them at a bank to keep for himself or his descendants?'

'I don't understand.'

Mark gave her one his sneaky grins. 'I can pretend to be John Bishop and take the bars to have them assayed at Mathey's, like I did last time. But instead of selling the bars I can leave them with a bank and collect them as one of John's descendants.'

'Are you sure? It seems a bit of a gamble.'

'It's worked before with the journals and the stamps for Makoto. No reason it won't work again.'

An hour of research and Mark decided to use the *London and County Banking Company* on Lombard Street to deposit his gold. By 2012 it would be the *NatWest Bank* and their headquarters were, appropriately, on Bishopsgate, where he had his own bank account.

Although Mark decided to keep the large nugget Pauline had found as a souvenir, after four days of hot work in the basement, he had sixteen one-pound bars of gold. Even if the purity was only eighty-five percent, the bars would still be worth almost a quarter of a million pounds.

Mark arrived at the same place in Hyde Park he had used six years earlier, although this time is was a nice spring morning, tenth of April, 1854. Mark found the cab ride to Matthey's as uncomfortable and noisy as the last time, and the smell was worse with the warmer weather.

At Matthey's, he presented his business card and introduced himself as John Bishop. 'I have just returned from America and wish to have this gold assayed,' he said to the clerk and removed the gold bars from his backpack.

When a more senior person arrived, he repeated his introduction. 'I realise there are silver and other impurities, that is why I wish to have them assayed and marked appropriately.'

'Mr Bishop, this will take three days. Where can we contact you when we have competed the assay?'

'I will be visiting friends in the country, I will return on Thursday.'

An hour later, after the bars had been weighed, Mark left with his receipt for the gold and took a cab back to Hyde Park. Between the grime and stench, he was not about to hang around for three more days. He would rest at home and pop back in the evening to collect the bars and visit Lombard Street.

Pauline was too nervous to eat and enjoy her dinner. 'Are you sure this will work?'

'So far everything has gone smoothly. If it is not meant to be, then something will prevent it from happening. At least I'll have assay marked gold bars, even if they were assayed nearly one hundred and sixty years ago.'

He was soon back at Matthey's and the manager greeted him on arrival. 'Good morning, Mr Bishop. We have completed your assay and here are your stamped bars and letter of confirmation. The purity varies from eighty-five to ninety-one percent.'

Mark paid for the assay from the five hundred pounds he had left over from his time in Chesterfield. Packing the bars in his backpack, he had the doorman hail a cab and headed to Lombard Street.

This is where everything succeeds or fails he thought as he alighted in front of the bank.

Mark took a deep breath, entered the banking hall and approached a teller. 'I wish to open an account and store some valuables in your vault.'

When Mark showed the teller the three hundred and fifty pounds in Bank of England notes and a hundred pounds in gold sovereigns, the teller called the manager.

Mark presented his business card and explained his request. 'I wish to open an account and use it to pay for storing some valuables in your vault, will that be possible?'

'Mr Bishop, what is the nature of these valuables, may I ask?'

Mark opened his back pack and removed the sixteen bars, each measuring two by one by half-an-inch. 'These. Sixteen pounds of gold bars.'

The manager's eyes widened before he regained his composure. 'Er... Mr Bishop, we do provide this service. Might I ask for how long you wish us to keep them?'

'I am not certain. I mined the gold in California and I intend to go back there and try my luck again. It may be some time before I return, possibly a few years, will that be a problem?'

'No, not a problem at all, sir. We can offer you three percent interest on your deposit. How long a term are you considering?'

'Is a fifty year term possible?'

'Certainly we can arrange that. Any charges for storage of your gold in our vaults will be deducted from the final sum when withdrawn.'

Half-an-hour later, Mark was in possession of receipts for the account and for the gold. 'There is one more item of business. As I am travelling back to the Americas, I would like to have a contract or agreement that either I, or a family member, shall collect the gold. Proof of ownership will be this receipt and a copy of the agreement. Is this possible?'

'Certainly. I will have an agreement drafted at once, one copy to be held by the bank and another for yourself.'

By the time the agreement had been signed and witnessed, Mark was hungry. He had been in 1854 for five hours and although it was just past one o'clock in the afternoon, his stomach was telling him it was way past midnight in 2012. He took a cab back to Hyde Park, but the fine dry weather had enticed crowds of people to stroll the grounds and he had to walk around for almost two hours to find somewhere secluded to open the gateway. Behind some trees to the east of the park, Mark checked no-one was around and stepped back into 2012.

Chapter 27

Keldthorpe Farm, 28th August, 2012

'How was it? Any problems?' Pauline asked, as he stepped through the gateway.

'I'm starving. Let's raid the kitchen and I'll tell you all about it.'

After Mark had made himself a massive roast beef and chutney sandwich and a mug of tea, he recounted all that had happened and showed her the documents from the bank.

'These look so new. The bank will never accept them,' Pauline told him.

'I know. I'm going to have to bury them like last time.'

'You can't keep discovering things in the byre,' Pauline protested.

'This time I don't have to. It doesn't matter if there are no witnesses, the important thing is they are genuinely old,.'

'Then how're you going to find them this time?'

'Come on, I'll show you.'

Mark swigged the last of his tea and headed to his study. He took out the family Bible, lay it on the desk and showed her the back cover. 'See how thick this is? If I carefully open the inside cloth binding, I can hide those documents and glue it back. Then I'll call John Prentis to come over to help me sort out some legal stuff and 'accidentally' drop it. If I use a weak glue mixture, the back cover will come away and we can examine it and find the documents.'

The next morning, Mark wrapped the documents in oilskin and placed them in a brass box from the museum store. After sealing the box with wax and wrapping it in more oilskin, he and Pauline rode their horses to the byre.

Pauline looked around what was now a neat refreshment centre. 'You're running out of places to dig up.'

Mark pointed to the floor a few feet from the wall to the storage area. 'There, near the door. That flagstone is not so big and should be easier to remove.'

Mark packed the crowbar and shovel onto Lucky and changed into period clothes. 'Here we go again.' He opened a gateway to 1855 and kissed his wife. 'See you in an hour.'

He exited on Richmond road as before and rode up to the byre which was still the ruin it had been in on his last visit in 1840. He kicked aside a pile of dead leaves and found the flagstone he wanted. An hour later, the box was buried and the replaced flagstone covered with dead leaves and other debris. Minutes later he was back in 2012.

'I'll change and then I can start digging again.'

The box was exactly where he had left it a hundred and fifty-seven years earlier.

'Let's get it back to my study and we can check it, then hide the documents in the Bible.'

Mark took the oil skin wrapped package to his climate controlled safe room and carefully cut open the wrapping and scraped the wax off the box—the documents were slightly stained, but otherwise still legible.

Pauline gasped. 'I can't believe it. Just yesterday they looked so new.'

'Wait here, I'll get the glue pot and glue from the workshop.'

Twenty minutes later, Mark dropped the animal glue pearls he and Bill used to repair furniture in a pot of water. 'Pass me the Bible. I'll tackle that while we wait for them to dissolve.'

Mark took the scalpel blade he used to trim photographs and gently sliced open the back cover of the Bible and then trimmed off the old cracked glue.

Pauline passed him the documents and he carefully arranged them in the centre of the Bible cover. The glue pearls had dissolved so Mark put them in the electric glue pot.

It was not long before Pauline wrinkled her nose, 'Urgh! Smells like something died. I'm going to make coffee. Call me when you're finished... and open a damn window!'

Mark applied a thin coating of glue and sealed the documents inside the Bible cover. He took the Bible to his safe room and placed half-a-dozen books on top to apply pressure; the cool dry air would allow the glue to set faster. He met Pauline in the living room. 'Time to call John. He'll make the perfect witness.'

When John arrived the following morning, Mark took him on a tour of the farm's facilities and explained the offer of more land. 'Good pasture land is hard to find, and this directly adjoins my land to the west. It's a great opportunity to expand the herd and that means more milk and other products.'

Back in Mark's office, they discussed the purchase details and drafted the necessary papers.

'I'll have these drawn up properly back in the office.' John said.

'John, would you like to see the stamp collection? You arranged the insurance and everything, least I can do is show you. Then we can have some lunch before you head back.'

'Yes, I would. I have always wondered what all the fuss was about.'

Mark and Pauline took John to his safe room and showed him the fifty-odd matching albums in which he had mounted his collection.

'There they are,' Mark opened several to show John the stamps, envelopes and the detailed annotations and maps he had made for each item.

'I know little about stamp collecting, but this is fantastic.'

Mark then took out the family Bible. 'Of all these, this is my most treasured item. Our family Bible going all the way back to 1740.'

When Mark passed it to John, he deliberately fumbled and dropped it. The 'poor' job he had done of sealing the back cover worked. When Mark picked it up, the inside cloth binding had split open and the corner of a piece of paper was visible.

John pointed. 'What's that?'

Mark lay the book on the table and carefully prised open the cloth lining to reveal the documents he had hidden the day before.

John examined the papers with Mark and exclaimed, 'These are legal documents.' He pointed to the agreement. 'That's a contract between a John Bishop and the London and County Banking Company to store sixteen gold bars, the cost of storing the gold in their vaults to be deducted from the account on withdrawal of the money.' John looked at the deposit receipt. 'There. Four hundred and fifty pounds deposited on the thirteenth of April, 1854 at three percent for fifty years. That was a fortune in those days.'

'John Bishop was one of my ancestors. I'll show you.' Mark opened the Bible to the entry for John's birth on the fourteenth of September, 1818. 'In my cousin's research of the family tree, he mentions John Bishop going to California during the gold rush in 1849, but he died in Longtown, Cumberland on twentieth of May, 1854.'

John looked amazed. 'Well, it looks like he came back and deposited this gold in a London bank.'

'Would it still be there?' Pauline asked.

John turned to her, his brow furrowed. 'It should be. London and County Banking Company was the precursor for the NatWest. I'll contact one of their lawyers—he and I went to university together.'

'How difficult will it be to claim it?'

'Might take a while, but with these documents, the proof that John Bishop was Mark's ancestor, it should only be a matter of time, but it will depend a lot on the bank's policy on dormant accounts. Also, you would need to find any other descendants.'

'There aren't any.' Mark deliberately did not mention his 'Aunt' Penelope. 'I'm the last Bishop, except for the kids, of course.'

'Well, in that case, I'll call Bruce at NatWest straightaway and set up a meeting.'

Over lunch, the whole conversation revolved around the legalities of claiming, and finding, the gold bars. Afterwards John took a witness statement from Pauline while Mark packed an overnight bag, the Bible and the documents they had found, and followed John back to London.

Mark and John met Bruce Hancock in the main lobby of the bank on Bishopsgate.

Bruce shook Mark's hand. 'Come to my office, I'm dying to see these documents Mr Bishop.'

After scrutinising them, Bruce called his manager. John, as Mark's solicitor, did most of the talking. He explained how they had found the documents and showed them the family Bible as proof that John Bishop was Mark's ancestor and Mark, the only living adult descendant.

'Mr Bishop, this is most unusual,' the manager told them. 'This deposit receipt and contract appears to be almost one-hundred and sixty years old. Amazing! Please, you understand that before we can initiate a search, you need to complete a dormant accounts claim form and we will have to verify the authenticity of these documents, and your claim as the sole beneficiary?'

Mark leaned forward. 'That is perfectly understandable. How long do you think it will take?'

'Normally a search for a dormant account, which is certainly the case in this instance, takes three months. However, as this is so extraordinary, I will personally ensure we expedite this matter as soon as you complete a claim form.'

As the manager stood to shake hands, Mark mentioned, 'There is one other matter I would like to discuss while I am here. I would like to arrange a short term loan to buy some land next to my farm.'

'I am sure we can accommodate that request, Mr Bishop. Exactly how large a loan are you considering?'

'Two-hundred and twenty-thousand pounds.'

'After a few minutes checking Mark's account, the manager replied, 'That is not a problem, Mr Bishop. Mr Hancock will make the arrangements and be in touch with you.'

Mark now stood, shook hands and he and John left with Bruce who helped him complete the form.

Four hours later, Mark was on a train to Darlington. Pauline met him at the station that evening and asked about his trip.

'I thought you didn't want to take a loan?' Pauline asked when he related his trip to London.

'Yeah, but I can't wait three months or more for them to find that gold. I hate the idea of a further loan, but if Ben doesn't hear something soon, he may well sell to somebody else.'

Two weeks after visiting the bank, Mark and John Prentis met Ben Attwood at his farm. Mark and Ben signed the transfer papers and Mark arranged the purchase fee to be deposited in Ben's account. Back at the farm, Mark sat with Bill to plan for the expanded farm, now over six hundred acres, with three hundred and thirty acres of grazing land for his dairy herd.

Mark was discussing the plans for the extension of the greenhouses with Chris when his phone rang. It was John Prentis. 'Great news. Bruce has just called me and NatWest have tracked down the gold *and* the original account ledger. How soon can you come down?'

'Fantastic! I was beginning to wonder whether they would find anything. It's been nearly four months. We'll be there tomorrow afternoon.'

After Mark introduced his wife, the manager told them. 'Mr and Mrs Bishop, we have verified the authenticity of these documents and one of our archivists found a ledger containing details of an account for John Bishop at the address on the receipt, from the London and County Banking Company. We also traced the gold bars to one of our vaults. They were in a wooden box and inside we found an identical copy of the agreement you presented. Additionally, our legal department has checked and verified your claim to being the sole descendant and, as such, the collateral heir. Congratulations.'

'And that means what exactly?' Pauline asked.

'It means your husband is the legal claimant of these assets, Mrs Bishop.'

'So when can I claim the gold?' Mark asked.

'It has been moved to our vaults here and can be claimed as soon as Legal have you sign some paperwork. Another thing, Mr Bishop, there is one thousand, nine hundred and seventy pounds and fifteen shillings in the account. In view of the unusual nature of this particular dormant account, the bank has agreed to waive any storage fees for the gold.'

John Prentis, who until now had kept quiet, chipped in. 'Mark, all this is subject to Inheritance Tax of forty percent on any amount above three-hundred and twenty-five-thousand pounds and it has to be paid before you can take possession of these assets. It all depends on whatever price you get for the gold.'

'That still leaves me with a Hell of a lot more than I had this morning.'

Mark asked John to make the arrangements with the bank to pay any inheritance tax to Her Majesty's Revenue and Customs from his account.

The gold was finally valued at almost two-hundred and ten-thousand pounds and John declared he did not have any tax to pay. A week before Mark's thirty-eighth birthday, he had an extra two-hundred and seventy-three-thousand pounds in the bank. He had figured that gold ingots with antiquarian provenance would be worth more than just the value of the gold itself. He was correct—they realised thirty percent more than the actual gold price.

The publishing of the journals and his encyclopaedic knowledge of the postal history of north-east Derbyshire had not only made Mark the go-to expert on the subject but had sated his thirst for postal history. With the shop and museum closed for winter, and the extra money in his account covering the loan for Ben's land, he could now relax. He started thinking about extending his family tree again; he had done nothing with it since discovering Penelope was his great-aunt.

'We can start with Henry Bishop and work back from there,' he told Pauline one evening after the children were in bed.

'We? It's your family, you go. I had enough of the Fifteenth Century looking for Simon and I'm not interested in the Sixteenth

Century. I'll stick to Victorian history.'

'Alright. I'll wait until winter is over, probably end of April before we open the shop and museum full time for Bank Holiday.'

On the twenty-third of April, Mark came through the gateway near Kershope Burn, six miles north-east of Crofthead—it was eight o'clock on a warm evening in July 1550. He gave Lucky his head and let him run, slowing to a walk before reaching Moat. By the time he arrived at the farm, they were both well coated with dust. The house was different from the prosperous farm he had visited in 1767, now only a simple single-storey stone building with slate roof and a smaller stone shelter next to it.

A white-haired old man sat on a bench in front of the house talking to a young lad. On Mark's approach, he stood and sent the lad indoors; Mark stopped and waved.

The lad came out and handed a loaded crossbow to the old man, who aimed it at Mark. 'Anythin' I can do for yer?'

Mark raised his hand clear of his sword. 'I intend no harm and bring no trouble. I only want to ask how far it is to Carlisle.'

'Yer English? Where yer from?' the man asked, the crossbow not wavering an inch.

'I'm from Yorkshire. Been visiting kin in Blackpool Gate on my way to Penrith to visit more kin over there.'

The man lowered the crossbow slightly. 'Ye'll never make Carlisle afore dark and the roads are none too safe for a lone traveller at night.' He stared at Mark for a moment. 'Looks like yon horse could do wi' a drink. Yer can pump some water from 'well aside o' house.'

After watering Lucky, Mark approached the old man and introduced himself. 'Michael Holmes from York.'

'William Bishop. Bide a while, me son'll be back soon. Mayhap he'll let you stay the night.'

'That's generous of you, sir, I appreciate it.'

William, now satisfied Mark was a *bona fide* traveller and not a bandit, proved to be a chatty old fellow and Mark learned the family used to live in Longtown where his son, Henry, had joined the warden's army when the Scots invaded in 1542. Henry and two others had captured the leader of the Scots, *Robert Maxwell* at Solway Moss. For this, *Thomas Wharton*, the deputy warden of Western Marches granted them their own land.

'After that, me and me sons built this 'ere farm.'

No sooner said than a tall auburn-haired man entered the farmyard carrying two rabbits. William introduced Mark to his son, Henry, and explained Mark's situation.

'Yer welcome to rest a night. As me father said, it's none too safe ridin' at night.'

Mark collected his bedroll and saddle bags and followed Henry into the house.

'Alice, here's a couple o' cunny to roast, bring some ale oe'r for oor guest. This 'ere is Mister 'olmes, he'll be staying the night. He can sleep in front o' fire.'

His wife nodded and brought three clay mugs of ale before going to tend the stew over the fire.

The three men sat at the table on the only chairs available, the two boys sat on the floor near the fire watching the stranger. Mark looked around. Bare stone walls, hard earth floor covered in rushes and small windows. The fireplace had a flagstone hearth and a stack of wood piled by the well-constructed chimney. A doorway led to a bedroom off the combined living, dining and kitchen area and on a low shelf by the far wall, near the fireplace, lay a stack of rolled-up mattresses.

After a second mug of ale, William became quite garrulous while Henry nodded from time to time as his father told his tale. William related how his sister, Agnes, had died in 1472 and his wife Jane had passed away six years ago of lung fever.

'Ad another son, Jeremiah, Henry's older brother, born in 1505, but he died at Ancrum Moor five years ago under *Sir Brian Layton* fighting against them Scots.'

Mark knew this from his own and David's research. What he really wanted to know was more about William himself and his ancestors, but Alice ladled out stew into wooden bowls and placed a loaf of bread and a block of cheese on the table. After the meal, Henry took out a bottle of whisky and each had a dram; William more than one.

The sun set as they finished eating and the two boys laid out the straw-filled mattresses on wooden trestle beds they brought in from the bedroom. Henry offered one to Mark who unrolled his blanket and lay near the banked fire. It was some time before he could sleep. He had to pump William for more information in the morning before he left on his ostensible trip to Penrith.

After a breakfast of oats, bread and cheese, and more ale, Henry left to tend the sheep. Mark sat with William and asked about his sister.

'She died o' the bloody flux back in 1472. A couple o' years after Agnes's death, me father moved the family down 'ere t' England.'

Mark stared. *Moved to England! Damn, I'm going to have to start searching in Scotland.* 'Why did you move to England?'

'Me father wuz involved in a dispute with some o' them Armstrongs. Some o' the young 'uns didna' have their own land

and were jealous abart him bein' well off. Then in 1474, his twin brother, Angus, wuz killed in a fight wi' 'em. I remember cos I'd just turned ten and started going out on t' hills wi' t' sheep.'

William took a long swig of his ale and called to Alice for a refill. 'He wuz worried they might come after the family, so 'e sold the farm to Alex Armstrong and moved us all down to Longtown. When I wuz fifteen, me ma died of a fever and he made our names more English.'

'You mean he changed the family name?' Mark asked.

'Aye. We'd had enough trouble from the Armstrongs and Johnstons, so he changed our names tae Bishop, tae make it harder to find us, you see.'

Damn! This is going to complicate things. First Scotland, now this.'

'What was your name before?'

'Viscof,' William said. 'My great grandpa come all the way from Germany and settled near Langholm.'

Mark froze. His senses numb. He barely heard William's further explanation that William's father was Jamie, one of the twins he had met on his visit to Clement's farm. 'Excuse me. I, er... I need to go to the privy.'

Mark, not sure how he made it outside, leaned against the wall, his breath coming in short pants. *Simon was his ancestor... and his descendant!*

Excitement slowly overcame his shock—he had to learn more. He was grateful his buttonhole camera was recording all this; Pauline would never believe him otherwise. He returned and sat with William and listened to him relate how Jamie's two younger siblings, Meg and Alan, born in 1447 and 1449 had died in 1455. After he listened to William's stories of growing up in Scotland, and the move to Longtown, Mark started to saddle Lucky when Henry came back.

Mark thanked Henry for his hospitality and bought a jug of the whisky they had been drinking the night before from him; he figured this an appropriate souvenir to celebrate with back home.

Mark had a huge smile on his face when he walked in to the byre. He rushed over to Pauline, picked her up and whirled her around.

'What's the matter with you? What happened?'

'You'll never believe what I've found out.' he exclaimed, and hugged her.

'What? What did you find?'

'Come on, I'll show you. You won't believe it until you see for yourself.'

In the study she watched Mark download the video, his hands shaking. 'Watch this.'

Pauline watched Mark approach the farm and tensed when the old man pointed the crossbow at him. Her shoulders slumped in relief when William told him to water Lucky. She studied the interior of the farmhouse and listened to William's story.

When the video jumped to the next morning, she grimaced at the mugs of ale served for breakfast. She then heard William mention his father's original name. She stared at Mark. 'I don't believe it. That's... that's fantastic!'

'I'll update my family tree and wait for Penelope to come back from York. I can't wait to see her face when she sees this.'

He updated the now complex genealogical chart to include Simon and Donald Armstrong, adding copious notes and photographs. When Penelope came back from her studies at York, Mark and

Pauline showed her and Tony the new chart.

Tony gasped. 'You have got to be joking. You mean Simon is actually your ancestor as well as descendant?'

Penelope dropped to a chair, her mouth opening and closing, yet unable to speak.

'You had better watch the video,' Mark said and played it from just after he had finished breakfast.

Penelope grabbed Tony's arm when William mentioned 'Viscof'.

Her voice hoarse, Penelope asked, 'How can this be? It's not possible.'

'Not really,' Mark replied. 'I've done a lot of reading on time paradoxes ever since we learned Nicholas was our descendant. The Novikov principle states, *if an event exists that would cause a paradox or any 'change' to the past whatsoever, then the probability of that event is zero.* This would make time paradoxes impossible, *but*, it does permit closed causal loops where an event has no external causes or effects since time isn't really being altered, it's just going round in circles.'

Penelope recovered her voice. 'So where does it all start?'

Mark smirked. 'It doesn't. It goes round and round, where it starts, where it stops, nobody knows.'

'So where does that leave us and what's next?' Tony asked.

'It leaves us with a farm, a shop and a museum to run, greenhouses to expand and the brood to raise, as well as a need to get ready for Christmas, that's what.' Pauline declared.

'That's right,' Mark added. 'And we can concentrate on collecting plants and seeds for the seed bank. No need for any more forays to find my ancestors.'

Penelope stared at the genealogical chart. 'You know, there are still arguments where the Battle of Hastings actually happened—at Senlac Hill, Caldbec Hill or the village of Crowhurst and whether

King Harold died from an arrow to the eye or not... and there's still the Armstrong branch of the family to track down.'

Pauline looked startled at the idea and Tony groaned softly.

Mark, however, was thinking more of the future than the past. He knew what was coming over the next couple of hundred years and wondered how his family would be involved, and what *he* could do about it.

About the Author

Peter was born in Derbyshire, England and after graduating with an Honours degree in Geology in 1970 was offered a position to pursue a Master's Degree studying Iceland's volcanoes. He decided to find a geology job instead and soon after he found himself in the traditional geologists' fall back career, as a barman! After a year as a Mines Geologist with the National Coal Board in Doncaster, Yorkshire, Peter moved to Singapore in 1972 to work in the oil and gas industry. After seventeen years on oil rigs he moved in to management and held positions in Training, Human Resource and Health and Safety involving travel to over thirty countries over a forty-two year career.

On retiring in 2014, after twenty-five years of writing technical training material and manuals, Peter now splits his time between family, grandson duty and writing fiction.

'I used to collect British stamps principally from 1840-1841 and the postal history of my home area in north-east Derbyshire, England, but became frustrated at not finding new material. Then, one of my cousins sent me our family tree going back to 1660. I thought how great it would be to have a time machine to travel back in time to find the stamps I wanted as well more about the life of my ancestors. Since this wasn't going to happen, I decided to write a story about someone who did.'

Peter Martin

Bibliography

- Bestall, J M 1978 History of Chesterfield, Volume III, Early Victorian Chesterfield
- Comock, Richard 2010 A Year on a Dairy Farm
- Ekirch, A Roger 2006 At Day's Close Night in Times Past
- Flanders, Judith 2013 The Victorian City, Everyday Life in Dickens' London
- Foy, Karen 2014 Life in the Victorian Kitchen, Culinary Secrets and Servants' Stories
- Goodman, Ruth 2014 How to be a Victorian
- Goodman, Ruth 2016 How to be a Tudor
- Higgs, Michelle 2014 A Visitor's guide to Victorian England
- Higgs, Michelle 2015 Servants' Stories, Life Below Stairs in their Own word 1800-1950
- Houghton, Walter E 1957 The Victorian Frame of Mind, 1830-1870
- Hughes, Kristine 1998 The Writer's Guide to Everyday Life in Regency and Victorian England from 1811-1901
- Jackson, Lee 2015 Dirty Old London, The Victorian Fight Against Filth
- Langland, Alex, Ginn, Peter and Goodman, Ruth 2009 Victorian Farm
- Mortimer, Ian 2009 The Time Traveller's guide to Medieval England

- Mortimer, Ian 2013 The Time Traveller's Guide to Elizabethan England
- Pool, Daniel 1993 What Jane Austen Ate and Charles Dickens Knew
- Stanley, Liz (Ed.) 1984 The Diaries of Hannah Cullwick, Victorian Maidservant
- Redding Ware, J 1909 Passing English of the Victorian era, a dictionary of heterodox English, Slang and Phrase
- Young, G M (Ed.) 1934 Early Victorian England Vol. I and II

Printed in Great Britain
by Amazon